The Price of the Prairie: A Story of Kansas

Margaret Hill McCarter

Illustrated by J. N. Marchand

"Come, Phil," she cried, "come, crown me Queen of May here in April!"

THE PRICE
OF THE PRAIRIE

A STORY OF KANSAS

By

MARGARET HILL McCARTER

Author of "THE COTTONWOOD'S STORY," "CUDDY'S BABY," ETC.

WITH FIVE ILLUSTRATIONS

BY J. N. MARCHAND

FIFTEENTH EDITION

December 28, 1912

"AT EVENING TIME IT SHALL BE LIGHT"

This little love story of the prairies is dedicated to all who believe that the defence of the helpless is heroism; that the protection of the home is splendid achievement; and, that the storm, and stress, and patient endurance of the day will bring us at last to the peace of the purple twilight.

CONTENTS

ILLUSTRATIONS

PROEM

"Nature never did betray the heart that loved her"

I can hear it always—the Call of the Prairie. The passing of sixty Winters has left me a vigorous man, although my hair is as white as the January snowdrift in the draws, and the strenuous events of some of the years have put a tax on my strength. I shall always limp a little in my right foot—that was left out on the plains one freezing night with nothing under it but the earth, and nothing over it but the sky. Still, considering that although the sixty years were spent mainly in that pioneer time when every day in Kansas was its busy day, I am not even beginning to feel old. Neither am I sentimental and inclined to poetry. Life has given me mostly her prose selections for my study.

But this love of the Prairie is a part of my being. All the comedy and tragedy of these sixty years have had them for a setting, and I can no more put them out of my life than the Scotchman can forget the heather, or the Swiss emigrant in the flat green lowland can forget the icy passes of the glacier-polished Alps. Geography is an element of every man's life. The prairies are in the red corpuscles of my blood. Up and down their rippling billows my memory runs. For always I see them,—green and blossom-starred in the Springtime; or drenched with the driving summer deluge that made each draw a brimming torrent; or golden, purple, and silver-rimmed in the glorious Autumn. I have seen them gray in the twilight, still and tenderly verdant at noonday, and cold and frost-wreathed under the white star-beams. I have seen them yield up their rich yellow sheaves of grain, and I have looked upon their dreary wastes marked with the dull black of cold human blood. Plain practical man of affairs that I am, I come back to the blessed prairies for my inspiration as the tartan warmed up the heart of Argyle.

CHAPTER I

SPRINGVALE BY THE NEOSHO

Sweeter to me than the salt sea spray, the fragrance of summer rains;
Nearer my heart than the mighty hills are the wind-swept Kansas plains.
Dearer the sight of a shy wild rose by the road-side's dusty way,
Than all the splendor of poppy-fields ablaze in the sun of May.
Gay as the bold poinsettia is, and the burden of pepper trees,
The sunflower, tawny and gold and brown, is richer to me than these;
And rising ever above the song of the hoarse, insistent sea,
The voice of the prairie calling, calling me.

—ESTHER M. CLARKE.

Whenever I think of these broad Kansas plains I think also of Marjie. I cannot now remember the time when I did not care for her, but the day when O'mie first found it out is as clear to me as yesterday, although that was more than forty years ago. O'mie was the reddest-haired, best-hearted boy that ever laughed in the face of Fortune and made friends with Fate against the hardest odds. His real name was O'Meara, Thomas O'Meara, but we forgot that years ago.

"If O'mie were set down in the middle of the Sahara Desert," my Aunt Candace used to say, "there'd be an oasis a mile across by the next day noon, with never failing water and green trees right in the middle of it, and O'mie sitting under them drinking the water like it was Irish rum."

O'mie would always grin at this saying and reply that, "by the nixt day noon follerin' that, the rascally gover'mint at Washin'ton would come along an' kick him out into the rid san', claimin' that that particular oasis was an Injun riservation, specially craayted by Providence fur the dirthy Osages,—the bastes!"

O'mie hated the Indians, but he was a friend to all the rest of mankind. Indeed if it had not been for him I should not have had that limp in my right foot, for both of my feet would have been mouldering these many years under the curly mesquite of the Southwest plains. But that comes later.

We were all out on the prairie hunting for our cows that evening—the one when O'mie guessed my secret. Marjie's pony was heading straight to the west, flying over the ground. The big red sun was slipping down a flame-wreathed sky, touching with fire the ragged pennons of a blue-black storm cloud hanging sullenly to the northward, and making an indescribable splendor in the far southwest.

Riding hard after Marjie, coming at an angle from the bluff above the draw, was an Osage Indian, huge as a giant, and frenzied with whiskey. I must have turned a white despairing face toward my comrades, and I was glad afterward that I was against the background of that flaming sunset so that my features were in the shadow. It was then that O'mie, who was nearest me, looking steadily in my eyes said in a low voice:

"Bedad, Phil! so that's how it is wid ye, is it? Then we've got to kill that Injun jist fur grandeur."

I knew O'mie for many years, and I never saw him show a quiver of fear, not even in those long weary days when, white and hollow-cheeked, he waited for his last enemy, Death,—whom he vanquished, looking up into my face with eyes of inexpressible peace, and murmuring softly,

"Safe in the arms of Jasus."

Old men are prone to ramble in their stories, and I am not old. To prove that, I must not jiggle with these heads and tails of Time, but I must begin earlier and follow down these eventful years as if I were a real novel-writer with consecutive chapters to set down.

Springvale by the Neosho was a favorite point for early settlers. It nestled under the sheltered bluff on the west. There were never-failing springs in the rocky outcrop. A magnificent grove of huge oak trees, most rare in the plains country, lined the river's banks and covered the fertile lowlands. It made a landmark of the spot, this beautiful natural forest, and gave it a place on the map as a meeting-ground for the wild tribes long before the days of civilized occupation. The height above the valley commands all that wide prairie that ripples in treeless fertility from as far as even an Indian can see until it breaks off with that cliff that walls the Neosho bottom lands up and down for many a mile. To the southwest the open black lowlands along Fingal's Creek beckoned as temptingly to the settler as did the Neosho Valley itself. The divide between the two, the river and its tributary, coming down from the northwest makes a high promontory. Its eastern side is the rocky ledge of the bluff. On the west it slopes off to the fertile draws of Fingal's Creek, and the sunset prairies that swell up and away beyond them.

Just where the little stream joins the bigger one Springvale took root and flourished amazingly. It was an Indian village site and trading-point since tradition can remember. The old tepee rings show still up in the prairie cornfield where even the plough, that great weapon of civilization and obliteration, has not quite made a dead level of the landmarks of the past. I've bumped across those rings many a time in the days when we went from Springvale up to the Red Range schoolhouse in the broken country where Fingal's Creek has its source. It was the hollow beyond the tepee ring that caused his pony to stumble that night when Jean Pahusca, the big Osage, was riding like fury between me and that blood-red sky.

The early Indians always built on the uplands although the valleys ran close beneath them. They had only arrows and speed to protect them from their foes. It was not until they had the white man's firearms that they dared to make their homes in the lowlands. Black Kettle in the sheltered Washita Valley might never have fallen before General Custer had the Cheyennes kept to the high places after the custom of their fathers. But the early white settlers had firearms and skill in building block-houses, so they took to the valleys near wood and water.

On the day that Kansas became a Territory, my father, John Baronet, with all his household effects started from Rockport, Massachusetts, to begin life anew in the wild unknown West. He was not a poor man, heaven bless his memory! He never knew want except the pinch of pioneer life when money is of no avail because the necessities are out of reach. In the East he had been a successful lawyer and his success followed him. They will tell you in Springvale to-day that "if Judge Baronet were alive and on the bench things would go vastly better," and much more to like effect.

My mother was young and beautiful, and to her the world was full of beauty. Especially did she love the sea. All her life was spent beside it, and it was ever her delight. It must have been from her that my own love of nature came as a heritage to me, giving me capacity to take and keep those prairie scenes of idyllic beauty that fill my memory now.

In the Summer of 1853 my father's maiden sister Candace had come to live with us. Candace Baronet was the living refutation of all the unkind criticism ever heaped upon old maids. She was a strong, comely, unselfish woman who lived where the best thoughts grow.

One day in late October, a sudden squall drove landward, capsizing the dory in which my mother was returning from a visit to old friends on an island off the Rockport coast. She was in sight of home when that furious gust of wind and rain swept across her path. The next morning the little waves rippled musically against the beach whither they had borne my dead mother and left her without one mark of cruel usage. Neither was there any sign of terror on her face, white and peaceful under her damp dark hair.

I know now that my father and his sister tried hard to suppress their sorrow for my sake, but the curtains on the seaward side of the house were always lowered now and my father's face looked more and more to the westward. The sea became an unbearable thing to him. Yet he was a brave, unselfish man and in all the years following that one Winter he lived cheerfully and nobly—a sunshiny life.

In the early Spring he gave up his law practice in Rockport.

"The place for me is on the frontier," he said to my Aunt Candace one day. "I'm sick of the sight of that water. I want to try the prairies and I want to be in the struggle that is beginning beyond the Missouri. I want to do one man's part in the making of the West."

Aunt Candace looked steadily into her brother's face.

"I am sick of the sea, too, John," she said. "Will the prairies be kinder to us, I wonder."

I did not know till long afterward, when the Kansas blue-grass had covered both their graves, that the blue Atlantic had in its keeping the form of the one love of my aunt's life. Rich am I, Philip Baronet, to have had such a father and such a mother-hearted aunt. They made life full and happy for me with never from that day any doleful grieving over the portion Providence had given them. And the blessed prairie did bring them peace. Its spell was like a benediction on their lives who lived to bless many lives.

It was late June when our covered wagon and tired ox-team stopped on the east bluff above the Neosho just outside of Springvale. The sun was dropping behind the prairie far across the river valley when another wagon and ox-team with pioneers like ourselves joined us. They were Irving Whately and his wife and little daughter, Marjory. I was only seven and I have forgotten many things of these later years, but I'll never forget Marjie as I first saw her. She was stiff from long sitting in the big covered wagon, and she stretched her pudgy little legs to get the cramp out of them, as she took in the scene. Her pink sun-bonnet had fallen back and she was holding it by both strings in one hand. Her rough brown hair was all in little blowsy ringlets round her face and the two braids hanging in front of her shoulders ended each in a big blowsy curl. Her eyes were as brown as her hair. But what I noted then and many a time afterward was the exceeding whiteness of her face. From St. Louis I had seen nothing but dark-skinned Mexicans, tanned Missourians, and Indian, Creole, and French Canadian, all coppery or bronze brown, in this land of glaring sunshine. Marjie made me think of Rockport and the pink-cheeked children of the country lanes about the town. But most of all she called my mother back, white and beautiful as she looked in her last peaceful sleep, the day the sea gave her to us again. "Star Face," Jean Pahusca used to call Marjie, for even in the Kansas heat and browning winds she never lost the pink tint no miniature painting on ivory could exaggerate.

We stood looking at one another in the purple twilight.

"What's your name?"

"Marjory Whately. What's yours?"

"Phil Baronet, and I'm seven years old." This, a shade boastingly.

"I'm six," Marjory said. "Are you afraid of Indians?"

"No," I declared. "I won't let the Indians hurt you. Let's run a race," pointing toward where the Neosho lay glistening in the last light of day, a gap in the bluff letting the reflection from great golden clouds illumine its wave-crumpled surface.

We took hold of hands and started down the long slope together, but our parents called us back. "Playmates already," I heard them saying.

In the gathering evening shadows we all lumbered down the slope to the rock-bottomed ford and up into the little hamlet of Springvale.

That night when I said my prayers to Aunt Candace I cried softly on her shoulder. "Marjie makes me homesick," I sobbed, and Aunt Candace understood then and always afterward.

The very air about Springvale was full of tradition. The town had been from the earliest times a landmark of the old Santa Fé trail. When the freighters and plainsmen left the village and climbed to the top of the slope and set their faces to the west there lay before them only the wilderness wastes. Here Nature, grown miserly, offered not even a stick of timber to mend a broken cart-pole in all the thousand miles between the Neosho and the Spanish settlement of New Mexico.

Here the Indians came with their furs and beaded garments to exchange for firearms and fire-water. People fastened their doors at night for a purpose. No curfew bell was needed to call in the children. The wooded Neosho Valley grew dark before the evening lights had left the prairies beyond the west bluff, and the waters that sang all day a song of cheer as they rippled over the rocky river bed seemed always after nightfall to gurgle murderously as they went their way down the black-shadowed valley.

The main street was as broad as an Eastern boulevard. Space counted for nothing in planning towns in a land made up of distances. At the end of this street stood the "Last Chance" general store, the outpost of civilization. What the freighter failed to get here he would do without until he stood inside the brown adobe walls of the old city of Santa Fé. Tell Mapleson, the proprietor of the "Last Chance," was a tall, slight, restless man, quick-witted, with somewhat polished manners and a gift of persuasion in his speech.

Near this store was Conlow's blacksmith shop, where the low-browed, black-eyed Conlow family have shod horses and mended wagons since anybody can remember. They were the kind of people one instinctively does not trust, and yet nobody could find a true bill against them. The shop had thick stone walls. High up under the eaves on the north side a long narrow slit, where a stone was missing, let out a bar of sullen red light. Old Conlow did not know about that chink for years, for it was only from the bluff above the town that the light could be seen.

Our advent in Springvale was just at the time of its transition from a plains trading-post to a Territorial town with ambition for settlement and civilization. I can see now that John Baronet deserved the place he came to hold in that frontier community, for he was a State-builder.

"I should feel more dacent fur all etarnity jist to be buried in the same cimet'ry wid Judge Bar'net," O'mie once declared. "I should walk into kingdom-come, dignified and head up, saying to the kaper av the pearly gates, kind o' careless-like, 'I'm from that little Kansas town av Springvale an' ye'll check up my mortial remains over in the cimet'ry, be my neighbor, Judge Bar'net, if ye plaze.'"

It was O'mie's way of saying what most persons of the community felt toward my father from the time he drove into Springvale in the purple twilight of that June evening in 1854.

Irving Whately's stock of merchandise was installed in the big stone building on the main corner of the village, where the straggling Indian trails from the south and the trail from the new settlement out on Fingal's Creek converged on the broad Santa Fé trail. Amos

Judson, a young settler, became his clerk and general helper. In the front room over this store was John Baronet's law office, and his sign swinging above Whately's seemed always to link those two names together.

Opposite this building was the village tavern. It was a wide two-story structure, also of stone, set well back from the street, with a double veranda along the front and the north side. A huge oak tree grew before it, and a flagstone walk led up to the veranda steps. In big black lettering its inscription over the door told the wayfarer on the old trail that this was

THE CAMBRIDGE HOUSE.
C. C. GENTRY, PROP.

Cam Gentry (his real name was Cambridge, christened from the little Indiana town of Cambridge City) was a good-souled, easy-going man, handicapped for life by a shortness of vision no spectacle lens could overcome. It might have been disfiguring to any other man, but Cam's clear eye at close range, and his comical squint and tilt of the head to study out what lay farther away, were good-natured and unique. He was in Kansas for the fun of it, while his wife, Dollie, kept tavern from pure love of cooking more good things to eat than opportunity afforded in a home. She was a Martha whose kitchen was "dukedom large enough." Whatever motive, fine or coarse, whatever love of spoils or love of liberty, brought other men hither, Cam had come to see the joke—and he saw it. While as to Dollie, "Lord knows," she used to say, "there's plenty of good cooks in old Wayne County, Indiany; but if they can get anything to eat out here they need somebody to cook it for 'em, and cook it right."

Doing chores about the tavern for his board and keep was the little orphan boy, Thomas O'Meara, whose story I did not know for many years. We called him O'mie. That was all. Marjie and O'mie and Mary Gentry, Cam and Dollie's only child, were my first Kansas playmates. Together we waded barefoot in the shallow ripples of the Neosho, and little by little we began to explore that wide, sweet prairie land to the west. There was just one tree standing up against the horizon; far away to us it seemed, a huge cottonwood, that kept sentinel guard over the plains from the highest level of the divide.

Whately built a home a block or more beyond that of his young clerk, Amos Judson. It was farther up the slope than any other house in Springvale except my father's. That was on the very crest of the west bluff, overlooking the Neosho Valley. It fronted the east, and across the wide street before it the bluff broke precipitously four hundred feet to the level floor of the valley below. Sometimes the shelving rocks furnished a footing where one could clamber down half way and walk along the narrow ledge. Here were cunning hiding-places, deep crevices, and vine-covered heaps of jagged stone outcrop invisible from the height above or the valley below. It was a bit of rugged, untamable cliff rarely found in the plains country; and it broke so suddenly from the level promontory sloping down to the south and away to the west, that a stranger sitting by our east windows would never have guessed that the seeming bushes peering up across the street were really the tops of tall trees with their roots in the side of the bluff not half way to the bottom.

From our west window the green glory of the plains spread out to the baths of sunset. No wonder this Kansas land is life of my life. The sea is to me a wavering treachery, but these firm prairies are the joy of my memory.

Our house was of stone with every corner rounded like a turret wall. It was securely built against the winter winds that swept that bluff when the Kansas blizzard unchained its fury, for it stood where it caught the full wrath of the elements. It caught, too, the splendor of all the sunrise beyond the mist-filled valley, and the full moon in the level east above the oak treetops made a dream of chastened glory like the silver twilight gleams in Paradise.

"I want to watch the world coming and going," my father said when his house was finished; "and it is coming down that Santa Fé trail. It is State-making that is begun here. The East doesn't understand it yet, outside of New England. And these Missourians, Lord pity them! they think they can kill human freedom with a bullet, like thrusting daggers into the body of Julius Cæsar to destroy the Roman Empire. What do they know of the old Puritan blood, and the strength of the grip of a Massachusetts man? Heaven knows where they came from, these Missouri ruffians; but," he added, "the devil has it arranged where they will go to."

"Oh, John, be careful," exclaimed Aunt Candace.

"Are you afraid of them, Candace?"

"Well, no, I don't believe I am," replied my aunt.

She was not one of those blustering north-northwest women. She squared her life by the admonition of Isaiah, "In quietness and in confidence shall be your strength." But she was a Baronet, and although they have their short-comings, fear seems to have been left out of their make-up.

CHAPTER II

JEAN PAHUSCA

In even savage bosoms
There are longings, yearnings, strivings
For the good they comprehend not.

—LONGFELLOW.

The frontier broke all lines of caste. There was no aristocrat, autocrat, nor plutocrat in Springvale; but the purest democracy was among the children. Life was before us; we loved companionship, and the same dangers threatened us all. The first time I saw Marjie she asked, "Are you afraid of Indians?" They were the terror of her life. Even to-day the mere press despatch of an Indian uprising in Oklahoma or Arizona will set the blood bounding through my veins and my first thought is of her.

I shall never forget the day my self-appointed guardianship of her began. Before we had a schoolhouse, Aunt Candace taught the children of the community in our big living-room. One rainy afternoon, late in the Fall, the darkness seemed to drop down suddenly. We could not see to study, and we were playing boisterously about the benches of our improvised schoolroom, Marjie, Mary Gentry, Lettie and Jim Conlow, Tell Mapleson,—old Tell's boy,—O'mie, both the Mead boys, and the four Anderson children. Suddenly Marjie, who was watching the rain beating against the west window, called, "Phil, come here! What is that long, narrow, red light down by the creek?"

Marjie had the softest voice. Amid the harsh jangle of the Andersons and Bill Mead's big whooping shouts it always seemed like music to me. I stared hard at the sullen block of flame in the evening shadows.

"I don't know what it is," I said.

She slipped her fingers into the pocket of my coat as I turned away, and her eyes looked anxiously into mine. "Could it be an Indian camp-fire?" she queried.

I looked again, flattening my nose against the window pane. "I don't know, Marjie, but I'll find out. Maybe it's somebody's kitchen fire down west. I'll ask O'mie."

In truth, that light had often troubled me. It did not look like the twinkling candle-flare I could see in so many windows of the village. I turned to O'mie, who, with his face to the wall, waited in a game of hide-and-seek. Before I could call him Marjie gave a low cry of terror. We all turned to her in an instant, and I saw outside a dark face close against the window. It was gone so quickly that only O'mie and I caught sight of it.

"What was it, Marjie?" the children cried.

"An Indian boy," gasped Marjie. "He was right against the window."

"I'll bet it was a spook," shouted Bill Mead.

"I'll bet it wasn't nothin' at all," grinned Jim Conlow. "Possum Conlow" we called him for that secretive grin on his shallow face.

"I'll bet it wath a whole gang of Thiennes," lisped tow-headed Bud Anderson.

"They ain't no Injuns nearer than the reserve down the river, and ain't been no Injuns in Springvale for a long time, 'cept annuity days," declared Tell Mapleson.

"Well, let's foind out," shouted O'mie, "I ain't afraid av no Injun."

"Neither am I," I cried, starting after O'mie, who was out of the door at the word.

But Marjie caught my arm, and held it.

"Let O'mie go. Don't go, Phil, please don't."

I can see her yet, her brown eyes full of pleading, her soft brown hair in rippling waves about her white temples. Did my love for her spring into being at that instant? I cannot tell. But I do know that it was a crucial moment for me. Sixty years have I seen, and my life has grown practical and barren of sentiment. But I know that the boy, Phil Baronet, who stood that evening with Marjie and the firelight and safety on one side, and darkness and uncertainty on the other, had come to one of those turning-points in a life, unrecognized for the time, whose decision controls all the years that follow. For suddenly came the query "How can I best take care of her? Shall I stay with her in the light, or go into the dark and strike the danger out of it?" I didn't frame all this into words. It was all only an intense feeling, but the mental judgment was very real. I turned from her and cleared the doorstep at a leap, and in a moment was by O'mie's side, chasing down the hill-slope toward town.

We never thought to run to the bluff's edge and clamber down the shelving, precipitous sides. Here was the only natural hiding-place, but like children we all ran the other way. When we had come in again with the report of "No enemy in sight," and had shut the door against the rain, I happened to glance out of the east window. Climbing up to the street from the cliff I saw the lithe form of a young Indian. He came straight to the house and stood by the east window where he could see inside. Then with quick, springing step he walked down the slope. I crossed to the west window and watched him shutting out that red bar of light now and then, till he melted into the shadows.

Meanwhile the children were chattering like sparrows and had not noticed me.

"Would you know it, Marjie, if you thaw it again?" lisped Bud Anderson.

"Oh, yes! His hair was straight across like this." Marjie drew one hand across her curl-shaded forehead, to show how square the black hair grew about the face she had seen.

"That's nothin'," said Bill Mead. "They change scalps every time they catch a white man,—just take their own off an' put his on, an' it grows. There's lots of men in Kansas look like white men's just Injuns growed a white scalp on 'em."

"Really, is there?" asked Mary Gentry credulously.

"Sure, I've seen 'em," went on Bill with a boy's love of that kind of lying.

"Wouldn't a Injun look funny with my thcalp?" Bud Anderson put in. "I'll bet I'm jutht a Injun mythelf."

"Then you've got some little baby girl's scalp," grinned Jim Conlow.

"'Tain't no 'pothum'th, anyhow," rejoined Bud; and we laughed our fears away.

That evening Aunt Candace sent me home with Marjie to take some fresh doughnuts to Mrs. Whately. I can see the little girl now as we splashed sturdily down Cliff Street through the wet gloom, her face like a white blossom in the shadowy twilight, her crimson jacket open at the throat, and the soft little worsted scarf about her damp fluffy curls making a glow of rich coloring in the dim light.

"You'll never let the Indians get you, will you, Phil?" she asked, when we stood a moment by the bushes just at the steepest bend of the street.

I stood up proudly. I was growing very fast in this gracious climate. "The finest-built boy in Springvale," the men called me. "No, Marjie. The Indians won't get me, nor anybody else I don't want them to have."

She drew close to me, and I caught her hand in mine a moment. Then, boylike, I flipped her heavy braid of hair over her shoulder and shook the wettest bushes till their drops scattered in a shower about her. Something, a dog we thought, suddenly slid out from the bush and down the cliff-side. When I started home after delivering the cakes, Marjie held the candle at the door to light my way. As I turned at the edge of the candle's rays to wave my hand, I saw her framed in the doorway. Would that some artist could paint that picture for me now!

"I'll whistle up by the bushes," I cried, and strode into the dark.

On the bend of the crest, where the street drops down almost too steep for a team of horses to climb, I turned and saw Marjie's light in the window, and the shadow of her head on the pane. I gave a long, low whistle, the signal call we had for our own. It was not an echo, it was too near and clear, the very same low call in the bushes just over the cliff beside me as though some imitator were trying to catch the notes. A few feet farther on my path I came face to face with the same Indian whom I had seen an hour before. He strode by me in silence.

Without once looking back I said to myself, "If you aren't afraid of me, I'm not afraid of you. But who gave that whistle, I wonder. That's my call to Marjie."

"Marjie's awful 'fraid of Injuns," I said to Aunt Candace that night. "Didn't want me to find who it was peeked, but I went after him, clear down to Amos Judson's house, because I thought that was the best way, if it was an Injun. She isn't afraid of anything else. She's the only girl that can ride Tell Mapleson's pony, and only O'mie and Tell and I among the boys can ride him. And she killed the big rattlesnake that nearly had Jim Conlow, killed it with a hoe. And she can climb where no other girl dares to, on the bluff below town toward the Hermit's Cave. But she's just as 'fraid of an Injun! I went to hunt him, though."

"And you did just right, Phil. The only way to be safe is to go after what makes you afraid. I guess, though, there really was nobody. It was just Marjie's imagination, wasn't it?"

"Yes, there was, Auntie; I saw him climb up from the cliff over there and go off down the hill after we came in."

"Why didn't you say so?" asked my aunt.

"We couldn't get him, and it would have scared Marjie," I answered.

"That's right, Phil. You are a regular Kansas boy, you are. The best of them may claim to come from Massachusetts,"—with a touch of pride,—"but no matter where they come from, they must learn how to be quick-witted and brave and manly here in Kansas. It's what all boys need to be here."

A few days later the door of our schoolroom opened and an Indian boy strode in and seated himself on the bench beside Tell Mapleson. He was a lad of fifteen, possibly older. His dress was of the Osage fashion and round his neck he wore a string of elk teeth. His face was thoroughly Indian, yet upon his features something else was written. His long black hair was a shade too jetty and soft for an Indian's, and it grew squarely across his forehead, suggesting the face of a French priest. We children sat open-mouthed. Even Aunt Candace forgot herself a moment. Bud Anderson first found his voice.

"Well, I'll thwan!" he exclaimed in sheer amazement.

Bill Mead giggled and that broke the spell.

"How do you do?" said my aunt kindly.

"How," replied the young brave.

"What is your name, and what do you want?" asked our teacher.

"Jean Pahusca. Want school. Want book—" He broke off and finished in a jargon of French and Indian.

"Where is your home, your tepee?" queried Aunt Candace.

The Indian only shook his head. Then taking from his beads a heavy silver cross, crudely shaped and wrought, he rose and placed it on the table. Taking up a book at the same time he seated himself to study like the rest of us.

"He has paid his tuition," said my aunt, smiling. "We'll let him stay."

So Jean Pahusca was established in our school.

CHAPTER III

THE HERMIT'S CAVE

The secret which the mountains kept
The river never told.

The bluff was our continual delight. It was so difficult, so full of surprises, so enchanting in its dangers. All manner of creeping things in general, and centipedes and rattlesnakes in particular, made their homes in its crevices. Its footing was perilous to the climber, and its hiding-places had held outlaws and worse. Then it had its haunted spots, where tradition told of cruel tragedies in days long gone by; and of the unknown who had found here secret retreat, who came and went, leaving never a name to tell whom they were nor what their story might be. All these the old cliff had in its keeping for the sturdy boys and girls of parents who had come here to conquer the West.

Just below the town where the Neosho swings away to the right, the bottom lands narrow down until the stream sweeps deep and swift against a stone wall almost two hundred feet in height. From the top of the cliff here the wall drops down nearly another hundred feet, leaving an inaccessible heap of rough cavernous rocks in the middle stratum.

Had the river been less deep and dangerous we could not have gotten up from below; while to come down from above might mean a fall of three hundred feet or more to the foam-torn waters and the jagged rocks beneath them. Here a stranger hermit had hidden himself years before. Nobody knew his story, nor how he had found his way hither, for he spoke in a strange tongue that nobody could interpret. That this inaccessible place was his home was certain. Boys bathing in the shallows up-stream sometimes caught a glimpse of him moving about among the bushes. And sometimes at night from far to the east a light could be seen twinkling half way up the dark cliff-side. Every boy in Springvale had an ambition to climb to the Hermit's Cave and explore its mysteries; for the old man died as he had lived, unknown. One winter day his body was found on the sand bar below the rapids where the waters had carried him after his fall from the point of rock above the deep pool. There was no mark on his coarse clothing to tell a word of his story, and the Neosho kept his secret always.

What boy after that would not have braved any danger to explore the depths of this hiding-place? But we could not do it. Try as we might, the hidden path leading up, or down, baffled us.

After Jean Pahusca came into our school we had a new interest and for a time we forgot that tantalizing river wall below town. Jean was irregular in his attendance and his temper. He learned quickly, for an Indian. Sometimes he was morose and silent; sometimes he was affable and kind, chatting among us like one of our own; and sometimes he found the white man's fire-water. Then he murdered as he went. He was possessed of a demon to kill, kill the moment he became drunk. Every living thing in his way had to flee or perish then. He would stop in his mad chase to crush the life out of a sleeping cat, or to strike at a bird or a chicken. Whiskey to him meant death, as we learned to our sorrow. Nobody knew where he lived. He dressed like an Osage but he was supposed to make his home with the Kaws, whose reservation was much nearer to us. Sometimes in the cool weather he slept in our sheds. In warm weather he lay down on the ground wherever he chose to sleep. There was a fascination about him unlike all the other Indians who came up to the village, many of whom we knew. He could be so gentle and winning in his manner at times, one forgot he was an Indian. But the spirit of the Red Man was ever present to overcome the strange European mood in a moment.

"He's no Osage, that critter ain't," Cam Gentry said to a group on his tavern veranda one annuity day when the tribes had come to town for their quarterly allowances. "He's second cousin on his father's side to some French missionary, you bet your life. He's got a gait like a Jessut priest. An' he's not Osage on't other side, neither. I'll bet his mother was a Kiowa, an' that means his maternal grandad was a rattlesnake, even if his paternal grandpop was a French markis turned religious an' gone a-missionaryin' among the red heathen.

You dig fur enough into that buck's hide an' you'll find cussedness big as a sheep, I'm tellin' you."

"Where does he live?" inquired my father.

"Lord knows!" responded Cam. "Down to the Kaws' nests, I reckon."

"He was cuttin' east along the Fingal Creek bluff after he'd made off to the southwest, the other night, when I was after the cows," broke in O'mie, who was sitting on the lowest step listening with all his ears. "Was cuttin' straight to the river. Only that's right by the Hermit's Cave an' he couldn't cross to the Osages there."

"Reckon he zigzagged back to town to get somethin' he forgot at Conlow's shop," put in Cam. "Didn't find any dead dogs nor children next mornin', did ye, O'mie?"

Conlow kept the vilest whiskey ever sold to a poor drink-thirsty Redskin. Everybody knew it except those whom the grand jury called into counsel. I saw my father's brow darken.

"Conlow will meet his match one of these days," he muttered.

"That's why we are runnin' you for judge," said Cam. "This cussed country needs you in every office it's got to clean out that gang that robs an' cheats the Injuns, an' then makes 'em ravin' crazy with drinkin'. They's more 'n Conlow to blame, though, Judge. Keep one eye on the Government agents and Indian traders."

"I wonder where Jean did go anyhow," O'mie whispered to me. "Let's foind out an' give him a surprise party an' a church donation some night."

"What does he come here so much for, anyhow?" I questioned.

"I don't know," replied O'mie. "Why can't he stay Injun? What'll he do wid the greatest common divisor an' the indicative mood an' the Sea of Azov, an' the Zambezi River, when he's learned 'em, anyhow? Phil, begorra, I b'lave that cussed Redskin is in this town fur trouble, an' you jist remember he'll git it one av these toimes. He ain't natural

Injun. Uncle Cam is right. He's not like them Osages that comes here annuity days. All that's Osage about him is his clothes."

While we were talking, Jean Pahusca came silently into the company and sat down under the oak tree shading the walk. He never looked less like an Indian than he did that summer morning lounging lazily in the shade. The impenetrable savage face had now an expression of ease and superior self-possession, making it handsome. Unlike the others of his race who came and went about Springvale, Jean's trappings were always bright and fresh, and his every muscle had the poetry of motion. In all our games he was an easy victor. He never clambered about the cliff as we did, he simply slid up and down like a lizard. Jim Conlow was built to race, but Jean skimmed the ground like a bird. He could outwrestle every boy except O'mie (nobody had ever held that Irishman if he wanted to get away), and his grip was like steel. We all fought him by turns and he defeated everyone until my turn came. From me he would take no chance of defeat, however much the boys taunted him with being afraid of Phil Baronet. For while he had a quickness that I lacked, I knew I had a muscular strength he could not break. I disliked him at first on Marjie's account; and when she grew accustomed to his presence and almost forgot her fear, I detested him. And never did I dislike him so much before as on this summer morning when we sat about the shady veranda of the Cambridge House. Nobody else, however, gave any heed to the Indian boy picturesquely idling there on the blue-grass.

Down the street came Lettie Conlow and Mary Gentry with Marjory Whately, all chatting together. They turned at the tavern oak and came up the flag-stone walk toward the veranda. I could not tell you to-day what my lady wears in the social functions where I sometimes have the honor to be a guest. I am a man, and silks and laces confuse me. Yet I remember three young girls in a frontier town more than forty years ago. Mary Gentry was slender—"skinny," we called her to tease her. Her dark-blue calico dress was clean and prim. Lettie Conlow was fat. Her skin was thick and muddy, and there was a brown mole below her ear. Her black, slick braids of hair were my especial dislike. She had no neck to speak of, and when she turned her head the creases above her fat shoulders deepened. I might have liked Lettie but for her open preference for me. Everybody knew this preference, and she annoyed me exceedingly. This morning she wore a thin old red lawn cut down from her mother's gown. A ruffle of the same lawn flopped about her neck. As they came near, her black eyes sought mine as usual, but I saw only the floppy red ruffle—and Marjie. Marjie looked sweet and cool in a fresh starched gingham, with her round white arms bare to the elbows, and her white shapely neck, with its dainty curves and dimples. The effect was heightened by the square-cut bodice, with its green and white gingham bands edged with a Hamburg something, narrow and spotless. How unlike she was to Lettie in her flimsy trimmings! Marjie's hair was coiled in a knot on the top of her head, and the little ringlets curved about her forehead and at the back of her neck. Somehow, with her clear pink cheeks and that pale green gown, I could think only of the wild roses that grew about the rocks on the bluff this side of the Hermit's Cave.

Marjie smiled kindly down at Jean as she passed him. There was always a tremor of fear in that smile; and he knew it and gloried in it.

"Good-morning, Jean," she said in that soft voice I loved to hear.

"Good-morning, Star-face," Jean smiled back at her; and his own face was transfigured for the instant, as his still black eyes followed her. The blood in my veins turned to fire at that look. Our eyes met and for one long moment we gazed steadily at each other. As I turned away I saw Lettie Conlow watching us both, and I knew instinctively that she and Jean Pahusca would sometime join forces against me.

"Well, if you lassies ain't a sight good for sore eyes, I'll never tell it," Cam shouted heartily, squinting up at the girls with his good-natured glance. "You're cool as October an' twicet as sweet an' fine. Go in and let Dollie give you some hot berry pie."

"To cool 'em off," O'mie whispered in my ear. "Nothin' so coolin' as a hot berry pie in July. Let's you and me go to the creek an' thaw out."

That evening Jean Pahusca found the jug supposed to be locked in Conlow's chest of tools inside his shop. I had found where that red forge light came from, and had watched it from my window many a night. When it winked and blinked, I knew somebody inside the shop was passing between it and the line of the chink. I did not speak of it. I was never accused of telling all I knew. My father often said I would make a good witness for my attorney in a suit at law.

Among the Indians who had come for their stipend on this annuity day was a strong young Osage called Hard Rope, who always had a roll of money when he went out of town. I remember that night my father did not come home until very late; and when Aunt Candace asked him if there was anything the matter, I heard him answer carelessly:

"Oh, no. I've been looking after a young Osage they call Hard Rope, who needed me."

I was sleepy, and forgot all about his words then. Long afterwards I had good reason for knowing through this same Hard Rope, how well an Indian can remember a kindness. He never came to Springvale again. And when I next saw him I had forgotten that I had ever known him before. However, I had seen the blinking red glare down the slope that evening and I knew something was going on. Anyhow, Jean Pahusca, crazed with drink, had stolen Tell Mapleson's pony and created a reign of terror in the street until he disappeared down the trail to the southwest.

"It's a wonder old Tell doesn't shoot that Injun," Irving Whately remarked to a group in his store. "He's quick enough with firearms."

"Well," said Cam Gentry, squinting across the counter with his shortsighted eyes, "there's somethin' about that 'Last Chance' store and about this town I don't understand. There's a nigger in the wood-pile, or an Injun in the blankets, somewhere. I hope it won't be long till this thing is cleared up and we can know whether we do know anything, or don't know it. I'm gettin' mystifieder daily." And Cam sat down chuckling.

"Anyhow, we won't see that Redskin here for a spell, I reckon," broke in Amos Judson, Whately's clerk. And with this grain of comfort, we forgot him for a time.

One lazy Saturday afternoon in early August, O'mie and I went for a swim on the sand-bar side of the Deep Hole under the Hermit's Cave. I had something to tell O'mie. All the boys trusted him with their confidences. We had slid quietly down the river; somehow, it was too hot to be noisy, and we were lying on a broad, flat stone letting the warm water ripple over us. A huge bowlder on the sand just beyond us threw a sort of shadow over our brown faces as we rested our heads on the sand.

"O'mie," I began, "I saw something last night."

"Well, an' phwat did somethin' do to you?" He was blowing at the water, which was sliding gently over his chest.

"That's what I want to tell you if you will shut up that red flannel mouth a minute."

"The crimson fabric is now closed be order av the Coort," grinned O'mie.

"O'mie, I waked up suddenly last night. It was clear moonlight, and I looked out of the window. There right under it, on a black pony just like Tell Mapleson's, was Jean Pahusca. He was staring up at the window. He must have seen me move for he only stayed a minute and then away he went. I watched him till he had passed Judson's place and was in the shadows beyond the church. He had on a new red blanket with a circle of white right in the middle, a good target for an arrow, only I'd never sneak up behind him. If I fight him I'll do it like a white man, from the front."

"Then ye'll be dead like a white man, from the front clear back," declared O'mie. "But hadn't ye heard? This mornin' ould Tell was showin' Tell's own pony he said he brought back from down at Westport. He got home late las' night. An' Tell, he pipes up an' says, 'There was a arrow fastened in its mane when I see it this mornin', but his dad took no notice whatsoever av the boy's sayin'; just went on that it was the one Jean Pahusca had stole when he was drunk last. What does it mean, Phil? Is Jean hidin' out round here again? I wish the cuss would go to Santy Fee with the next train down the trail an' go to Spanish bull fightin'. He's just cut out for that, begorra; fur he rides like a Comanche. It ud be a sort av disgrace to the bull though. I've got nothin' agin bulls."

"O'mie, I don't understand; but let's keep still. Some day when he gets so drunk he'll kill one of the grand jury, maybe the rest of them and the coroner can indict him for something."

We lay still in the warm water. Sometimes now in the lazy hot August afternoons I can hear the rippling song of the Neosho as it prattled and gurgled on its way. Suddenly O'mie gave a start and in a voice low and even but intense he exclaimed:

"For the Lord's sake, wud ye look at that? And kape still as a snake while you're doin' it."

Lying perfectly still, I looked keenly about me, seeing nothing unusual.

"Look up across yonder an' don't bat an eye," said O'mie, low as a whisper.

I looked up toward the Hermit's Cave. Sitting on a point of rock overhanging the river was an Indian. His back was toward us and his brilliant red blanket had a white circle in the centre.

"He's not seen us, or he'd niver set out there like that," and O'mie breathed easier. "He could put an arrow through us here as aisy as to snap a string, an' nobody'd live to tell the tale. Phil Bar'net, he's kapin' den in that cave, an' the devil must have showed him how to git up there."

A shout up-stream told of other boys coming down to our swimming place. You have seen a humming bird dart out of sight. So the Indian on the rock far above us vanished at that sound.

"That's Bill Mead comin'; I know his whoop. I wish I knew which side av that Injun's head his eyes is fastened on," said O'mie, still motionless in the water. "If he's watchin' us up there, I'm a turtle till the sun goes down."

A low peal of thunder rolled out of the west and a heavy black cloud swept suddenly over the sun. The blue shadow of the bluff fell upon the Neosho and under its friendly cover we scrambled into our clothes and scudded out of sight among the trees that covered the east bottom land.

"Now, how did he ever get to that place, O'mie?" I questioned.

"I don't know. But if he can get there, I can too."

Poor O'mie! he did not know how true a prophecy he was uttering.

"Let's kape this to oursilves, Phil," counselled my companion. "If too many knows it Tell may lose another pony, or somebody's dead dog may float down the stream like the ould hermit did. Let's burn him out av there oursilves. Then we can adorn our own tepee wid that soft black La Salle-Marquette-Hennepin French scalp."

I agreed, and we went our way burdened by a secret dangerous but fascinating to boys like ourselves.

CHAPTER IV

IN THE PRAIRIE TWILIGHT

The spacious prairie is helper to a spacious life.
Big thoughts are nurtured here, with little friction.

—QUAYLE.

By the time I was fifteen I was almost as tall and broad-shouldered as my father. Boy-like, I was prodigal of my bounding vigor, which had not tempered down to the strength of my mature manhood. It was well for me that a sobering responsibility fell on me early, else I might have squandered my resources of endurance, and in place of this sturdy story-teller whose sixty years sit lightly on him, there would have been only a ripple in the sod of the curly mesquite on the Plains and a little heap of dead dust, turned to the inert earth again. The West grows large men, as it grows strong, beautiful women; and I know that the boys and girls then differed only in surroundings and opportunity from the boys and girls of Springvale to-day. Life is finer in its appointments now; but I doubt if it is any more free or happy than it was in those days when we went to oyster suppers and school exhibitions up in the Red Range neighborhood. Among us there was the closest companionship, as there needs must be in a lonely and spacious land. What can these lads and lasses of to-day know of a youth nurtured in the atmosphere of peril and uncertainty such as every one of us knew in those years of border strife and civil war? Sometimes up here, when I see the gay automobile parties spinning out upon the paved street and over that broad highway miles and miles to the west, I remember the time when we rode our Indian ponies thither, and the whole prairie was our boulevard.

Marjie could ride without bridle or saddle, and she sat a horse like a cattle queen. The four Anderson children were wholesome and good-natured, as they were good scholars, and they were good riders. They were all tow-headed and they all lisped, and Bud was the most hopeless case among them. Flaxen-haired, baby-faced youngster that he was, he was the very first in all our crowd to learn to drop on the side of his pony and ride like a Comanche. O'mie and I also succeeded in learning that trick; Tell Mapleson broke a collar-bone, attempting it; and Jim Conlow, as O'mie said, "knocked the 'possum' aff his mug thryin' to achave the art." He fractured the bones of his nose, making his face a degree more homely than it was before. Then there were the Mead boys to be counted on everywhere. Dave went West years ago, made his fortune, and then began to traffic with the Orient. His name is better known in Hong-Kong now than it is in Springvale. He never married, and it used to be said that a young girl's grave up in the Red Range graveyard held all his hope and love. I do not know; for he left home the year I came up to Topeka to enlist, and Springvale was like the bitter waters of Marah to my spirit. But that comes later.

Bill Mead married Bessie Anderson, and the seven little tow-headed Meads, stair-stepping down the years, played with the third generation here as we used to play in the years gone by. Bill is president of the bank on the corner where the old Whately store stood and is a share-holder in several big Kansas City concerns. Bessie lost her rosy cheeks years ago, but she has her seven children; the youngest of them, Phil, named for me, will graduate from the Kansas University this year. Lettie Conlow was always on the uncertain list with us. No Conlow could do much with a horse except to put shoes under it. It was a trick of hers to lag behind and call to me to tighten a girth, while Marjie raced on with Dave Mead or Tell Mapleson. Tell liked Lettie, and it rasped my spirit to be made the object of her preference and his jealousy. Once when we were alone his anger boiled hot, and he shook his fist at me and cried:

"You mean pup! You want to take my girl from me. I can lick you, and I'm going to do it."

I was bigger than Tell, and he knew my strength.

"I wish to goodness you would," I said. "I'd rather be licked than to have a girl I don't care for always smiling at me."

Tell's face fell, and he grinned sheepishly.

"Don't you really care for Lettie, Phil? She says you like Bess Anderson."

Was that a trick of Lettie's to put Marjie out of my thought, I wondered, or did she really know my heart? I distrusted Lettie. She was so like her black-eyed father. But I had guarded my own feelings, and the boys and girls had not guessed what Marjie was to me.

It was about this time that Father Le Claire, a French priest who had been a missionary in the Southwest, began to come and go about Springvale. His work lay mostly with the Osages farther down the Neosho, but he labored much among the Kaws. He was a kindly-spirited man, reserved, but gentle and courteous ever, and he was very fond of children. He was always in town on annuity days, when the tribes came up for their quarterly stipend from the Government. Mapleson was the Indian agent. The "Last Chance," unable to compete with its commercial rival, the Whately house, had now a drug store in the front, a harness shop in the rear and a saloon in the cellar. It was to this "Last Chance" that the Indians came for their money; and it was Father Le Claire who piloted many of them out to the trails leading southward and started them on the way to their villages, sober and possessed of their Government allowance or its equivalent in honest merchandise.

From the first visit the good priest took to Jean Pahusca, and he helped to save the young brave from many a murdering spell.

To O'mie and myself, however, remained the resolve to drive him from Springvale; for, boylike, we watched him more closely than the men did, and we knew him better. He was not the only one of our town who drank too freely. Four decades ago the law was not the righteous force it is to-day, and we looked upon many sights which our children, thank Heaven, never see in Kansas.

"Keep out of that Redskin's way when he's drunk," was Cam Gentry's advice to us. "You know he'd scalp his grandmother if he could get hold of her then."

We kept out of his way, but we bided our time.

Father Le Claire had another favorite in Springvale, and that was O'mie. He said little to the Irish orphan lad, but there sprang up a sort of understanding between the two. Whenever he was in town, O'mie was not far away from him; and the boy, frank and confidential in everything else, grew strangely silent when we talked of the priest. I spoke of this to my father one day. He looked keenly at me and said quietly:

"You would make a good lawyer, Phil, you seem to know what a lawyer must know; that is, what people think as well as what they say."

"I don't quite understand, father," I replied.

"Then you won't make a good lawyer. It's the understanding that makes the lawyer," and he changed the subject.

My mind was not greatly disturbed over O'mie, however. I was young and neither I nor my companions were troubled by anything but the realities of the day. Limited as we were by circumstances in this new West, we made the most of our surroundings and of one another. How much the prairies meant to us, as they unrolled their springtime glory! From the noonday blue of the sky overhead to the deep verdure of the land below, there ranged every dainty tint of changeful coloring. Nature lavished her wealth of loveliness here, that the dream of the New Jerusalem might not seem a mere phantasy of the poet disciple who walked with the Christ and was called of Him "The Beloved."

The prairies were beautiful to me at any hour, but most of all I loved them in the long summer evenings when the burst of sunset splendor had deepened into twilight. Then the afterglow softened to that purple loveliness indescribably rare and sweet, wreathed round by gray cloudfolds melting into exquisite pink, the last far echo of the daylight's glory. It is said that any land is beautiful to us only by association. Was it the light heart of my boyhood, and my merry comrades, and most of all, the little girl who was ever in my thoughts, that gave grandeur to these prairies and filled my memory with pictures no artist could ever color on canvas? I cannot say, for all these have large places in my mind's treasury.

From early spring to late October it was a part of each day's duty for the youngsters of Springvale to go in the evening after the cows that ranged on the open west. We went together, of course, and, of course, we rode our ponies. Sometimes we went far and hunted long before we found the cattle. The tenderest grasses grew along the draws, and these often formed a deep wrinkle on the surface where our whole herd was hidden until we came to the very edge of the depression. Sometimes the herd was scattered, and every one must be rounded up and headed toward town before we left the prairie. And then we loitered on the homeward way and sang as only brave, free-spirited boys and girls can sing. And the prairie caught our songs and sent them rippling far and far over its clear, wide spaces.

As the twilight deepened, we drew nearer together, for comradeship meant protection. Some years before, a boy had been stolen out on these prairies one day by a band of Kiowas, and that night the mother drowned herself in the Neosho above town. Her home had been in a little stone cabin round the north bend of the river. It was in the sheltered draw just below where the one lone cottonwood tree made a landmark on the Plains—a deserted habitation now, and said to be haunted by the spirit of the unhappy mother. The child's father, a handsome French Canadian, had turned Plainsman and gone to the Southwest and had not been heard of afterwards. While we had small grounds for fear, we kept our ponies in a little group coming in side by side on the home stretch. All the purple shadows of those sweet summer twilights are blended with the memories of those happy care-free hours.

In the long summer days the cows ranged wider to the west, and we wandered farther in our evening jaunts and lingered later in the fragrant draws where the sweet grasses were starred with many brilliant blossoms. That is how we happened to be away out on the northwest prairie that evening when Jean Pahusca found us, the evening when O'mie read my secret in my tell-tale face. Even to-day a storm cloud in the northwest with the sunset flaming against its jagged edges recalls that scene. The cattle had all been headed homeward, and we were racing our ponies down the long slope to the south. On the right the draw, watched over by the big cottonwood, breaks through the height and finds its way to the

Neosho. The watershed between the river and Fingal's Creek is here only a high swell, and straight toward the west it is level as a floor.

The air of a hot afternoon had begun to ripple in cool little waves against our faces. All the glory of the midsummer day was ending in the grandeur of a crimson sunset shaded northward by that threatening thundercloud. With our ponies lined up for one more race we were just on the point of starting, when a whoop, a savage yell, and Jean Pahusca rose above the edge of the draw behind us and dashed toward us headlong. We knew he was drunk, for since Father Le Claire's coming among us he had come to be a sort of gentleman Indian when he was sober; and we caught the naked gleam of the short sharp knife he always wore in a leather sheath at his belt. We were thrown into confusion, and some ponies became unmanageable at once. It is the way of their breed to turn traitor with the least sign of the rider's fear. At Jean's second whoop there was a stampede. Marjie's pony gave a leap and started off at full gallop toward the level west. Hers was the swiftest horse of all, but the Indian coming at an angle had the advantage of space, and he singled her out in a moment. Her hair hung down in two heavy braids, and as she gave one frightened glance backward I saw her catch them both in one hand and draw them over her shoulder as if to save them from the scalping knife.

My pony leaped to follow her but my quick eye caught the short angle of the Indian's advantage. I turned, white and anguish-stricken, toward my companions. Then it was that I heard O'mie's low words:

"Bedad, Phil, an' that's how it is wid ye, is it? Then we've got to kill that Injun, just for grandeur."

His voice set a mighty force tingling in every nerve. The thrill of that moment is mine after all these years, for in that instant I was born again. I believe no terror nor any torture could have stayed me then, and death would have seemed sublime if only I could have flung myself between the girl and this drink-crazed creature seeking in his irresponsible madness to take her life. It was not alone that this was Marjie, and there swept over me the full realization of what she meant to me. Something greater than my own love and life leaped into being within me. It was the swift, unworded comprehension of a woman's worth, of the sacredness of her life, and her divine right to the protection of her virtue; a comprehension of the beauty and blessing of the American home, of the obedient daughter, the loving wife, the Madonna mother, of all that these mean as the very foundation rock of our nation's strength and honor. It swept my soul like a cleansing fire. The words for this came later, but the force of it swayed my understanding in that instant's crisis. Some boys grow into manhood as the years roll along, and some leap into it at a single bound. It was a boy, Phil Baronet, who went out after the cows that careless summer day so like all the other summer days before it. It was a man, Philip Baronet, who followed them home that dark night, fearing neither the roar of the angry storm cloud that threshed in fury above us, nor any human being, though he were filled with the rage of madness.

At O'mie's word I dashed after Marjie. Behind me came Bud Anderson and Dave Mead, followed by every other boy and girl. O'mie rode beside me, and not one of us thought of himself. It was all done in a flash, and I marvel that I tell its mental processes as if they were a song sung in long-metre time. But it is all so clear to me. I can see the fiery radiance of that sky blotted by the two riders before me. I can hear the crash of the ponies' feet, and I can even feel the sweep of wind out of that storm-cloud turning the white underside of the big cottonwood's leaves uppermost and cutting cold now against the hot air. And then there rises up that ripple of ground made by the ring of the Osage's tepee in the years gone by. Marjie deftly swerved her pony to the south and skirted that little ridge of ground with a graceful curve, as though this were a mere racing game and not a life-and-death ride. Jean's horse plunged at the tepee ring, leaped to the little hollow beyond it, stumbled and fell, and, pellmell, like a stampede of cattle, we were upon him.

I never could understand how Dave Mead headed the crowd back and kept the whole mass from piling up on the fallen Indian and those nearest to him. Nor do I understand why some of us were not crushed or kicked out of life in that *mêlée* of ponies and riders struggling madly together. What I do know is that Bud Anderson, who was not thrown from his horse, caught Jean's pony by the bridle and dragged it clear of the mass. It was O'mie's quick hand that wrested that murderous knife from the Indian's grasp, and it was my strong arm that held him with a grip of iron. The shock sobered him instantly. He struggled a moment, and then the cunning that always deceived us gained control. The Indian spirit vanished, and with something masterful in his manner he relaxed all effort. Lifting his eyes to mine with no trace of resentment in their impenetrable depths, he said evenly:

"Let me go. I was drunk. I was fool."

"Let him go, Phil. He did act kinder drunk," Bill Mead urged, and I loosed my hold. I knew instinctively that we were safe now, as I knew also that this submission of Jean Pahusca's must be paid for later with heavy interest by somebody.

"Here'th your horth; s'pothe you thkite," lisped Bud Anderson.

Jean sprang upon his pony and dashed off. We watched him ride away down the long slope. In a few moments another horseman joined him, and they took the trail toward the Kaw reservation. It was Father Le Claire riding with the Indian into the gathering shadows of the south.

I turned to Marjie standing beside me. Her big brown eyes were luminous with tears, and her face was as white as my mother's face was on the day the sea left its burden on the Rockport sands. It was hate that made Jean Pahusca veil his countenance for me a moment before. Something of which hate can never know made me look down at her calmly. O'mie's hand was on my shoulder and his eyes were on us both. There was a quaint approval in his glance toward me. He knew the self-control I needed then.

"Phil saved you, Marjie," Mary Gentry exclaimed.

"No, he saved Jean," put in Lettie.

"And O'mie saved Phil," Bess Anderson urged. "Just grabbed that knife in time."

"Well, I thaved mythelf," Bud piped in.

He never could find any heroism in himself who, more than any other boy among us, had a record for pulling drowning boys out of the Deep Hole by the Hermit's Cave, and killing rattlesnakes in the cliff's crevices, and daring the dark when the border ruffians were hiding about Springvale.

An angry growl of thunder gave us warning of the coming storm. In our long race home before its wrath, in the dense darkness wrapping the landscape, we could only trust to the ponies to keep the way. Marjie rode close by my side that night, and more than once my hand found hers in the darkness to assure her of protection. O'mie, bless his red head! crowded Lettie to the far side of the group, keeping Tell on the other side of her.

When I climbed the hill on Cliff Street that night I turned by the bushes and caught the gleam of Marjie's light. I gave the whistling call we had kept for our signal these years, and I saw the light waver as a good-night signal.

That night I could not sleep. The storm lasted for hours, and the rain swept in sheets across the landscape. The darkness was intense, and the midsummer heat of the day was lost in the chill of that drouth-breaking torrent. After midnight I went to my father's room. He had not retired, but was sitting by the window against which the rain beat heavily. The light burned low, and his fine face was dimly outlined in the shadows. I sat down beside his knee as I was wont to do in childhood.

"Father," I began hesitatingly, "Father, do you still love my mother? Could you care for anybody else? Does a man ever—" I could not say more. Something so like tears was coming into my voice that my cheeks grew hot.

My father's hand rested gently on my head, his fingers stroking the ripples of my hair. White as it is now, it was dark and wavy then, as my mother's had been. It was the admiration of the women and girls, which admiration always annoyed and embarrassed me. In and out of those set waves above my forehead his fingers passed caressingly. He knew the heart of a boy, and he sat silent there, letting me feel that I could tell him anything.

"Have you come to the cross-roads, Phil?" he asked gently. "I was thinking of you as I sat here. Maybe that brought you in. Your boyhood must give way to manhood soon. These times of civil war change conditions for our children," he mused to himself, rather than spoke to me. "We expect a call to the front soon, Phil. When I am gone, I want you to do a man's part in Springvale. You are only a boy, I know, but you have a man's strength, my son."

"And a man's spirit, too," I cried, springing up and standing erect before him. "Let me go with you, Father."

"No, Phil, you must stay here and help to protect these homes, just as we men must go out to fight for them. To the American people war doesn't mean glory nor conquest. It means safety and freedom, and these begin and end in the homes of our land."

The impulse wakened on the prairie that evening at the sight of Marjie's peril leaped up again within me.

"I'll do my best. But tell me, Father," I had dropped down beside him again, "do you still love my mother? Does a man love the same woman always?"

Few boys of my age would have asked such a question of a man. My father took both of my hands into his own strong hands and in the dim light he searched my face with his keen eyes.

"Men differ in their natures, my boy. Even fathers and sons do not always think alike. I can speak only for myself. Do I love the woman who gave you birth? Oh, Phil!"

No need for him to say more. Over his face there swept an expression of tenderness such as I have never seen save as at long intervals I have caught it on the face of a sweet-browed mother bending above a sleeping babe. I rose up before him, and stooping, I kissed his forehead. It was a sacred hour, and I went out from his presence with a new bond binding us together who had been companions all my days. My dreams when I fell asleep at last were all of Marjie, and through them all her need for a protector was mingled with a still greater need for my guardianship. It came from two women who were strangers to me, whose faces I had never seen before.

CHAPTER V

A GOOD INDIAN

Underneath that face like summer's ocean,
Its lips as moveless, and its brow as clear,
Slumbers a whirlwind of the heart's emotion,
Love, hatred, pride, hope, sorrow,—all save fear.

Cast in the setting of to-day, after such an attempt on human life as we broke up on the prairie, Jean Pahusca would have been hiding in the coverts of Oklahoma, or doing time at the Lansing penitentiary for attempted assault with intent to kill. The man who sold him the whiskey would be in the clutches of the law, carrying his case up to the Supreme Court, backed by the slush fund of the brewers' union. The Associated Press would give the incident a two-inch heading and a one-inch story; and the snail would stay on the thorn, and the lark keep on the wing.

Even in that time Springvale would not have tolerated the Indian among us had it not been that the minds of the people were fermenting with other things. We were on the notorious old border between free and slave lands, whose tragedies rival the tales of the Scottish border. Kansas had been a storm centre since the day it became a Territory, and the overwhelming theme was negro slavery. Every man was marked as "pro" or "anti." There was no neutral ground. Springvale was by majority a Free-State town. A certain element with us, however, backed up by the Fingal's Creek settlement, declared openly and vindictively for slavery. It was from this class that we had most to fear. While the best of our people were giving their life-blood to save a nation, these men connived with border raiders who would not hesitate to take the life and property of every Free-State citizen. When our soldiers marched away to fields of battle, they knew they were leaving an enemy behind them, and no man's home was safe. Small public heed was paid then to the outbreak of a drunken Indian boy who had been overcome in a scrap out on the prairie when the youngsters were hunting their cows.

Where the bushes grow over the edge of the bluff at the steep bend in Cliff Street, a point of rock projects beyond the rough side. By a rude sort of stone steps beside this point we could clamber down many feet to the bush-grown ledge below. This point had been a meeting-place and playground for Marjie and myself all those years. We named it "Rockport" after the old Massachusetts town. Marjie could hear my call from the bushes and come up to the half-way place between our two homes. The stratum of rock below this point was full of cunning little crevices and deep hiding-places. One of these, known only to Marjie and myself, we called our post-office, and many a little note, scrawled in childish hand, but always directed to "Rockport" like a real address on the outside fold, we left for each other to find. Sometimes it was a message, sometimes it was only a joke, and sometimes it was just a line of childish love-making. We always put our valentines in this private house of Uncle Sam's postal service. Maybe that was why the other boys and girls did not couple our names together oftener. Everybody knew who got valentines at the real post-office and where they came from.

On the evening after the storm there was no loitering on the prairie. While we knew there was no danger, a half-dozen boys brought the cows home long before the daylight failed. At sunset I went down to "Rockport," intending to whistle to Marjie. How many a summer evening together here we had watched the sunset on the prairie! To-night, for no reason that I could give, I parted the bushes and climbed down to the ledge below, intending in a moment to come up again. I paused to listen to the lowing of some cows down the river. All the sweet sounds and odors of evening were in the air, and the rain-washed woodland of the Neosho Valley was in its richest green. I did not notice that the bushes hid me until, as I turned, I caught a glimpse of a red blanket, with a circular white centre, sliding up that stairway. An instant later, a call, my signal whistle, sounded from the rock above. I stood on the ledge under the point, my heart the noisiest thing in all that summer landscape full of soft twilight utterances. I was too far below the cliff's edge to catch any answering call, but I determined to fling that blanket and its wearer off the height if any harm should even threaten. Presently I heard a light footstep, and Marjie parted the bushes above me. Before she could cry out, Jean spoke to her. His voice was clear and sweet as I had never heard it before, and I do not wonder it reassured her.

"No afraid, Star-face, no afraid. Jean wants one word."

Marjie did not move, and I longed to let her know how near I was to her, and yet I dared not till I knew his purpose.

"Star-face," he began, "Jean drink no more. Jean promise Padre Le Claire, never, never, Star-face, not be afraid anymore, never, never. Jean good Indian now. Always keep evil from Star-face."

How full of affection were his tones. I wondered at his broken Indian tongue, for he had learned good English, and sometimes he surpassed us all in the terse excellence and readiness of his language. Why should he hesitate so now?

"Star-face,"—there was a note of self-control in his pleading voice,— "I will never drink again. I would not do harm to you. Don't be afraid."

I heard her words then, soft and sweet, with that tremor of fear she could never overcome.

"I hope you won't, Jean."

Then the bushes crackled, as she turned and sped away.

I was just out of sight again when that red blanket slipped down the rocks and disappeared over the side of the ledge in the jungle of bushes below me.

A little later, when Mary Gentry and O'mie and I sat with Marjie on the Whately doorstep, she told us what Jean had said.

"Do you really think he will be good now?" asked Mary. She was always credulous.

"Yes, of course," Marjie answered carelessly.

Her reply angered me. She seemed so ready to trust the word of this savage who twenty-four hours before had tried to scalp her. Did his manner please Marjie? Was the foolish girl attracted by this picturesque creature? I clenched my fists in the dark.

"Girls are such silly things," I said to myself. "I thought better of Marjie, but she is like all the rest." And then I blushed in the dark for having such mean thoughts.

"Don't you think he will be good now, Phil?"

I did not know how eagerly she waited for my answer. Poor Marjie! To her the Indian name was always a terror. Before I could reply O'mie broke in:

"Marjory Whately, ye'll excuse me fur referrin' to it, but I ain't no bigger than you are."

O'mie had not grown as the most of us had, and while he had a lightning quickness of movement, and a courage that never faltered, he was no match for the bigger boys in strength and endurance. Marjie was rounding into graceful womanhood now, but she was not of the slight type. She never lost her dimples, and the vigorous air of the prairies gave her that splendid physique that made her a stranger to sickness and kept the wild-rose bloom on her fair cheeks. O'mie did not outweigh her.

"Ye'll 'scuse me," O'mie went on, "fur the embarrassin' statement; but I ain't big, I run mostly to brains, while Phil here, an' Bill, an' Dave, an' Bud, an' Possum Conlow runs mostly to beef; an' yet, bein' small, I ain't afraid none of your good Injun. But take this warnin' from me, an old friend that knew your grandmother in long clothes, that you kape wide of Jean Pahusca's trail. Don't you trust him."

Marjie gave a little shiver. Had I been something less a fool then I should have known that it was a shiver of fear, but I was of the age to know everything, and O'mie sitting there had learned my heart in a moment on the prairie the evening before. And then I wanted Marjie to trust to me. Her eyes were like stars in the soft twilight, and her white face lost its color, but she did not look at me.

"Don't you trust that mock-turtle Osage, Marjorie, don't." O'mie was more deeply in earnest than we thought.

"But O'mie," Marjie urged, "Jean was just as earnest as you are now; and you'd say so, too, Phil, if you had heard him."

She was right. The words I had heard from above the rock rang true.

"And if he really wants to do better, what have we all been told in the Sunday-school? 'Thou shalt love thy neighbor as thyself.'"

I could have caught that minor chord of fear had I been more master of myself at that moment.

"Have ye talked wid Father Le Claire?" asked O'mie. "Let's lave the baste to him. Phil, whin does your padre and his Company start to subdue the rebillious South?"

"Pretty soon, father says."

"My father is going too," Marjie said gently, "and Henry Anderson and Cris Mead, and all the men."

"Oh, well, we'll take care of the widders an' orphans." O'mie spoke carelessly, but he added, "It's grand whin such min go out to foight fur a country. Uncle Cam wants to go if he's aqual to the tests; you know he's too near-sighted to see a soldier. Why don't you go too, Phil? You're big as your dad, an' not half so essential to Springvale. Just lave it to sich social ornimints as me an' Marjie's 'good Injun.'"

Again Marjie shivered.

"I want to go, but father won't let me leave—Aunt Candace."

"An' he's right, as is customary wid him. You nade your aunt to take care of you. He couldn't be stoppin' the battle to lace up your shoes an' see that you'd washed your neck. Come, Mary, little girls must be gettin' home." And he and Mary trotted down the slope toward the twinkling lights of the Cambridge House.

Before I reached home, O'mie had overtaken me, saying:

"Come, Phil, let's rest here a minute."

We were just by the bushes that shut off my "Rockport," so we parted them and sat down on the point of rock. The moon was rising, red in the east, and the Neosho Valley below us was just catching its gleams on the treetops, while each point of the jagged bluff stood out silvery white above the dark shadows. A thousand crickets and katydids were chirping in the grass. It was only on the town side that the bushes screened this point. All the west prairie was in that tender gloom that would roll back in shadowy waves before the rising moon.

"Phil," O'mie began, "don't be no bigger fool than nature cut you out fur to be. Don't you trust that 'good Injun' of Marjie's, but kape one eye on him comin' an t' other 'n on him goin'."

"I don't trust him, O'mie, but he has a voice that deceives. I don't wonder, being a girl, Marjie is caught by it."

"An' you, bein' a boy," O'mie mimicked,—"Phil, you're enough to turn my hair rid. But never mind, ye can't trust him. Fur why? He's not to be trusted. If he was aven Injun clean through you could a little, maybe. Some Osages has honor to shame a white man,—aven an Irishman,—but he's not Osage. He's a Kiowa, the kind that stole that little chap years ago up toward Rid Range. An' he ain't Kiowa altogether nather. The Injun blood gives him cuteness, but half his cussedness is in that soft black scalp an' that soft voice sayin', 'Good Injun.' There's some old Louis XIV somewhere in his family tree. The roots av it may be in the Plains out here, but some branch is a graft from a Orleans rose-bush. He's got the blossoms an' the thorns av a Frenchman. An' besides," O'mie added, "as if us two wise men av the West didn't know, comes Father Le Claire to me to-day. He's Jean's guide an' counsellor. An' Phil, begorra, them two looks alike. Same square-cut kind o' foreheads they've got. Annyhow, I was waterin' the horses down to the ford, an' Father Le Claire comes on me sudden, ridin' up on the Kaw trail from the south. He blessed me wid his holy hand and then says quick:

"'O'mie, ye are a lad I can trust!'"

"I nodded, not knowin' why annybody can't be trusted who goes swimmin' once a week, an' never tastes whiskey, an' don't practise lyin', nor shirkin' his stunt at the Cambridge House."

"'O'mie,' says he, 'I want to tell you who you must not trust. It is Jean Pahusca,' says he; 'I wish I didn't nade to say it, but it is me duty to warn ye. Don't mistreat him, but O'mie, for Heaven's sake, kape your eyes open, especially when he promises to be good.' It's our stunt, Phil, to watch him close now he's took to reformin' to the girls."

"O'mie, we know, and Father Le Claire knows, but how can we make those foolish girls understand? Mary believes everything that's said to her anyhow, and you heard Marjie to-night. She thinks she should take Jean at his word."

"Phil, you are all right, seemin'ly. You can lick any av us. You've got the build av a giant, an' you've beautiful hair an' teeth. An' you are son an' heir to John Bar'net, which is an asset some av us would love to possess, bein' orphans, an' the lovely ladies av Springvale is all bewitched by you; but you are a blind, blitherin' ijit now an' again."

"Well, you heard what Marjie said, and how careless she was."

"Yes, an' I seen her shiver an' turn white the instant too. Phil, she's doin' that to kape us from bein' unaisy, an' it's costin' her some to do it. Bless her pretty face! Phil, don't be no bigger fool than ye can kape from."

In less than a week after the incident on the prairie my father's Company was called to the firing line of the Civil War and the responsibilities of life fell suddenly upon me. There was a great gathering in town on the day the men marched away. Where the opera house stands now was the corner of a big vacant patch of ground reaching out toward the creek. To-day it was filled with the crowd come to see the soldiers and bid them good-bye. A speaker's stand was set up in the yard of the Cambridge House and the boys in blue were in the broad street before it. It was the last civilian ceremony for many of them, for that Kansas Company went up Missionary Ridge at Chattanooga, led the line as Kansans will ever do, and in the face of a murderous fire they drove the foeman back. But many of them never came home to wear their laurels of victory. They lie in distant cemeteries under the shadow of tall monuments. They lie in old neglected fields, in sunken trenches, by lonely waysides, and in deep Southern marshes, waiting all the last great Reunion. If I should live a thousand years, the memory of that bright summer morning would not fade from my mind.

Dr. Hemingway, pastor of the Presbyterian Church, presided over the meeting, and the crowd about the soldiers was reinforced by all the countryside beyond the Neosho and the whole Red Range neighborhood.

Skulking about the edge of the company, or gathered in little groups around the corners just out of sight, were the pro-slavery sympathizers, augmented by the Fingal's Creek crowd, who were of the Secession element clear through. In the doorway of the "Last Chance" sat the Rev. Dodd, pastor of the Springvale Methodist Church South, taking no part in this patriotic occasion. Father Le Claire was beside Dr. Hemingway. He said not a word, but Springvale knew he was a power for peace. He did not sanction bloodshed even in a righteous cause. Neither would he allow those who followed his faith to lift a hand against those who did go out to battle. We trusted him and he never betrayed that trust. This morning I recalled what O'mie had said about his looking like Jean Pahusca. His broad hat was pushed back from his square dark forehead; and the hair, soft and jetty, had the same line about the face. But not one feature there bespoke an ignoble spirit. I did not understand him, but I was drawn toward him, as I was repelled by the Indian from the moment I first saw his head above the bluff on the rainy October evening long ago.

How little the Kansas boys and girls to-day can understand what that morning meant to us, when we saw our fathers riding down the Santa Fé Trail to the east, and waving good-bye to us at the far side of the ford! How the fire of patriotism burned in our hearts, and how the sudden loss of all our strongest and best men left us helpless among secret cruel enemies! And then that spirit of manhood leaped up within us, the sudden sense of responsibility come to "all the able-bodied boys" to stand up as a wall of defence about the homes of Springvale. Too well we knew the dangers. Had we not lived on this Kansas border in all those plastic years when the mind takes deepest impressions? The ruffianism of Leavenworth and Lawrence and Osawatomie had been repeated in the unprotected surroundings of Springvale. The Red Range schoolhouse had been burned, and the teacher, a Massachusetts man, had been drowned in a shallow pool near the source of Fingal's Creek, his body fastened face downward so that a few inches of water were enough for the fiendish purpose. Eastward the settlers had fled to our town, time and again, to escape the border raiders, whose coming meant death to the free-spirited father, and a widow and orphans left destitute beside the smoking embers of what had been a home. Those were busy days in Kansas, and the memory of them can yet stir the heart of a man of sixty years.

That morning Dr. Hemingway offered prayer, the prayer of a godly man, for the souls of men about to be baptized with a baptism of blood that other men might be free, and a peaceful generation might walk with ease where their feet trod red-hot ploughshares; a prayer for the strong arm of God Almighty, to uphold every soldier's hands until the cause of right should triumph; a prayer for the heavenly Father's protection about the homes left fatherless for the sake of His children.

And then he prayed for us, "for Philip Baronet, the strong and manly son of his noble father, John Baronet; for David and William Mead, for John and Clayton and August Anderson." He prayed for Tell Mapleson, too (Tell was always square in spite of his Copperhead father), and for "Thomas O'Meara." We hardly knew whom he meant.

Bud Anderson whispered later, "Thay, O'mie, you'll never get into kingdom come under an athumed name. Better thtick to 'O'mie.'"

And last of all the good Doctor prayed for the wives and daughters, that they "be strong and very courageous," doing their part of working and waiting as bravely as they do who go out to stirring action. Then ringing speeches followed. I remember them all; but most of all the words of my father and of Irving Whately are fixed in my mind. My father lived many years and died one sunset hour when the prairies were in their autumn glory, died with his face to the western sky, his last earthly scene that peaceful prairie with the grandeur of a thousand ever-changing hues building up a wall like to the walls of the New Jerusalem which Saint John saw in a vision on the Isle of Patmos. There was

No moaning of the bar
When he put out to sea

for he died beautifully, as he had lived. I never saw Irving Whately again, for he went down before the rebel fire at Chattanooga; but the sound of his voice I still can hear.

The words of these men seemed to lift me above the clouds, and what followed is like a dream. I know that when the speeches were done, Marjie went forward with the beautiful banner the women of Springvale had made with their own hands for this Company. I could not hear her words. They were few and simple, no doubt, for she was never given to display. But I remember her white dress and her hair parted in front and coiled low on her neck. I remember the sweet Madonna face of the little girl, and how modestly graceful she was. I remember how every man held his breath as she came up to the group seated on the stage, how pink her cheeks were and how white the china aster bloom nestling against the ripples of her hair, and how the soldiers cheered that flag and its bearer. I remember Jean Pahusca, Indian-like, standing motionless, never taking his eyes from Marjie's face. It was that flag that this Company followed in its awful charge up Missionary Ridge. And it was Irving Whately who kept it aloft, the memory of his daughter making it doubly sacred to him.

And then came the good-byes. Marjie's father gripped my hand, and his voice was full of tears.

"Take care of them, Phil. I have no son to guard my home, and if we never come back you will not let harm come to them. You will let me feel when I am far away that you are shielding my little girl from evil, won't you, Phil?"

I clenched his hand in mine. "You know I'll do that, Mr. Whately." I stood up to my full height, young, broad-shouldered, and muscular.

"It will be easier for me, Phil, to know you are here."

I understood him. Mrs. Whately was, of all the women I knew, least able to do for herself. Marjie was like her father, and, save for her fear of Indians, no Kansas girl was ever more capable and independent. It has been my joy that this father trusted me. The flag his daughter put into his hands that day was his shroud at Chattanooga, and his last moments were happier for the thought of his little girl in my care.

Aunt Candace and I walked home together after we had waved the last good-byes to the soldiers. From our doorway up on Cliff Street we watched that line of men grow dim and blend at last into the eastern horizon's purple bound. When I turned then and looked down at the town beyond the slope, it seemed to me that upon me alone rested the burden of its protection. Driven deep in my boyish soul was the sense of the sacredness of these homes, and of a man's high duty to keep harm from them. My father had gone out to battle, not alone to set free an enslaved race, but to make whole and strong a nation whose roots are in the homes it defends. So I, left to fill his place, must be the valiant defender of the defenceless. Such moments of exaltation come to the young soul, and by such ideals a life is squared.

That evening our little crowd of boys strolled out on the west prairie. The sunset deepened to the rich afterglow, and all the soft shadows of evening began to unfold about us. In that quiet, sacred time, standing out on the wide prairie, with the great crystal dome above us, and the landscape, swept across by the free winds of heaven, unrolled in all its dreamy beauty about us, our little company gripped hands and swore our fealty to the Stars and Stripes. And then and there we gave sacred pledge and promise to stand by one another and to give our lives if need be for the protection and welfare of the homes of Springvale.

Busy days followed the going of the soldiers. Somehow the gang of us who had idled away the summer afternoons in the sand-bar shallows beyond the Deep Hole seemed suddenly to grow into young men who must not neglect school nor business duties. Awkwardly enough but earnestly we strove to keep Springvale a pushing, prosperous community, and while our efforts were often ludicrous, the manliness of purpose had its effect. It gave us breadth, this purpose, and broke up our narrow prejudices. I believe in those first months I would have suffered for the least in Springvale as readily as for the greatest. Even Lettie Conlow, whose father kept on shoeing horses as though there were no civil strife in the nation, found such favor with me as she had never found before. I know now it was only a boy's patriotic foolishness, but who shall say it was ignoble in its influence? Marjie was my especial charge. That Fall I did not retire at night until I had run down to the bushes and given my whistle, and had seen her window light waver a good-night answer, and I knew she was safe. I was not her only guardian, however. One crisp autumn night there was no response to my call, and I sat down on the rocky outcrop of the steep hill to await the coming of her light in the window. It was a clear starlight night, and I had no thought of being unseen as I was quietly watching. Presently, up through the bushes a dark form slid. It did not stand erect when the street was reached, but crawled with head up and alert in the deeper shadow of the bluff side of the road. I knew instinctively that it was Jean Pahusca, and that he had not been expecting me to be there after my call and had failed to notice me in his eagerness to creep unseen down the slope. Sometimes in these later years in a great football game I have watched the Haskell Indians crawling swiftly up and down the side-lines following the surge of the players on the gridiron, and I always think of Jean as he crept down the hill that night. It was late October and the frost was glistening, but I pulled off my boots in a moment and silently followed the fellow. Inside the fence near Marjie's window was a big circle of lilac bushes, transplanted years ago from the old Ohio home of the Whatelys. Inside this clump Jean crept, and I knew by the quiet crackle of twigs and dead leaves he was making his bed there. My first thought was to drag him out and choke him. And then my better judgment prevailed. I slipped away to find O'mie for a council.

"Phil, I'd like to kill him wid a hoe, same as Marjie did that other rattlesnake that had Jim Conlow charmed an' flutterin' toward his pisen fangs, only we'd better wait a bit. By Saint Patrick, Philip, we can't hang up his hide yet awhoile. I know what the baste's up to annyhow."

"Well, what is it?" I queried eagerly.

"He's bein' a good Injun he is, an' he's got a crude sort o' notion he's protectin' that dear little bird. She may be scared o' him, an' he knows it; but bedad, I'd not want to be the border ruffian that went prowlin' in there uninvited; would you?"

"Well, he's a dear trusty old Fido of a watchdog, O'mie. We will take Father Le Claire's word, and keep an eye on him though. He will sleep where he will sleep, but we'll see if the sight of water affects him any. A dog of his breed may be subject to rabies. You can't always trust even a 'good Injun.'"

After that I watched for Jean's coming and followed him to his lilac bed, a half-savage, half-educated Indian brave, foolishly hoping to win a white girl for his own.

All that Fall Jean never missed a night from the lilac bush. As long as he persisted in passing the dark hours so near to the Whately home my burden of anxiety and responsibility was doubled. In silent faithfulness he kept sentinel watch. I dared not tell Marjie, for I knew it would fill her nights with terror, and yet I feared her accidental discovery of his presence. Jean was doing more than this, however. His promise to be good seemed to belie Father Le Claire's warning. In and out of the village all that winter he went, orderly, at times even affable, quietly refusing every temptation to drunkenness. "A good Indian" he was, even to the point where O'mie and I wondered if we might not have been wrong in our judgment of him. He was growing handsomer too. He stood six feet in his moccasins, stalwart as a giant, with grace in every motion. Somehow he seemed more like a picturesque Gipsy, a sort of semi-civilized grandee, than an Indian of the Plains. There was a dominant courtliness in his manner and his bearing was kingly. People spoke kindly of him. Regularly he took communion in the little Catholic chapel at the south edge of town on the Kaw trail. Quietly but persistently he was winning his way to universal favor. Only the Irish lad and I kept our counsel and, waited.

After the bitterly cold New Year's Day of '63 the Indian forsook the lilac bush for a time. But I knew he never lost track of Marjie's coming and going. Every hour of the day or night he could have told just where she was. We followed him down the river sometimes at night, and lost him in the brush this side the Hermit's Cave. We did not know that this was a mere trick to deceive us. To make sure of him we should have watched the west prairie and gone up the river for his real landing place. How he lived I do not know. An Indian can live on air and faith in a promise, or hatred of a foe. At last he lulled even our suspicion to sleep.

"Ask the priest what to do," I suggested to O'mie when we grew ashamed of our spying. "They are together so much the rascal looks and walks like him. See him on annuity day and tell him we feel like chicken thieves and kidnappers."

O'mie obeyed me to the letter, and ended with the query to the good Father:

"Now phwat should a couple of young sleuth-hounds do wid such a dacent good Injun?"

Father Le Claire's reply stunned the Irish boy.

"He just drew himself up a mile high an' more," O'mie related to me, "just stood up like the angel av the flamin' sword, an' his eyes blazed a black, consumin' fire. 'Watch him,' says the praist, 'for God's sake, watch him. Don't ask me again phwat to do. I've told you twice. Thirty years have I lived and labored with his kind. I know them.' An' then," O'mie went on, "he put both arms around me an' held me close as me own father might have done, somewhere back, an' turned an' left me. So there's our orders. Will ye take 'em?"

I took them, but my mind was full of queries. I did not trust the Indian, and yet I had no visible reason to doubt his sincerity.

CHAPTER VI

WHEN THE HEART BEATS YOUNG

A patch of green sod 'neath the trees brown and bare,
A smell of fresh mould on the mild southern air,
A twitter of bird song, a flutter, a call,
And though the clouds lower, and threaten and fall—
There's Spring in my heart!

—BERTA ALEXANDER GARVEY.

When the prairies blossomed again, and the Kansas springtime was in its daintiest green, when a blur of pink was on the few young orchards in the Neosho Valley, and the cottonwoods in the draws were putting forth their glittering tender leaves—in that sweetest time of all the year, a new joy came to me. Most girls married at sixteen in those days, and were grandmothers at thirty-five. Marjie was no longer a child. No sweeter blossom of young womanhood ever graced the West. All Springvale loved her, except Lettie Conlow. And Cam Gentry summed it all up in his own quaint way, brave old Cam fighting all the battles of the war over again on the veranda of the Cambridge House, since his defective range of vision kept him from the volunteer service. Watching Marjie coming down the street one spring morning Cam declared solemnly:

"The War's done decided, an' the Union has won. A land that can grow girls like Marjory Whately's got the favorin' smile of the Almighty upon it."

For us that season all the world was gay and all the skies were opal-hued, and we almost forgot sometimes that there could be sorrow and darkness and danger. Most of all we forgot about an alien down in the Hermit's Cave, "a good Indian" turned bad in one brief hour. Dear are the memories of that springtide. Many a glorious April have I seen in this land of sunshine, but none has ever seemed quite like that one to me. Nor waving yellow wheat, nor purple alfalfa bloom, nor ramparts of dark green corn on well-tilled land can hold for me one-half the beauty of the windswept springtime prairie. No sweet odor of new-ploughed ground can rival the fragrance of the wild grasses in their waving seas of verdure.

We were coming home from Red Range late one April day, where we had gone to a last-day-of-school affair. The boys and girls did not ride in a group now, but broke up into twos and twos sauntering slowly homeward. The tender pink and green of the landscape with the April sunset tinting in the sky overhead, and all the far south and west stretching away into limitless waves of misty green blending into the amethyst of the world's far bound, gave setting for young hearts beating in tune with the year's young beauty.

Tell Mapleson and Lettie had been with Marjie and me for a time, but at last Tell had led Lettie far away. When we reached the draw beyond the big cottonwood where Jean Pahusca threw us into such disorder on that August evening the year before, we found a rank profusion of spring blossoms. Leading our ponies by the bridle rein we lingered long in the fragrant draw, gathering flowers and playing like two children among them. At length Marjie sat down on the sloping ground and deftly wove into a wreath the little pink blooms of some frail wild flower.

"Come, Phil," she cried, "come, crown me Queen of May here in April!"

I was as tall then as I am now, and Marjie at her full height came only to my shoulder. I stooped to lay that dainty string of blossoms above her brow. They fell into place in her wavy hair and nestled there, making a picture only memory can keep. The air was very sweet and the whole prairie about the little draw was still and dewy. The purple twilight, shot through with sunset coloring, made an exquisite glory overhead, and far beyond us. It is all sacred to me even now, this moment in Love's young dream. I put both my hands gently against her fair round cheeks and looked down her into her brown eyes.

"Oh, Marjie," I said softly, and kissed her red lips just once.

She said never a word while we stood for a moment, a moment we never forgot. The day's last gleam of gold swept about us, and the ripple of a bird's song in the draw beyond the bend fell upon the ear. An instant later both ponies gave a sudden start. We caught their bridle reins, and looked for the cause. Nothing was in sight.

"It must have been a rattlesnake in that tall grass, Phil," Marjie exclaimed. "The ponies don't like snakes, and they don't care for flowers."

"There are no snakes here, Marjie. This is the garden of Eden without the Serpent," I said gayly.

All the homeward way was a dream of joy. We forgot there was a Civil War; that this was a land of aching hearts and dreary homes, and bloodshed and suffering and danger and hate. We were young, it was April on the prairies, and we had kissed each other in the pink-wreathed shadows of the twilight. Oh, it was good to live!

The next morning O'mie came grinning up the hill.

"Say, Phil, ye know I cut the chape Neosho crowd last evening up to Rid Range fur that black-eyed little Irish girl they call Kathleen. So I came home afterwhoile behind you, not carin' to contaminate meself wid such a common set after me pleasant company at Rid Range."

"Well, we managed to pull through without you, O'mie, but don't let it happen again. It's too hard on the girls to be deprived of your presence. Do be more considerate of us, my lord."

O'mie grinned more broadly than ever.

"Well, I see a sight worth waitin' fur on my homeward jaunt in the gloamin'."

"What was it, a rattlesnake?"

"Yes, begorra, it was just that, an' worse. You remember the draw this side of the big cottonwood, the one where the 'good Injun' come at us last August, the time he got knocked sober at the old tepee ring?"

I gave a start and my cheeks grew hot. O'mie pretended not to notice me.

"Well," he went on, "just as I came beyont that ring on this side and dips down toward the draw where Jean come from when he was aimin' to hang a certain curly brown-haired scalp—"

A thrill of horror went through me at the picture.

"Ye needn't shiver. Injuns do that; even little golden curls from babies' heads. You an' me may live to see it, an' kill the Injun that does it, yit. Now kape quiet. In this draw aforesaid, just like a rid granite gravestone sat a rid granite Injun, 'a good Injun,' mind you. In his hands was trailin' a broken wreath of pink blossoms, an' near as an Injun can, an' a Frenchman can't, he was lovin' 'em fondly. My appearance, unannounced by me footman, disconcerted him extramely. He rose up an' he looked a mile tall. They moved some clouds over a little fur his head up there," pointing toward the deep blue April sky where white cumulus clouds were heaped, "an' his eyes was one blisterin' grief, an' blazin' hate. He walks off proud an' erect, but some like a wounded bird too. But mostly and importantly, remember, and renew your watchfulness. It's hate an' a bad Injun now. Mark my words. The 'good Injun' went out last night wid the witherin' of them pink flowers lyin' limp in his cruel brown hands."

"But whose flower wreath could it have been?" I asked carelessly.

"O, phwat difference! Just some silly girl braided 'em up to look sweet for some silly boy. An' maybe he kissed her fur it. I dunno. Annyhow she lost this bauble, an' looking round I found it on the little knoll where maybe she sat to do her flower wreathin'."

He held up an old-fashioned double silver scarf-pin, the two pins held together by a short silver chain, such as shawls were fastened with in those days. Marjie had had the pin in the light scarf she carried on her arm. It must have slipped out when she laid the scarf beside her and sat down to make the wreath. I took the pin from O'mie's hand, my mind clear now as to what had frightened the ponies. A new anxiety grew up from that moment. The "good Indian" was passing. And yet I was young and joyously happy that day, and I did not feel the presence of danger then.

The early May rains following that April were such as we had never known in Kansas before. The Neosho became bank-full; then it spread out over the bottom lands, flooding the wooded valley, creeping up and up towards the bluffs. It raced in a torrent now, and the song of its rippling over stony ways was changed to the roar of many waters, rushing headlong down the valley. On the south of us Fingal's Creek was impassable. Every draw was brimming over, and the smaller streams became rivers. All these streams found their way to the Neosho and gave it impetus to destroy—which it did, tearing out great oaks and sending them swirling and plunging, in its swiftest currents. It found the soft, uncertain places underneath its burden of waters and with its millions of unseen hands it digged and scooped and shaped the thing anew. When at last the waters were all gone down toward the sea and our own beautiful river was itself again, singing its happy song on sunny sands and in purple shadows, the valley contour was much changed. To the boys who had known it, foot by foot, the differences would have been most marked. Especially would we have noted the change about the Hermit's Cave, had not that Maytime brought its burden of strife to us all.

That was the black year of the Civil War, with Murfreesboro, Chancellorsville, Gettysburg, Chattanooga and Chickamauga all on its record. Here in Kansas the minor tragedies are lost in the great horror of the Quantrill raid at Lawrence. But the constant menace of danger, and the strain of the thousand ties binding us to those from every part of the North who had gone out to battle, filled every day with its own care. When the news of Chancellorsville reached us, Cam Gentry sat on the tavern veranda and wept.

"An' to think of me, strong, an' able, an' longin' to fight for the Union, shut out because I can only see so far."

"But Uncle Cam," Dr. Hemingway urged, "Stonewall Jackson was killed by his own men just when victory was lost to us. You might do the same thing,—kill some man the country needs. And I believe, too, you are kept here for a purpose. Who knows how soon we may need strong men in this town, men who can do the short-range work? The Lord can use us all, and your place is here. Isn't that true, Brother Dodd?"

I was one of the group on the veranda steps that evening where the men were gathered in eager discussion of the news of the great Union loss at Chancellorsville, brought that afternoon by the stage from Topeka. I glanced across at Dodd, pastor of the Methodist Church South. A small, secretive, unsatisfactory man, he seemed to dole out the gospel grudgingly always, and never to any outside his own denomination.

He made no reply and Dr. Hemingway went on: "We have Philip here, and I'd count on him and his crowd against the worst set of outlaws that ever rode across the border. Yet they need your head, Uncle Cam, although their arms are strong."

He patted my shoulder kindly.

"We need you, too," he continued, "to keep us cheered up. When the Lord says to some of us, 'So far shalt thou see, and no farther,' he may give to that same brother the power to scatter sunshine far and wide. Oh, we need you, Brother Gentry, to make us laugh if for nothing else."

Uncle Cam chuckled. He was built for chuckling, and we all laughed with him, except Mr. Dodd. I caught a sneer on his face in the moment.

Presently Father Le Claire and Jean Pahusca joined the group. I had not seen the latter since the day of O'mie's warning. Indian as he was, I could see a change in his impassive face. It made me turn cold, me, to whom fear was a stranger. Father Le Claire, too, was not like himself. Self-possessed always, with his native French grace and his inward spiritual calm, this evening he seemed to be holding himself by a mighty grip, rather than by that habitual self-mastery that kept his life in poise.

I tell these impressions as a man, and I analyze them as a man, but, boy as I was, I felt them then with keenest power. Again the likeness of Indian and priest possessed me, but raised no query within me. In form, in gait and especially in the shape of the head and the black hair about their square foreheads they were as like as father and son. Just once I caught Jean's eye. The eye of a rattlesnake would have been more friendly. O'mie was right. The "good Indian" had vanished. What had come in his stead I was soon to know. But withal I could but admire the fine physique of this giant.

While the men were still full of the Union disaster, two horsemen came riding up to the tavern oak. Their horses were dripping wet. They had come up the trail from the southwest, where the draws were barely fordable. Strangers excited no comment in a town on the frontier. The trail was always full of them coming and going. We hardly noted that for ten days Springvale had not been without them.

"Come in, gentlemen," called Cam. "Here, Dollie, take care of these friends. O'mie, take their horses."

They passed inside and the talk outside went eagerly on.

"Father Le Claire, how do the Injuns feel about this fracas now?" inquired Tell Mapleson.

The priest spoke carefully.

"We always counsel peace. You know we do not belong to either faction."

His smile was irresistible, and the most partisan of us could not dislike him that he spoke for neither North nor South.

"But," Tell persisted, "how do the Injuns themselves feel?"

Tell seemed to have lost his usual insight, else he could have seen that quick, shrewd, penetrating glance of the good Father's reading him through and through.

"I have just come from the Mission," he said. "The Osages are always loyal to the Union. The Verdigris River was too high for me to hear from the villages in the southwest."

Tell was listening eagerly. So also were the two strangers who stood in the doorway now. If the priest noted this he gave no sign. Mr. Dodd spoke here for the first time.

"Well," he said in his pious intonation, "if the Osages are loyal, that clears Jean here. He's an Osage, isn't he?"

Jean made no reply; neither did Le Claire, and Tell Mapleson turned casually to the strangers, engaging them in conversation.

"We shall want our horses at four sharp in the morning," one of the two came out to say to Cam. "We have a long hard day before us."

"At your service," answered Cam. "O'mie, take the order in your head."

"Is that the biggest hostler you've got?" looking contemptuously at little O'mie standing beside me. "If you Kansas folks weren't such damned abolitionists you'd have some able-bodied niggers to do your work right."

O'mie winked at me and gave a low whistle. Neither the wink nor the whistle was lost on the speaker, who frowned darkly at the boy.

Cam squinted up at the men good-naturedly. "Them horses dangerous?" he asked.

"Yes, they are," the stranger replied. "Can we have a room downstairs? We want to go to bed early. We have had a hard day."

"You can begin to say your 'Now I lay me' right away in here if you like," and the landlord led the way into a room off the veranda. One of the two lingered outside in conversation with Mapleson for a brief time.

"Come, go home with me, O'mie," I said later, when the crowd began to thin out.

"Not me," he responded. "Didn't ye hear, 'four A. M. sharp'? It's me flat on me bed till the dewy morn an' three-thirty av it. Them's vicious horses. An' they'll be to curry clane airly. Phil," he added in a lower voice, "this town's a little overrun wid strangers wid no partic'lar business av their own, an' we don't need 'em in ours. For one private citizen, I don't like it. The biggest one of them two men in there's named Yeager, an' he's been here three toimes lately, stayin' only a few hours each toime."

O'mie looked so little to me this evening! I had hardly noted how the other boys had outgrown him.

"You're not very big for a horseman after all, my son, but you're grit clear through. You may do something yet the big fellows couldn't do," I said affectionately.

He was Irish to the bone, and never could entirely master his brogue, but we had no social caste lines, and Springvale took him at face value, knowing his worth.

At Marjie's gate I stopped to make sure everything was all right. Somehow when I knew the Indian was in town I could never feel safe for her. She hurried out in response to my call.

"I'm so glad to see you to-night, Phil," she said, a little tremulously. "I wish father were here. Do you think he is safe?"

She was leaning on the gate, looking eagerly into my eyes. The shadows of the May twilight were deepening around us, and Marjie's white face looked never so sweet to me as now, in her dependence on my assurance.

"I'm sure Mr. Whately is all right. It is the bad news that gets here first. I'm so glad our folks weren't at Chancellorsville."

"But they may be in as dreadful a battle soon. Oh, Phil, I'm so—what? lonesome and afraid to-night. I wish father could come home."

It was not like Marjie, who had been a dear brave girl, always cheering her dependent mother and hopefully expecting the best. To-night there swept over me anew that sense of the duty every man owes to the home. It was an intense feeling then. Later it was branded with fire into my consciousness. I put one of my big hands over her little white hand on the gate.

"Marjie," I said gently, "I promised your father I would let no harm come to you. Don't be afraid, little girl. You can trust me. Until he comes back I will take care of you."

The twilight was sweet and dewy and still. About the house the shadows were darkening. I opened the gate, and drawing her hand through my arm, I went up the walk with her.

"Is that the lilac that is so fragrant?" I caught a faint perfume in the air.

"Yes," sadly, "what there is of it." And then she laughed a little. "That miserable O'mie came up here the day after we went to Red Range and persuaded mother to cut it all down except one straight stick of a bush. He told her it was dying, and that it needed pruning, and I don't know what. And you know mother. I was over at the Anderson's, and when I came home the whole clump was gone. I dreamed the other night that somebody was hiding in there. It was all dead in the middle. Do you remember when we played hide-and-seek in there?"

"I never forget anything you do, Marjie," I answered; "but I'm glad the bushes are thinned out."

She broke off some plumes of the perfumy blossoms.

"Take those to Aunt Candace. Tell her I sent them. Don't let her think you stole them," she was herself now, and her fear was gone.

"May I take something else to Aunt Candace, too, Marjie?"

"What else?" She looked up innocently into my face. We were at the door-step now.

"A good-night kiss, Marjie."

"I'll see her myself about that," she replied mischievously but confusedly, pushing me away. I knew her cheek was flushed as my own, and I caught her hand and held it fast.

"Good-night, Phil." That sweet voice of hers I could not disobey. In a moment I was gone, happy and young and confident. I could have fought the whole Confederate army for the sake of this girl left in my care—my very own guardianship.

CHAPTER VII

THE FORESHADOWING OF PERIL

O clear-eyed Faith, and Patience thou
So calm and strong!
Lend strength to weakness, teach us how
The sleepless eyes of God look through
This night of wrong!

—WHITTIER.

While these May days were slipping by, strange history was making itself in Kansas. I marvel now, as I recall the slender bonds that stayed us from destruction, that we ever dared to do our part in that record-building day. And I rejoice that we did not know the whole peril that menaced us through those uncertain hours, else we should have lost all courage.

Father Le Claire held himself neutral to the North and the South, and was sometimes distrusted by both factions in our town; but he went serenely on his way, biding his time patiently. At sunrise on the morning after O'mie had surprised Jean Pahusca with Marjie's wreath of faded blossoms held caressingly in his brown hands, Le Claire met him in the little chapel. What he confessed led the priest to take him at once to the Osages farther down on the Neosho.

"I had hoped to persuade Jean to stay at the Mission," Le Claire said afterwards. "He is the most intelligent one of his own tribe I have ever known, and he could be invaluable to the Osages, but he would not stay away from Springvale. And I thought it best to come back with him."

The good man did not say why he thought it best to keep Jean under his guardianship. Few people in Springvale would have dreamed how dangerous a foe we had in this superbly built, picturesque, handsome Indian.

In the early hours of the morning after his return, the priest was roused from a sound sleep by O'mie. A storm had broken over the town just after midnight. When it had spent itself and roared off down the valley, the rain still fell in torrents, and O'mie's clothes were dripping when he rushed into Le Claire's room.

"For the love av Heaven," he cried, "they's a plot so pizen I must git out of me constitution quick. They're tellin' it up to Conlow's shop. Them two strangers, Yeager and his pal, that's s'posed to be sleepin' now to get an airly start, put out 'fore midnight for a prowl an' found theirsilves right up to Conlow's. An' I wint along behind 'em—respectful," O'mie grinned; "an' there was Mapleson an' Conlow an' the holy Dodd, mind ye. M. E. South's his rock o' defence. An' Jean was there too. They're promisin' him somethin', the strangers air. Tell an' Conlow seemed to kind o' dissent, but give in finally."

"Is it whiskey?" asked the priest.

"No, no. Tell says he can't have nothin' from the 'Last Chance.' Says the old Roman Catholic'll fix his agency job at Washington if he lets Jean get drunk. It's somethin' else; an' Tell wants to git aven with you, so he gives in."

The priest's face grew pale.

"Well, go on."

"There's a lot of carrion birds up there I never see in this town. Just lit in there somehow. But here's the schame. The Confederates has it all planned, an' they're doin' it now to league together all the Injun tribes av the Southwest. They's more 'n twinty commissioned officers, Rebels, ivery son av 'em, now on their way to meet the chiefs av these tribes. An' all the Kansas settlements down the river is to be fell upon by the Ridskins, an' nobody to be spared. Wid them Missouri raiders on the east and the Injuns in the southwest where'll anybody down there be, begorra, betwixt two sich grindin' millstones? I couldn't gather it all in, ye see. I was up on a ladder peeking in through a long hole laid down sideways. But that's the main f'ature av the rumpus. They're countin' big on the Osages becase the Gov'mint trusts 'em to do scout duty down beyont

Humboldt, and Jean says the Osages is sure to join 'em. Said it is whispered round at the Mission now. And phwat's to be nixt?"

Father Le Claire listened intently to O'mie's hurried recital. Then he rose up before the little Irishman, and taking both of the boy's hands in his, he said: "O'mie, you must do your part now."

"Phwat can I do? Show me, an' bedad, I'll do it."

"You will keep this to yourself, because it would only make trouble if it were repeated now, and we may outwit the whole scheme without any unnecessary anxiety and fright. Also, you must keep your eyes and ears open to all that's done and said here. Don't let anything escape you. If I can get across the Neosho this morning I can reach the Mission in time to keep the Osages from the plot, and maybe break it up. Then I'll come back here. They might need me if Jean"—he did not finish the sentence. "In two days I can do everything needful; while if the word were started here now, it might lead to a Rebel uprising, and you would be outnumbered by the Copperheads here, backed by the Fingal's Creek crowd. You could do nothing in an open riot."

"I comprehend ye," said O'mie. "It's iverything into me eyes an' ears an' nothin' out av me mouth."

"Meanwhile," the priest spoke affectionately, "you must be strong, my son, to choose the better part. If it's life or death,—O God, that human life should be held so cheap!—if it's left to you to choose who must be the sacrifice, you will choose right. I can trust you. Remember, in two or three days at most, I can be back; but keep your watch, especially of Jean. He means mischief, but I cannot stay here now, much less take him with me. He would not go."

So it happened that Father Le Claire hurried away in the darkness and the driving rain, and at a fearful risk swam his horse across the Neosho, and hastened with all speed to the Mission.

When that midnight storm broke over the town, on the night when O'mie followed the strangers and found out their plot, I helped Aunt Candace to fasten the windows and make sure against it until I was too wide awake to go to bed. I sat down by my window, in the lightning flashes watching the rain, wind-driven across the landscape. The night was pitch black. In all the southwest there was only one light, a sullen red bar of flame that came up from Conlow's forge fire. I watched it indifferently at first because it was there. Then I began to wonder why it should gleam there red and angry at this dead hour of darkness. As I watched, the light flared up as though it were fanned into a blaze. Then it began to blink and I knew some one was inside the shop. It was blotted out for a time, then it glowed again, as if there were many passing and re-passing. I wondered what it could all mean in such an hour, on such a night as this. Then I thought of old Conlow's children, of "Possum" in his weak, good-natured homeliness, and of Lettie. How I disliked her, and wished she would keep out of my way, which she never would do. Her face was clear to me, there in the dark. It grew malicious; then it hardened into wickedness, and I slipped from watching into a drowsy, half-waking sleep in my chair. The red bar of light became the flame of cannon on a battlefield, I saw our men in a life-and-death struggle with the enemy on a rough, wild mountainside. Everywhere my father was leading them on, and by his side Irving Whately bore the Springvale flag aloft. And then beside me lay the color-bearer with white, agonized face, pleading with me. His words were ringing in my ears, "Take care of Marjie, Phil; keep her from harm."

I woke with a start, stiff and shivering. With one half-dazed glance at the black night and that sullen tell-tale light below me, I groped my way to my bed and slept then the dreamless sleep of vigorous youth.

The rain continued for many hours. Yeager and his company could not get away from town on account of the booming Neosho. Also several other strange men seemed to have rained down from nobody asked where, and while the surface of affairs was smooth there was a troubled undercurrent. Nobody seemed to know just what to expect, yet a sense of calamity pervaded the air. Meanwhile the rain poured down in intermittent torrents. On the second evening of this miserable gloom I strolled down to the tavern stables to find O'mie. Bud and John Anderson and both the Mead boys were there, sprawled out on the hay. O'mie sat on a keg in the wagon way, and they were all discussing affairs of State like sages. I joined in and we fought the Civil War to a finish in half an hour. In all the "solid North" there was no more loyal company on that May night than that group of brawny young fellows full of the fire of patriotism, who swore anew their eternal allegiance to the Union.

"It's a crime and a disgrace," declared Dave Mead, "that because we're only boys we can't go to the War, and every one of us, except O'mie here, muscled like oxen; while older, weaker men are being shot down at Chancellorsville or staggering away from Bull Run."

"O'mie 'thgot the thtuff in him though. I'd back him againth David and Goliath," Bud Anderson insisted.

"Yes, or Sodom and Gomorrah, or some other Bible characters," observed Bill Mead. "You'd better join the Methodist Church South, Bud, and let old Dodd labor with you."

Then O'mie spoke gravely:

"Boys, we've got a civil war now in our middust. Don't ask me how I know. The feller that clanes the horses around the tavern stables, trust him fur findin' which way the Neosho runs, aven if he is small an' insignificant av statoor. I've seen an' heard too much in these two dirty wet days."

He paused, and there came into his eyes a pathetic pleading look as of one who sought protection. It gave place instantly to a fearless, heroic expression that has been my inspiration in many a struggle. I know now how he longed to tell us all he knew, but his word to Le Claire held him back.

"I can't tell you exactly phwat's in the air, fur I don't know it all yit. But there's trouble brewin' here, an' we must be ready, as we promised we would be when our own wint to the front."

O'mie had hit home. Had we not sworn our fealty to the flag, and protection to our town in our boyish patriotism the Summer before?

"Boys," O'mie went on, "if the storm breaks here in Springvale we've got to forgit ourselves an' ivery son av us be a hero for the work that's laid before him. Safe or dangerous, it's duty we must be doin', like the true sons av a glorious commonwealth, an' we may need to be lightnin' swift about it, too."

Tell Mapleson and Jim Conlow had come in as O'mie was speaking. We knew their fathers were bitter Rebels, although the men made a pretence to loyalty, which kept them in good company. But somehow the boys had not broken away from young Tell and Jim. From childhood we had been playmates, and boyish ties are strong. This evening the two seemed to be burdened with something of which they dared not or would not speak. There was a sort of defiance about them, such as an enemy may assume toward one who has been his friend, but whom he means to harm. Was it the will of Providence made O'mie appeal to them at the right moment?

"Say, boys," he had a certain Celtic geniality, and a frank winning smile that was irresistible. "Say, boys, all av the crowd's goin' to stand together no matter what comes, just as we've done since we learned how to swim in the shallows down by the Deep Hole. We're goin' to stand shoulder to shoulder, an' we'll save this town from harm, whativer may come in betwane, an' whoiver av us it's laid on to suffer, in the ind we'll win. For why? We are on the right side, an' can count on the same Power that's carried men aven to the inds av the earth to fight an' die fur what's right. Will ye be av us, boys? We've niver had no split in our gang yet. Will ye stay wid us?"

Tell and Jim looked at each other. Then Tell spoke. He had the right stuff in him at the last test always.

"Yes, boys, we will, come what will come."

Jim grinned at Tell. "I'll stand by Tell, if it kills me," he declared.

We put little trust in his ability. It is the way of the world to overlook the stone the Master Builder sometimes finds useful for His purpose.

"An' you may need us real soon, too," Tell called back as the two went out.

"By cracky, I bet they know more 'n we do," Bud Anderson declared.

Dave Mead looked serious.

"Well, I believe they'll hold with us anyhow," he said. "What they know may help us yet."

The coming of another tremendous downpour sent us scampering homeward. O'mie and I had started up the hill together, but the underside of the clouds fell out just as we reached Judson's gate, and by the time we had come to Mrs. Whately's we were ready to dive inside for shelter. When the rain settled down for an all-night stay, Mrs. Whately would wrap us against it before we left her. She put an old coat of Mr. Whately's on me. I had gone out in my shirt sleeves. Marjie looked bravely up at my tall form. I knew she was thinking of him who had worn that coat. The only thing for O'mie was Marjie's big water proof cloak. The old-fashioned black-and-silver mix with the glistening black buttons, such as women wore much in those days. It had a hood effect, with a changeable red silk lining, fastened at the neck. To my surprise O'mie made no objection at all to wearing a girl's wrap. But I could never fully forecast the Irish boy. He drew the circular garment round him and pulled the hood over his head.

"Come, Philip, me strong protector," he called, "let's be skiting."

At the door he turned back to Marjie and said in a low voice, "Phil will mistake me fur a girl an' be wantin' me to go flower-huntin' out on the West Prairie, but I won't do it."

Marjie blushed like the June roses, and slammed the door after him. A moment later she opened it again and held the light to show us the dripping path to the gate. Framed in the doorway with the light held up by her round white arm, the dampness putting a softer curl in every stray lock of her rich brown hair, the roses still blooming on her cheeks, she sent us away. Too young and sweet-spirited she seemed for any evil to assail her in the shelter of that home.

Late at night again the red light of the forge was crossed and re-crossed by those who moved about inside the shop. Aunt Candace and I had sat long together talking of the War, and of the raiding on the Kansas border. She was a balm to my spirit, for she was a strong, fearless woman, always comforting in the hour of sorrow, and self-possessed in the face of danger. I wonder how the mothers of Springvale could have done without her. She decked the brides for their weddings, and tenderly laid out the dead. The new-born babe she held in her arms, and dying eyes looking back from the Valley of the Shadow, sought her face. That night I slept little, and I welcomed the coming of day. When the morning dawned the world was flooded with sunshine, and a cool steady west wind blew the town clear of mud and wet, the while the Neosho Valley was threshed with the swollen, angry waters.

With the coming of the sunshine the strangers disappeared. Nowhere all that day were there any but our own town's people to be seen. Some of these, however, I knew afterwards, were very busy. I remember seeing Conlow and Mapleson and Dodd sauntering carelessly about in different parts of the town, especially upon Cliff Street, which was unusual for them. Just at nightfall the town was filled with strangers again. Yeager and his companion, who had been water-bound, returned with half a dozen more to the Cambridge House, and other unknown men were washed in from the west. That night I saw the red light briefly. Then it disappeared, and I judged the shop was deserted. I did not dream whose head was shutting off the light from me, nor whose eyes were peering in through that crevice in the wall. The night was peacefully beautiful, but its beauty was a mockery to me, filled as I was with a nameless anxiety. I had no reason for it, yet I longed for the return of Father Le Claire. He had not taken Jean with him, and I judged that the Indian was near us somewhere and in the very storm centre of all this uneasiness.

At midnight I wakened suddenly. Outside, a black starless sky bent over a cool, quiet earth. A thick darkness hid all the world. Dead stillness everywhere. And yet, I listened for a voice to speak again that I was sure I had heard as I wakened. I waited only a moment. A quick rapping under my window, and a low eager call came to my ears. I sprang up and groped my way to the open casement.

"What's the matter down there?" I called softly.

"Phil, jump into your clothes and come down just as quick as you can." It was Tell Mapleson's voice, full of suppressed eagerness. "For God's sake, hurry. It's life and death. Hurry! Hurry!"

"Run to the side door, Tell, and call Aunt Candace. She'll let you in."

I heard him make a plunge for the side door. By the time my aunt wakened to open it, I was down stairs. Tell stood inside the hallway, white and haggard. Our house was like a stone fort in its security, and Aunt Candace had fastened the door behind him. She seemed a perfect tower of strength to me, standing there like a strong guardian of the home.

"Stop a minute, Tell. We'll save time by knowing what we are about. What's the matter?" My aunt's voice gave him self-control.

He held himself by a great effort.

"There's not a second to lose, but we can't do anything without Phil. He must lead us. There's been a plot worked up here for three nights in Conlow's shop, to burn' every Union man's house in town. Preacher Dodd and that stranger named Yeager and the other fellow that's been stayin' at the tavern are backin' the whole thing. The men that's been hanging round here are all in the plot. They're to lay low a little while, and at two o'clock the blazin's to begin. Jim's run to Anderson's and Mead's, but we'll do just what Phil says. We'll get the boys together and you'll tell us what to do. The men'll kill Jim an' me if they find out we told, but we swore we'd stay by you boys. We'll help clear through, but don't tell on us. Don't never tell who told on 'em. Please don't." Tell never had seemed manly to me till that moment. "They're awful against O'mie. They say he knows too much. He heard 'em talking too free round the stables. They're after you too, Phil. They think if they get you out of the way, they can manage all the rest. I heard old Dodd tell 'em to make sure of John Baronet's cub. Said you were the worst in town, to come against. They'll kill you if they lay hands on you. They'll come right here after you."

"Then they'll go back without him," my aunt said firmly.

"They say the Indians are to come from the south at daylight," Tell hurried on, "an' finish up all that's left without homes. They're the Kiowas. They'll not get here till just about daylight." Tell's teeth were chattering, and he trembled as with an ague.

"Worst of all,"—he choked now,—"Whately's home's to be left alone, and Jean's to get Marjie and carry her off. They hate her father so, they've let Jean have her. They know she was called over to Judson's late to stay with Mrs. Judson. He's away, water-bound, and the baby's sick, and just as she gets home, he's to get her. If she screams, or tries to get away, he'll scalp her."

I heard no more. My heart forgot to beat. I had seen Marjie's signal light at ten o'clock and I was sure of her safety. The candle turned black before me. The cry of my dreams, Irving Whately's pleading cry, rang in my ears: "Take care of Marjie, Phil! Keep her from harm!"

"Phil Baronet, you coward," Tell fairly hissed in my ear, "come and help us! We can't do a thing without you."

I, a coward! I sprang to the door and with Tell beside me we sped away in the darkness. A faint light glimmered in the Whately home. At the gate, Dave Mead hailed us.

"It's too late, boys," he whispered, "Jean's gone and she's with him. He rode by me like the devil, going toward the ford. They'll be drowned and that's better than for her to live. The whole Indian Territory may be here by morning."

I lifted my face to the pitiless black sky above me, and a groan, the agony of a breaking heart, burst from my lips. In that instant, I lived ages of misery.

"Oh, Phil, what shall we do? The town's full of helpless folks." Dave caught my arm to steady himself. "Can't you, can't you put us to work?"

Could I? His appeal brought me to myself. In the right moment the Lord sends us to our places, and forsakes us not until our task is finished. On me that night, was laid the duty of leadership in a great crisis; and He who had called me, gave me power. Every Union household in the town must be roused and warned of the impending danger. And whatever was done must be done quickly, noiselessly, and at a risk of life to him who did it. My plan sprang into being, and Dave and Tell ran to execute it. In a few minutes we were to meet under the tavern oak. I dashed off toward the Cambridge House. Uncle Cam had not yet gone to bed.

"Where's O'mie?" I gasped.

"I dunno. He flew in here ten minutes or more ago, but he never lit. In ten seconds he was out again an' gone. He's got some sense an' generally keeps his red head level. I'm waitin' to see what's up."

In a word I gave Cam the situation, all except Jean's part. As I hurried out to meet the boys at the oak, I stumbled against something in the dense darkness. Cam hastened after me. The flare of the light from the opening of the door showed a horse, wet and muddy to the throat latch. It stared at the light in fright and then dashed away in the darkness.

All the boys, Tell and Jim, the Meads, John, Clayton, and Bud Anderson,—all but O'mie, met in the deep shadow of the oak before the tavern door. Our plans fell into form with Cam's wiser head to shape them here and there. The town was districted and each of us took his portion. In the time that followed, I worked noiselessly, heroically, taking the most dangerous places for my part. The boys rallied under my leadership, for they would have it so. Everywhere they depended on my word to direct them, and they followed my direction to the letter. It was not I, in myself, but John Baronet's son on whom they relied. My father's strength and courage and counsel they sought for in me. But all the time I felt myself to be like a spirit on the edge of doom. I worked as one who feels that when his task is ended, the blank must begin. Yet I left nothing undone because of the dead weight on my soul.

What happened in that hour, can never all be told. And only God himself could have directed us among our enemies. Since then I have always felt that the purpose crowns the effort. In Springvale that night was a band of resolute lawless men, organized and armed, with every foot of their way mapped out, every name checked, the lintel of every Union doorway marked, men ready and sworn to do a work of fire and slaughter. Against them was a group of undisciplined boys, unorganized, surprised, and unequipped, groping in the darkness full of unseen enemies. But we were the home-guard, and our own lives were nothing to us, if only we could save the defenceless.

CHAPTER VIII

THE COST OF SAFETY

In the dark and trying hour,
In the breaking forth of power,
In the rush of steeds and men,
His right hand will shield thee then.

—LONGFELLOW.

It was just half past one o'clock when the sweet-toned bell in the Presbyterian Church steeple began to ring. Dr. Hemingway was at the rope in the belfry. His part was to give us our signal. At the first peal the windows of every Union home blazed with light. The doors were flung wide open, and a song—one song—rose on the cool still night.

O say, can you see by the dawn's early light
What so proudly we hailed at the twilight's last gleaming?—
Whose broad stripes and bright stars, through the perilous fight
O'er the ramparts we watched, were so gallantly streaming!
O say, does that star-spangled banner yet wave
O'er the land of the free and the home of the brave?

It was sung in strong, clear tones as I shall never hear it sung again; and the echoes of many voices, and the swelling music of that old church bell, floated down the Neosho Valley, mingling with the rushing of the turbulent waters.

It was Cam Gentry's plan, this weapon of light and song. The Lord did have a work for him to do, as Dr. Hemingway had said.

"Boys," he had counselled us under the oak, "we can't match 'em in a pitched battle. They're armed an' ready, and you ain't and you can't do nothing in the dark. But let every house be ready, just as Phil has planned. Warn them quietly, and when the church bell rings, let every winder be full of light, every door wide open, and everybody sing."

He could roar bass himself to be heard across the State line, and that night he fairly boomed with song.

"They're dirty cowards, and can't work only in the dark and secret quiet. Give 'em light and song. Let 'em know we are wide awake and not afraid, an' if Gideon ever had the Midianites on the hike, you'll have them pisen Copperheads goin'. They'll never dast to show a coil, the sarpents! cause that's not the way they fight; an' they'll be wholly onprepared, and surprised."

Just before the ringing of the signal bell, the boys had met again by appointment under the tavern oak. Two things we had agreed upon when we met there first. One was a pledge of secrecy as to the part of young Tell and Jim in our work and to the part of Mapleson and Conlow in the plot, for the sake of their boys, who were loyal to the town. The other was to say nothing of Jean's act. Marjie was the light of Springvale, and we knew what the news would mean. We must first save the homes, quietly and swiftly. Other calamities would follow fast enough. In the darkness now, Bud Anderson put both arms around me.

"Phil," he whispered, "you're my king. You muth go to her mother now. In the morning, your Aunt Candathe will come to her. Maybe in the daylight we can find Marjie. He can't get far, unleth the river—"

He held me tight in his arms, that manly, tender-hearted boy. Then I staggered away like one in a dream toward the Whately house. We had not yet warned Mrs. Whately, for we knew her home was to be spared, and our hands were full of what must be done on the instant. Time never seemed so precious to me as in those dreadful minutes when we roused that sleeping town. I know now how Paul Revere felt when he rode to Lexington.

But now my cold knuckles fell like lead against Mrs. Whately's door, and mechanically I gave the low signal whistle I had been wont to give to Marjie. Like a mockery came the clear trill from within. But there was no mockery in the quick opening of the casement above me, where a dim light now gleamed, nor in the flinging up of the curtain, and it was not a spirit but a real face with a crown of curly hair that was outlined in the gloom. And a voice, Marjie's sweet voice, called anxiously:

"Is that you, Phil? I'll be right down." Then the light disappeared, and I heard the patter of feet on the stairs; then the front door opened and I walked straight into heaven. For there stood Marjie, safe and strong, before me—my Marjie, escaped from the grave, or from that living hell that is worse than death, captivity in the hands of an Indian devil.

"What's the matter, Phil?"

"Marjie, can it be you? How did you ever get back?"

She looked at me wonderingly.

"Why, I was only down there at Judson's. The baby's sick and Mrs. Judson sent for me after ten o'clock. I didn't come away till midnight. She may send for me again at any minute,—that's why I'm not in bed. I wanted to stay with her, but she made me come home on mother's account. I ran home by myself. I wasn't afraid. I heard a horse galloping away just before I got up to the gate. But what is the matter, Phil?"

I stood there wholly sure now that I was in Paradise. Jean had not tried to get her after all. She was here, and no harm had touched her. Tell had not understood. Jean had been in the middle of this night's business somewhere, I felt sure, but he had done no one any harm. After all he had been true to his promise to be a good Indian, and Le Claire had misjudged him.

"You didn't see who was on the horse, did you?"

"No. Just as I started from Mrs. Judson's, O'mie came flying by me. He looked so funny. He had on the waterproof cloak I loaned him last night, hood and all, and his face was just as white as milk. I thought he was a girl at first. He called to me almost in a whisper. 'Don't hurry a bit, Marjie,' he said; 'I'm taking your cloak home.' But I couldn't find it anywhere about the door. O'mie is always doing the oddest things!"

Just then the church bell began to ring, and together we put on the lights and joined in the song. Its inspiration drove everything before it. I did not stay long with Marjie, however, for there was much for me to do, and I seemed to have stepped from a world of horror and darkness into a heaven of light. How I wished O'mie would come in! I had not found him in all that hour, ages long to us, in which we had done this much of our work for the town. But I was sure of O'mie.

"He's doing good business somewhere," I said. "Bless his red head. He'll never quit so long as there's a thing to do."

There was no rest for anybody in Springvale that night. As Cam Gentry had predicted, not a torch blazed; and the attacking party, thrown into confusion by the sudden blocking of their secret plan of assault, did not rally. Our next task was to make sure against the Indians, the rumor of whose coming grew everywhere, and the fear of a daybreak massacre kept us all keyed to the pitch of terrible expectancy.

The town had four strongholds, the tavern, the Whately store, the Presbyterian Church, and my father's house. All these buildings were of stone, with walls of unusual thickness. Into these the women and children were gathered as soon as we felt sure the enemy in our midst was outdone. Dr. Hemingway took command of the church. Cam Gentry at his own door was a host.

"I can see who goes in and out of the Cambridge House; I reckon, if I can't tell a Reb from a Bluecoat out in a battle," he declared, as he opened his doors to the first little group of mothers and children who came to him for protection. "I can see safety for every one of you here," he added with that cheery laugh that made us all love him. Aunt Candace was the strong guardian in our home up on Cliff Street. We looked for O'mie to take care of the store, but he was nowhere to be seen and that duty was given to Grandpa Mead, whose fiery Union spirit did not accord with his halting step and snowy hair.

A patrol guard was quickly formed, and sentinels were stationed on the south and west. On the north and east the flooded Neosho was a perfect wall of water round about us.

Since that Maytime, I have lived through many days of peril and suffering, and I have more than once walked bravely as I might along the path at whose end I knew was an open grave, but never to me has come another such night of terror. In all the town there were not a dozen men, loyal supporters of the Union cause, who had a fighting strength. On the eight stalwart boys, and the quickness and shrewdness of little O'mie, the salvation of Springvale rested. After that awful night I was never a boy again. Henceforth I was a man, with a man's work and a man's spirit.

The daylight was never so welcome before, and never a grander sunrise filled the earth with its splendor. I was up on the bluff patrolling the northwest boundary when the dawn began to purple the east. Oh, many a time have I watched the sunrise beyond the Neosho Valley, but on this rare May morning every shaft of light, every tint of roseate beauty along the horizon, every heap of feathery mist that decked the Plains, with the Neosho, bank-full, sweeping like molten silver below it—all these took on a new loveliness. Eagerly, however, I scanned the southwest where the level beams of day were driving back the gray morning twilight, and the green prairie billows were swelling out of the gloom. Point by point, I watched every landmark take form, waiting to see if each new blot on the landscape might not be the first of the dreaded Indian bands whose coming we so feared.

With daybreak, came assurance. Somehow I could not believe that a land so beautiful and a village so peaceful could be threshed and stained and blackened by the fire and massacre of a savage band allied to a disloyal, rebellious host. And yet, I had lived these stormy years in Kansas and the border strife has never all been told. I dared not relax my vigilance, so I watched the south and west, trusting to the river to take care of the east.

And so it happened that, sentinel as I was, I had not seen the approach of a horseman from the northwest, until Father Le Claire came upon me suddenly. His horse was jaded with travel, and he sat it wearily. A pallor overspread his brown cheeks. His garments were wet and mud-splashed.

"Oh, Father Le Claire," I cried, "nobody except my own father could be more welcome. Where have you been?"

"I am not too late, then!" he exclaimed, ignoring my question. His eyes quickly took in the town. No smoke was rising from the kitchen fires this morning, for the homes were deserted. "You are safe still?" He gave a great gasp of relief. Then he turned and looked steadily into my eyes.

"It has been bought with a price," he said simply. "Three days ago I left you a boy. I come back to find you a man. Where's O'mie?"

"D—down there, I think."

It dawned on me suddenly that not one of us had seen or heard of O'mie since he left Tell and Jim at the shop just before midnight. Marjie had seen him a few minutes later, and so had Cam Gentry. But where was he after that? Much as we had needed him, we had had no time to hunt for him. Places had to be filled by those at hand in the dreadful necessity before us. We could count on O'mie, of course. He was no coward, nor laggard; but where could he have kept himself?

"What has happened, Philip?" the priest asked.

Briefly I told him, ending with the story of the threatening terror of an Indian invasion.

"They will not come, Philip. Do not fear. That danger is cut off. The Kiowas, who were on their way to Springvale, have all turned back and they are far away. I know."

His assurance was balm to my soul. And my nerves, on the rack for these three days, with the culmination of the last six hours seemed suddenly to snap within me.

"Go home and rest now," said Father Le Claire. "I will take the word along the line. Come down to the tavern at nine o'clock."

Aunt Candace had hot coffee and biscuit and maple syrup from old Vermont, with ham and eggs, all ready for me. The blessed comfort of a home, safe from harm once more, filled me with a sense of rest. Not until it was lifted did I realize how heavy was the burden I had carried through those May nights and days.

Long before nine o'clock, the tavern yard was full of excited people, all eagerly talking of the events of the last few hours. We had hardly taken our bearings yet, but we had an assurance that the perils of the night no longer threatened us. The strange men who had filled the town the evening before had all disappeared, but in the company here were many whom we knew to be enemies in the dark. Yet they mingled boldly with the others, assuming a loyalty for their own purposes. In the crowd, too, was Jean Pahusca, impenetrable of countenance, indifferent to the occasion as a thing that could not concern him. His red blanket was gone and his leather trousers and dark flannel shirt displayed his superb muscular form. There was no knife in his belt now, and he carried no other weapon. With his soft dark hair and the ruddy color showing in his cheeks, he was dangerously handsome to a romantic eye. Among all its enemies, he had been loyal to Springvale. My better self rebuked my distrust, and my heart softened toward him. His plan with the raiders to seize Marjie must have been his crude notion of saving her from a worse peril. When he knew she was safe he had dropped out of sight in the darkness.

The boys who had done the work of the night before suddenly became heroes. Not all of us had come together here, however. Tell was keeping store up at the "Last Chance," and Jim was seeing to the forge fire, while the father of each boy sauntered about in the tavern yard.

"You won't tell anybody about father," Tell pleaded before he left us. "He never planned it, indeed he didn't. It was old man Dodd and Yeager and them other strangers."

I can picture now the Reverend Mr. Dodd, piously serious, sitting on the tavern veranda at that moment, a disinterested listener to what lay below his spiritual plane of life. Just above his temple was a deep bruise, and his right hand was bound with a white bandage. Five years later, one dark September night, by the dry bed of the Arickaree Creek in Colorado, I heard the story of that bandage and that bruise.

"And you'll be sure to keep still about my dad, too, won't you?" Jim Conlow urged. "He's bad, but—" as if he could find no other excuse, he added grinning, "I don't believe he's right bright; and Tell and me done our best anyhow."

Their best! These two had braved the worst of foes, with those of their own flesh and blood against them. We would keep their secret fast enough, nor should anyone know from the boys who of our own townspeople were in the plot. I believe now that Conlow would have killed Jim had he suspected the boy's part in that night's work. I have never broken faith with Jim, although Heaven knows I have had cause enough to wish never to hear the name of Conlow again.

One more boy was not in our line, O'mie, still missing from the ranks, and now my heart was heavy. Everybody else seemed to forget him in the excitement, however, and I hoped all was well.

On the veranda a group was crowding about Father Le Claire, listening to what he had to say. Nobody tried to do business in our town that day. Men and women and children stood about in groups, glad to be alive and to know that their homes were safe. It was a sight one may not see twice in a lifetime. And the thrill within me, that I had helped a little toward this safety, brought a pleasure unlike any other joy I have ever known.

"Where's Aunt Candace?" I asked Dollie Gentry, who had grasped my arm as if she would ring it from my shoulder.

"Hadn't you heard?" Dollie's eyes filled with tears. "Judson's baby died this mornin'. Judson he can't get across Fingal's Creek or some of the draws, to get home, and the fright last night was too much for Mis' Judson. She fainted away, an' when she come to, the baby was dead. I'm cookin' a good meal for all of 'em. Land knows, carin' for the little corpse is all they can do without botherin' to cook."

Good Mrs. Gentry used her one talent for everybody's comfort. And as for the Judsons, theirs was one of the wayside tragedies that keep ever alongside the line of civil strife.

They made room for us on the veranda, six husky Kansas bred fellows, hardly more than half-way through our teens, and we fell in with the group about Father Le Claire. He gave us a searching glance, and his face clouded. Good Dr. Hemingway beside him was eager for his story.

"Tell us the whole thing," he urged. "Then we can understand our part in it. Surely the arm of the Lord was not shortened for us last night."

"It is a strange story, Dr. Hemingway, with a strange and tragic ending," replied the priest. He related then the plot which O'mie had heard set forth by the strangers in our town. "I left at once to warn the Osages, believing I could return before last night."

"Them Osages is a cussed ornery lot, if that Jean out on the edge of the crowd there is a sample," a man from the west side of town broke in.

"They are true blue, and Jean is not an Osage; he's a Kiowa," Le Claire replied quietly.

"What of him ain't French," declared Cam Gentry. "That's where his durned meanness comes in biggest. Not but what a Kiowa's rotten enough. But sence he didn't seem to take part in this doings last night, I guess we can stand him a little while longer."

Father Le Claire's face flushed. Then a pallor overspread the flame. His likeness to the Indian flashed up with that flush. So had I seen Pahusca flush with anger, and a paleness cover his coppery countenance. Self-mastery was a part of the good man's religion, however, and in a voice calm but full of sympathy he told us of the tragic events whose evil promise had overshadowed our town with an awful peril.

It was a well-planned, cold-blooded horror, this scheme of the Southern Confederacy, to unite the fierce tribes of the Southwest against the unprotected Union frontier. And with the border raiders on the one side and the hostile Indians on the other, small chance of life would have been left to any Union man, woman, or child in all this wide, beautiful Kansas. In the four years of the Civil War no cruelty could have exceeded the consequences of this conspiracy.

Unity of purpose has ever been lacking to the red race. No federation has been possible to it except as that federation is controlled by the European brain. The controlling power in the execution of this dastardly crime lay with desperate but eminently able white men. Their appeal to the Osages, however, was a fruitless one. For a third of a century the faithful Jesuits had labored with this tribe. Not in vain was their seed-sowing.

Le Claire reached the Osages only an hour before an emissary from the leaders of this infamous plot came to the Mission. The presence of the priest counted so mightily, that this call to an Indian confederacy fell upon deaf ears, and the messenger departed to rejoin his superiors. He never found them, for a sudden and tragic ending had come to the conspiracy.

It was a busy day in Kansas annals when that company of Rebel officers came riding up from the South to band together the lawless savages and the outlawed raiders against a loyal commonwealth. Humboldt was the most southern Union garrison in Kansas at that time. South of it the Osages did much scout duty for the Government, and it held them responsible for any invasion of this strip of neutral soil between the North and the South. Out in the Verdigris River country, in this Maytime, a little company of Osage braves on the way from their village to visit the Mission came face to face with this band of invaders in the neutral land. The presence of a score of strange men armed and mounted, though they were dressed as Union soldiers, must be accounted for, these Indians reasoned.

The scouts were moved only by an unlettered loyalty to the flag. They had no notion of the real purpose of these invaders. The white men had only contempt for the authority of a handful of red men calling them to account, and they foolishly fired into the Indian band. It was a fatal foolishness. Two braves fell to the earth, pierced by their bullets. The little body of red men dropped over on the sides of their ponies and were soon beyond gun range, while their opponents went on their way. But briefly only, for, reinforced by a hundred painted braves, the whole fighting strength of their little village, the Osages came out for vengeance. Near a bend in the Verdigris River the two forces came together. Across a scope five miles wide they battled. The white men must have died bravely, for they fought stubbornly, foot by foot, as the Indians drove them into that fatal loop of the river. It is deep and swift here. Down on the sands by its very edge they fell. Not a white man escaped. The Indians, after their savage fashion, gathered the booty, leaving a score of naked, mutilated bodies by the river's side. It was a cruel bit of Western warfare, yet it held back from Kansas a diabolical outrage, whose suffering and horror only those who know the Southwest tribes can picture. And strangely enough, the power that stayed the evil lay with a handful of faithful Indian scouts.

The story of the massacre soon reached the Mission. Dreadful as it was, it lifted a burden from Le Claire's mind; but the news that the Comanches and the Kiowas, unable to restrain their tribes, were already on the war-path, filed him with dread.

A twenty-four hours' rain, with cloudbursts along the way, was now sending the Neosho and Verdigris Rivers miles wide, across their valleys. It was impossible for him to intercept these tribes until the stream should fall. The priest perfected his plans for overtaking them by swift messengers to be sent out from the Mission at the earliest moment, and then he turned his horse upstream toward Springvale. All day he rode with all speed to the northward. The ways were sodden with the heavy rains, and the smaller streams were troublesome to the horseman. Night fell long before he had come to the upper Neosho Valley. With the darkness his anxiety deepened. A thousand chances might befall to bring disaster before he could reach us.

The hours of the black night dragged on, and northward still the priest hurried. It was long after midnight when he found himself on the bluff opposite the town. Between him and Springvale the Neosho rushed madly, and the oak grove of the bottom land was only black treetops above, and water below. All hope of a safe passage across the river here vanished, for he durst not try the angry waters.

"There must have been heavier rains here than down the stream," he thought. "Pray Heaven the messengers may reach the Kiowas before they fall upon any of the settlements in the south. I must go farther up to cross. O God, grant that no evil may threaten that town over there!"

Turning to look once more at the dark valley his eye caught a gleam of light far down the river.

"That must be Jean down at the Hermit's Hole," he said to himself. "I wonder I never tried to follow him there. But if he's down the river it is better for Springvale, anyhow."

All this the priest told to the eager crowd on the veranda of the Cambridge House that morning. But regarding the light and his thought of it, he did not tell us then, nor how, through all and all, his great fear for Springvale was on account of Jean Pahusca's presence there. He knew the Indian's power; and now that the fierce passion of love for a girl and hatred of a rival, were at fever pitch, he dared not think what might follow, neither did he tell us how bitterly he was upbraiding himself for having charged O'mie with secrecy.

He had not yet caught sight of the Irish boy; and Jean, who had himself kept clear of the evil intent against Springvale the night before, had studiously kept the crowd between the priest and himself. We did not note this then, for we were spell-bound by the story of the Confederate conspiracy and of Father Le Claire's efforts for our safety.

"The Kiowas, who were on the war-path, have been cut off by the Verdigris," he concluded. "The waters, that kept me away from Springvale on this side, kept them off in the southwest. The Osages did us God's service in our peril, albeit their means were cruel after the manner of the savage."

A silence fell upon the group on the veranda, as the enormity of what we had escaped dawned upon us.

"Let us thank God that in his ways, past finding out, He has not forsaken his children." Dr. Hemingway spoke fervently.

I looked out on the broad street and down toward the river shining in the May sunlight. The air was very fresh and sweet. The oak trees, were in their heaviest green, and in the glorious light of day the commonest things in this little frontier town looked good to me. Across my vision there swept the picture of that wide, swift-flowing Verdigris River, and of the dead whose blood stained darkly that fatal sand-bar, their naked bodies hacked by savage fury, waiting the coming of pitiful hands to give them shelter in the bosom of the earth. And then I thought of all these beautiful prairies which the plough was beginning to subdue, of the homesteads whose chimney smoke I had seen many a morning from my windows up on Cliff Street. I thought of the little towns and unprotected villages, and of what an Indian raid would mean to these,—of murdered men and burning houses, and women dragged away into a slavery too awful to picture. I thought of Marjie and of what she had escaped. And then clear, as if he were beside me, I heard O'mie's voice:

"Phil, oh, Phil, come, come!" it pleaded.

I started up and stared around me.

CHAPTER IX

THE SEARCH FOR THE MISSING

Also Time runnin' into years—
A thousand Places left be'ind;
An' Men from both two 'emispheres
Discussin' things of every kind;
So much more near than I 'ad known,
So much more great than I 'ad guessed—
An' me, like all the rest, alone,
But reachin' out to all the rest!

—KIPLING.

"Uncle Cam, where is O'mie? I haven't seen him yet," I broke in upon the older men in the council. "Could anything have happened to him?"

The priest rose hurriedly.

"I have been hoping to see him every minute," he said. "Has anybody seen him this morning?"

A flurry followed. Everybody thought he had seen somebody else who had been with O'mie, but nobody, first hand, could report of him.

"Why, I thought he was with the boys," Cam Gentry exclaimed. "Nobody could keep track of nobody else last night."

"I thought I saw him this morning," said Dr. Hemingway. "But"—hesitatingly—"I do not believe I did either. I just had him in mind as I watched Henry Anderson's boys go by."

"All three of us are not equal to one O'mie," Clayton Anderson declared.

"What part of town did he have, Philip?" asked Le Claire.

"No part," I answered. "We had to take the boys that were out there under the oak."

Dr. Hemingway called a council at once, and all who knew anything of the missing boy reported. I could give what had been told to Aunt Candace and myself only in a general way, in order to shield Tell Mapleson. Cam had seen O'mie only a minute, just before midnight.

"He went racin' out draggin' somethin' after him, an' jumped over the porch railin' here," pointing to the north, "stid o' goin' down the steps. O'mie's double-geared lightin' for quickness anyhow, but last night he jist made lightnin' seem slow the way he got off the reservation an' into the street. It roused me up. I was half asleep settin' here waitin' to put them strangers to bed again. So I set up an' waited fur the boy to show up an' apologize fur his not bein' no quicker, when in comes Phil; an' ye all know the rest. I've not laid an eye on O'mie sence, but bein' short on range I took it he was here but out of sight. Oh, Lord!" Cam groaned, "can anything have happened to him?"

While Cam was speaking I noticed that Jean Pahusca who had been loafing about at the far side of the crowd, was standing behind Father Le Claire. No one could have told from his set, still face what his thoughts were just then.

The last one who had seen O'mie was Marjie.

"I had left the door open so I could find the way better," she said. "At the gate O'mie came running up. I thought he was a girl, for he had my cloak around him and the hood over his head. His face was very white.

"I supposed it was just the light behind me, made it look so, for he wasn't the least bit scared. He called to me twice. 'Don't hurry,' he said; 'I'm taking your cloak home.' Mrs. Judson shut the door just then, thinking I had gone on, and I ran home, but O'mie flew ahead of me. Just before I came around the corner I heard a horse start up and dash off to the river. I ran in to mother and shut the door."

"I met a horse down by the river as I ran to grandpa's after Bill. He was staying over there last night." It was Dave Mead who spoke. "I made a grab at the rein. I was crazy to think of such a thing, but—" Dave didn't say why he tried to stop the horse, for that would mean to repeat what Tell had told us, and we had to keep Tell's part to ourselves. "The horse knocked me twenty feet and tore off toward the river."

And then for the first time we noticed Dave Mead's right arm in a sling. Too much was asked of us in those hours for us to note the things that mark our common days.

"It put my shoulder out of place," Dave said simply. "Didn't get it in again for so long, it's pretty sore. I was too busy to think about it at first."

Dave Mead never put his right hand to his head again. And to-day, if the broad-shouldered, fine-looking American should meet you on the streets of Hong Kong, he would offer you his left hand. For hours he forgot himself to save others. It is his like that have filled Kansas and made her story a record of heroism like to the story of no other State in all the nation.

But as to O'mie we could find nothing. There was something strange and unusual about his returning the borrowed cloak at that late hour. The whole thing was so unlike O'mie.

"They've killed him and put him in the river," wailed Dollie Gentry.

"I'm afraid he's been foully dealt with. They suspected he knew too much," and Dr. Hemingway bowed his head in sorrow.

"He's run straight into a coil of them pisen Copperheads an' they've made way with him; an' to think we hadn't missed him," sobbed Cam in his chair.

Father Le Claire gripped his hands, and his face grew as expressionless as the Indian's behind him. It dawned upon us now that O'mie was lost, there was no knowing how. O'mie, who belonged to the town and was loved as few orphan boys are loved. Oh, any of us would have suffered for him, and to think that he should be made the victim of rebel hate, that the blow should fall on him who had given no offence. All his manliness, his abounding kindness, his sunny smile and joy in living, swept up in memory in the instant. Instinctively the boys drew near to one another, and there came back to me the memory of that pathetic look in his eyes as we talked of our troubles down in the tavern stables two nights before: "Whoiver it's laid on to suffer," I could almost hear him saying it. And then I did hear his voice, low and clear, a faint call again, as I had heard it before.

"Phil, oh Phil, come!"

It shot through my brain like an arrow. I turned and seized Le Claire by the hand.

"O'mie's not dead," I cried. "He's alive somewhere, and I'm going to find him."

"You bet your life he'th not dead," Bud Anderson echoed me. "Come on."

The boys with Le Claire started in a body through the crowd; a shout went up, a sudden determination that O'mie must be alive seemed to possess Springvale.

"Stay with Cam and Dollie," Le Claire turned Dr. Hemingway back with a word. "They need you now. We can do all that can be done."

He strode ahead of us; a stalwart leader of men he would make in any fray. It flashed into my mind that it was not the Kiowa Indian blood that made Jean Pahusca seem so stately and strong as he strode down the streets of Springvale. A red blanket over Le Claire's broad shoulders would have deceived us into thinking it was the Indian brave leading on before us.

The river was falling rapidly, and the banks were slimy. Fingal's Creek was almost at its usual level and the silt was crusting along its bedraggled borders. Just above where it empties into the Neosho we noted a freshly broken embankment as though some weight had crushed over the side and carried a portion of the bank with it. Puddles of water and black mud filled the little hollows everywhere. Into one of these I stepped as we were eagerly searching for a trace of the lost boy. My foot stuck to something soft like a garment in the puddle. I kicked it out, and a jet button shone in the ooze. I stooped and lifted the grimy thing. It was Marjie's cloak.

"This is the last of O'mie," Dave Mead spoke reverently.

"Here's where they pushed him in," said John Anderson pointing to the break in the bank.

There was a buzzing in my ears, and the sunlight on the river was dancing in ten thousand hideous curls and twists. The last of O'mie, until maybe, a bloated sodden body might be found half buried in some flood-wrought sand-bar. The May morning was a mockery, and every green growing leaf seemed to be using the life force that should be in him.

"Yes, there's where he went in." It was Father Le Claire's voice now, "but he fought hard for his life."

"Yeth, and by George, yonder'th where he come out. Thee that thaplin' on the bank? It'th thplit, but it didn't break; an' that bank'th brokener'n thith."

Oh, blessed Bud! His tow head will always wear a crown to me.

On the farther bank a struggle had wrenched the young trees and shrubs away and a slide of slime marked where the victim of the waters had fought for life. We knew how to swim, and we crossed the swollen creek in a rush. But here all trace disappeared. Something or somebody had climbed the bank. A horse's hoofs showed in the mud, but on the ground beyond the horse's feet had not seemed to leave a track. The cruel ruffians must have pushed him back when he tried to gain the bank here. We hunted and hunted, but to no avail. No other mark of O'mie's having passed beyond the creek could be found.

It was nearly sunset before we came back to town. Not a mouthful had been eaten, and with the tenseness of the night's excitement stretching every nerve, the loss of sleep, the constant searching, and the heaviness of despair, mud-stained, wearied, and haggard, we dragged ourselves to the tavern again. Other searchers had been going in different directions. In one of these parties, useful, quick and wisely counselling, was Jean Pahusca. His companions were loud in their praise of his efforts. The Red Range neighborhood had received the word at noon and turned out in a mass, women and children joining in the quest. But it was all in vain. Wild theories filled the air, stories of strangers struggling with somebody in the dark; the sound of screams and of some one running away. But none of these stories could be substantiated. And all the while what Tell Mapleson had said to Aunt Candace and me when he came to warn us, kept repeating itself to me. "They're awful against O'mie. They think he knows too much."

Early the next morning the search was renewed, but at nightfall no further trace of the lost boy had been discovered. On the second evening, when we gathered at the Cambridge House, Dr. Hemingway urged us to take a little rest, and asked that we come later to a prayer meeting in the church.

"O'mie is our one sacrifice beside the dear little babe of Judson's. All the rest of us have been spared to life, and our homes have been protected. We must look to the Lord for comfort now, and thank Him for His goodness to us."

Then the Rev. Mr. Dodd spoke sneeringly:

"You've made a big ado for two days about a little coward who cut and run at the first sound of danger. Disguised himself like a girl to do it. He will come sneaking in fast enough when he finds the danger is over. A lot of us around town are too wise to be deceived. The Lord did save us," how piously he spoke, "but we should not disgrace ourselves."

He got no further. I had been leaning limply against the veranda post, for even my strength was giving way, more under the mental strain than the physical tax. But at the preacher's words all the blood of my fighting ancestry took fire. There was a Baronet with Cromwell's Ironsides, the regiment that was never defeated in battle. There was a Baronet color-bearer at Bunker Hill and later at Saratoga, and it was a Baronet who waited till the last boat crossed the Delaware when Washington led his forces to safety. There were Baronets with Perry on Lake Erie, and at that moment my father was fighting for the life of a nation. I cleared the space between us at a bound, and catching the Reverend Dodd by throat and thigh, I lifted him clear of the railing and flung him sprawling on the blue-grass.

"If you ever say another word against O'mie I'll break your neck," I cried, as he landed.

Father Le Claire was beside him at once.

"He's killed me," groaned Dodd.

"Then he ought to bury his dead," Dr. Hemingway said coldly, which was the only time the good old man was ever known to speak unkindly to any one among us.

The fallen preacher gathered himself together and slipped away.

Dollie Gentry had a royal supper for everybody that night. Jean Pahusca sat by Father Le Claire with us at the long table in the dining-room. Again my conscience, which upbraided me for doubting him, and my instinct, which warned me to beware of him, had their battle within me.

"I just had to do something or I'd have jumped into the Neosho myself," Dollie explained in apology for the abundant meal, as if cooking were too worldly for that grave time. "I know now," she said, "how that poor woman felt whose little boy was took by the Kiowas years ago out on the West Prairie. They said she did jump into the river. Anyhow, she disappeared."

"Did you know her or her husband?" Father Le Claire asked quietly.

"Yes, in a way," Dollie replied. "He was a big, fine-looking man built some like you, an' dark. He was a Frenchman. She was a little, small-boned woman. I saw her in the 'Last Chance' store the day she got here from the East. She was fair and had red hair, I should say; but they said the woman that drowned herself was a black-haired French woman. She didn't look French to me. She lived in that little cabin up around the bend toward Red Range, poor dear! That cabin's always been haunted, they say."

"Was she never heard of again?" the priest went on. We thought he was keeping Dollie's mind off O'mie.

"Ner him neither. He cut out west toward Santy Fee with some Mexican traders goin' home from Westport. I heard he left 'em at Pawnee Rock, where they had a regular battle with the Kiowas; some thought he might have been killed by the Kiowas, and others by the Mexicans. Anyhow, he never was heard of in Springvale no more."

"Mrs. Gentry," Le Claire asked abruptly, "where did you find O'mie?"

"Why, we've had him so long I forget we never hadn't him." Dollie seemed confused, for O'mie was a part of her life. "He was brought up here from the South by a missionary. Seems to me he found the little feller (he was only five years old) trudgin' off alone, an' sayin' he wouldn't stay at the Mission 'cause there was Injuns there. Said the Injuns killed his father, an' he kicked an' squalled till the missionary just brought him up here. He was on his way to St. Mary's, up on the Kaw, an' he was takin' the little one on with him. He stopped here with O'mie an' the little feller was hungry—"

"And you fed him; naked, and you clothed him," the priest added reverently.

"Poor O'mie!" and Dollie made a dive for the kitchen to weep out her grief alone.

It seemed to settle upon Springvale that O'mie was lost; had been overcome in some way by the murderous raiders who had infested our town.

In sheer weariness and hopelessness I fell on my bed, that night, and sleep, the "sleep that knits up the ravelled sleave of care," fell upon me. Just at daybreak I woke with a start. I had not dreamed once all night, but now, wide awake, with my face to the open east window where the rose tint of a grand new day was deepening into purple on the horizon's edge, feeling and knowing everything perfectly, I saw O'mie's face before me, white and drawn with pain, but gloriously brave. And his pleading voice, "Phil, ye'll come soon, won't ye?" sounded low and clear in my ears.

I sprang up and dressed myself. I was so sure of O'mie, I could hardly wait to begin another search. Something seemed to impel me to speed. "He won't last long," was a vague, persistent thought that haunted me.

"What is it, Phil?" my aunt called as I passed her door.

"Aunt Candace, it's O'mie. He's not dead yet, I'm sure. But I must go at once and hunt again."

"Where will you go now?" she queried.

"I don't know. I'm just being led," I replied.

"Phil," Aunt Candace was at the door now, "have you thought of the Hermit's Cave?"

Her words went through me like a sword-thrust.

"Why, why,—oh, Aunt Candace, let me think a minute."

"I've been thinking for twelve hours," said my aunt. "Until you try that place don't give up the hunt."

"But I don't know how to get there."

"Then make a way. You are not less able to do impossible things than the Pilgrim Fathers were. If you ever find O'mie it will be in that place. I feel it, I can't say why. But, Phil, you will need the boys and Father Le Claire. Take time to get breakfast and get yourself together. You will need all your energy. Don't squander it the first thing."

Dear Aunt Candace! This many a year has her grave been green in the Springvale cemetery, but greener still is her memory in the hearts of those who knew her. She had what the scholars of to-day strive to possess—the power of poise.

I ate my breakfast as calmly as I could, and before I left home Aunt Candace made me read the Ninety-first Psalm. Then she kissed me good-bye and bade me God-speed. Something kept telling me to hurry, hurry, as I tried to be deliberate, and quickened my thought and my step. At the tavern Cam Gentry met us.

"It ain't no use to try, boys, O'mie's down in the river where the cussed Copperheads put him; but you're good to keep tryin'." He sat down in a helpless resignation, so unlike his natural buoyant spirit it was hard to believe that this was the same Cam we had always known.

"Judson's baby's to be buried to-day, but we can't even bury O'mie. Oh, it's cruel hard." Cam groaned in his chair.

The dew had not ceased to glitter, and the sun was hardly more than risen when Father Le Claire and the crowd of boys, reinforced now by Tell Mapleson and Jim Conlow, started bravely out, determined to find the boy who had been missing for what seemed ages to us.

"If we find O'mie, we'll send word by the fastest runner, and you must ring the church bell," Le Claire arranged with Cam. "All the town can have the word at once then."

"We'll go to the Hermit's Cave first," I announced.

The company agreed, but only Bud Anderson seemed to feel as I did. To the others it was a wasted bit of heroism, for if none of us had yet found the way to this retreat, why should we look for O'mie there? So the boys argued as we hurried to the river. The Neosho was inside its banks again, but, deep and swift and muddy, it swept silently by us who longed to know its secrets.

"Philip, why do you consider the cave possible?" Le Claire asked as we followed the river towards the cliff.

"Aunt Candace says so," I replied.

"Well, it's worth the trial if only to prove a woman's intuition—or whim," he said quietly.

The same old cliff confronted us, although the many uprooted trees showed a jagged outcrop this side the sheer wall. We looked up helplessly at the height. It seemed foolish to think of O'mie being in that inaccessible spot.

"If he is up there," Dave Mead urged, "and we can get to him, it will be to put him alongside Judson's baby this afternoon."

All the other boys were for turning back and hunting about Fingal's Creek again, all except Bud. Such a pink and white boy he was, with a dimple in each cheek and a blowsy tow head.

"Will you stay with me, Bud, till I get up there?" I asked him.

"Yeth thir! or down there. Let'th go round an' try the other thide."

"Well, I guess we'll all stay with Phil, you cottontop," Tell Mapleson put in.

We all began to circle round the bluff to get beyond this steep, forbidding wall. Our plan was to go down the river beyond the cave, and try to climb up from that point. Crossing along by the edge of the bluff we passed the steepest part and were coming again to where the treetops and bushes that clung to the side of the high wall reached above the crest, as they do across the street from my own home. Just ahead of us, as we hurried, I caught sight of a flat slab of the shelving rock slipped aside and barely balancing on the edge, one end of it bending down the treetops as if newly slid into that place. All about the stone the thin sod of the bluff's top was cut and trampled as if a struggle had been there. We examined it carefully. A horse's tracks were plainly to be seen.

"Something happened here," Le Claire said. "Looks like a horse had been urged up to the very edge and had kept pulling back."

"And that stone is just slipped from its place," Clayton Anderson declared. "Something has happened here since the rains."

As we came to the edge, we saw a pile of earth recently scraped from the stone outcrop above.

"Somebody or something went over here not long ago," I cried.

"Look out, Phil," Bill Mead called, "or somebody else will follow somebody before 'em—"

Bill's warning came too late. I had stepped on the balanced slab. It tipped and went over the side with a crash. I caught at the edge and missed it, but the effort threw me toward the cliff and I slid twenty feet. The bushes seemed to part as by a well-made opening and I caught a strong limb, and gained my balance. I looked back at the way I had come. And then I gave a great shout. The anxious faces peering down at me changed a little.

"What is it?" came the query.

I pointed upward.

"The nicest set of hand-holds and steps clear up," I called. "You can't see for the shelf. But right under there where Bud's head is, is the best place to get a grip and there's a foothold all the way down." I stared up again. "There's a rope fastened right under there. Bend over, Bud, careful, and you'll find it. It will let you over to the steps. Swing in on it."

In truth, a set of points for hand and foot partly natural, partly cut there, rude but safe enough for boy climbers like ourselves, led down to my tree lodge.

"And what's below you?" shouted Tell.

"Another tree like this. I don't know how far down if you jump right," I answered back.

"Well, jump right, for I'm nekth. Ever thee a tow-headed flying thquirrel?" And Bud was shinning down over the edge clawing tightly the stone points of vantage.

Many a time in these sixty years have I seen a difficult and dreaded way grow suddenly easy when the time came to travel it. When we were only boys idling away the long summer afternoons the cliff was always impossible. We had rarely tried the downward route, and from below with the river, always dangerously deep and swift, at the base, our exploring had brought failure. That hand-hold of leather thongs, braided into a rope and fastened securely under the ledge out of sight from above, gave the one who knew how the easy passage to the points of rock. Then for nearly a hundred feet zigzagging up stream by leaping cautiously to the right place, by clinging and swinging, the way opened before us. I took the first twenty feet at a slide. The others caught the leather rope, testing to see if it was securely fastened. Its two ends were tied around the deeply grooved stone.

Father Le Claire and Jim Conlow stayed at the top. The one to help us back again; the other, as the swiftest-footed boy among us, to run to town with any message needful to be sent. The rest of us, taking all manner of fearful risks, crashed down over the side of that bluff in headlong haste.

The Hermit's Cave opened on a narrow ledge such as runs below the "Rockport" point, where Marjie and I used to play, off Cliff Street. We reached this ledge at last, hot and breathless, hardly able to realize that we were really here in the place that had baffled us so long. It was an almost inaccessible climb to the crest above us, and the cliff had to be taken at an angle even then. I believe any one accustomed only to the prairie would never have dared to try it.

The Hermit's Cave was merely a deep recess under the overhanging shelf. It penetrated far enough to offer a retreat from the weather. The thick tangle of vines before it so concealed the place that it was difficult to find it at first. Just beyond it the rock projected over the line of wall and overhung the river. It was on this point that the old Hermit had been wont to sit, and from which tradition says he fell to his doom. It was here we had seen Jean Pahusca on that hot August afternoon the summer before. How long ago all that seemed now as the memory of it flashed up in my mind, and I recalled O'mie's quiet boast, "If he can get up there, so can I!"

I was a careless boy that day. I felt myself a man now, with human destiny resting on my shoulders. As we came to this rocky projection I was leading the file of cliff-climbers. The cave was concealed by the greenery. I stared about and then I called, "O'mie! O'mie!"

Faintly, just beside me, came the reply: "Phil, you 've come? Thank God!"

I tore through the bushes and vines into the deep recess. The dimness blinded me at first. What I saw when the glare left my eyes was O'mie stretched on the bare stones, bound hand and foot. His eyes were burning like stars in the gloom. His face was white and drawn with suffering, but he looked up bravely and smiled upon me as I bent over him to lift him. Before I could speak, Bud had cut the bands and freed him. He could not move, and I lifted him like a child in my strong arms.

"Is the town safe?" he asked feebly.

"Yes, now we've found you," Dave Mead replied.

"How did you get here, O'mie?" Clayton Anderson asked.

But O'mie, lying limply in my arms, murmured deliriously of the ladder by the shop, and wondered feebly if it could reach from the river up to the Hermit's Cave. Then his head fell forward and he lay as one dead on my knee.

A year before we would have been a noisy crew that worked our way to this all but inaccessible place, and we would have filled the valley with whoops of surprise at finding anything in the cavern. To-day we hardly spoke as we carried O'mie out into the light. He shivered a little, though still unconscious, and then I felt the hot fever begin to pulse throughout his body.

Dave Mead was half way up the cliff to Father Le Claire. Out on the point John Anderson waved, to the crest above, the simple message, "We've found him."

Bud dived into the cavern and brought out an empty jug, relic of Jean Pahusca's habitation there.

"What he needeth ith water," Bud declared. "I'll bet he'th not had a drop for two dayth."

"How can you get some, Bud? We can't reach the river from here," I said.

"Bah! all mud, anyhow. I'll climb till I find a thpring. They're all around in the rockth. The Lord give Motheth water. I'll hunt till He thoweth me where it ith."

Bud put off in the bushes. Presently his tow head bobbed through the greenery again and a jug dripping full of cool water was in his hands.

"Thame leadin' that brought uth here done it," he lisped, moistening O'mie's lips with the precious liquid.

Bud had a quaint use of Bible reference, although he disclaimed Dr. Hemingway's estimate of him as the best scholar in the Presbyterian Sunday-school.

It seemed hours before relief came. I held O'mie all that time, hoping that the gracious May sunshine might win him to us again, but his delirium increased. He did not know any of us, but babbled of strange things.

At length many shouts overhead told us that half of Springvale was above us, and a rude sort of hammock was being lowered. "It's the best we can do," shouted Father Le Claire. "Tie him in and we'll pull him up."

It was rough handling even with the tenderest of care, and a very dangerous feat as well. I watched those above draw up O'mie's body and I was the last to leave the cave. As I turned to go, by merest chance, my eye caught sight of a knife handle protruding from a crevice in the rock. I picked it up. It was the short knife Jean Pahusca always wore at his belt. As I looked closely, I saw cut in script letters across the steel blade the name, *Jean Le Claire*.

I put the thing in my pocket and soon overtook the other boys, who were leaping and clinging on their way to the crest.

That night Kansas was swept across by the very worst storm I have known in all these sixty years. It lifted above the town and spared the beautiful oak grove in the bottom lands beside us. Further down it swept the valley clean, and the bluff about the cave had not one shrub on its rough sides. The lightning, too, played strange pranks.

The thunderbolts shattered trees and rocks, up-rooting the one and rending and tumbling the other in huge masses of debris upon the valley. It broke even the rough way we had traversed to the Hermit's Cave, and a great heap of fallen stone now shut the cavern in like a rock tomb. Where O'mie had lain was sealed to the world, and it was a full quarter of a century before a path was made along that dangerous cliff-side again.

CHAPTER X

O'MIE'S CHOICE

And how can man die better
Than facing fearful odds
For the ashes of his fathers
And the temples of his gods?

—MACAULAY.

There was only one church bell in Springvale for many years. It called to prayers, or other public service. It sounded the alarm of fire, and tolled for the dead. It was our school-bell and wedding-bell. It clanged in terror when the Cheyennes raided eastward in '67, and it pealed out solemnly for the death of Abraham Lincoln. It chimed on Christmas Eve and rang in each New Year. Its two sad notes that were tolled for the years of the little Judson baby had hardly ceased their vibrations when it broke forth into a ringing, joyous resonance for the finding of O'mie alive.

O'mie was taken to our home. No other woman's hands were so strong and gentle as the hands of Candace Baronet. Everybody felt that O'mie could be trusted nowhere else. It was hard for Cam and Dollie at first, but when Dollie found she might cook every meal and send it up to my aunt, she was more reconciled; while Cam came and went, doing a multitude of kindly acts. This was long before the days of telephones, and a hundred steps were needed for every one taken to-day.

In the weeks that followed, O'mie hung between life and death. With all the care and love given him, his strength wasted away. He had been cruelly beaten, and cuts and bruises showed how terrible had been his fight for freedom.

At first he talked deliriously, but in the weakness that followed he lay motionless hour on hour. And with the fever burning out his candle of life, we waited the end. How heavy-hearted we were in those days! It seemed as though all Springvale claimed the orphan boy. And daily, morning and evening, a messenger from Red Range came for word of him, bearing always offers of whatever help we would accept from the kind-hearted neighborhood.

Father Le Claire had come into our home with the bringing of O'mie, and gentle as a woman's were his ministrations. One evening, when the end of earthly life seemed near for O'mie, the priest took me by the arm, and we went down to the "Rockport" point together. The bushes were growing very rank about my old playground and trysting place. I saw Marjie daily, for she came and went about our house with quiet usefulness. But our hands and hearts were full of the day's sad burden, and we hardly spoke to each other. Marjie's nights were spent mostly with poor Mrs. Judson, whose grief was wearing deep grooves into the young mother face.

To-night Le Claire and I sat down on the rock and breathed deeply of the fresh June air. Below us, for many a mile, the Neosho lay like a broad belt of silver in the deepening shadows of the valley, while all the West Prairie was aflame with the sunset lights. The world was never more beautiful, and the spirit of the Plains seemed reaching out glad hands to us who were so strong and full of life. All day we had watched beside the Irish boy. His weakened pulse-beat showed how steadily his strength was ebbing. He had fallen asleep now, and we dared not think what the waking might be for us.

"Philip, when O'mie is gone, I shall leave Springvale," the priest began. "I think that Jean Pahusca has at last decided to go to the Osages. He probably will never be here again. But if he should come—" Le Claire paused as if the words pained him—"remember you cannot trust him. I have no tie that binds me to you. I shall go to the West. I feel sure the Plains Indians need me now more than the Osages and the Kaws."

I listened silently, not caring to question why either O'mie or Jean should bind him anywhere. The former was all but lost to me already. Of the latter I did not care to think.

"And before I go, I want to tell you something I know of O'mie," Le Claire went on.

I had wondered often at the strange sort of understanding I knew existed between himself and O'mie. I began to listen more intently now, and for the first time since leaving the Hermit's Cave I thought of the knife with the script lettering. I shrank from questioning him or showing him the thing. I had something of my father's patience in letting events tell me what I wanted to know. So I asked no questions, but let him speak.

"O'mie comes by natural right into a dislike, even hatred, of the red race. It may be I know something more of him than anyone else in Springvale knows. His story is a romance and a tragedy, stranger than fiction. In the years to come, when hate shall give place to love in our nation, when the world is won to the church, a younger generation will find it hard to picture the life their forefathers lived."

The priest's brow darkened and his lips were compressed, as if he found it hard to speak what he would say.

"I come to you, Philip, because your experience here has made you a man who were only a boy yesterday; because you love O'mie; because you have been able to keep a quiet tongue; and most of all, because you are John Baronet's son, and heir, I believe, to his wisdom. Most of O'mie's story is known to your father. He found it out just before he went to the war. It is a tragical one. The boy was stolen by a band of Indians when he was hardly more than a baby. It was a common trick of the savages then; it may be again as our frontier creeps westward."

The priest paused and looked steadily out over the Neosho Valley, darkening in the twilight.

"You know how you felt when O'mie was lost. Can you imagine what his mother felt when she found her boy was stolen? Her husband was away on a trapping tour, had been away for a long time, and she was alone. In a very frenzy, she started out on the prairie to follow the Indians. She suffered terrible hardship, but Providence brought her at last to the Osage Mission, whose doors are always open to the distressed. And here she found a refuge. A strange thing happened then. While Patrick O'Meara, O'mie's father, was far from home, word had reached him that his wife was dead.

Coming down the Arkansas River, O'Meara chanced to fall in with some Mexicans who had a battle with a band of Indians at Pawnee Rock. With these Indians was a little white boy, whom O'Meara rescued. It was his own son, although he did not know it, and he brought the little one to the Mission on the Neosho.

"Philip, it is vouchsafed to some of us to know a bit of heaven here on earth. Such a thing came to Patrick O'Meara when he found his wife alive, and the baby boy was restored to her. They were happy together for a little while. But Mrs. O'Meara never recovered from her hardships on the prairie, and her husband was killed by the Comanches a month after her death. Little O'mie, dying up there now, was left an orphan at the Mission. You have heard Mrs. Gentry tell of his coming here. Your father is the only one here who knows anything of O'mie's history. If he never comes back, you must take his place."

The purple shadows of twilight were folding down upon the landscape. In the soft light the priest's face looked dark and set.

"Why not tell me now what father knows?" I asked.

"I cannot tell you that now, Philip. Some day I may tell you another story. But it does not concern you or O'mie. What I want you to do is what your father will do if he comes home. If he should not come, he has written in his will what you must do. I need not tell you to keep this to yourself."

"Father Le Claire, can you tell me anything about Jean Pahusca, and where he is now?"

He rose hastily.

"We must not stay here." Then, kindly, he took my hand. "Yes, some day, but not now, not to-night." There was a choking in his voice, and I thought of O'mie.

We stood up and let the cool evening air ripple against our faces. The Neosho Valley was black now. Only here and there did we catch the glitter of the river. The twilight afterglow was still pink, but the sweep of the prairie was only a purple blur swathed in gray mist.

Out of this purple softness, as we parted the bushes, we saw Marjie hurrying toward us.

"Phil, Phil!" she cried, "O'mie's taken a change for the better. He's been asleep for three hours, and now he is awake. He knew Aunt Candace and he asked for you. The doctor says he has a chance to live. Oh, Phil!" and Marjie burst into tears.

Le Claire took her hand and, putting it through my arm, he said, gently as my father might have done, "You are both too young for such a strain as this. Oh, this civil war! It robs you of your childhood. Too soon, too soon, you are men and women. Philip, take Marjory home. Don't hurry." He smiled as he spoke. "It will do you good to leave O'mie out of mind for a little while."

Then he hurried off to the sick room, leaving us together. It seemed years since that quiet April sunset when we gathered the pink flowers out in the draw, and I crowned Marjie my queen. It was now late June, and the first little yellow leaves were on the cottonwoods, telling that midsummer was near.

"Marjie," I said, putting the hand she had withdrawn through my arm again, "the moon is just coming up. Let's go out on the prairie a little while. Those black shadows down there distress me. I must have some rest from darkness."

We walked slowly out on Cliff Street and into the open prairie, which the great summer moon was flooding with its soft radiance. No other light is ever so regal as the full moon above the prairie, where no black shadows can checker and blot out and hem in its limitless glory. Marjie and I were young and full of vigor, but the steady drain on mind and heart, and the days and nights of broken rest, were not without effect. And yet to-night, with hope once more for O'mie's life, with a sense of lifted care, and with the high tide of the year pouring out its riches round about us, the peace of the prairies fell like a benediction on us, as we loitered about the grassy spaces, quiet and very happy.

Then the care for others turned our feet homeward. I must relieve Aunt Candace to-night by O'mie's side, and Marjie must be with her mother. The moonlight tempted us to linger a little longer as we passed by "Rockport," and we parted the bushes and stood on our old playground rock.

"Marjie, the moonlight makes a picture of you always," I said gently.

She did not answer, but gazed out across the valley, above whose dark greenery the silvery mists lay fold on fold. When she turned her face to mine, something in her eyes called up in me that inspiration that had come to be a part of my thought of her, that sense of a woman's worth and of her right to tenderest guardianship.

"Marjie"—I put both arms around her and drew her to me—"the best thing in the world is a good girl, and you are the best girl in the world." I held her close. It was no longer a boy's admiration, but a man's love that filled my soul that night. Marjie drew gently away.

"We must go now, Phil, indeed we must. Mother needs me."

Oh, I could wait her time. I took her arm and led her out to the street. The bushes closed behind us, and we went our way together. It was well we could not look back upon the rock. We had hardly left it when two figures climbed up from the ledge below and stood where we had been—two for whom the night had no charm and the prairie and valley had no beauty, a low-browed, black-eyed girl with a heart full of jealousy, and a tall, graceful, picturesquely handsome young Indian. They had joined forces, just as I had once felt they would sometime do. As I came whistling up the street on my way home I paused by the bushes, half inclined to go beyond them again. I was happy in every fiber of my being. But duty prodded me sharply to move on. I believe now that Jean Pahusca would have choked the life out of me had I met him face to face that moonlit night. Heaven turns our paths away from many an unknown peril, and we credit it all to our own choice of ways.

Slowly but steadily O'mie came back to us. So far had he gone down the valley of the shadow, he groped with difficulty up toward the light again. He slept much, but it was life-giving sleep, and he was not overcome by delirium after that turning point in his illness. I think I never fully knew my father's sister till in those weeks beside the sickbed. It was not the medicine, nor the careful touch, it was herself—her wholesome, hopeful, trustful spirit—that seemed to enter into the very life of the sick one, and build him to health. I had rarely known illness, I who had muscles like iron, and the frame of a giant. My father was a man of wonderful vigor. It was not until O'mie was brought to our house that I understood why he should have been trusted to no one else.

We longed to know his story. The town had settled into its old groove. The victories of Gettysburg and Vicksburg had thrilled us, as the loss at Chancellorsville had depressed our spirits; and the war was our constant theme. And then the coming and going of traders and strangers on the old trail, the undercurrent of anxiety lest another conspiracy should gather, the Quantrill raid at Lawrence, all helped to keep us from lethargy. We had had our surprise, however. Strangers had to give an account of themselves to the home guard now. But we were softened toward our own townspeople. They were very discreet, and we must meet and do business with them daily. For the sake of young Tell and Jim, we who knew would say nothing. Jean came into town at rare intervals, meeting the priest down in the chapel. Attending to his own affairs, walking always like a very king, or riding as only a Plains Indian can ride, he came and went unmolested. I never could understand that strange power he had of commanding our respect. He seldom saw Marjie, and her face blanched at the mention of his name. I do not know when he last appeared in our town that summer. Nobody could keep track of his movements. But I do know that after the priest's departure, his disappearance was noted, and the daylight never saw him in Springvale again. What the dark hours of the night could have told is another story.

With O'mie out of danger, Le Claire left us. His duties, he told us, lay far to the west. He might go to the Kiowas or the Cheyennes. In any event, it would be long before he came again.

"I need not ask you, Philip, to take good care of O'mie. He could not have better care. You will guard his interests. Until you know more than you do now, you will say nothing to him or any one else of what I have told you."

He looked steadily into my eyes, and I understood him.

"I think Jean Pahusca will never trouble you, nor even come here now. I have my reasons for thinking so. But, Philip, if you should know of his being here, keep on your guard. He is a man of more than savage nature. What he loves, he will die for. What he hates, he will kill. Cam Gentry is right. The worst blood of the Kiowas and of the French nationality fills his veins. Be careful."

Brave little O'mie struggled valiantly for health again. He was patient and uncomplaining, but the days ran into weeks before his strength began to increase. Only one want was not supplied: he longed for the priest.

"You're all so good, it's mighty little in me to say it, an' Dr. Hemingway's gold, twenty-four karat gold; but me hair's red, an' me rale name's O'Meara, an' naturally I long for the praist, although I'm a proper Presbyterian."

"How about Brother Dodd?" I inquired.

"All the love in his heart fur me put in the shell of a mustard seed would rattle round loike a walnut in a tin bushel box, begorra," the sick boy declared.

It was long before he could talk much and we did not ask a question we could avoid, but waited his own time to know how he had been taken from us and how he had found himself a prisoner in that cavern whence we had barely cheated Death of its pitiful victim. As he could bear it he told us, at length, of his part in the night the town was marked for doom. Propped up on his pillows, his face to the open east window, his thin, white hands folded, he talked quietly as of a thing in which he had had little part.

"Ye see, Phil, the Almighty made us all different, so He could know us, an' use us when He wanted some partic'lar thing that some partic'lar one could do. When folks puts on a uniform in their dress or their thinkin', they belong to one av two classes—them as is goin' to the devil like convicts an' narrow churchmen, or them as is goin' after 'em hard to bring 'em into line again, like soldiers an' sisters av charity; an' they just have to act as one man. But mainly we're singular number. The Lord didn't give me size."

He looked up at my broad shoulders. I had carried him in my arms from his bed to the east window day after day.

"I must do me own stunt in me own way. You know mebby, how I tagged thim strangers till, if they'd had the chance at me they'd have fixed me. Specially that Dick Yeager, the biggest av the two who come to the tavern."

"The chance! Didn't they have their full swing at you?"

"Well, no, not regular an' proper," he replied.

I wondered if the cruelty he had suffered might not have injured his brain and impaired his memory.

"You know I peeked through that hole up in the shop that Conlow seems to have left fur such as me. Honorable business, av coorse. But Tell and Jim, they was hid behind the stack av wagon wheels in the dark corner—just as honorable an' high-spirited as meself, on their social level. I was a high-grader up on that ladder. Well, annyhow, I peeked an' eavesdropped, as near as I could get to the eaves av the shop, an' I tould Father Le Claire all I could foind out. An' then he put it on me to do my work. 'You can be spared,' he says. 'If it's life and death, ye'll choose the better part.' Phil, it was laid on all av us to choose that night."

His thin, blue-veined hand sought mine where he lay reclining against the pillows. I took it in my big right hand, the hand that could hold Jean Pahusca with a grip of iron.

"There was only one big enough an' brainy enough an' brave enough to lead the crowd to save this town an' that was Philip Baronet. There was only one who could advise him well an' that was Cam Gentry. Poor old Cam, too near-sighted to tell a cow from a catfish tin feet away. Without you, Cam and the boys couldn't have done a thing.

"Can ye picture what would be down there now? I guess not, fur you'd not be making pictures now, You'd be a picture yourself, the kind they put on the carbolic acid bottle an' mark 'pizen.'"

O'mie paused and looked out dreamily across the valley to the east plains beyond them.

"I can't tell how fast things wint through me moind that night. You did some thinkin' yourself, an' you know. 'I can't do Phil's part if I stay here,' I raisoned, 'an' bedad, I don't belave he can do my part. Bein' little counts sometimes. It's laid on me to be the sacrifice, an' I'll kape me promise an' choose the better part. I'll cut an' run.'"

He looked up at my questioning face with a twinkle in his eye.

"'There's only one to save this town. That's Phil's stunt,' I says; 'an' there's only one to save Marjie. That's my stunt.'"

I caught my breath, for my heart stood still, and I felt I must strangle.

"Do you mean to say, Thomas O'Meara—?" I could get no fuither.

"I mane, either you or me's got to tell this. If you know it better'n I do, go ahead." And then more gently he went on: "Yes, I mane to say, kape still, dear; I'm not very strong yet. If I'd gone up to Cliff Street afther you to come to her, she'd be gone. If Jean got hands on her an' she struggled or screamed, as she'd be like to do, bein' a sensible girl, he had that murderous little short knife, an' he'd swore solemn he'd have her or her scalp. He's not got her, nor her scalp, nor that knife nather now. I kept that much from doin' harm. I dunno where the cruel thing wint to, but it wint, all right.

"And do ye mane to say, Philip Baronet, that ye thought I'd lost me nerve an' was crude enough to fall in wid a nest av thim Copperheads an' let 'em do me to me ruin? Or did you think His Excellency, the Reverend Dodd was right, an' I'd cut for cover till the fuss was over? Well, honestly now, I'm not that kind av an Irishman."

My mind was in a tumult as I listened. I wondered how O'mie could be so calm when I durst not trust myself to speak.

"So I run home, thinkin' ivery jump, an' I grabbed the little girl's waterproof cloak. Your lady friends' wraps comes in handy sometimes. Don't niver despise 'em, Phil, nor the ladies nather. You woman-hater!" O'mie's laugh was like old times and very good to hear.

"I flung that thing round me, hood on me brown curls, an' all, an' then I flew. I made the ground just three times in thim four blocks and a half to Judson's. You know how the kangaroo looks in the geography picture av Australia, illustratin' the fauna an' flora, with a tall, thin tree beyont, showin' lack of vegetation in that tropic, an' a little quilly cus they call a ornithorynchus, its mouth like Jim Conlow's? Well, no kangaroo'd had enough self-respect to follow me that night. I caught Marjie just in time, an' I puts off before her toward her home. At the corner I quit kangarooin' an' walks quick an' a little timid-like, just Marjie to a dimple. If you'd been there, you'd wanted to put some more pink flowers round where they'd do the most good."

I squeezed his hand.

"Quit that, you ugly bear. That's a lady's hand yet a whoile an' can't stand too much pressure.

"It was to save her loife, Phil." O'mie spoke solemnly now. "You could save the town. I couldn't. I could save her. You couldn't. In a minute, there in the dark by the gate, Jean Pahusca grabs me round me dainty waist. His horse was ready by him an' he swung me into the saddle, not harsh, but graceful like, an' gintle. I never said a word, but gave a awful gasp like I hadn't no words, appreciative enough. 'I'm saving' you, Star-face,' he says. 'The Copperheads will burn your mother's house an' the Kiowas will come and steal Star-face—' an' he held me close as if he would protect me—he got over that later—an' I properly fainted. That's the only way the abducted princess can do in the novel—just faint. It saves hearin' what you don't want to know. An' me size just suited the case. Don't never take on airs, you big hulkin' fellow. No graceful prince is iver goin' to haul you over the saddle-bow thinkin' you're the choice av his heart. It saved Marjie, an' it got Jean clear av town before he found his mistake, which wa'n't bad for Springvale. Down by Fingal's Creek I come to, an' we had a rumpus. Bein' a dainty girl, I naturally objected to goin' into that swirlin' water, though I didn't object to Jean's goin'—to eternity. In the muss I lost me cloak—the badge av me business there. I never could do nothin' wid thim cussed hooks an' eyes on a collar an' the thing wasn't anchored securely at me throat. It was awful then. I can't remember it all. But it was dark, and Jean had found me out, and the waters was deep and swift. The horse got away on the bank an' slid back, I think. It must have been then it galloped up to town; but findin' Jean didn't follow, it came back to him. I didn't know annything fur some toime. I'd got too much av Fingal's Creek mixed into me constitution an' by-laws to kape my thoughts from floatin' too. I'll never know rightly whin I rode an' whin I was dragged, an' whin I walked. It was a runnin' fight av infantry and cavalry, such as the Neosho may never see again, betwixt the two av us."

Blind, trustful fool that I had been, thinking after all Le Claire's warnings that Jean had been a good, loyal, chivalrous Indian, protecting Marjie from harm.

"And to think we have thought all this time there were a dozen Rebels making away with you, and never dreamed you had deliberately put yourself into the hands of the strongest and worst enemy you could have!"

"It was to save a woman, Phil," O'mie said simply. "He could only kill me. He wouldn't have been that good to her. You'd done the same yoursilf to save anny woman, aven a stranger to you. Wait an' see."

How easily forgotten things come back when we least expect them. There came to me, as O'mie spoke, the memory of my dream the night after Jean had sought Marjie's life out on the Red Range prairie. The night after I talked with my father of love and of my mother. That night two women whom I had never seen before were in my dreams, and I had struggled to save them from peril as though they were of my own flesh and blood.

"You will do it," O'mie went on. "You were doing more. Who was it wint down along the creek side av town where the very worst pro-slavery fellows is always coiled and ready to spring, wint in the dark to wake up folks that lived betwixt them on either side, who was ready to light on 'em at a minute's notice? Who wint upstairs above thim as was gettin' ready to burn 'em in their beds, an' walked quiet and cool where one wrong step meant to be throttled in the dark? Don't talk to me av courage."

"But, O'mie, it was all chance with us. You went where danger was certain."

"It was my part, Phil, an' I ain't no shirker just because I'm not tin feet tall an' don't have to be weighed on Judson's stock scales." O'mie rested awhile on the pillows. Then he continued his story.

"They was more or less border raidin' betwixt Jean an' me till we got beyont the high cliff above the Hermit's Cave. When I came to after one of his fists had bumped me head he was urgin' his pony to what it didn't want. The river was roarin' below somewhere an' it was black as the grave's insides. It was way up there that in a minute's lull in the hostilities, I caught the faint refrain:

'Does the star-spangled banner yit wave,
O'er the land av the free and the home av the brave?'

"I didn't see your lights. They was tin thousand star-spangled banners wavin' before me eyes ivery second. But that strain av song put new courage into me soul though I had no notion what it really meant. I was half dead an' wantin' to go the other half quick, an' it was like a drame, till that song sent a sort of life-givin' pulse through me. The next minute we were goin' over an' over an' over, betwane rocks, an' hanging to trees, down, down, down, wid that murderous river roarin' hungry below us. Jean jumpin' from place to place an' me clingin' to him an' hittin' iverything that could be hit at ivery jump. An' then come darkness over me again. There was a light somewhere when I come to. I was free an' I made a quick spring. I got that knife, an' like a flash I slid the blade down a crack somewhere. An' then he tied me solid, an' standin' over me he says slow an' cruel: 'You—may—stay—here—till—you—starve—to—

death. Nobody—can—get—to—you—but—me—an'—I'm—niver—comin'—back. I hate you.' An' his eyes were just loike that noight whin I found him with thim faded pink flowers out on the prairie."

"O'mie, dear, you are the greatest hero I ever heard of. You poor, beaten, tortured sacrifice."

I put my arm around his shoulder and my tears fell on his red hair.

"I didn't do no more than ivery true American will do—fight an' die to protect his home; or if not his'n, some other man's. Whin the day av choosin' comes we can't do no more 'n to take our places. We all do it. Whin Jean put it on me to lay there helpless an' die o' thirst, I know'd I could do it. Same as you know'd you'd outwit that gang ready to burn an' kill, that I'd run from. I just looked straight up at Jean—the light was gettin' dim—an' I says, 'You—may—go—plum—to—the—divil, —but—you—can't—hurt—that—part—av—me—that's—never—hungry—nor —thirsty.' When you git face to face wid a thing like that," O'mie spoke reverently, "somehow the everlastin' arms, Dr. Hemingway's preaches of, is strong underneath you. The light wint out, an' Jean in his still way had slid off, an' I was alone. Alone wid me achin' and me bonds, an' wid a burnin' longin' fur water, wid a wish to go quick if I must go; but most av all—don't never furgit it, Phil, whin the thing overtakes you aven in your strength—most av all, above all sufferin' and natural longin' to live—there comes the reality av the words your Aunt Candace taught us years ago in the little school:

"'Though I walk through the valley av the shadow av death, I will fear no evil.'

"I called for you, Phil, in my misery, as' I know'd somehow you'd hear me. An' you did come."

His thin hand closed over mine, and we sat long in silence—two boys whom the hand of Providence was leading into strange, hard lines, shaping us each for the work the years of our manhood were waiting to bring to us.

CHAPTER XI

GOLDEN DAYS

There are days that are kind
As a mother to man, showing pathways that wind
Out and in, like a dream, by some stream of delight;
Never hinting of aught that they hold to affright;
Only luring us on, since the way must be trod,
Over meadows of green with their velvety sod,
To the steeps, that are harder to climb, far before.
There are nights so enchanting, they seem to restore
The original beauty of Eden; so tender,
They woo every soul to a willing surrender
Of feverish longing; so holy withal,
That a broad benediction seems sweetly to fall
On the world.

We were a busy folk in those years that followed the close of the war. The prairies were boundless, and the constant line of movers' wagons reaching out endlessly on the old trail, with fathers and mothers and children, children, children, like the ghosts of Banquo's lineal issue to King Macbeth, seemed numerous enough to people the world and put to the plough every foot of the virgin soil of the beautiful Plains. With the downfall of slavery the strife for commercial supremacy began in earnest here, and there are no idle days in Kansas.

When I returned home after two years' schooling in Massachusetts, I found many changes. I had beaten my bars like a caged thing all those two years. Rockport, where I made my home and spent much of my time, was so unlike Springvale, so wofully and pridefully ignorant of all Kansas, so unable to get any notion of my beautiful prairies and of the free-spirited, cultured folk I knew there, that I suffered out my time there and was let off a little early for good behavior. Only one person did I know who had any real interest in my West, a tall, dark-eyed, haughty young lady, to whom I talked of

Kansas by the hour. Her mother, who was officiously courteous to me, didn't approve of that subject, but the daughter listened eagerly.

When I left Rockport, Rachel—that was her name, Rachel Melrose—asked me when I was coming back. I assured her, never, and then courteously added if she would come to Kansas.

"Well, I may go," she replied, "not to your Springvale, but to my aunt in Topeka for a visit next Fall. Will you come up to Topeka?"

Of course, I would go to Topeka, but might she not come to Springvale? There were the best people on earth in Springvale. I could introduce her to boys who were gentlemen to the core. I'd lived and laughed and suffered with them, and I knew.

"But I shouldn't care for any of them except you." Rachel's voice trembled and I couldn't help seeing the tears in her proud dark eyes.

"Oh, I've a girl of my own there," I said impulsively, for I was always longing for Marjie, "but Clayton Anderson and Dave Mead are both college men now." And then I saw how needlessly rude I had been.

"Of course I want you to come to Springvale. Come to our house. Aunt Candace will make you royally welcome. The Baronets and Melroses have been friends for generations. I only wanted the boys to know you; I should be proud to present my friend to them. I would take care of you. You have been so kind to me this year, I should be glad to do much for you." I had taken her hand to say good-bye.

"And you would let that other girl take care of herself, wouldn't you, while I was there? Promise me that when I go to Kansas you will come up to Topeka to see me, and when I go to your town, if I do, you will not neglect me but will let that Springvale girl entirely alone."

I did not know much of women then—nor now—although I thought then I knew everything. I might have read behind that fine aristocratic face a supremely selfish nature, a nature whose pleasure increased only as her neighbor's pleasure decreased. There are such minds in the world.

I turned to her, and taking both of her willing hands in mine, I said frankly: "When you visit your aunt, I'll be glad to see you there. If you visit my aunt I would be proud to show you every courtesy. As for that little girl, well, when you see her you will understand. She has a place all her own with me." I looked straight into her eyes as I said this.

She smiled coquettishly. "Oh, I'm not afraid of her," she said indifferently; "I can hold my own with any Kansas, girl, I'm sure."

She was dangerously handsome, with a responsive face, a winning smile and gracious manners. She seemed never to accept anything as a gift, but to take what was her inherent right of admiration and devotion. When I bade her good-bye a look of sadness was in her eyes. It rebuked my spirit somehow, although Heaven knows I had given her no cause to miss me. But my carriage was waiting and I hurried away. For a moment only her image lingered with me, and then I forgot her entirely; for every turn of the wheel was bringing me to Kansas, to the prairies, to the beautiful Neosho Valley, to the boys again, to my father and home, but most of all to Marjie.

It was twenty months since I had seen her. She had spent a year in Ohio in the Girls' College at Glendale, and had written me she would reach Springvale a month before I did. After that I had not heard from her except through a marked copy of the *Springvale Weekly Press*, telling of her return. She had not marked that item, but had pencilled the news that "Philip Baronet would return in three weeks from Massachusetts, where he had been enjoying the past two years in school."

Enjoying! Under this Marjie had written in girlish hand, "Hurry up, Phil."

On the last stage of my journey I was wild with delight. It was springtime on the prairies, and a verdure clothed them with its richest garments. I did not note the growing crops, and the many little freeholds now, where there had been only open unclaimed land two years before. I was longing for the Plains again, for one more ride, reckless and free, across their broad stretches, for one more gorgeous sunset out on Red Range, one more soft, iridescent twilight purpling down to the evening darkness as I had seen it on "Rockport" all those years. How the real Rockport, the Massachusetts town, faded from me, and the sea, and the college halls, and city buildings. The steam and steel and brick and marble of an older civilization, all gave place to Nature's broad handiwork and the generous-hearted, capable, unprejudiced people of this new West. However crude and plain Springvale might have seemed to an Eastern boy suddenly transplanted here, it was fair and full of delight for me.

The stage driver, Dever, by name, was a stranger to me, but he knew all about my coming. Also he was proud to be the first to give me the freshest town gossip. That's the stage-driver's right divine always. I was eager to hear of everybody and in this forty miles' ride I was completely informed. The story rambled somewhat aimlessly from topic to topic, but it never lagged.

"Did I know Judson? He'd got a controlling interest now in Whately's store. He was great after money, Judson was. They do say he's been a little off the square getting hold of the store. The widder Whately kept only about one-third, or maybe one-fourth of the stock. Mrs. Whately, she wa'n't no manager. Marjie'd do better, but Marjie wa'n't twenty yet. And yet if all they say's true she wouldn't need to manage. Judson is about the sprucest widower in town, though he did seem to take it so hard when poor Mis' Judson was taken." She never overcame the loss of her baby, and the next Summer they put her out in the prairie graveyard beside it. "But Judson now, he's shyin' round Marjie real coltish.

"It'd be fine fur her, of course," my driver went on, "an' she was old a-plenty to marry. Marjie was a mighty purty girl. The boys was nigh crazy about her. Did I know her?"

I did; oh, yes, I remembered her.

"They's another chap hangin' round her, too; his name's—lemme see, uh—common enough name when I was a boy back in

Kentucky—uh—Tillhurst, Richard Tillhurst. Tall, peaked, thin-visaged feller. Come out from Virginny to Illinois. Got near dead with consumption 'nd come on to Kansas to die. Saw Springvale 'nd thought better of it right away. Was teachin' school and payin' plenty of attention to the girls, especially Marjie. They was an old man Tillhurst when I was a boy. He was from Virginny, too—" but I pass that story.

"Tell Mapleson's pickin' up sence he's got the post-office up in the 'Last Chance'; put that doggery out'n his sullar, had in wall paper now, an' drugs an' seeds, an' nobody was right sure where he got his funds to stock up, so—they was some sort of story goin' about a half-breed named Pahusky when I first come here, bein' 'sociated with Mapleson—Cam Gentry's same old Cam, squintin' round an' jolly as ever. O'mie? Oh, he's leadin' the band now. By jinks, that band of his'n will just take the cake when it goes up to Topeky this Fall to the big political speak-in's." On and on the driver went, world without end, until we caught the first faint line along the west that marked the treetops of the Neosho Valley. We were on the Santa Fé Trail now, and we were coming to the east bluff where I had first seen the little Whately girl climb out of the big wagon and stretch the stiffness out of her fat little legs. The stage horses were bracing for the triumphal entry into town, when a gang of young outlaws rushed up over the crest of the east slope. They turned our team square across the way and in mock stage-robbery style called a halt. The driver threw up his hands in mock terror and begged for mercy, which was granted if he would deliver up one Philip Baronet, student and tenderfoot. But I was already down from the stage and O'mie was hugging me hard until Bud Anderson pulled him away and all the boys and girls were around me. Oh, it was good to see them all again, but best of all was it to see Marjie. She had been a pretty picture of a young girl. She was beautiful now. No wonder she had many admirers. She was last among the girls to greet me. I took her hand and our eyes met. Oh, I had no fear of widower nor of school-teacher, as I helped her to a seat beside me in the stage.

"I'm so glad to see you again, Phil," she looked up into my face. "You are bigger than ever."

"And you are just the same Marjie."

The crowd piled promiscuously about us and we bumped down the slope and into the gurgling Neosho, laughing and happy.

With all the rough and tumble years of a boyhood and youth on the frontier, the West has been good to me, and I look back along the way glad that mine was the pioneer's time, and that the experiences of those early days welded into my building and being something of their simplicity, and strength, and capacity for enjoyment. But of all the seasons along the way of these sixty years, of all the successes and pleasures, I remember best and treasure most that glorious summer after my return from the East. My father was on the Judge's bench now and his legal interests and property interests were growing. I began the study of law under him at once, and my duties were many, for he put responsibility on me from the first. But I was in the very heyday of life, and had no wish ungratified.

"Phil, I want you to go up the river and take a look at two quarters of Section 29, range 14, this afternoon. It lies just this side of the big cottonwood," my father said to me one June day.

"Make a special note of the land, and its natural appurtenances. I want the information at once, or you needn't go out on such a hot day. It's like a furnace in the courthouse. It may be cooler out that way." He fanned his face with his straw hat, and the light breeze coming up the valley lifted the damp hair about his temples.

"There's a bridle path over the bluff a mile or so out, where you can ride a horse down and go up the river in the bottom. It's a much shorter way, but you'd better go out the Red Range road and turn north at the third draw well on to the divide. It gets pretty steep near the river, so you have to keep to the west and turn square at the draw. If it wasn't so warm you might go on to Red Range for some depositions for me. But never mind, Dave Mead is going up there Monday, anyhow. Will you ride the pony?"

"No, I'll go out in the buggy."

"And take some girl along? Well, don't forget your errand. Be sure to note the lay of the land. There's no building, I believe, but a little stone cabin and it's been empty for years; but you can see. Be sure to examine everything in that cabin carefully. Stop at the courthouse as you go out, and get the surveyor's map and some other directions."

It was a hot summer day, with that thin, dry burning in the air that the light Kansas zephyr fanned back in little rippling waves. My horses were of the Indian pony breed, able to go in heat or cold. Most enduring and least handsome of the whole horse family, with temper ranging from moderately vicious to supremely devilish, is this Indian pony of the Plains.

Marjie was in the buggy beside me when I stopped at the courthouse for instructions. Lettie Conlow was passing and came to the buggy's side.

"Where are you going, Marjie?" she asked. There was a sullen minor tone in her voice.

"With Phil, out somewhere. Where is it you are going, Phil?"

I was tying the ponies. They never learned how to stand unanchored a minute.

"Out north on the Red Range prairie to buy a couple of quarters," I replied carelessly and ran up the courthouse steps.

"Well, well, well," Cam Gentry roared as he ambled up to the buggy. Cam's voice was loud in proportion as his range of vision was short. "You two gettin' ready to elope? An' he's goin' to git his dad to back him up gettin' a farm. Now, Marjie, why'd you run off? Let us see the performance an' hear Dr. Hemingway say the words in the Presbyterian Church. Or maybe you're goin' to hunt up Dodd. He went toward Santy Fee when he put out of here after the War."

Cam could be heard in every corner of the public square. I was at the open window of my father's office. Looking out, I saw Lettie staring angrily at Cam, who couldn't see her face. She had never seemed less attractive to me. She had a flashy coloring, and she made the most of ornaments. Some people called her good-looking. Beside Marjie, she was as the wild yoncopin to the calla lily. Marjie knew how to dress. To-day, shaded by the buggy-top, in her dainty light blue lawn, with the soft pink of her cheeks and her clear white brow and throat, she was a most delicious thing to look upon in that hot summer street. Poor Lettie suffered by contrast. Her cheeks were blazing, and her hair, wet with perspiration, was adorned with a bow of bright purple ribbon tied butterfly-fashion, and fastened on with a pin set with flashing brilliants.

"Baronet, I think we are marching straight into Hell's jaws"

"Oh, Uncle Cam," Marjie cried, blushing like the pink rambler roses climbing the tavern veranda, "Phil's just going out to look at some land for his father. It's up the river somewhere and I'm going to hold the ponies while he looks."

"Well, he'd ort to have somebody holdin' 'em fur him. I'll bet ye I'd want a hostler if I had the lookin' to do. Land's a mighty small thing an' hard to look at, sometimes; 'specially when a feller's head's in the clouds an' he's walkin' on air. Goin' northwest? Look out, they's a ha'nted house up there. But, by hen, I'd never see a ha'nt long's I had somethin' better to look at."

I saw Lettie turn quickly and disappear around the corner. My father was busy, so I sat in the office window and whistled and waited, watching the ponies switch lazily at the flies.

When we were clear of town, and the open plain swept by the summer breezes gave freedom from the heat, Marjie asked:

"Where is Lettie Conlow going on such a hot afternoon?"

"Nowhere, is she? She was talking to you at the courthouse."

"But she rushed away while Uncle Cam was joking, and I saw her cross the alley back of the courthouse on Tell's pony, and in a minute she was just flying up toward Cliff Street. She doesn't ride very well. I thought she was afraid of that pony. But she was making it go sailing out toward the bluff above town."

"Well, let her go, Marjie. She always wears on my nerves."

"Phil, she likes you, I know. Everybody knows."

"Well, I know and everybody knows that I never give her reason to. I wish she would listen to Tell. I thought when I first came home they were engaged."

"Before he went up to Wyandotte to work they were—he said so, anyhow."

Then we forgot Lettie. She wasn't necessary to us that day, for there were only two in our world.

Out on the prairie trail a mile or more is the point where the bridle path leading to the river turns northwest, and passing over a sidling narrow way down the bluff, it follows the bottom lands upstream. As we passed this point we did not notice Tell Mapleson's black pony just making the top from the sidling bluff way, nor how quickly its rider wheeled and headed back again down beyond sight of the level prairie road. We had forgotten Lettie Conlow and everybody else.

The draw was the same old verdant ripple in the surface of the Plains. The grasses were fresh and green. Toward the river the cottonwoods were making a cool, shady way, delightfully refreshing in this summer sunshine.

We did not hurry, for the draw was full of happy memories for us.

"I'll corral these bronchos up under the big cottonwood, and we'll explore appurtenances down by the river later," I said. "Father says every foot of the half-section ought to be viewed from that tree, except what's in the little clump about the cabin."

We drove up to the open prairie again and let the horses rest in the shade of this huge pioneer tree of the Plains. How it had escaped the prairie fires through its years of sturdy growth is a marvel, for it commanded the highest point of the whole divide. Its shade was delicious after the glare of the trail.

For once the ponies seemed willing to stand quiet, and Marjie and I looked long at the magnificent stretch of sky and earth. There were a few white clouds overhead, deepening to a dull gray in the southwest. All the sunny land was swathed in the midsummer yellow green, darkening in verdure along the river and creeks, and in the deepest draws. Even as we rested there the clouds rolled over the horizon's edge, piling higher and higher, till they hid the afternoon sun, and the world was cool and gray. Then down the land sped a summer shower; and the sweet damp odor of its refreshing the south wind bore to us, who saw it all. Sheet after sheet of glittering raindrops, wind-driven, swept across the prairie, and the cool green and the silvery mist made a scene a master could joy to copy.

I didn't forget my errand, but it was not until the afternoon was growing late that we left the higher ground and drove down the shady draw toward the river. The Neosho is a picture here, with still expanses that mirror the trees along its banks, and stony shallows where the water, even in midsummer, prattles merrily in the sunshine, as it hurries toward the deep stillnesses.

We sat down in a cool, grassy space with the river before us, and the green trees shading the little stone cabin beyond us, while down the draw the vista of still sunlit plains was like a dream of beauty.

"Marjie,"—I took her hand in mine—"since you were a little girl I have known you. Of all the girls here I have known you longest. In the two years I was East I met many young ladies, both in school and at Rockport. There were some charming young folks. One of them, Rachel Melrose, was very pretty and very wealthy. Her mother made considerable fuss over me, and I believe the daughter liked me a little; for she—but never mind; maybe it was all my vanity. But, Marjie, there has never been but one girl for me in all this world; there will never be but one. If Jean Pahusca had carried you off—Oh, God in Heaven! Marjie, I wonder how my father lived through the days after my mother lost her life. Men do, I know."

I was toying with her hand. It was soft and beautifully formed, although she knew the work of our Springvale households.

"Marjie," my voice was full of tenderness, "you are dear to me as my mother was to my father. I loved you as my little playmate; I was fond of you as my girl when I was first beginning to care for a girl as boys will; as my sweetheart, when the liking grew to something more. And now all the love a man can give, I give to you."

I rose up before her. They call me vigorous and well built to-day. I was in my young manhood's prime then. I looked down at her, young and dainty, with the sweet grace of womanhood adorning her like a garment. She stood up beside me and lifted her fair face to mine. There was a bloom on her cheeks and her brown eyes were full of peace. I opened my arms to her and she nestled in them and rested her cheek against my shoulder.

"Marjie," I said gently, "will you kiss me and tell me that you love me?"

Her arms were about my neck a moment. Sometimes I can feel them there now. All shy and sweet she lifted her lips to mine.

"I do love you, Phil," she murmured, and then of her own will, just once, she kissed me.

"It is vouchsafed sometimes to know a bit of heaven here on earth," Le Claire had said to me when he talked of O'mie's father.

It came to me that day; the cool, green valley by the river, the vine-covered old stone cabin, the sunlit draw opening to a limitless world of summer peace and beauty, and Marjie with me, while both of us were young and we loved each other.

The lengthening shadows warned me at last.

"Well, I must finish up this investigation business of Judge Baronet's," I declared. "Come, here's a haunted house waiting for us. Father says it hasn't been inhabited since the Frenchman left it. Are you afraid of ghosts?"

We were going up a grass-grown way toward the little stone structure, half buried in climbing vines and wild shrubbery.

"What a cunning place, Phil! It doesn't look quite deserted to me, somehow. No, I'm not afraid of anything but Indians."

My arm was about her in a moment. She looked up laughing, but she did not put it away.

"Why, there are no Indians here, Phil," and she looked out on the sunny draw.

My face was toward the cabin. I was in a blissful waking dream, else I should have taken quicker note. For sure as I had eyes, I caught a flash of red between the far corner of the cabin and the thick underbrush beyond it. It was just a narrow space, where one might barely pass, between the corner of the little building and the surrounding shrubbery; but for an instant, a red blanket with a white centre flashed across this space, and was gone. So swift was its flight and so full was my mind of the joy of living, I could not be sure I had seen anything. It was just a twitch of the eyelid. What else could it be?

We pushed open the solid oak door, and stood inside the little room. The two windows let in a soft green light. It was a rude structure of the early Territorial days, made for shelter and warmth. There was a dark little attic or loft overhead. A few pieces of furniture—a chair, a table, a stone hearth by the fireplace, and a sort of cupboard—these, with a strong, old worn chest, were all that the room held. Dust was everywhere, as might have been expected. And yet Marjie was right. The spirit of occupation was there.

"Do you know, Marjie, this cabin has hardly been opened since the poor woman drowned herself in the river, down there. They found her body in the Deep Hole. The Frenchman left the place, and it has been called haunted. An Indian and a ghost can't live together. The race fears them of all things. So the Indians would never come here."

"But look there, Phil!"—Marjie had not heeded my words—"there's a stick partly burned, and these ashes look fresh." She was bending over the big stone hearth.

As I started forward, my eye caught a bit of color behind the chair by the table. I stooped to see a purple bow of ribbon, tied butterfly fashion—Lettie Conlow's ribbon. I put it in my pocket, determined to find out how it had found its way here.

"Ugh! Let's go," said Marjie, turning to me. "I'm cold in here. I'd want a home up under the cottonwood, not down in this lonely place. Maybe movers on the trail camp in here." Marjie was at the door now.

I looked about once more and then we went outside and stood on the broad, flat step. The late afternoon was dreamily still here, and the odor of some flowers, faint and woodsy, came from the thicket beside the doorway.

"It is dreary in there, Marjie, but I'll always love this place outside. Won't you?" I said, and with a lover's happiness in my face, I drew her close to me.

She smiled and nodded. "I'll tell you all I think after a while. I'll write it to you in a letter."

"Do, Marjie, and put it in our 'Rockport' post-office, just like we used to do. I'll write you every day, too, and you'll find my letter in the same old crevice. Come, now, we must go home."

"We'll come again." Marjie waved her hand to the silent gray cabin. And slowly, as lovers will, we strolled down the walk and out into the open where the ponies neighed a hurry-up call for home.

Somehow the joy of youth and hope drove fear and suspicion clear from my mind, and with the opal skies above us and the broad sweet prairies round about us for an eternal setting of peace and beauty, we two came home that evening, lovers, who never afterwards might walk alone, for that our paths were become one way wherein we might go keeping step evermore together down the years.

CHAPTER XII

A MAN'S ESTATE

When I became a man I put away childish things.

The next day was the Sabbath. I was twenty-one that day. Marjie and I sang in the choir, and most of the solo work fell to us. Dave Mead was our tenor, and Bess Anderson at the organ sang alto. Dave was away that day. His girl sweetheart up on Red Range was in her last illness then, and Dave was at her bedside. Poor Dave! he left Springvale that Fall, and he never came back. And although he has been honored and courted of women, I have been told that in his luxurious bachelor apartments in Hong Kong there is only one woman's picture, an old-fashioned daguerreotype of a sweet girlish face, in an ebony frame.

Dr. Hemingway always planned the music to suit his own notions. What he asked for we gave. On this Sabbath morning there was no surprise when he announced, "Our tenor being absent, we will omit the anthem, and I shall ask brother Philip and sister Marjory to sing Number 549, 'Oh, for a Closer Walk with God.'"

He smiled benignly upon us. We were accustomed to his way, and we knew everybody in that little congregation. And yet, somehow, a flutter went through the company when we stood up together, as if everybody knew our thoughts. We had stood side by side on Sabbath mornings and had sung from the same book since childhood, with never a thought of embarrassment. It dawned on Springvale that day as a revelation what Marjie meant to me. All the world, including our town, loves a lover, and it was suddenly clear to the town that the tall, broad-shouldered young man who looked down at the sweet-browed little girl-woman beside him as he looked at nobody else, whose hand touched hers as they turned the leaves, and who led her by the arm ever so gently down the steps from the choir seats, was reading for himself

That old fair story
Set round in glory
Wherever life is found.

And Marjie, in spotless white, with her broad-brimmed hat set back from her curl-shaded forehead, the tinted lights from the memorial window which Amos Judson had placed there for his wife, falling like an aureole about her, who could keep from loving her?

"Her an' Phil Baronet's jist made fur one another," Cam Gentry declared to a bunch of town gossips the next day.

"Now'd ye ever see a finer-lookin' couple?" broke in Grandpa Mead. "An' the way they sung that hymn yesterday—well, I just hope they'll repeat it over my remains." And Grandpa began to sing softly in his quavering voice:

Oh, for a closer walk with God,
A cam and heavenli frame,
A light toe shine upon tha road
That leads me toe tha Lamb.

Everybody agreed with Cam except Judson. He was very cross with O'mie that morning. O'mie was clerk and manager for him now, as Judson himself had been for Irving Whately. He rubbed his hands and joined the group, smiling a trifle scornfully.

"Seems to me you're all gossiping pretty freely this morning. The young man may be pretty well fixed some day. But he's young, he's young. Mrs. Whately's my partner, and I know their affairs very well, very well. She'll provide her daughter with a man, not a mere boy."

"Well, he was man enough to keep this here town from burnin' up, an' no tellin' how many bloodsheds," Grandpa Mead piped in.

"He was man enough to find O'mie and save his life," Cam protested.

"Well, we'll leave it to Dr. Hemingway," Judson declared, as the good doctor entered the doorway. Judson paid liberally into the church fund and accounted that his wishes should weigh much with the good minister. "We—these people here—were just coupling the name of Marjory Whately with that boy of Judge Baronet's. Now I know how Mrs. Whately is circumstanced. She is peculiarly situated, and it seems foolish to even repeat such gossip about this young man, this very young man, Philip."

The minister smiled upon the group serenely. He knew the life-purpose of every member of it, and he could have said, as Kipling wrote of the Hindoo people:

I have eaten your bread and salt,
I have drunk your water and wine;
The deaths ye died I have watched beside,
And the lives ye led were mine.

"I never saw a finer young man and woman in my life," he said gently. "I know nothing of their intentions—as yet. They haven't been to me," his eyes twinkled, "but they are good to look upon when they stand up together. Our opinions, however, will cut little figure in their affairs. Heaven bless them and all the boys and girls! How soon they grow to be men and women."

The good man made his purchase and left the store.

"But he's a young man, a very boy yet," Amos Judson insisted, unable to hide his disappointment at the minister's answer.

The very boy himself walked in at that instant. Judson turned a scowling face at O'mie, who was chuckling among the calicoes, and frowned upon the group as if to ward off any further talk. I nodded good-morning and went to O'mie.

"Aunt Candace wants some Jane P. Coats's thread, number 50 white, two spools."

"That's J. & P. Coats, young man." Judson spoke more sharply than he need to have done. "Goin' East to school doesn't always finish a boy; size an' learnin' don't count," and he giggled.

I was whistling softly, "Oh, for a Closer Walk with God," and I turned and smiled down on the little man. I was head and shoulders above him.

"No, not always. I can still learn," I replied good-naturedly, and went whistling on my way to the courthouse.

I was in a good humor with all the world that morning. Out on "Rockport" in the purple twilight of the Sabbath evening I had slipped my mother's ring on Marjie's finger. I was on my way now for a long talk with my father. I was twenty-one, a man in years, as I had been in spirit since the night the town was threatened by the Rebel raiders—aye, even since the day Irving Whately begged me to take care of Marjie. I had no time to quarrel with the little widower.

"He's got the best of you, Judson," Cam declared. "No use to come, second hand, fur a girl like that when a handsome young feller like Phil Baronet, who's run things his own way in this town sence he was a little feller, 's got the inside track. Why, the young folks, agged on by some older ones, 'ud jist natcherly mob anybody that 'ud git in Phil's way of whatever he wanted. Take my word, if he wants Marjie he kin have her; and likewise take it, he does want her."

"An' then," Grandpa spoke with mock persuasion, "Amos, ye know ye've been married oncet. An' ye're not so young an' ye're a leetle bald. D'ye just notice Phil's hair, layin' in soft thick waves? Allers curled that way sence he was a little feller."

Amos Judson went into an explosive combustion.

"I've treated my wife's memory and remains as good as a man ever did. She's got the biggest stone in the cemet'ry, an' I've put a memorial window in the church. An' what more could a man do? It's more than any of you have done." Amos was too wrought up to reason.

"Well, I acknowledge," said Cam, "I've ben a leetle slack about gittin' a grave-stun up fur Dollie, seein' she's still livin', but I have threatened her time an' agin to put a winder to her memory in the church an' git her in shape to legalize it if she don't learn how to git me up a good meal. Darned poor cook my wife is."

"An' as for this boy," Judson broke in, not noticing Cam's joke, "as to his looks," he stroked his slick light brown hair, "a little baldness gives dignity, makes a man look like a man. Who'd want to have hair like a girl's? But Mrs. Whately's too wise not to do well by her daughter. She knows the value of a dollar, and a man makin' it himself."

"Well, why not set your cap fur the widder? You'd make a good father to her child, an' Phil would jest na'chelly be proud of you for a daddy-in-law." This from the stage driver, Dever, who had caught the spirit of the game in hand. "Anyhow you'd orter seen them two young folks meet when he first got back home, out there where the crowd of 'em helt up the stage. Well, sir, she was the last to say 'howdy do.' Everybody was lookin' the other way then, 'cept me, and I didn't have sense enough. Well, sir, he jist took her hand like somethin' he'd been reachin' fur about two year, an' they looked into each other's eyes, hungry like, an' a sort of joy such as any of us 'ud long to possess come into them two young faces. I tell you, if you're goin' to gossip jist turn it onto Judson er me, but let them two alone."

Judson was too violently angry to be discreet.

"It's all silly scand'lous foolishness, and I won't hear another word of it," he shouted.

Just as he spoke, Marjie herself came in. Judson stepped forward in an officious effort to serve her, and unable to restrain himself, he called out to O'mie, "Put four yards of towelling, twelve and a half cents a yard, to Mrs. Whately's standing account."

It was not the words that offended, so much as the tone, the proprietary sound, the sense of obligation it seemed to put upon the purchaser, unrelieved by his bland smile and attempt at humor in his after remark, "We don't run accounts with everybody, but I guess we can trust you."

It cut Marjie's spirit. A flush mounted to her cheeks, as she took her purchase and hurried out of the door and plump into my father, who was passing just then.

Judge Baronet was a man of courtly manners. He gently caught Marjie's arm to steady her.

"Good-morning, Marjie. How is your mother to-day?"

The little girl did not speak for a moment. Her eyes were full of tears. Presently she said, "May I come up to your office pretty soon? I want to ask you something—something of our business matters."

"Yes, yes, come now," he replied, taking her bundle and putting himself on the outer side of the walk. He had forgotten my appointment for the moment.

When they reached the courthouse he said: "Just run into my room there; I've got to catch Sheriff Karr before he gets away."

He opened the door of his private office, thrusting her gently inside, and hurried away. I turned to meet my father, and there was Marjie. Tear drops were on her long brown lashes, and her cheeks were flushed.

"Why, my little girl!" I exclaimed in surprise as she started to hurry away.

"I didn't know you were in here; your father sent me in"—and then the tears came in earnest.

I couldn't stand for that.

"What is it, Marjie?" I had put her in my father's chair and was bending over her, my face dangerously near her cheek.

"It's Amos Judson—Oh, Phil, I can't tell you. I was going to talk to your father."

"All right," I said gayly. "Ask papa. It's the proper thing. He must be consulted, of course. But as to Judson, don't worry. O'mie promised me just this morning to sew him up in a sack and throw him off the cliff above the Hermit's Cave into the river. O'mie says it's safe; he's so light he'll float."

Marjie smiled through her tears. A noise in the outer office reminded us that some one was there, and that the outer door was half ajar. Then my father came in. His face was kindly impenetrable.

"I had forgotten my son was here. Phil, take these papers over to the county attorney's office. I'll call you later." He turned me out and gave his attention to Marjie.

I loafed about the outer office until she and my father came out. He led her to the doorway and down the steps with a courtesy he never forgot toward women. When we were alone in his private office I longed to ask Marjie's errand, but I knew my father too well.

"You wanted to see me, Phil?" He was seated opposite to me, his eyes were looking steadily into mine, and clear beyond them down into my soul.

"Yes, Father," I replied; "I am a man now—twenty-one years and one day over. And there are a few things, as a man, I want to know and to have you know."

He was sharpening a pencil carefully. "I'm listening," he said kindly.

"Well, Father—" I hesitated. It was so much harder to say than I had thought it would be. I toyed with the tassel of the window cord confusedly. "Father, you remember when you were twenty-one?"

"Yes, my son, I was just out of Harvard. And like you I had a father to whom I went to tell him I was in love, just as you are. When your own son comes to you some day, help him a little."

I felt a weight lifted from my mind. It was good of him to open the way.

"Father, I have never seen any other girl like Marjie."

"No, there isn't any—for you. But how about her?"

"I think, I know she—does care. I think—" I was making poor work of it after all his help. "Well, she said she did, anyhow." I blurted out defiantly.

"The court accepts the evidence," he remarked, and then more seriously he went on: "My son, I am happy in your joy. I may have been a little slow. There was much harmless coupling of her name with young Tillhurst's while you were away. I did not give it much thought. Letters from Rockport were also giving you and Rachel Melrose some consideration. Rachel is an only child and pretty well fixed financially."

"Oh, Father, I never gave her two thoughts."

"So the letters intimated, but added that the Melrose blood is persistent, and that Rachel's mother was especially willing. She is of a good family, old friends of Candace's and mine. She will have money in her own right, is handsome and well educated. I thought you might be satisfied there."

"But I don't care for her money nor anybody else's. Nobody but Marjie will ever suit me," I cried.

"So I saw when I looked at you two in church yesterday. It was a revelation, I admit; but I took in the situation at once." And then more affectionately he added: "I was very proud of you, Phil. You and Marjie made a picture I shall keep. When you want my blessing, I have part of it in the strong box in my safe. All I have of worldly goods will be yours, Phil, if you do it no dishonor; and as to my good-will, my son, you are my wife's child, my one priceless treasure. When by your own efforts you can maintain a home, nor feel yourself dependent, then bring a bride to me. I shall do all I can to give you an opportunity. I hope you will not wait long. When Irving Whately lay dying at Chattanooga he told me his hopes for Marjie and you. But he charged me not to tell you until you should of your own accord come to me. You have his blessing, too."

How good he was to me! His hand grasped mine.

"Phil, let me say one thing; don't ever get too old to consult your father. It may save some losses and misunderstandings and heart-aches. And now, what else?"

"Father, when O'mie seemed to be dying, Le Claire told me something of his story one evening. He said you knew it."

My father looked grave.

"How does this concern you, Phil?"

"Only in this. I promised Le Claire I would see that O'mie's case was cared for if he lived and you never came back," I replied. "He is of age now, and if he knows his rights he does not use them."

"Have you talked to O'mie of this?" he asked quickly.

"No, sir; I promised not to speak of it."

"Phil, did Le Claire suggest any property?"

"No, sir. Is there any?"

My father smiled. "You have a lawyer's nose," he said, "but fortunately you can keep a still tongue. I'm taking care of O'mie's case right now. By the way," he went on after a short pause. "I sent you out on an errand Saturday. That's another difficult case, a land claim I'm trying to prove for a party. There are two claimants. Tell Mapleson is the counsel for the other one. It's a really dangerous case in some ways. You were to go and spy out the land. What did you see? Anything except a pretty girl?" My face was burning. "Oh, I understand. You found a place out there to stand, and now you think you can move the world."

"I found something I want to speak of besides. Oh, well—I'm not ashamed of caring for Marjie."

"No, no, my boy. You are right. You found the best thing in the world. I found it myself once, by a moonlit sea, not on the summer prairie; but it is the same eternal blessing. Now go on."

"Well, father, you said the place was uninhabited. But it isn't. Somebody is about there now."

"Did you see any one, or is it just a wayside camp for movers going out on the trail?"

"I am not sure that I saw any one, and yet—"

"Tell me all you know, and all you suspect, and why you have conclusions," he said gravely.

"I caught just a glimpse, a mere flirt of a red blanket with a white centre, the kind Jean Pahusca used to wear. It was between the corner of the house and the hazel-brush thicket, as if some one were making for the timber."

"Did you follow it?"

"N—no, I could hardly say I saw anything; but thinking about it afterwards, I am sure somebody was getting out of sight."

"I see." My father looked straight at me. I knew his mind, and I blushed and pulled at the tassel of the window cord. "Be careful. The county has to pay for curtain fixtures. What else?"

"Well, inside the cabin there were fresh ashes and a half-burned stick on the hearth. By a chair under the table I picked this up." I handed him the bow of purple ribbon with the flashing pin.

"It must be movers, and as to that red flash of color, are you real sure it was not just a part of the rose-hued world out there?" He smiled as he spoke.

"Father, that bow was on Lettie Conlow's head not an hour before it was lost out there. She found out where we were going, and she put out northwest on Tell Mapleson's pony. She may have taken the river path. It is the shortest way. Why should she go out there?"

"Do some thinking for yourself. You are a man now, twenty-one, and one day over. You can unravel this part." He sat with impenetrable face, waiting for me to speak.

"I do not know. Lettie Conlow has always been silly about—about the boys. All the young folks say she likes me, has always liked me."

"How much cause have you given her? Be sure your memory is clear." My father spoke sternly.

"Father," I stood before him now, "I am a man, as you say, and I have come up through a boyhood no better nor worse than the other boys whom you know here. We were a pretty decent gang even before you went away to the War. After that we had to be men. But all these years, Father, there has been only one girl for me. I never gave Lettie Conlow a ghost of a reason for thinking I cared for her. But she is old Conlow's own child, and she has a bitter, jealous nature."

"Well, what took her to the—to the old cabin out there?"

"I do not know. She may have been hidden out there to spy what we—I was doing."

"Did she have on a red blanket too, Saturday afternoon?"

"Well, now I wonder—." My mind was in a whirl. Could she be in league against me? What did it mean? I sat down to think.

"Father, there's something I've never yet understood about this town," I burst out impetuously. "If it is to have anything to do with my future I ought to know it. Father Le Claire would tell me only half his story. You know more of O'mie than you will tell me. And here is a jealous girl whose father consented to give Marjie to a brutal Indian out of hatred for her father; and it is his daughter who trails me over the prairie because I am with Marjie. Why not tell me now what you know?"

My father sat looking thoughtfully at me. At last he spoke.

"I know nothing of girls' love affairs and jealousies," he said; "pass that now. I am O'mie's attorney and am trying to adjust his claims for him as I can discover them. I cannot get hold of the case myself as I should like. If Le Claire were here I might find out something."

"Or nothing," I broke in. "It would depend on circumstances."

"You are right. He has never told me all he knows, but I know much without his telling."

"Do you know how Jean Pahusca came to carry a knife for years with the name, 'Jean Le Claire,' cut in the blade? Do you know why the half-breed and the priest came to look so much alike, same square-cut forehead, same build, same gait, same proud way of throwing back the head? You've only to look at them to see all this, except that with a little imagination the priest's face would fit a saint and Jean's is a very devil's countenance."

"I do not know the exact answer to any of these questions. They are points for us to work out together now you are a man. Jean is in some way bound to Le Claire. If by blood ties, why does the priest not own, or entirely disown him? If not, why does the priest protect him?

"In some way, too, both are concerned with O'mie. Le Claire is eager to protect the Irishman. I do not know where Jean is, but I believe sometimes he is here in concealment. He and Tell Mapleson are counselling together. I think he furnishes Tell with some booty, for Tell is inordinately prosperous. I look at this from a lawyer's place. You have grown up with the crowd here, and you see as a young man from the social side, where personal motives count for much. Together we must get this thing unravelled; and it may be in doing it some love matters and some church matters may get mixed and need straightening. You must keep me informed of every thing you know." He paused a moment, then added: "I am glad you have let me know how it is with you, Phil. In your life I can live my own again. Children do so bless us. Be happy in your love, my boy. But be manly, too. There are some hard climbs before you yet. Learn to bear and wait. Yours is an open sunlit way to-day. If the shadows creep across it, be strong. They will lift again. Run home now and tell Aunt Candace I'll be home at one o'clock. Tell her what you have told me, too. She will be glad to know it."

"She does know it; she has known it ever since the night we came into Springvale in 1854."

My father turned to the door. Then he put his arms about me and kissed my forehead. "You have your mother's face, Phil." How full of tenderness his tones were!

In the office I saw Judson moving restlessly before the windows. He had been waiting there for some time, and he frowned on me as I passed him. He was a man of small calibre. His one gift was that of money-getting.

By the careful management of the Whately store in the owner's absence he began to add to his own bank account. With the death of Mr. Whately he had assumed control, refusing to allow any investigation of affairs until, to put it briefly, he was now in entire possession. Poor Mrs. Whately hardly knew what was her own, while her husband's former clerk waxed pompous and well-to-do. Being a vain man, he thought the best should come to him in social affairs, and being a man of medium intellect, he lacked self-control and tact.

This was the nature of the creature who strode into Judge Baronet's private office, slamming the door behind him and presenting himself unannounced. The windows front the street leading down to where the trail crossed the river, and give a view of the glistening Neosho winding down the valley. My father was standing by one of these windows when Judson fired himself into the room. John Baronet's mind was not on Springvale, nor on the river. His thoughts were of his son and of her who had borne him, the sweet-browed woman whose image was in the sacredest shrine of his heart.

Judson's advent was ill-timed, and his excessive lack of tact made the matter worse.

"Mr. Baronet," he began pompously enough, "I must see you on a very grave matter, very grave indeed."

Judge Baronet gave him a chair and sat down across the table from him to listen. Judson had grated harshly on his mood, but he was a man of poise.

"I'll be brief and blunt. That's what you lawyers want, ain't it?" The little man giggled. "But I must advise this step at once as a necessary, a very necessary one."

My father waited. Judson hadn't the penetration to feel embarrassed.

"You see it's like this. If you'll just keep still a minute I can show you, though I ain't no lawyer; I'm a man of affairs, a commercialist, as you would say. A producer maybe is a better term. In short, I'm a money-maker."

My father smiled. "I see," he remarked. "I'll keep still. Go on."

"Well, now, I'm a widower that has provided handsome for my first wife's remains. I've earned and paid for the right to forget her."

The great broad-shouldered, broad-minded man before the little boaster looked down to hide his contempt.

"I've did my part handsome now, you'll admit; and being alone in the world, with no one to enjoy my prosperity with me, I'm lonesome. That's it, I'm lonesome. Ain't you sometimes?"

"Often," my father replied.

"Now I know'd it. We're in the same boat barring a great difference in ages. Why, hang it, Judge, let's get married!" He giggled explosively and so failed to see the stern face of the man before him.

"I want a young woman, a pretty girl, I've a right to a pretty girl, I think. In fact, I want Marjory Whately. And what's more, I'm going to have her. I've all but got the widder's consent now. She's under considerable obligation to me."

Across John Baronet's mind there swept a picture of the Chattanooga battle field. The roar of cannon, the smoke of rifles, the awful charge on charge, around him. And in the very heart of it all, Irving Whately wounded unto death, his hands grasping the Springvale flag, his voice growing faint.

"You will look after them, John? Phil promised to take care of Marjie. It makes this easier. I believe they will love each other, John. I hope they may. When they do, give them my blessing. Good-bye." Across this vision Judson's thin sharp voice was pouring out words.

"Now, Baronet, you see, to be plain, it's just this way. If I marry Marjory, folks'll say I'm doing it to get control of the widder's stock. It's small; but they'll say it."

"Why should it be small?" My father's voice was penetrating as a knife-thrust. Judson staggered at it a little.

"Business, you know, management you couldn't understand. She's no hand at money matters."

"So it seems," my father said dryly.

"But you'd not understand it. To resume. Folks'll say I'm trying to get the whole thing, when all I really want is the girl, the girl now. She'll not have much at best; and divided between her and her mother, there'll be little left for Mrs. Whately to go on livin' on, with Mrs. Judson's share taken out. Now, here's my point precisely, precisely. You take the widder yourself. You need a wife, and Mrs. Whately's still good-looking most ways. She was always a pretty, winsome-faced woman.

"You've got a plenty and getting more all the time. You could provide handsome for her the rest of her life. You'd enjoy a second wife, an' she'd be out of my way. You see it, don't you? I'll marry Marjie, an' you marry her mother, kind of double wedding. Whew! but we'd make a fine couple of grooms. What's in gray hair and baldness, anyhow? But there's one thing I can't stand for. Gossip has begun to couple the name of your boy with Miss Whately. Now he's just a very boy, only a year or two older'n she, and nowise able to take care of her properly, you'll admit; and it's silly. Besides, Conlow was telling me just an hour or more ago, that Phil and Lettie was old-time sweethearts. I've nothing to do with Phil's puppy love, however. I'm here to advise with you. Shall we clinch the bargain now, or do you want to think about it a little while? But don't take long. It's a little sudden maybe to you. It's been on my mind since the day I got that memorial window in an' Marjory sang 'Lead Kindly Light,' standing there in the light of it. It was a service for my first wife sung by her that was to be my second, you might almost say. Dr. Hemingway talked beautiful, too, just beautiful. But I've got to go. Business don't bother you lawyers,"—he was growing very familiar now,—"but us merchants has to keep a sharp eye to time. When shall I call?" He rose briskly. "When shall I call?" he repeated.

My father rose up to his full height. His hands were clasped hard behind his back. He did not lift his eyes to the expectant creature before him, and the foxy little widower did not dream how near to danger he was. With the self-control that was a part of John Baronet's character, he replied in an even voice:

"You will come when I send for you."

That evening my father told me all that had taken place.

"You are a man now, and must stand up against this miserable cur. But you must proceed carefully. No hot-headed foolishness will do. He will misjudge your motives and mine, and he can plant some ugly seeds along your way. Property is his god. He is daily defrauding the defenceless to secure it. When I move against him it will be made to appear that I do it for your sake. Put yourself into the place where, of your own wage-earning power, you can keep a wife in comfort, not luxury yet. That will come later, maybe. And then I'll hang this dog with a rope of his own braiding. But I'll wait for that until you come fully into a man's estate, with the power to protect what you love."

CHAPTER XIII

THE TOPEKA RALLY

And men may say what things they please, and none dare stay their tongue.
But who has spoken out for these—the women and the young?

—KIPLING.

Henceforth I had one controlling purpose. Mine was now the task to prove myself a man with power to create and defend the little kingdom whose throne is builded on the hearthstone. I put into my work all the energy of my youth and love and hope.

I applied myself to the study of law, and I took hold of my father's business interests with a will. I was to enter into a partnership with him when I could do a partner's work. He forebore favors, but he gave me opportunity to prove myself. Stories of favoritism on account of my father's position, of my wasteful and luxurious habits, ludicrous enough in a little Kansas town in the sixties, were peddled about by the restless little widower. By my father's advice I let him alone and went my way. I knew that silently and persistently John Baronet was trailing him. And I knew the cause was a righteous one. I had lived too long in the Baronet family to think the head of it would take time to follow after a personal dislike, or pursue a petty purpose.

There may have been many happy lovers on these sunny prairies that idyllic summer, now forty years gone by. The story of each, though like that of all the others, seems best to him who lived it. Marjie and I were going through commonplace days, but we were very happy with the joy of life and love. Our old playground was now our trysting place. Together on our "Rockport" we planned a future wherein there were no ugly shadows.

"Marjie, I'll always keep 'Rockport' for my shrine now," I said to her one evening as we were watching the sunset lights on the prairie and the river upstream. "If you ever hear me say I don't care for 'Rockport,' you will know I do not care for you. Now, think of that!"

"Don't ever say it, Phil, please, if you can help it." Marjie's mood was more serious than mine just then. "I used to be afraid of Indians. I am still, if there were need to be, and I looked to you always somehow to keep them away. Do you remember how I would always get on your side of the game when Jean Pahusca played with us?"

"Yes, Marjie. That's where you belong—on my side. That's the kind of game I'm playing."

"Phil, I am troubled a little with another game. I wish Amos Judson would stay away from our house. He can make mother believe almost anything. I don't feel safe about some matters. Judge Baronet tells me not to worry, that he will keep close watch."

"Well, take it straight from me that he will do it," I assured her. "Let's let the widower go his way. He talks about me; says I'm 'callow, that's it, just callow.' I don't mind being callow, as long as it's not catching. Look at the river, how it glistens now. We can almost see the shallows up by the stone cabin below the big cottonwood. The old tree is shapely, isn't it?"

We were looking upstream to where the huge old tree stood out against the golden horizon.

"Let's buy that land, Phil, and build a house under the big cottonwood some day."

"All right, I'm to go out there again soon. Will you go too?"

"Of course," Marjie assented, "if you want me to."

"I am sure I'd never want to take any other girl out there, but just you, dear," I declared.

And then we talked of other things, and promised to put our letters next day, into the deep crevice we had called our post-office these many years. Before we parted that night, I said:

"I'm thinking of going up to Topeka when the band goes to the big political speaking, next week. I will write to you. And be sure to let me find a letter in 'Rockport' when I get back. I'll be so lonely up there."

"Well, find some pretty girl and let her kill time for you."

"Will you and Judson kill time down here?"

"Ugh! no," Marjie shivered in disgust. "I can't bear the sight of his face any more."

"Good! I'll not try to be any more miserable by being bored with somebody I don't care for at Topeka. But don't forget the letter. Good-night, little sweetheart," and after the fashion of lovers, I said good-bye.

Kansas is essentially a land of young politicians. When O'mie took his band to the capital city to play martial music for the big political rally, there were more young men than gray beards on the speakers' stand and on the front seats. I had gone with the Springvale crowd on this jaunt, but I did not consider myself a person of importance.

"There's Judge Baronet's son; he's just out of Harvard. He's got big influence with the party down his way. His father always runs away ahead of his ticket and has the whole district about as he wants it. That's the boy that saved Springvale one night when the pro-slavery crowd was goin' to burn it, the year of the Quantrill raid."

So, I heard myself exploited in the hotel lobby of the old Teft House.

"What's Tell Mapleson after this year, d'ye reckon? Come in a week ago. He's the doggondest feller to be after somethin', an' gets it, too, somehow." The speaker was a seasoned politician of the hotel lobby variety.

"Oh, he's got a big suit of some kind back East. It's a case of money bein' left to heirs, and he's looking out that the heirs don't get it."

"Ain't it awful about the Saline country?" a bystander broke in here. "Just awful! Saw a man from out there last night by the name of Morton. He said that them Cheyennes are raidin' an' murderin' all that can't get into the towns. Lord pity the unprotected settlers way out in that lonely country. This man said they just killed the little children before their mothers' eyes, after they'd scalped and tomahawked the fathers. Just beat them to death, and then carried off the women. Oh, God! but it's awful."

Awful! I lived through the hours of that night from the time young Tell Mapleson had told of Jean Pahusca's plan to seize Marjie, to the moment when I saw her safe in the shelter of her mother's doorway. Awful! And this sort of thing was going on now in the Saline Valley. How could God permit it?

"There was one family out there, they got the mother and baby and just butchered the other children right before her eyes. They hung the baby to a tree later, and when they got ready they killed its mother. It was the only merciful thing they done, I guess, in all their raid, for they made her die a thousand deaths before they really cut off her poor pitiful life."

So I heard the talk running on, and I wondered at the bluff committeeman who broke up the group to get the men in line for a factional caucus.

Did the election of a party favorite, the nomination of a man whose turn had come, or who would be favorable to "our crowd" in his appointments match in importance this terrible menace to life on our Indian frontier? I had heard much of the Saline and the Solomon River valleys. Union soldiers were homesteading those open plains. My father's comrades-in-arms they had been, and he was intensely interested in their welfare. These Union men had wounds still unhealed from service in the Civil War. And the nation they bore these wounds to save, the Government at Washington, was ignorant or indifferent to this danger that threatened them hourly—a danger infinitely worse than death to women. And the State in the vital throes of a biennial election was treating the whole affair as a deplorable incident truly, but one the national government must look out for.

I was young and enthusiastic, but utterly without political ambition. I was only recently out of college, with a scholar's ideals of civic duty. And with all these, I had behind me the years of a frontier life on the border, in which years my experience and inspiration had taught me the value of the American home, and a strong man's duty toward the weak and defenceless. The memories of my mother, the association and training of my father's sister, and my love for Marjie made all women sacred to me. And while these feelings that stirred the finest fibres of my being, and of which I never spoke then, may have been the mark of a less practical nature than most young men have to-day, I account my life stronger, cleaner and purer for having had them.

I could take only a perfunctory interest in the political game about me, and I felt little elation at the courteous request that I should take a seat in the speakers' stand, when the clans did finally gather for a grand struggle for place.

The meeting opened with O'mie's band playing "The Star-Spangled Banner." It brought the big audience to their feet, and the men on the platform stood up. I was the tallest one among them. Also I was least nervous, least anxious, and least important to that occasion. Perfunctorily, too, I listened to the speeches, hearing the grand old Republican party's virtues lauded, and the especial fitness of certain of its color-bearers extolled as of mighty men of valor, with "the burning question of the hour" and "the vital issue of the time" enlarged upon, and "the State's most pernicious evil" threatened with dire besetments. And through it all my mind was on the unprotected, scattered settlements of the Saline Valley, and the murdered children and the defenceless women, even now in the cruel slavery of Indian captivity.

I knew only a few people in the capital city and I looked at the audience with the indifference of a stranger who seeks for no familiar face. And yet, subconsciously, I felt the presence of some one who was watching me, some one who knew me well. Presently the master of ceremonies called for the gifted educator, Richard Tillhurst of Springvale. I knew he was in Topeka, but I had not hunted for him any more than he had sought me out. We mutually didn't need each other. And yet local pride is strong, and I led the hand-clapping that greeted his appearance. He was visibly embarrassed, and ultra-dignified. Education had a representative above reproach in him. Pompously, after the manner of the circumscribed instructor, he began, and for a limited time the travelling was easy. But he made the fatal error of keeping on his feet after his ideas were exhausted. He lost the trail and wandered aimlessly in the barren, trackless realms of thought, seeking relief and finding none, until at length in sheer embarrassment he forced himself to retreat to his seat. Little enthusiasm was expressed and failure was written all over his banner.

The next speaker was a politician of the rip-roaring variety who pounded the table and howled his enthusiasm, whose logic was all expressed in the short-story form, sometimes witty, sometimes far-fetched and often profane. He interested me least of all, and my mind abstracted by the Tillhurst feature went back again to the Plains. I could not realize what was going on when the politician had finished amid uproarious applause, and the chairman was introducing the next speaker, until I caught my father's name, coupled with lavish praise of his merits. There was a graceful folding of his mantle on the shoulders of "his gifted son, just out of Harvard, but a true child of Kansas, with a record for heroism in the war time, and a growing prominence in his district, and an altogether good-headed, good-hearted, and, the ladies all agree, good-looking young man, the handsome giant of the Neosho." And I found myself thrust to the front of the speakers' stand, with applause following itself, and O'mie, the mischievous rascal, striking off a few bars of "See, the Conquering Hero Comes!"

I was taken so completely by surprise that I thought the earth especially unkind not to open at once and let me in. It must have been something of my inheritance of my father's self-control, coupled with my life experience of having to meet emergencies quickly, which all the children of Springvale knew, that pulled me through. The prolonged cheering gave me a moment to get the mastery. Then like an inspiration came the thought to break away from the beaten path of local politics and to launch forth into a plea for larger political ideals. I cited the Civil War as a crucible, testing men. I did not once mention my father, but the company knew his proud record, and there were many present who had fought and marched and starved and bled beside him, men whom his genius and his kindness had saved from peril, even the peril of death. And then out of the fulness of a heart that had suffered, I pled for the lives and homes of the settlers on our Plains frontier. I pictured, for I knew how to picture, the anguish of soul an Indian raid can leave in its wake, and the duty we owe to the homes, our high privilege as strong men and guardians to care for the defenceless, and our opportunity to repay a part at least of the debt we owe to the Union soldier by giving a State's defence to these men, who were homesteading our hitherto unbroken, trackless plains, and building empire westward toward the baths of sunset.

The effort was so boyish, so unlike every other speech that had been made, and yet so full of a young man's honest zeal and profound convictions from a soul stirred to its very depths, that the audience rose to their feet at my closing words, and cheer followed cheer, making the air ring with sound.

When the meeting had finished, I found myself in the centre of a group of men who knew John Baronet and just wouldn't let his son get away without a handshake. I was flushed with the pleasure of such a reception and was doing my best to act well, when a man grasped my hand with a grip unlike any other hand I had ever felt, so firm, so full of friendship, and yet so undemonstrative, that I instinctively returned the clasp. He was a man of some thirty years, small beside me, and there was nothing unusual in his face or dress or manner to attract my attention. A stranger might not turn to him a second time in a crowd, unless they had once spoken and clasped hands.

"My name is Morton," he said. "I know your father, I knew him in the army and before, back in Massachusetts. I am from the Saline River country, and I came down here hoping to find the State more interested in the conditions out our way. You were the only speaker who thought of the needs of the settlers. There are terrible things being done right now."

He spoke so simply that a careless ear would not have detected the strength of the feeling back of the words.

"I'll tell my father I met you," I said cordially, "and I hope, I hope to heaven the captives may be found soon, and the Indians punished. How can a man live who has lost his wife, or his sweetheart, in that way?"

I knew I was blushing, but the matter was so terrible to me. Before he could answer, Richard Tillhurst pushed through the crowd and caught my arm.

"There's an old friend of yours here, who wants to meet you, Mr. Baronet," and he pulled me away.

"I hope I'll see you again," I turned to Mr. Morton to say, and in a moment more, I was face to face with Rachel Melrose. It was she whose presence I had somehow felt in that crowd of strangers. She was handsomer even than I had remembered her, and she had a style of dress new and attractive. One would know that she was fresh from the East, for our own girls and women for the most part had many things to consider besides the latest fashions.

I think Tillhurst mistook my surprise for confusion. He was a man of good principles, but he was a human being, not a saint, and he pursued a purpose selfishly as most of us who are human do.

The young lady grasped my hand in both of hers impulsively.

"Oh, Mr. Baronet, I'm so glad to see you again. I knew you would come to Topeka as soon as you knew I had come West. I just got here two days ago, and I could hardly wait until you came. It's just like old times to see you again."

Then she turned to Tillhurst, standing there greedily taking in every word, his face beaming as one's face may who finds an obstacle suddenly lifted from his way.

"We are old friends, the best kind of friends, Mr. Tillhurst. Mr. Baronet and I have recollections of two delightful years when he was in Harvard, haven't we?"

"Yes, yes," I replied. "Miss Melrose was the only girl who would listen to my praising Kansas while I was in Massachusetts. Naturally I found her delightful company."

"Did he tell you about his girl here?" Tillhurst asked, a trifle maliciously, maybe.

"Of course, I didn't," I broke in. "We don't tell all we know when we go East."

"Nor all you have done in the East when you come back home, evidently," Tillhurst spoke significantly. "I've never heard him mention your name once, Miss Melrose."

"Has he been flirting with some one, Mr. Tillhurst? He promised me faithfully he wouldn't." Her tone took on a disappointed note.

"I'll promise anybody not to flirt, for I don't do it," I cried. "I came home and found this young educator trying to do me mischief with the little girl I told you about the last time I saw you. Naturally he doesn't like me."

All this in a joking manner, and yet a vein of seriousness ran through it somewhere.

Rachel Melrose was adroit.

"We won't quarrel," she said sweetly, "now we do meet again, and when I go down to Springvale to visit your aunt, as you insisted I must do, we'll get all this straightened out. You'll come and take tea with us of course. Mr. Tillhurst has promised to come, too."

The young man looked curiously at me at the mention of Rachel's visit to Springvale. A group of politicians broke in just here.

"We can't have you monopolize 'the handsome giant of the Neosho' all the time," they said, laughing, with many a compliment to the charming young monopolist. "We don't blame him, of course, now, but we need him badly. Come, Baronet," and they hurried me away, giving me time only to thank her for the invitation to dine with her.

At the Teft House letters were waiting for me. One from my father asking me to visit Governor Crawford and take a personal message of some importance to him, with the injunction, "Stay till you do see him." The other was a fat little envelope inscribed in Marjie's handwriting. Inside were only flowers, the red blossoms that grow on the vines in the crevices of our "Rockport," and a sheet of note paper about them with the simple message:

"Always and always yours, Marjie."

Willing or unwilling, I found myself in the thick of the political turmoil, and had it not been for that Indian raiding in Northwest Kansas, I should have plunged into politics then and there, so strong a temptation it is to control men, if opportunity offers. It was late before I could get out of the council and rush to my room to write a hurried but loving letter to Marjie. I had to be brief to get it into the mails. So I wrote only of what was first in my thoughts; herself, and my longing to see her, of the noisy political strife, and of the Saline River and Solomon River outrages, I hurried this letter to the outgoing stage and fell in with the crowd gathering late in the dining-room. I was half way through my meal before I remembered Rachel's invitation.

"I can only be rude to her, it seems, but I'll offer my excuses, and maybe she will let me have the honor of her company home. She will hunt me up before I get out of the hall, I am sure." So I satisfied myself and prepared for the evening gathering.

It was much on the order of the other meeting, except that only seasoned party leaders were given place on the programme.

I asked Rachel for her company home, but she laughingly refused me.

"I must punish you," she said. "When do you go home?"

"Not for two days," I replied. "I have business for my father and the person I am to see is called out of town."

"Then there will be plenty of time later for you. You go home to-morrow, Mr. Tillhurst," she said coquettishly. "Tell his friends in

Springvale, he is busy up here." She was a pretty girl, but slow as I was, I began to see method in her manner of procedure. I could not be rude to her, but I resolved then not to go one step beyond the demands of actual courtesy.

In the crowd passing up to the hotel that night, I fell into step with my father's soldier friend, Morton.

"When you get ready to leave Springvale, come out and take a claim on the Saline," he said. "That will be a garden of Eden some day."

"It seems to have its serpent already, Mr. Morton," I replied.

"Well, the serpent can be crushed. Come out and help us do it. We need numbers, especially in men of endurance." We were at the hotel door. Morton bade me good-bye by saying, "Don't forget; come our way when you get the Western fever."

Governor Crawford returned too late for me to catch the stage for Springvale on the same day. Having a night more to spend in the capital, it seemed proper for me to make amends for my unpardonable forgetfulness of Rachel Melrose's invitation to tea by calling on her in the evening. Her aunt's home was at the far side of the town beyond the modest square stone building that was called Lincoln College then. It was only a stone's throw from the State Capitol, the walls of the east wing of which were then being built.

I remember it was a beautiful moonlit night, in early August, and Rachel asked me to take a stroll over the prairie to the southwest. The day had been very hot, and the west had piled up some threatening thunderheads. But the evening breezes fanned them away over the far horizon line and the warm night air was light and dry. The sky was white with the clear luminous moonlight of the open Plains country.

Rachel and I had wandered idly along the gentle rise of ground until we could quite overlook the little treeless town with this Lincoln College and the jagged portion of the State House wing gleaming up beyond.

"Hadn't we better turn back now? Your aunt cautioned us two strangers here not to get lost." I was only hinting my wishes.

"Oh, let's go on to that tree. It's the only one here in this forsaken country. Let's pay our respects to it," Rachel urged.

She was right. To an Easterner's eye it was a forsaken country. From the Shunganunga Creek winding beneath a burden of low, black underbrush, northward to the river with its fringe of huge cottonwoods, not a tree broke the line of vision save this one sturdy young locust spreading its lacy foliage in dainty grace on the very summit of the gentle swell of land between the two streams. Up to its pretty shadowed spaces we took our way. The grass was dry and brown with the August heat, and we rested awhile on the moonlit prairie.

Rachel was strikingly handsome, and the soft light lent a certain tone to her beauty. Her hair and eyes were very dark, and her face was clear cut. There was a dash of boldness, an assumption of authority all prettily accented with smiles and dimples that was very bewitching. She was a subtle flatterer, and even the wisest men may be caught by that bait. It was the undercurrent of sympathy, product of my life-long ideals, my intense pity for the defenceless frontier, that divided my mind and led me away from temptation that night.

"Rachel Melrose, we must go home," I insisted at last. "This tree is all right, but I could show you a cottonwood out above the Neosho that dwarfs this puny locust. And yet this is a gritty sort of sapling to stand up here and grow and grow. I wonder if ever the town will reach out so far as this."

I am told the tree is green and beautiful to-day, and that it is far inside the city limits, standing on the old Huntoon road. About it are substantial homes. South of it is a pretty park now, while near it on the west is a handsome church, one of the city's lions to the stranger, for here the world-renowned author of "In His Steps" has preached every Sabbath for many years. But on that night it seemed far away from the river and the town nestling beside it.

"I'll go down and take a look at your cottonwood before I go home. May I? You promised me last Spring." Rachel's voice was pleasant to hear.

"Why, of course. Come on. Mr. Tillhurst will be there, I am sure, and glad as I shall be to see you."

"Oh, you rogue! always hunting for somebody else. I am not going to loose you from your promise. Remember that you said you'd let everybody else alone when I came. Now your Mr. Tillhurst can look after all the girls you have been flirting with down there, but you are my friend. Didn't we settle that in those days together at dear old Rockport? We'll just have the happiest time together, you and I, and nobody shall interfere to mar our pleasure."

She was leaning toward me and her big dark eyes were full of feeling. I stood up before her. "My dear friend," I took her hand and she rose to her feet. "You have been very, very good to me. But I want to tell you now before you come to Springvale"—she was close beside me, her hand on my arm, gentle and trembling. I seemed like a brute to myself, but I went on. "I want you to know that as my aunt's guest and mine, your pleasure will be mine. But I am not a flirt, and I do not care to hide from you the fact that my little Springvale girl is the light of my life. You will understand why some claims are unbreakable. Now you know this, let me say that it will be my delight to make your stay in the West pleasant." She bowed her proud head on my arm and the tears fell fast. "Oh, Rachel, I'm a beast, a coarse, crude Westerner. Forgive my plain speech. I only wanted you to know."

But she didn't want to know. She wanted me to quit saying anything to her and her beautiful dark hair was almost against my cheek. Gently as I could, I put her from me. Drawing her hand through my arm, I patted it softly, and again I declared myself the bluntest of speakers. She only wept the more, and asked me to take her to her aunt's. I was glad to do it, and I bade her a humble good-bye at the door. She said not a word, but the pressure of her hand had speech. It made me feel that I had cruelly wronged her.

As I started for town beyond the college, I shook my fist at that lone locust tree. "You blamed old sapling! If you ever tell what you saw to-night I hope you'll die by inches in a prairie fire."

Then I hurried to my room and put in the hours of the night, wakeful and angry at all the world, save my own Springvale and the dear little girl so modest and true to me. The next day I left Topeka, hoping never to see it again.

CHAPTER XIV

DEEPENING GLOOM

A yellow moon in splendor drooping,
A tired queen with her state oppressed,
Low by rushes and sword-grass stooping,
Lies she soft on the waves at rest.
The desert heavens have felt her sadness;
The earth will weep her some dewy tears;
The wild beck ends her tune of gladness,
And goeth stilly, as soul that fears.

—JEAN INGELOW.

The easiest mental act I ever performed was the act of forgetting the existence of Rachel Melrose. Before the stage had reached the divide beyond the Wakarusa on its southward journey, I was thinking only of Springvale and of what would be written in the letter that I knew was waiting for me in our "Rockport." Oh, I was a fond and foolish lover. I was only twenty-one and Judson may have been right about my being callow. But I was satisfied with myself, as youth and inexperience will be.

Travelling was slow in those rough-going times, and a breakdown on a steep bit of road delayed us. Instead of reaching home at sunset, we did not reach the ford of the Neosho until eight o'clock. As I went up Cliff Street I turned by the bushes and slid down the rough stairway to the ledge below "Rockport." I had passed under the broad, overhanging shelf that made the old playground above, when I suddenly became aware of the nearness of some one to me, the peculiar consciousness of the presence of a human being. The place was in deep shadow, although the full moon was sailing in glory over the prairies, as it had done above the lone Topeka locust tree. My daily visits here had made each step familiar, however. I was only a few feet from the cunningly hidden crevice that had done post-office duty for Marjie and me in the days of our childhood. Just beside it was a deep niche in the wall. Ordinarily I was free and noisy enough in my movements, but to-night I dropped silently into the niche as some one hurried by me, groping to find the way. Instinctively I thought of Jean Pahusca, but Jean never blundered like this. I had had cause enough to know his swift motion. And besides, he had been away from Springvale so long that he was only a memory now. The figure scrambled to the top rapidly.

"I'll guess that's petticoats going up there," I said mentally, "but who's hunting wild flowers out here alone this time of night? Somebody just as curious about me as I am about her, no doubt. Maybe some girl has a lover's haunt down that ledge. I'll have to find out. Can't let my stairway out to the general climbing public."

I was feeling for the letter in the crevice.

"Well, Marjie has tucked it in good and safe. I didn't know that hole was so deep."

I found my letter and hurried home. It was just a happy, loving message written when I was away, and a tinge of loneliness was in it. But Marjie was a cheery, wholesome-spirited lass always, and took in the world from the sunny side.

"There's a party down at Anderson's to-night, Phil," Aunt Candace announced, when I was eating my late supper. "The boys sent word for you to come over even if you did get home late. You are pretty tired, aren't you?"

"Never, if there's a party on the carpet," I answered gayly.

I had nearly reached the Anderson home, and the noisy gayety of the party was in my ears, when two persons met at the gate and went slowly in together.

It was Amos Judson and Lettie Conlow.

"Well, of all the arrangements, now, that is the best," I exclaimed, as I went in after them.

Tillhurst was talking to Marjie, who did not see me enter.

"Phil Baronet! 'The handsome young giant of the Neosho,'" O'mie shouted. "Ladies and gentlemen: This is the very famous orator who got more applause in Topeka this week than the very biggest man there. Oh, my prophetic soul! but we were proud av him."

"Well, I guess we were," somebody else chimed in. "Why didn't you come home with the crowd, handsome giant?"

"He was charmed by that pretty girl, an old sweetheart of his from Massachusetts." Tillhurst was speaking. "You ought to have seen him with her, couldn't even leave when the rest of us did."

There was a sudden silence. Marjie was across the room from me, but I could see her face turn white. My own face flamed, but I controlled myself. And Bud, the blessed old tow-head, came to my rescue.

"Good for you, Phil. Bet we've got one fellow to make a Bothton girl open her eyeth even if Tillhurtht couldn't. He'th jutht jealouth. But we all know Phil! Nobody'll ever doubt old Philip!"

It took the edge off the embarrassment, and O'mie, who had sidled over into Marjie's neighborhood, said in a low voice:

"Tillhurst is a consummit liar, beautiful to look upon. That girl tagged Phil. He couldn't get away an' be a gintleman."

I did not know then what he was saying, but I saw her face bloom again.

Later I had her alone a moment. We were eating water melon on the back porch, half in the shadow, which we didn't mind, of course.

"May I take you home, Marjie, and tell you how sweet that letter was?" I asked.

"Phil, I didn't know you were coming, and Richard Tillhurst asked me just as you came in. I saw Amos Judson coming my way, so I made for the nearest port."

"And you did right, dearie," I said very softly; "but, Marjie, don't forget you are my girl, my only girl, and I'll tell you all about this

Topeka business to-morrow night. No, I'll write you a letter to-night when I go home. You'll find it at 'Rockport' to-morrow."

She smiled up at me brightly, saying contentedly, "Oh, you are always all right, Phil."

As we trailed into the kitchen from the water melon feast, Lettie Conlow's dress caught on a nail in the floor. I stooped to loose it, and rasped my hand against a brier clinging to the floppy ruffle (Lettie was much given to floppy things in dress), and behold, a sprig of little red blossoms was sticking to the prickles. These blooms were the kind Marjie had sent me in her letter to Topeka. They grew only in the crevices about the cliff. It flashed into my mind instantly that it was Lettie who had passed me down on that ledge.

"I suppose I'll find her under my plate some morning when I go to breakfast," I said to myself. "She is a trailer of the Plains. Why should she be forever haunting my way, though?"

Fate was against me that night. Judson was called from the party to open the store. A messenger from Red Range had come posthaste for some merchandise. We did not know until the next day that it was the burial clothes for the beautiful young girl whose grave held Dave Mead's heart.

Before Judson left, he came to me with Lettie.

"Will you take this young lady home for me? I must go to the store at once. Business before pleasure with me. That's it, business first. Very sorry, Miss Lettie; Phil will see you safely home."

I was in for the obligation. The Conlows lived four blocks beyond the shop down toward the creek. The way was shadowy, and Lettie clung to my arm. I was tired from my stage ride of a day and a half, and I had not slept well for two nights. I distrusted Lettie, for I knew her disposition as I knew her father's before her.

"Phil, why do you hate me?" she asked at the gate.

"I don't hate you, Lettie. You use an ugly word when you say 'hate,'" I replied.

"There's one person I do hate," she said bitterly.

"Has he given you cause?"

"It's not a man; it's a woman. It's Marjie Whately," she burst out. "I hate her."

"Well, Lettie, I'm sorry, for I don't believe Marjie deserves your hate."

"Of course, you'd say so. But never mind. Marjie's not going to have my hate alone. You'll feel like I do yet, when her mother forces her away from you. Marjie's just a putty ball in her mother's hands, and her mother is crazy about Amos Judson. Oh, I've said too much," she exclaimed.

"You have, Lettie; but stop saying any more." I spoke sternly. "Good-night."

She did not return my greeting, and I heard her slam the door behind her.

That night, late as it was, I wrote a long letter to Marjie. I had no pangs of jealousy, and I felt that she knew me too well to doubt my faith, and yet I wanted just once more to assure her. When I had finished, I went out softly and took my way down to "Rockport." It was one of those glorious midsummer moonlit nights that have in their subdued splendor something more regal than the most gorgeous midday. I was thankful afterwards for the perfect beauty of that peaceful night, with never a hint of the encroaching shadows, the deep gloom of sorrow creeping toward me and my loved one. The town was sleeping quietly. The Neosho was "chattering over stony ways," and whispering its midnight melody. The wooded bottoms were black and glistening, and all the prairies were a gleaming, silvery sea of glory. The peace of God was on the world, the broad benediction of serenity and love. Oh, many a picture have I in my memory's treasure house, that imperishable art gallery of the soul. And among them all, this one last happy night with its setting of Nature's grand handiwork stands clear evermore.

I had put my letter safe in its place, deep where nobody but Marjie would find it. I knew that if even the slightest doubt troubled her this letter would lift it clean away. I told her of Rachel Melrose and of my fear of her designing nature, a fear that grew, as I reflected on her acts and words. I did not believe the young lady cared for me. It was a selfish wish to take what belonged to somebody else. I assured my little girl that only as a gentleman should be courteous, had been my courtesy to Rachel. And then for the first time, I told Marjie of her father's dying message. I had wanted her to love me for myself. I did not want any sense of duty to her father's wishes to sway her. I knew now that she did love me. And I closed the affectionate missive with the words:

"To my father and Aunt Candace you are very dear. Your mother has always been kind to me. I believe she likes me. But most of all, Marjie, your father, who lies wrapped in the folds of that Springvale flag, who gave his life to make safe and happy the land we love and the home we hope to build, your father, sent us his blessing. When the roar of cannon was changing for him to the chant of seraphim, and the glare of the battle field was becoming 'a sea of glass mingled with fire' that burst in splendor over the jewelled walls and battlements of the New Jerusalem, even in that moment, his last thought was of us two. 'I hope they will love each other,' he said to my father. 'If they do, give them my blessing.' And then the night shut down for him. But in the eternal day where he waits our coming and loves us, Marjie, if he knows of what we do here, he is blessing our love.

"Good-night, my dear, dear girl, my wife that is to be, and know now and always there is for me only one love. In sunny ways or shadow-checkered paths, whatever may come, I cannot think other than as I do now. You are life of my life. And so again, good-night."

I had climbed to the rock above the crevice and was standing still as the night about me for the moment when a grip like steel suddenly closed on my neck and an arm like the tentacle of a devilfish slid round my waist. Then the swift adroitness of knee and shoulder bent me backward almost off my feet. I gave a great wrench, and with a power equal to my assailant, struggled with him. It was some moments before I caught sight of his face. It was Jean Pahusca. I think my strength grew fourfold with that glimpse. It was the first time in our lives that we had matched muscle. He must have been the stronger of the two, but discipline and temperate habits had given me endurance and judgment. It was a life-and-death strife between us. He tried to drag me to the edge of the rock. I strove to get him through the bushes into the street. At length I gained the mastery and with my hand on his throat and my knee on his chest I held him fast.

"You miserable devil!" I muttered, "you have the wrong man. You think me weak as O'mie, whose body you could bind. I have a mind to choke you here, you murderer. I could do it and rid the world of you, now." He struggled and I gave him air. There was something princely about him even as he lay in my power. And, fiend as he was, he never lost the spirit of a master. To me also, brute violence was repulsive now that the advantage was all mine.

"You deserve to die. Heaven is saving you for a fate you may well dread. You would be in jail in ten minutes if you ever showed your face here in the daylight, and hanged by the first jury whose verdict could be given. I could save all that trouble now in a minute, but I don't want to be a murderer like you. For the sake of my own hands and for the sake of the man whose son I believe you to be, I'll spare your life to-night on one condition!"

I loosed my hold and stepped away from him. He rose with an effort, but he could not stand at first.

"Leave this country to-night, and never show your face here again. There are friends of O'mie's sworn to shoot you on sight. Go now to your own tribe and do it quickly."

Slowly, like a promise made before high heaven, he answered me.

"I will go, but I shall see you there. When we meet again, my hand will have you by the throat. And—I don't care whose son you are."

He slid down the cliff-side like a lizard, and was gone. I turned and stumbled through the bushes full into Lettie Conlow crouching among them.

"Lettie, Lettie," I cried, "go home."

"I won't unless you will come with me," she answered coaxingly.

"I have taken you home once to-night," I said. "Now you may go alone or stay here as you choose," and I left her.

"You'll live to see the day you'll wish you hadn't said that," I heard her mutter threateningly behind me.

A gray mist had crept over the low-hanging moon. The world, so glorious in its softened radiance half an hour ago, was dull and cheerless now. And with a strange heartache and sense of impending evil I sought my home.

The next day was a busy one in the office. My father was deep in the tangle of a legal case and more than usually grave. Early in the afternoon, Cam Gentry had come into the courthouse, and the two had a long conference. Toward evening he called me into his private office.

"Phil, this land case is troubling me. I believe the papers we want are in that old cabin. Could you go out again to-morrow?" He smiled now. "Go and make a careful search of the premises. If there are any boxes, open them. I will give you an order from Sheriff Karr. And Phil, I believe I wouldn't take Marjie this time. I want to have a talk with her to-morrow, anyhow. You can't monopolize all her time. I saw Mrs. Whately just now and made an appointment with her for Marjie."

When he spoke again, his words startled me.

"Phil, when did you see Jean Pahusca last?"

"Last night, no, this morning, about one o'clock," I answered confusedly.

My father swung around in his chair and stared at me. Then his face grew stern, and I knew my safety lay in the whole truth. I learned that when I was a boy.

"Where was he?" The firing had begun.

"On the point of rock by the bushes on Cliff Street."

"What were you doing there?"

"Looking at the moonlight on the river."

"Did you see him first?"

"No, or he would not have seen me."

"Phil, save my time now. It's a matter of great importance to my business. Also, it is serious with you. Begin at the party. Whose escort were you?"

"Lettie Conlow's."

My father looked me straight in the eyes. I returned his gaze steadily.

"Go on. Tell me everything." He spoke crisply.

"I was late to the party. Tillhurst asked Marjie for her company just as I went in. Judson was going her way, and she chose the lesser of two—pleasures, we'll say. Just before the party broke up, Judson was called out. He had asked Lettie for her company, and he shoved her over to my tender mercies."

"And you went strolling up on Cliff Street in the moonlight with her till after midnight. Is that fair to Marjie?" I had never heard his voice sound so like resonant iron before.

"I, strolling? I covered the seven blocks from Anderson's to Conlow's in seven minutes, and stood at the gate long enough to let the young lady through, and to pinch my thumb in the blamed old latch, I was in such a hurry; and then I made for the Baronets' roost."

"But why didn't you stay there?" he asked.

I blushed for a certainty now. My actions seemed so like a brain-sick fool's.

"Now, Phil," my father said more kindly, "you remember I told you when you came to let me know you were twenty-one, that you must not get too old to make a confidant of me. It is your only safe course now."

"Father, am I a fool, or is it in the Baronet blood to love deeply and constantly even unto death?"

The strong man before me turned his face to the window.

"Go on," he said.

"I had been away nearly a week. I sat up and wrote a long letter to Marjie. It would stand as clean evidence in court. I'm not ashamed of what I put on paper, although it is my own business. Then I went out to a certain place under the cliff where Marjie and I used to hide our valentines and put little notes for each other years ago."

"The post-office is safer, Phil."

"Not with Tell Mapleson as postmaster."

He assented, and I went on. "I had come to the top again and was looking at the beauty of the night, when somebody caught me by the throat. It was Jean Pahusca."

Briefly then I related what had taken place.

"And after that?" queried my questioner.

"I ran into Lettie Conlow. She may have been there all the time. I do not know, but I felt no obligation to take care of a girl who will not take care of herself. It was rude, I know, and against my creed, but that's the whole truth. I may be a certain kind of a fool about a girl I know. But I'm not the kind of gay fool that goes out after divers and strange women. Bill Mead told me this morning that he and Bud Anderson passed Lettie somewhere out west alone after one o'clock. He was in a hurry, but he stopped her and asked her why she should be out alone. I think Bud went home with her. None of the boys want harm to come to her, but she grows less pleasant every day. Bill would have gone home with her, but he was hurrying out to Red Range. Dave's girl died out there last night. Poor Dave!"

"Poor Dave!" my father echoed, and we sat in silence with our sympathy going out to the fine young man whose day was full of sorrow.

"Well," my father said, "to come back to our work now. There are some ugly stories going that I have yet to get hold of. Cam Gentry is helping me toward it all he can. This land case will never come to court if Mapleson can possibly secure the land in any other way. He'd like to ruin us and pay off that old grudge against you for your part in breaking up the plot against Springvale back in '63 and the suspicion it cast on him. Do you see?"

I was beginning to see a little.

"Now, you go out to the stone cabin to-morrow afternoon and make a thorough search for any papers or other evidence hidden there. The man who owned that land was a degenerate son of a noble house. There are some missing links in the evidence that our claim is incontestable. The other claimant to the land is entirely under Tell Mapleson's control. That's the way it shapes up to me. Meanwhile if it gets into court, two or more lines are ready to tighten about you. Keep yourself in straight paths and you are sure at last to win. I have no fear for you, Phil, but be a man every minute."

I understood him. As I left the courthouse, I met O'mie. There was a strange, pathetic look in his eyes. He linked his arm in mine, and we sauntered out under the oak trees of the courthouse grounds.

"Phil, do ye remimber that May mornin' when ye broke through the vines av the Hermit's Cave? I know now how the pityin' face av the Christ looked to the man who had been blind. I know how the touch av his hands felt to them as had been lepers. They was made free and safe. Wake as I was that sorry mornin' I had one thought before me brain wint dark, the thought that I might some day help you aven a little. I felt that way in me wakeness thin. To-day in me strength I feel it a hundred times more. Ye may not nade me, but whin ye do, I'm here. Whin I was a poor lost orphan boy, worth nothin' to nobody, you risked life an' limb to drag me back from the agony av a death by inches. And now, while I'm only a rid-headed Irishman, I can do a dale more thinkin' and I know a blamed lot more 'n this blessed little burg iver drames of. They ain't no bloodhound on your track, but a ugly octopus of a devilfish is gittin' its arms out after you. They's several av 'em. Don't forgit, Phil; I know I'd die for your sake."

"O'mie, I believe you, but don't be uneasy about me. You know me as well as anybody in this town. What have I to fear?"

"Begorra, there was niver a purer-hearted boy than you iver walked out of a fun-lovin', rollickin' boyhood into a clane, honest manhood. You can't be touched."

Just then the evening stage swung by and swept up the hill.

"Look at the ould man, now, would ye? Phil, he's makin' fur Bar'net's. Bet some av your rich kin's comin' from the East, bringing you their out-av-style clothes, an' a few good little books and Sunday-school tracts to improve ye."

There was only one passenger in the stage, a woman whose face I could not see.

That evening O'mie went to Judson at closing time.

"Mr. Judson, I want a lave of absence fur a week or tin days," he said.

"What for?" Judson was the kind of man who could never be pleasant to his employees, for fear of losing his authority over them.

"I want to go out av town on business," O'mie replied.

"Whose business?" snapped Judson.

"Me own," responded O'mie calmly.

"I can't have it. That's it. I just can't have my clerks and underlings running around over the country taking my time."

"Then I'll lave your time here whin I go," O'mie spoke coolly. He had always been respectful toward his employer, but he had no servile fear of him.

"I just can't allow it," Judson went on. "I need you here." O'mie was the life of the business, the best asset in the store. "It may be a slack time, but I can't have it; that's it, I just can't put up with it. Besides," he simpered a little, in spite of himself, "besides, I'm likely to be off a few days myself, just any time, I can get ready for a step I have in mind, an important step, just any minute, but it's different with some others, and we have to regard some others, you know; have to let some others have their way once in a while. We'll consider it settled now. You are to stay right here."

"Ye'll consider it settled that I'm nadin' a tin days' vacation right away, an' must have it."

"I can't do it, O'Meara; that's it. I would not give you your place again, and I won't pay you a cent of this quarter's salary."

Judson's foolish temper was always his undoing.

"You say you won't?" O'mie asked with a smile.

"No, I won't. Hereafter you may beg your way or starve!" Judson fairly shouted.

"Excuse me, Mr. Amos Judson, but I'm not to thim straits yit. Not yit. I've a little bank account an' a good name at Cris Mead's bank. Most as good as yours."

The shot went home. Judson had but recently failed to get the bank's backing in a business dealing he had hoped to carry through on loans, and it had cut his vanity deeply.

"Good-bye, Amos, I'll be back, but not any sooner than ye nade me," and he was gone.

The next day Dever the stage driver told us O'mie was going up to Wyandotte on business.

"Whose business?" I asked. "He doesn't know a soul in Wyandotte, except Tell and Jim, who were working up there the last I knew. Tell may be in Fort Scott now. Whose business was it?"

"That's what I asked him," Dever answered with a grin, "and he said, his own."

Whatever it was, O'mie was back again before the end of the week. But he idled about for the full ten days, until Judson grew frantic. The store could not be managed without him, and it was gratifying to O'mie's mischievous spirit to be solicited with pledge and courtesy to take his place again.

After O'mie had left me in the courthouse yard, the evening after the party, I stopped on my way home to see Marjie a moment. She had gone with the Meads out to Red Range, her mother said, and might not be back till late, possibly not till to-morrow. Judson was sitting in the room when I came to the door. I had no especial reason to think Mrs. Whately was confused by my coming. She was always kind to everybody. But somehow the gray shadows of the clouded moon of the night before were chilling me still, and I was bitterly disappointed at missing my loved one's face in her home. It seemed ages since I had had her to myself; not since the night before my trip to Topeka. I stopped long enough to visit the "Rockport" letter-box for the answer to my letter I knew she would leave before she went out of town. There was no letter there. My heart grew heavy with a weight that was not to lift again for many a long day. Up on the street I met Dr. Hemingway. His kind eyes seemed to penetrate to my very soul.

"Good-evening, Philip," he said pleasantly, grasping my hand with a firm pressure. "Your face isn't often clouded."

I tried to look cheerful. "Oh, it's just the weather and some loss of sleep. Kansas Augusts are pretty trying."

"They should not be to a young man," he replied. "All weathers suit us if we are at peace within. That's where the storm really begins."

"Maybe so," I said. "But I'm all right, inside and out."

"You look it, Philip." He took my hand affectionately. "You are the very image of clean, strong manhood. Let not your heart be troubled."

I returned his hand-clasp and went my way. However much courage it may take to push forward to victory or death on the battle field, not the least of heroism does it sometimes require to walk bravely toward the deepening gloom of an impending ill. I have followed both paths and I know what each one demands.

At our doorway, waiting to welcome me, stood Rachel Melrose, smiling, sure, and effusively demonstrative in her friendship. She must have followed me on the next stage out of Topeka. Behind her stood Candace Baronet, the only woman I have ever known who never in all my life doubted me nor misunderstood me. Somehow the sunset was colorless to me that night, and all the rippling waves of wide West Prairie were shorn of their glory.

CHAPTER XV

ROCKPORT AND "ROCKPORT"

Glitters the dew, and shines the river,
Up comes the lily and dries her bell;
But two are walking apart forever,
And wave their hands in a mute farewell.

—JEAN INGELOW.

The Melrose family was of old time on terms of intimacy with the house of Baronet. It was a family with a proud lineage, wealth, and culture to its credit. Rachel had an inherited sense of superiority. Too much staying between the White Mountains and the Atlantic Ocean is narrowing to the mental scope. The West to her was but a wilderness whereto the best things of life never found their way. She took everything in Massachusetts as hers by due right, much more did it seem that Kansas should give its best to her; and withal she was a woman who delighted in conquest.

Her arrival in Springvale made a topic that was soon on everybody's tongue. In the afternoon of the day following her coming, when I went to my father's office before starting out to the stone cabin, I found Marjie there. I had not seen her since the party, and I went straight to her chair.

"Well, little girl, it's ten thousand years since I saw you last," I spoke in a low voice. My father was searching for some papers in his cabinet, and his back was toward us. "Why didn't I get a letter, dearie?"

She looked up with eyes whose brown depths were full of pain and sorrow, but with an expression I had never seen on her face before, a kind of impenetrable coldness. It cut me like a sword-thrust, and I bent over her.

"Oh, Marjie, my Marjie, what is wrong?"

"Here is that paper at last," my father said before he turned around. Even as he spoke, Rachel Melrose swept into the room.

"Why, Philip, I missed you after all. I didn't mean to keep you waiting, but I can never get accustomed to your Western hurry."

She was very handsome and graceful, and always at ease with me, save in our interviews alone.

"I didn't know you were coming," I said frankly; "but I want you to meet Miss Whately. This is the young lady I have told you about."

I took Marjie's hand as I spoke. It was cold, and I gave it the gentle pressure a lover understands as I presented her. She gave me a momentary glance. Oh, God be thanked for the love-light in those brown eyes! The memory of it warmed my heart a thousand times when long weary miles were between us, and a desolate sky shut down around the far desolate plains of a silent, featureless land.

"And this is Miss Melrose, the young lady I told you of in my letter," I said to Marjie. A quick change came into her eyes, a look of surprise and incredulity and scorn. What could have happened to bring all this about?

Rachel Melrose had made the fatal mistake of thinking that no girl reared west of the Alleghenies could be very refined or at ease or appear well dressed in the company of Eastern people. She was not prepared for the quiet courtesy and self-possession with which the Kansas girl greeted her; nor had she expected, as she told me afterward, to find in a town like Springvale such good taste and exquisite neatness in dress. True, she had many little accessories of an up-to-date fashion that had not gotten across the Mississippi River to our girls as yet, but Marjie had the grace of always choosing the right thing to wear. I was very proud of my loved one at that moment. There was a show of cordiality between the two; then Rachel turned to me.

"I'm going with you this afternoon. Excuse me, Miss Whately, Mr. Baronet promised me up at Topeka to take me out to see a wonderful cottonwood tree that he said just dwarfed the little locust there, that we went out one glorious moonlight night to see. It was a lovely stroll though, wasn't it, Philip?"

This time it was my father's eyes that were fixed upon me in surprise and stern inquiry.

"He will believe I am a flirt after all. It isn't possible to make any man understand how that miserable girl can control things, unless he is on the ground all the time." So ran my thoughts.

"Father, must that trip be made to-day? Because I'd rather get up a party and go out when Miss Melrose goes."

But my father was in no mood to help me then. He had asked me to go alone. Evidently he thought I had forgotten business and constancy of purpose in the presence of this pretty girl.

"It must be done to-day. Miss Melrose will wait, I'm sure. It is a serious business matter—"

"Oh, but I won't, Mr. Baronet. Your son promised me to do everything for me if I would only come to Springvale; that was away last Spring, and my stay will be short at best. I must go back to-morrow afternoon. Don't rob us of a minute."

She spoke with such a pretty grace, and yet her words were so trifling that my father must have felt as I did. He could have helped me then had he thought that I deserved help, for he was a tactful man. But he merely assented and sent us away. When we were gone Marjie turned to him bravely.

"Judge Baronet, I think I will go home. I came in from Red Range this noon with the Meads. It was very warm, coming east, and I am not very well." She was as white as marble. "I will see you again; may I?"

John Baronet was a man of deep sympathy as well as insight. He knew why the bloom had left her cheeks.

"All right, Marjie. You will be better soon."

He had risen and taken her cold hand. There was a world of cheer and strength in that rich resonant voice of his. "Little girl, you must not worry over anything. All the tangles will straighten for you. Be patient, the sunshine is back of all shadows. I promised your father, Marjory, that no harm should come to you. I will keep my promise. 'Let not your heart be troubled.'" His words were to her what the good minister's had been to me.

In the months that came after that my father was her one strong defence. Poor Marjie! her days as well as mine were full of creeping shadows. I had no notion of the stories being poured into her ears, nor did I dream of the mischief and sorrow that can be wrought by a jealous-hearted girl, a grasping money lover, and a man whose business dealings will not bear the light of day.

It has ever been the stage-driver's province to make the town acquainted with the business of each passenger whom he imports or exports. Our man, Dever, was no exception. Judson's store had become the centre of all the gossip in Springvale. Judson himself was the prince of scandalmongers, who with a pretence of refusing to hear gossip, peddled it out most industriously. He had hurried to Mrs. Whately with the story of our guest, and here I found him when I went to see Marjie, before I myself knew what passenger the stage had carried up to Cliff Street.

After the party at Anderson's, Tillhurst had not lost the opportunity of giving his version of all he had seen and heard in Topeka. Marjie listened in amazement but sure in her trustful heart that I would make it all clear to her in my letter. And yet she wondered why I had never mentioned that name to her, nor given her any hint of any one with claim enough on me to keep me for two days in Topeka. After all, she did recall the name—something forgotten in the joy and peace of that sweet afternoon out by the river in the draw where the haunted house was. Had I tried to tell her and lost my courage, she wondered. Oh, no, it could not be so.

The next day Marjie spent at Red Range. It was noon of the day following Rachel's arrival before she reached home. The ride in the midday heat, sympathy for Dave Mead, and the sad funeral rites in the morning, together with the memory of Tillhurst's gossip and the long time since we had talked with each other alone, had been enough to check even her sunny spirit. Gentle Mrs. Whately, willing to believe everybody, met her daughter with a sad face.

"My dear, I have some unwelcome news for you," she said when Marjie was resting in the cool sitting-room after the hot ride. "There's an old sweetheart of Phil's came here last evening to visit him. Mr. Dever, the stage-driver, says she is the handsomest girl he ever saw. They say she and Phil were engaged and had a falling out back East. They met again in Topeka, and Phil stayed a day or two to visit with her after the political meeting was over. And now she has come down here at his request to meet his folks. Marjie, daughter, you need not care. There are more worthy men who would be proud to marry you."

Marjie made no reply.

"Oh, daughter, he isn't worth your grief. Be strong. Your life will get into better channels now. There are those who care for you more than you dream of. And you cannot care for Phil when I tell you all I must tell."

"I will be strong, mother. What else?" Marjie said quietly. In the shadows of the room darkened to keep out the noonday heat, Mrs. Whately did not note the white face and the big brown eyes burning with pain.

"It's too bad, but you ought to know it. Judge Baronet's got some kind of a land case on hand. There's a fine half-section he's trying to get away from a young man who is poor. The Judge is a clever lawyer and he is a rich man. Mr. Judson says Tell Mapleson is this young man's counsel, and he's fighting to keep the land for its real owner. Well, Phil was strolling around until nearly morning with Lettie Conlow, and they met this young man somewhere. He doesn't live about here. And, Marjie, right before Lettie, Phil gave him an awful beating and made him promise never to show himself in Springvale again. You know Judge Baronet could do anything in that court-room he wants to. He is a fine man. How your father loved him! But Phil goes out and does the dirty work to help him win. So Amos Judson says."

"Did Amos Judson tell you all this, Mother?" Marjie asked faintly.

"Most of it. And he is so interested in your welfare, daughter."

Marjie rose to her feet. "Mother, I don't know how much truth there may be in the circumstances, but I'll wait until somebody besides Amos Judson tells me before I accept these stories."

"Well, Marjie, you are young. You must lean on older counsel. There is no man living as good and true as your father was to me. Remember that."

"Yes, there is," Marjie declared.

"Who is he, daughter?"

"Philip Baronet," Marjie answered proudly.

That afternoon Richard Tillhurst called and detained Marjie until she was late in keeping her appointment with Judge Baronet. Tillhurst's tale of woe was in the main a repetition of Mrs. Whately's, but he knew better how to make it convincing, for he had hopes of winning the prize if I were out of the way. He was too keen to think Judson a dangerous rival with a girl of Marjie's good sense and independence. It was with these things in mind that Marjie had met me. Rachel Melrose had swept in on us, and I who had declared to my dear one that I should never care to take another girl out to that sunny draw full of hallowed memories for us two, I was going again with this beautiful woman, my sweetheart from the East. And yet Marjie was quick enough to note that I had tried to evade the company of Miss Melrose, and she had seen in my eyes the same look that they had had for her all these years. Could I be deceiving her by putting Rachel off in her presence? She did not want to think so. Had Judge Baronet not been my father, he could have taken her into his confidence. She could not speak to him of me, nor could he discuss his son's actions with her.

But love is strong and patient, and Marjie determined not to give up at the first onslaught against it.

"I'll write to him now," she said. "There will be sure to be a letter for me up under 'Rockport.' He said something about a letter this afternoon, the letter he promised to write after the party at Anderson's. He couldn't be deceiving me, I'm sure. I'll tell him everything, and if he really doesn't care for me,"—the blank of life lay sullen and dull before her,—"I'll know it any how. But if he does care, he'll have a letter for me all right."

And so she wrote, a loving, womanly letter, telling in her own sweet way all her faith and the ugly uncertainty that was growing up against it.

"But I know you, Phil, and I know you are all my own." So she ended the letter, and in the purple twilight she hastened up to the cliff and found her way down to our old shaded corner under the rock. There was no letter awaiting her. She held her own a minute and then she thrust it in.

"I'll do anything for Phil," she murmured softly. "I cannot help it. He was my own—he must be mine still."

A light laugh sounded on the rock above her.

"Are you waiting for me here?" a musical voice cried out. It was Rachel's voice. "Your aunt said you were gone out and would be back soon. I knew you would like me to meet you half way. It is beautiful here, you must love the place, but"—she added so softly that the unwilling listener did not catch her words—"it isn't so fine as our old Rockport!"

Quickly came the reply in a voice Marjie knew too well, although the tone was unlike any she had ever heard before.

"I hate Rockport; I did not tell you so when I left last Spring, but I hated it then."

Swiftly across the listener's mind swept the memory of my words. "If you ever hear me say I don't like 'Rockport' you will know I don't care for you."

She had heard me say these words, had heard them spoken in a tone of vehement feeling. There was no mistaking the speaker's sincerity, and then the quick step and swing of the bushes told her I had gone. The Neosho Valley turned black before her eyes, and she sank down on the stone shelving of the ledge.

My ride that afternoon had been a miserable one. Rachel was coy and sweet, yet cunningly bold. I felt indignant at my father for forcing her company on me, and I resented the circumstance that made me a victim to injustice. I detested the beautiful creature beside me for her assumption of authority over my actions, and above all, I longed with an aching, starved heart for Marjie. I knew she had only to read my letter to understand. She might not have gone after it yet, but I could see her that evening and all would be well.

I did not go near the old stone cabin. My father had failed to know his son if he thought I would obey under these hard conditions. We merely drove about beyond the draw. Then we rested briefly under the old cottonwood before we started home.

In the twilight I hurried out to our "Rockport" to wait for Marjie. I was a little late and so I did not know that Marjie was then under the point of rock. My rudeness to Rachel was unpardonable, but she had intruded one step too far into the sacred precincts of my life. I would not endure her in the place made dear to me from childhood, by association with Marjie. So I rashly blurted out my feelings and left her, never dreaming who had heard me nor what meaning my words would carry.

Down at the Whately home Richard Tillhurst sat, bland and smiling, waiting for Miss Whately's return. I sat down to wait also.

The August evening was dry and the day's hot air was rippling now into a slight breeze. The shadows deepened and the twilight had caught its last faint glow, when Marjie, white and cold, came slowly up the walk. Her brown hair lay in little curls about her temples and her big dark eyes were full of an utterable sorrow. I hurried out to the gate to meet her, but she would have passed by me with stately step.

"Marjie," I called softly, holding the gate.

"Good-evening, Philip. Please don't speak to me one word." Her voice was low and sweet as of yore save that it was cold and cutting.

She stood beside me for a moment. "I cannot be detained now. You will find your mother's ring in a package of letters I shall send you to-morrow. For my sake as well as for your own, please let this matter end here without any questions."

"But I will ask you questions," I declared.

"Then they will not be answered. You have deceived me and been untrue to me. I will not listen to one word. You may be very clever, but I understand you now. This is the end of everything for you and me." And so she left me.

I stood at the gate only long enough to hear her cordial greeting of Tillhurst. My Marjie, my own, had turned against me. The shadows of the deepening twilight turned to horrid shapes, and all the purple richness with that deep crimson fold low in the western sky became a chill gloom bordered on the horizon by the flame of hate. So the glory of a world gone wrong slips away, and the creeping shadows are typical only of pain and heartache.

I turned aimlessly away. I had told Marjie she was the light of my life: I did not understand the truth of the words until the light went out. Heavily, as I had staggered toward her mother's house on the night when I was sure Jean Pahusca had stolen her, I took my way now into the gathering shadows, slowly, to where I could hear the Neosho whispering and muttering in the deep gloom.

It comes sometimes to most of us, the wild notion that life, the gift of God alone, is a cheap thing not worth the keeping, and the impulse to fling it away uprears its ugly suggestion. Out in a square of light by the ford I saw Dave Mead standing, looking straight before him. The sorrows of the day were not all mine. I went to him, and we stood there silent together. At length we turned about in a purposeless way toward the open West Prairie. How many a summer evening we had wandered here! How often had our ponies come tramping home side by side, in the days when we brought the cows in late from the farthest draw! It seemed like another world now.

"Phil, you are very good to me. Don't pity me! I can't stand that." We never had a tenor in our choir with a voice so clear and rich as his.

"I don't pity you, Dave, I envy you." I spoke with an effort. "You have not lost, you have only begun a long journey. There is joy at the end of it."

"Oh, that is easy for you to say, who have everything to make you happy."

"I? Oh, Dave! I have not even a grave." The sudden sense of loss, driven back by the thought of another's sorrow, swept over me again. It was his turn now to forget himself.

"What is it, Phil? Have you and Marjie quarrelled? You never were meant for that, either of you. It can't be."

"No, Dave. I don't know what is wrong. I only wish—no, I don't. It is hard to be a man with the heart of a boy still, a foolish boy with foolish ideals of love and constancy. I can't talk to-night, Dave, only I envy you the sure possession, the eternal faith that will never be lost."

He pressed my hand in his left hand. His right arm had had only a limited usefulness since the night he tried to stop Jean Pahusca down by the mad floods of the Neosho. I have never seen him since we parted on the prairie that August evening. The next day he went to Red Range to stay for a short time. By the end of a week I had left Springvale, and we are to each other only boyhood memories now.

Out on the open prairie, where there was room to think and be alone, I went to fight my battle. There was only a sweep of silver sky above me and a sweep of moonlit plain about me. Dim to the southwest crept the dark shadow of the wooded Fingal's Creek Valley, while against the horizon the big cottonwood tree was only a gray blur. The mind can act swiftly. By the time the moon had swung over the midnight line I had mapped out my course. And while I seemed to have died, and another being had my personality, with only memory the same in both, I rose up armed in spirit to do a man's work in the world. But it cost me a price. I have been on a battle field with a thousand against fifty, and I was one of the fifty. Such a strife as I pray Heaven may never be in our land again. I have looked Death in the face day after day creeping slowly, surely toward me while I must march forward to meet it. Did the struggle this night out on the prairie strengthen my soul to bear it all, I wonder.

The next morning a package addressed in Marjie's round girlish hand was put before me. Forgetful of resolve, I sent back by its bearer an imploring appeal for a chance to meet her and clear up the terrible misunderstanding. The note came back unopened. I gave it with the bundle to Aunt Candace.

"Keep this for me, auntie, dear," I said, and my voice trembled. She took it from my hand.

"All right, Phil, I'll keep it. You are not at the end of things, dearie. You are only at the beginning. I'll keep this. It is only keeping, remember." She pointed to a stain on the unopened note, the round little blot only a tear can make. "It isn't yours, I know."

It was the first touch of comfort I had felt. However slender the thread, Hope will find it strong to cling to. Rachel's visit ended that day. Self-centred always, she treated me as one who had been foolish, but whom she considered her admirer still. It was not in her nature to be rejected. She shaped things to fit her vanity, and forgot what could not be controlled. I refused to allow myself to be alone with her again. Nobody was ever so tied to a woman's presence as I kept myself by Aunt Candace so long as I remained in the house.

My father, I knew, was grieved and indignant. With all my fair promises and pretended loyalty I seemed to be an idle trifler. How could my relation to Lettie Conlow be explained away in the light of this visit from a handsome cultured young lady, who had had an assurance of welcome or she would not have come. He loved Marjie as the daughter of his dearest friend. He had longed to call her, "daughter," and I had foolishly thrown away a precious prize.

Serious, too, was my reckless neglect of business. I had disregarded his request to manage a grave matter. Instead of going alone to the cabin, I had gone off with a pretty girl and reported that I had found nothing.

"Did you go near the cabin?" He drove the question square at me, and I had sullenly answered, "No, sir." Clearly I needed more discipline than the easy life in Springvale was giving me. I went down to the office in the afternoon, hoping for something, I hardly knew what. He was alone, and I asked for a few words with him. Somehow I seemed more of a man to myself than I had ever felt before in his presence.

"Father," I began. "When the sea did its worst for you—fifteen years ago—you came to the frontier here, and somehow you found peace. You have done your part in the making of the lawless Territory into a law-abiding State, this portion of it at least. The frontier moves westward rapidly now."

"Well?" he queried.

"I have lost—not by the sea—but, well, I've lost. I want to go to the frontier too. I must get away from here. The Plains—somewhere—may help me."

"But why leave here?" he asked. After all, the father-heart was yearning to keep his son.

"Why did you leave Massachusetts?" I could not say Rockport. I hated the sound of the name.

"Where will you go, my boy?" He spoke with deepest sorrow, and love mingled in his tones.

"Out to the Saline Country. They need strong men out there. I must have been made to defend the weak." It was not a boast, but the frank expression of my young manhood's ideal. "Your friend Mr. Morton urged me to come. May I go to him? It may be I can find my place out in that treeless open land; that there will come to me, as it came to you, the help that comes from helping others."

Oh, I had fought my battle well. I was come into a man's estate now and had put away childish things.

My father sitting before me took both my hands in his.

"My son, you are all I have. You cannot long deceive me. I have trusted you always. I love you even unto the depths of disgrace. Tell me truly, have you done wrong? I will soon know it. Tell me now."

"Father," I held his hands and looked steadily into his eyes. "I have no act to conceal from you, nor any other living soul. I must leave here because I cannot stay and see—Father, Marjie is lost to me. I do not know why."

"Well, find out." He spoke cheerily.

"It is no use. She has changed, and you know her father's firmness. She is his mental image."

"There is no stain somewhere, no folly of idle flirtation, no weakness? I hear much of you and Lettie."

"Father, I have done nothing to make me ashamed. Last night when I fought my battle to the finish, for the first time in my life I knew my mother was with me. Somehow it was her will guiding me. I know my place. I cannot stay here. I will go where the unprotected need a strength like mine."

The stage had stopped at the courthouse door, and Rachel Melrose ran up the steps and entered the outer office. My father went out to meet her.

"Are you leaving us?" he asked kindly.

"Yes, I had only a day or two that I could spend here. But where is Philip?"

John Baronet had closed his door behind him. I thanked him fervently in my heart for his protection. How could I meet this woman now? And yet she had seemed only selfishly mischievous, and I must not be a coward, so I came out of the inner room at once. A change swept over her face when I appeared. The haughty careless spirit gave place to gentleness, and, as always, she was very pretty. Nothing of the look or manner was lost on John Baronet, and his pity for her only strengthened his opinion of my insincerity.

"Good-bye, Philip. We shall meet again soon, I hope. Good-bye, Judge Baronet." Her voice was soft and full of sadness. She smiled upon us both and turned to go.

My father led her down the courthouse steps and helped her into the stage. When he came back I did not look up. There was nothing for me to say. Quietly, as though nothing had occurred, he took up his work, his face as impenetrable as Jean Pahusca's.

My resemblance to my mother is strong. As I bent over his desk to gather up some papers for copying, my heavy dark hair almost brushed his cheek. I did not know then how his love for me was struggling with his sense of duty.

"I have trusted him too much, and given him too free a rein. He doesn't know yet how to value a woman's feelings. He must learn his lesson now. But he shall not go away without my blessing."

So he mused.

"Philip," his voice was as kind as it was firm, "we shall see what the days will bring. Your mother's spirit may be guiding you, and your father's love is always with you. Whatever snarls and tangles have gotten into your threads, time and patience will straighten and unravel. Whatever wrong you may have done, willingly or unwillingly, you must make right. There is no other way."

"Father," I replied in a voice as firm as his own. "Father, I have done no wrong."

Once more he looked steadily into my eyes and through them down into my very soul. "Phil, I believe you. These things will soon pass away."

In the early twilight I went for the last time to "Rockport." There are sadder things than funeral rites. The tragedies of life do not always ring down the curtain leaving the stage strewn with the forms of the slain. Oftener they find the living actor following his lines and doing his part of the play as if all life were a comedy. The man of sixty years may smile at the intensity of feeling in the boy of twenty-one, but that makes it no easier for the boy. I watched the sun go down that night, and then I waited through the dark hour till the moon, now past the full, should once more illumine the Neosho Valley. Although I have always been a lover of nature, that sunset and the purple twilight following, the darkness of the early evening hour and the glorious moonrise are tinged with a sorrow I have never quite lost even in the happier years since then. I sat alone on the point of rock. At last the impulse to go down below and search for a letter from Marjie overcame me, although I laughed bitterly at the folly of such a notion. In the crevice where her letter had been placed for me the night before, I found nothing. What a different story I might have to tell had I gone down at sunset instead of waiting through that hour of darkness before the moon crept above the eastern horizon line! And yet I believe that in the final shaping-up the best thing for each one comes to all of us. Else the universe is without a plan and Love unwavering and eternal is only a vagary of the dreamer.

Early the next morning I left Springvale, and set my face to the westward, as John Baronet had done a decade and a half before, to begin life anew where the wilderness laps the frontier line. My father held my hand long when I said good-bye, and love and courage and trust were all in that hand-clasp.

"You'll win out, my boy. Keep your face to the light. The world has no place for the trifler, the coward, or the liar. It is open to homestead claims for all the rest. You will not fail." And with his kiss on my forehead he let me go.

Anything is news in a little town, and especially interesting in the dull days of late Summer. The word that I had gone away started from Conlow's shop and swept through the town like a prairie fire through a grassy draw.

No one man is essential to any community. Springvale didn't need me so much as I needed it. But when I left it there were many more than I deserved who not only had a good word for me; they went further, and demanded that good reason for my going must be shown, or somebody would be made to suffer. Foremost among these were Cam Gentry, Dr. Hemingway, and Cris Mead, president of the Springvale Bank, the father of Bill and Dave. Of course, the boys, the blessed old gang, who had played together and worked together and been glad and sorry with each other down the years, the boys were loyal to the last limit.

But we had our share of gossips who had a tale they could unfold—a dreadful tale! Beginning with my forging my father's name to get money to spend on Rachel Melrose and other Topeka girls, and to pay debts I had contracted at Harvard, on and on the tale ran, till, by the time the Fingal's Creek neighborhood got hold of the "real facts," it developed that I had all but murdered a man who stood in the way of a rich fee my father was to get out of a land suit somewhere; and lastly came an ominous shaking of the head and a keeping back of the "worst truth," about my gay escapades with girls of shady reputation whom I had deceived, and cruelly wronged, trusting to my standing as a rich man's son to pull me through all right.

Marjie was the last one in Springvale to be told of my sudden leave-taking. The day had been intolerably long for her, and the evening brought an irresistible temptation to go up to our old playground. Contrary to his daily habit my father had passed the Whately house on his way home, and Marjie had seen him climb the hill. I was as like him in form as Jean Pahusca was like Father Le Claire. Six feet and two inches he stood, and so perfectly proportioned that he never looked corpulent. I matched him in height and weight, but I had not his fine bearing, for I had seen no military service then. I do not marvel that Springvale was proud of him, for his character matched the graces Nature had given him.

As Marjie watched him going the way I had so often taken, her resolve to forget what we had been to each other suddenly fell to pieces. Her feelings could not change at once. Mental habits are harder to break up than physical appetites. For fourteen years my loved one had known me, first as her stanch defender in our plays, then as her boy sweetheart and lastly as her lover and betrothed husband. Could twenty-four hours of distrust and misunderstanding displace these fourteen years of happy thinking? And so after sunset Marjie went up the slope, hardly knowing why she should do so or what she would say to me if she should meet me there. It was a poor beginning for the new life she had carefully mapped out, but impulse was stronger than resolve in her just then. Just at the steep bend in the street she came face to face with Lettie Conlow. The latter wore a grin of triumph as the two met.

"Good-evening, Marjie. I s'pose you've heard the news?"

"What news?" asked Marjie. "I haven't heard anything new to-day."

"Oh, yes, you have, too. You know all about it; but I'd not care if I was you."

Marjie was on her guard in a moment.

"I don't care for what I don't know, Lettie," she replied.

"Nor what you do, neither. I wouldn't if I was you. He ain't worth it; and it gives better folks a chance for what they want, anyhow."

Lettie's low brows and cunning black eyes were unendurable to the girl she was tormenting.

"Well, I don't know what you are talking about," and Marjie would have passed on, but Lettie intercepted her.

"You know that rich Melrose girl's gone back to Topeka?"

"Oh, yes," Marjie spoke indifferently; "she went last evening, I was told."

"Well, this morning Phil Baronet went after her, left Springvale for good and all. O'mie says so, and he knows all Phil knows. Marjie, she's rich; and Phil won't marry nobody but a rich girl. You know you ain't got what you had when your pa was alive."

Yes, Marjie knew that.

"Well he's gone anyhow, and I don't care."

"Why should you care?" Marjie could not help the retort. She was stung to the quick in every nerve. Lettie's face blazed with anger.

"Or you?" she stormed. "He was with me last. I can prove it, and a lot more things you'd never want to hear. But you'll never be his girl again."

Marjie turned toward the cliff just as O'mie appeared through the bushes and stepped behind Lettie.

"Oh, good-evening, lovely ladies; delighted to meet you," he hailed them.

Marjie smiled at him, but Lettie gave a sudden start.

"Oh, O'mie, what are you forever tagging me for?" She spoke angrily and without another word to Marjie she hurried down the hill.

"I tag!" O'mie grinned. "I'd as soon tag Satan, only I've just got to do it." But his face changed when he turned to Marjie. "Little girl, I overheard the lady. Lovely spirit that! I just can't help dancin' attendance on it. But, Marjie, I've come up here, knowin' Phil had gone and wasn't in my way, 'cause I wanted to show you somethin'. Yes, he's gone. Left early this mornin'. Never mind that, right now."

He led the way through the bushes and they sat down together. I cannot say what Marjie thought as she looked out on the landscape I had watched in loneliness the night before. It was O'mie, and not his companion, who told me long afterwards of this evening.

"I thought you were away on a ten days' vacation, O'mie. Dever said you were." She could not bear the silence.

"I'm on a tin days' vacation, but I'm not away, Marjie, darlin'," O'mie replied.

"Oh, O'mie, don't joke. I can't stand it to-night." Her face was white and her eyes were full of pain.

"Indade, I'm not jokin'. I came up here to show you somethin' and to tell you somethin'."

He took an old note book from his pocket and opened it to where a few brown blossoms lay flatly pressed between the leaves.

"Thim's not pretty now, Marjie, but the day I got 'em they was dainty an' pink as the dainty pink-cheeked girl whose brown curls they was wreathed about. These are the flowers Phil Baronet put on your hair out in the West Draw by the big cottonwood one April evenin' durin' the war; the flowers Jean Pahusca kissed an' throwed away. But I saved 'em because I love you, Marjie."

She shivered and bent her head.

"Oh, not like thim two ornery tramps who had these blossoms 'fore I got 'em, but like I'd love a sister, if I had one; like Father Le Claire loves me. D'ye see?"

"You are a dear, good brother, O'mie," Marjie murmured, without lifting her head.

"Oh, yis, I'm all av that an' more. Marjie, I'm goin' to kape these flowers till—well, now, Marjie, shall I tell you whin?"

"Yes, O'mie," Marjie said faintly.

"Well, till I see the pretty white veil lifted fur friends to kiss the bride an' I catch the scent av orange blossoms in thim soft little waves." He put his hand gently on her bowed head. "I'll get to do it, too," he went on, "not right away, but not fur off, nather; an' it won't be a little man, ner a rid-headed Irishman, ner a sharp-nosed school-teacher; but—Heaven bless an' kape him to-night!—it'll be a big, broad-shouldered, handsome rascal, whose heart has niver changed an' niver can change toward you, little sister, 'cause he's his father's own son—lovin', constant, white an' clane through an' through. Be patient. It's goin' to be all right for you two." He closed the book and put it back in its place. "But I mustn't stay here. I've got to tag Lettie some more. Her an' some others. That's what my tin days' vacation's fur, mostly." And O'mie leaped through the bushes and was gone.

The twilight was deepening when Marjie at last roused herself.

"I'll go down and see if he did get my letter," she murmured, taking her way down the rough stair. There was no letter in the crevice where she had placed it securely two nights before. Lifting her face upward she clasped her hands in sorrow.

"He took it away, but he did not come to me. He knows I love him." Then remembering herself, "I would not let him speak. But he said he hated 'Rockport.' Oh, what can it all mean? How could he be so good to me and then deceive me so? Shall I believe Lettie, or O'mie?"

Kneeling there in the deep shadows of the cliff-side with the Neosho gurgling darkly below her, and the long shafts of pink radiance from the hidden sunset illumining the sky above her, Marjie prayed for strength to bear her burden, for courage to meet whatever must come to her, and for the assurance of divine Love although now her lover, as well as her father, was lost to her. The simple pleading cry of a grief-stricken heart it was. Heaven heard that prayer, and Marjie went down the hill with womanly grace and courage and faith to face whatever must befall her in the new life opening before her.

In the days that followed my little girl was more than ever the idol of Springvale. Her sweet, sunny nature now had a new beauty. Her sorrow she hid away so completely there were few who guessed what her thoughts were. Lettie Conlow was not deceived, for jealousy has sharp eyes. O'mie understood, for O'mie had carried a sad, hungry heart underneath his happy-go-lucky carelessness all the years of his life. Aunt Candace was a woman who had overcome a grief of her own, and had been cheery and bright down the years. She knew the mark of conquest in the face. And lastly, my father, through his innate power to read human nature, watched Marjie as if she were his own child. Quietly, too, so quietly that nobody noticed it, he became a guardian over her. Where she went and what she did he knew as well as Jean Pahusca, watching in the lilac clump, long ago. For fourteen years he had come and gone to our house on Cliff Street up and down the gentler slope two blocks to the west of Whately's. Nobody knew, until it had become habitual, when he changed his daily walk homeward up the steeper climb that led him by Marjie's house farther down the street. Nobody realized, until it was too common for comment, how much a part of all the social life of Springvale my father had become. He had come to Kansas a widower, but gossip long ago gave up trying to do anything with him. And now, as always, he was a welcome factor everywhere, a genial, courteous gentleman, whose dignity of character matched his stern uprightness and courage in civic matters. Among all the things for which I bless his memory, not the least of them was this strong, unostentatious guardianship of a girl when her need for protection was greatest, as that Winter that followed proved.

I knew nothing of all this then. I only knew my loved one had turned against me. Of course I knew that Rachel was the cause, but I could not understand why Marjie would listen to no explanation, why she should turn completely from me when I had told her everything in the letter I wrote the night of the party at Anderson's. And now I was many miles from Springvale, and the very thought of the past was like a knife-thrust. All my future now looked to the Westward. I longed for action, for the opportunity to do something, and they came swiftly, the opportunity and the action.

CHAPTER XVI

BEGINNING AGAIN

It matters not what fruit the hand may gather,
If God approves, and says, "This is the best."
It matters not how far the feet may wander,
If He says, "Go, and leave to Me the rest."

—ALBERT MACY.

I stood in the August twilight by the railway station in the little frontier town of Salina, where the Union Pacific train had abandoned me to my fate. Turning toward the unmapped, limitless Northwest, I suddenly realized that I was at the edge of the earth now. Behind me were civilization and safety. Beyond me was only a waste of gray nothingness. Yet this was the world I had come hither to conquer. Here were the spaces wherein I should find peace. I set my face with grim determination to work now, out of the thing before me, a purpose that controlled me.

Morton's claim was a far day's journey up the Saline Valley. It would be nearly a week before I could find a man to drive me thither; so I secured careful directions, and the next morning I left the town on foot and alone. I did not mind the labor of it. I was as vigorous as a young giant, fear of personal peril I had never known, and the love of adventure was singing its siren's song to me. I was clad in the strong, coarse garments, suited to the Plains. I was armed with two heavy revolvers and a small pistol. Hidden inside of my belt as a last defence was the short, sharp knife bearing Jean Le Claire's name in script lettering.

I shall never forget the moment when a low bluff beyond a bend in the Saline River shut off the distant town from my view and I stood utterly alone in a wide, silent world, left just as God had made it. Humility and uplift mingle in the soul in such a time and place. One question ran back and forth across my mind: What conquering power can ever bring the warmth of glad welcome to the still, hostile, impenetrable beauty of these boundless plains?

"The air is full of spirits out here," I said to myself. "There is no living thing in sight, and yet the land seems inhabited, just as that old haunted cabin down on the Neosho seemed last June."

And then with the thought of that June day Memory began to play her tricks on me and I cried out, "Oh, perdition take that stone cabin and the whole Neosho Valley if that will make me forget it all!"

I strode forward along the silent, sunshiny way, with a thousand things on my mind's surface and only one thought in its inner deeps. The sun swung up the sky, and the thin August air even in its heat was light and invigorating. The river banks were low and soft where the stream cuts through the alluvial soil a channel many feet below the level of the Plains. The day was long, but full of interest to me, who took its sight as a child takes a new picture-book, albeit a certain sense of peril lurked in the shadowing corners of my thought.

The August sun was low in the west when I climbed up the grassy slope to Morton's little square stone cabin. It stood on a bold height overlooking the Saline River. Far away in every direction the land billows lay fold on fold. Treeless and wide they stretched out to the horizon, with here and there a low elevation, and here and there the faint black markings of scrubby bushes clinging to the bank of a stream. The stream itself, now only a shallow spread of water, bore witness to the fierce thirst of the summer sun. Up and down the Saline Valley only a few scattered homesteads were to be seen, and a few fields of slender, stunted corn told the story of the first struggle for conquest in a beautiful but lonely and unfriendly land.

Morton was standing at the door of his cabin looking out on that sweep of plains with thoughtful eyes. He did not see me until I was fairly up the hill, and when he did he made no motion towards me, but stood and waited for my coming. In those few moments as I swung forward leisurely—for I was very tired now—I think we read each other's character and formed our estimates more accurately than many men have done after years of close business association.

He was a small man beside me, as I have said, and his quiet manner, and retiring disposition, half dignity, half modesty, gave the casual acquaintance no true estimate of his innate force. Three things, however, had attracted me to him in our brief meeting at Topeka: his voice, though low, had a thrill of power in it; his hand-clasp was firm and full of meaning; and when I looked into his blue eyes I recalled the words which the Earl of Kent said to King Lear:

Every movement of ours had been watched by Indian scouts

"You have that in your countenance which I would fain call master."

And when King Lear asked, "What's that?" Kent replied, "Authority."

It was in Morton's face. Although he was not more than a dozen years my senior, I instinctively looked upon him as a leader of men, and he became then and has always since been one of my manhood's ideals.

"I'm glad to see you, Baronet. Come in." He grasped my hand firmly and led the way into the house. I sat down wearily in the chair he offered me. It was well that I had walked the last stage of my journey. Had I been twenty-four hours later I should have missed him, and this one story of the West might never have been told.

The inside of the cabin was what one would expect to find in a Plainsman's home who had no one but himself to consider.

While I rested he prepared our supper. Disappointment in love does not always show itself in the appetite, and I was as hungry as a coyote. All day new sights and experiences had been crowding in upon me. The exhilaration of the wild Plains was beginning to pulse in my veins. I had come into a strange, untried world. The past, with its broken ties and its pain and loss, must be only a memory that at my leisure I might call back; but here was a different life, under new skies, with new people. The sunset lights, the gray evening shadows, and the dip and swell of the purple distances brought their heartache; but now I was hungry, and Morton was making johnny cakes and frying bacon; wild plums were simmering on the fire, and coffee was filling the room with the rarest of all good odors vouchsafed to mortal sense.

At the supper table my host went directly to my case by asking, "Have you come out here to prospect or to take hold?"

"To take hold," I answered.

"Are you tired after your journey?" he queried.

"I? No. A night's sleep will fix me." I looked down at my strong arms, and stalwart limbs.

"You sleep well?" His questions were brief.

"I never missed but one night in twenty-one years, except when I sat up with a sick boy one Summer," I replied.

"When was that one night?"

"Oh, during the war when the border ruffians and Copperheads terrorized our town."

"You are like your father, I see." He did not say in what particular; and I added, "I hope I am."

We finished the meal in silence. Then we sat down by the west doorway and saw the whole Saline Valley shimmer through the soft glow of twilight and lose itself at length in the darkness that folded down about it. A gentle breeze swept along from somewhere in the far southwest, a thousand insects chirped in the grasses. Down by the river a few faint sounds of night birds could be heard, and then loneliness and homesickness had their time, denied during every other hour of the twenty-four.

After a time my host turned toward me in the gloom and looked steadily into my eyes.

"He's taking my measure," I thought.

"Well," I said, "will I do?"

"Yes," he answered. "Your father told me once in the army that his boy could ride like a Comanche, and turn his back to a mark and hit it over his shoulder." He smiled.

"That's because one evening I shot the head off a scarecrow he had put up in the cherry tree when I was hiding around a corner to keep out of his sight. All the Springvale boys learned how to ride and shoot and to do both at once, although we never had any shooting to do that really counted."

"Baronet"—there was a tone in Morton's voice that gripped and held me—"you have come here in a good time. We need you now. Men of your build and endurance and skill are what this West's got to have."

"Well, I'm here," I answered seriously.

"I shall leave for Fort Harker to-morrow with a crowd of men from the valley to join a company Sheridan has called for," he went on. "You know about the Indian raid the first of this month. The

Cheyennes came across here, and up on Spillman Creek and over on the Solomon they killed a dozen or more people. They burned every farm-house, and outraged every woman, and butchered every man and child they could lay hands on. You heard about it at Topeka."

"Hasn't that Indian massacre been avenged yet?" I cried.

Clearly in my memory came the two women of my dream of long ago. How deeply that dream had impressed itself upon my mind! And then there flashed across my brain the image of Marjie, as she looked the night when she stood in the doorway with the lamplight on her brown curls, and it became clear to me that she was safe at home. Oh, the joy of that moment! The unutterable thankfulness that filled my soul was matched in intensity only by the horror that fills it even now when I think of a white woman in Indian slave-bonds. And while I was thinking of this I was listening to Morton's more minute account of what had been taking place about him, and why he and his neighbors were to start on the next day for Fort Harker down on the Smoky Hill River.

Early in that memorable August of 1868 a band of forty Cheyenne braves, under their chief Black Kettle, came riding up from their far-away villages in the southwest, bent on a merciless murdering raid upon the unguarded frontier settlements. They were a dirty, ragged, sullen crew as ever rode out of the wilderness. Down on the Washita River their own squaws and papooses were safe in their tepees too far from civilization for any retaliatory measure to reach them.

When Black Kettle's band came to Fort Hays, after the Indian custom they made the claim of being "good Indians."

"Black Kettle loves his white soldier brothers, and his heart feels glad when he meets them," the Chief declared. "We would be like white soldiers, but we cannot, for we are Indians; but we can all be brothers. It is a long way that we have come to see you. Six moons have come and gone, and there has been no rain; the wind blows hot from the south all day and all night; the ground is hot and cracked; the grass is burned up; the buffalo wallows are dry; the streams are dry; the game is scarce; Black Kettle is poor, and his band is hungry. He asks the white soldiers for food for his braves and their squaws and papooses. All other Indians may take the war-trail, but Black Kettle will forever keep friendship with his white brothers."

Such were his honeyed words. The commander of the fort issued to each brave a bountiful supply of flour and bacon and beans and coffee. Beyond the shadow of the fort they feasted that night. The next morning they had disappeared, these loving-hearted, loyal Indians, over whom the home missionary used to weep copious tears of pity. They had gone—but whither? Black Kettle and his noble braves were not hurrying southward toward their squaws and papooses with the liberal supplies issued to them by the Government. Crossing to the Saline Valley, not good Indians, but a band of human fiends, they swept down on the unsuspecting settlements. A homestead unprotected by the husband and father was their supreme joy. Then before the eyes of the mother, little children were tortured to death, while the mother herself—God pity her—was not only tortured, but what was more cruel, was kept alive.

Across the Saline Valley, over the divide, and up the Solomon River Valley this band of demons pushed their way. Behind them were hot ashes where homes had been, and putrid, unburied bodies of murdered men and children, mutilated beyond recognition. On their ponies, bound hand and foot, were wretched, terror-stricken women. The smiling Plains lay swathed in the August sunshine, and the richness of purple twilights, and of rose-hued day dawns, and the pitiless noontime skies of brass only mocked them in their misery. Did a merciful God forget the Plains in those days of prairie conquest? No force rose up to turn Black Kettle and his murderous horde back from the imperilled settlements until loaded with plunder, their savage souls sated with cruelty, with helpless captives for promise of further fiendish sport, they headed southward and escaped untouched to their far-away village in the pleasant, grassy lands that border the Washita River.

Not all their captives went with them, however. With these "good Indians," recipients of the Fort Hays bounty, were two women, mothers of a few months, not equal to the awful tax of human endurance. These, bound hand and foot, they staked out on the solitary Plains under the blazing August skies, while their tormentors rode gayly away to join their fat, lazy squaws awaiting them in the southland by the winding Washita.

This was the story Morton was telling to me as we sat in the dusk by his cabin door. This was the condition of those fair Kansas River valleys, for the Cheyennes under Black Kettle were not the only foes here. Other Cheyenne bands, with the Sioux, the Brules, and the Dog Indians from every tribe were making every Plains trail a warpath.

"The captives are probably all dead by this time; but the crimes are not avenged, and the settlers are no safer than they were before the raid," Morton was saying. "Governor Crawford and the Governor of Colorado have urged the authorities at Washington to protect our frontier, but they have done nothing. Now General Sheridan has decided to act anyhow. He has given orders to Colonel George A. Forsyth of the U. S. Cavalry, to make up a company of picked men to go after the Cheyennes at once. There are some two hundred of them hiding somewhere out in the Solomon or the Republican River country. It is business now. No foolishness. A lot of us around here are going down to Harker to enlist. Will you go with us, Baronet? It's no boys' play. The safety of our homes is matched against the cunning savagery of the redskins. We paid fifteen million dollars for this country west of the Mississippi. If these Indians aren't driven out and made to suffer, and these women's wrongs avenged, we'd better sell the country back to France for fifteen cents. But it's no easy piece of work. Those Cheyennes know these Plains as well as you know the streets of Springvale. They are built like giants, and they fight like demons. Don't underestimate the size of the contract. I know John Baronet well enough to know that if his boy begins, he won't quit till the battle is done. I want you to go into this with your eyes open. Whoever fights the Indians must make his will before the battle begins. Forsyth's company will be made up of soldiers from the late war, frontiersmen, and scouts. You're not any one of these, but—" he hesitated a little—"when I heard your speech at Topeka I knew you had the right metal. Your spirit is in this thing. You are willing to pay the price demanded here for the hearthstones of the West."

My spirit! My blood was racing through every artery in leaps and bounds. Here was a man calmly setting forth the action that had been my very dream of heroism, and here was a call to duty, where duty and ideal blend into one. And then I was young, and thought myself at the beginning of a new life; pain of body was unknown to me; the lure of the Plains was calling to me—daring adventure, the need for courage, the patriotism that fires the young man's heart, and, at the final analysis, my loyalty to the defenceless, my secret notions of the value of the American home, my horror of Indian captivity, a horror I had known when my mind was most impressible—all these were motives driving me on. I wondered that my companion could be so calm, sitting there in the dim twilight explaining carefully what lay before me; and yet I felt the power of that calmness building up a surer strength in me. I did not dream of home that night. I chased Indians until I wakened with a scream.

"What's the matter, Baronet?" Morton asked.

"I thought the Cheyennes had me," I answered sleepily.

"Don't waste time in dreaming it. Better go to sleep and let 'em alone," he advised; and I obeyed.

The next morning we were joined by half a dozen settlers of that scattered community, and together we rode across the Plains toward Fort Harker. I had expected to find a fortified stronghold at the end of our ride. Something in imposing stone on a commanding height. Something of frowning, impenetrable strength. Out on the open plain by the lazy, slow-crawling Smoky Hill River were low buildings forming a quadrangle about a parade ground. Officers' quarters, soldiers' barracks, and stables for the cavalry horses and Government mules, there were, but no fortifications were there anywhere. Yet the fort was ample for the needs of the Plains. The Indian puts up only a defensive fight in the region of Federal power. It is out in the wide blank lands where distance mocks at retreat that he leads out in open hostility against the white man. Here General Sheridan had given Colonel Forsyth commission to organize a Company of Plainsmen. And this Company was to drive out or annihilate the roving bands of redskins who menaced every home along the westward-creeping Kansas frontier in the years that followed the Civil War. It was to offer themselves to this cause that the men from Morton's community, whom I had joined, rode across the divide from the Saline Valley on that August day, and came in the early twilight to the solitary unpretentious Federal post on the Smoky Hill.

It is only to a military man in the present time that this picture of Fort Harker would be interesting, and there is nothing now in all that peaceful land to suggest the frontier military station which I saw on that summer day, now nearly four decades ago. But everything was interesting to me then, and my greatest study was the men gathered there for a grim and urgent purpose. My impression of frontiersmen had been shaped by the loud threats, the swagger, and much profanity of the border people of the Territorial and Civil War days. Here were quiet men who made no boasts. Strong, wiry men they were, tanned by the sun of the Plains, their hands hardened, their eyes keen. They were military men who rode like centaurs, scouts who shot with marvellous accuracy, and the sturdy settlers, builders of empire in this stubborn West. Had I been older I would have felt my own lack of training among them. My hands, beside theirs, were soft and white, and while I was accounted a good marksman in Springvale I was a novice here. But since the night long ago when Jean Pahusca frightened Marjie by peering through our schoolroom window I had felt myself in duty bound to drive back the Indians. I had a giant's strength, and no Baronet was ever seriously called a coward.

The hours at Fort Barker were busy ones for Colonel Forsyth and Lieutenant Fred Beecher, first in command under him. Their task of selecting men for the expedition was quickly performed. My heart beat fast when my own turn came. Forsyth's young lieutenant was one of the Lord's anointed. Soft-voiced, modest, handsome, with a nature so lovable, I find it hard to-day to think of him in the military ranks where war and bloodshed are the ultimate business. But young Beecher was a soldier of the highest order, fearless and resourceful. I cannot say how much it lay in Morton's recommendation, and how much in the lieutenant's kind heart that I was able to pass muster and be written into that little company of less than threescore picked men. The available material at Fort

Harker was quickly exhausted, and the men chosen were hurried by trains to Fort Hays, where the remainder of the Company was made up.

Dawned then that morning in late Summer when we moved out from the Fort and fronted the wilderness. On the night before we started I wrote a brief letter to Aunt Candace, telling her what I was about to do.

"If I never come back, auntie," I added, "tell the little girl down on the side of the hill that I tried to do for Kansas what her father did for the nation, that I gave up my life to establish peace. And tell her, too, if I really do fall out by the way, that I'll be lonely even in heaven till she comes."

But with the morning all my sentiment vanished and I was eager for the thing before me. Two hundred Indians we were told we should find and every man of us was accounted good for at least five redskins. At sunrise on the twenty-ninth day of August in the year of our Lord 1868, Colonel Forsyth's little company started on its expedition of defence for the frontier settlements, and for just vengeance on the Cheyennes of the plains and their allied forces from kindred bands. Fort Hays was the very outpost of occupation. To the north and west lay a silent, pathless country which the finger of the white man had not touched. We knew we were bidding good-bye to civilization as we marched out that morning, were turning our backs on safety and comfort and all that makes life fine. Before us was the wilderness, with its perils and lonely desolation and mysteries.

But the wilderness has a siren's power over the Anglo-Saxon always. The strange savage land was splendid even in its silent level sweep of distance. When I was a boy I used to think that the big cottonwood beyond the West Draw was the limit of human exploration. It marked the world's western bound for me. Here were miles on miles of landscape opening wide to more stretches of leagues and leagues of far boundless plains, and all of it was weird, unconquerable, and very beautiful. The earth was spread with a carpet of gold splashed with bronze and scarlet and purple, with here and there a shimmer of green showing through the yellow, or streaking the shallow waterways. Far and wide there was not a tree to give the eye a point of attachment; neither orchard nor forest nor lonely sentinel to show that Nature had ever cherished the land for the white man's home and joy. The buffalo herd paid little heed to our brave company marching out like the true knights of old to defend the weak and oppressed. The gray wolf skulked along in the shadows of the draws behind us and at night the coyotes barked harshly at the invading band. But there was no mark of civilized habitation, no friendly hint that aught but the unknown and unconquerable lay before us.

I was learning quickly in those days of marching and nights of dreamless sleep under sweet, health-giving skies. After all, Harvard had done me much service; for the university training, no less than the boyhood on the Territorial border, had its part in giving me mental discipline for my duties now. Camp life came easy to me, and I fell into the soldier way of thinking, more readily than I had ever hoped to do.

On we went, northward to the Saline Valley, and beyond that to where the Solomon River winds down through a region of summer splendor, its rippling waves of sod a-tint with all the green and gold and russet and crimson hues of the virgin Plains, while overhead there arched the sky, tenderly blue in the morning, brazen at noonday, and pink and gray and purple in the evening lights. But we found no Indians, though we followed trail on trail. Beyond the Solomon we turned to the southwest, and the early days of September found us resting briefly at Fort Wallace, near the western bound of Kansas.

The real power that subdues the wilderness may be, nay, is, the spirit of the missionary, but the mark of military occupation is a tremendous convincer of truth. The shotgun and the Bible worked side by side in the conquest of the Plains; the smell of powder was often the only incense on the altars, and human blood was sprinkled for holy water. Fort Wallace, with the Stars and Stripes afloat, looked good to me after that ten days in the trackless solitude. And yet I was disappointed, for I thought our quest might end here with nothing to show in results for our pains. I did not know Forsyth and his band, as the next twenty days were to show me.

While we were resting at the Fort, scouts brought in the news of an Indian attack on a wagon train a score of miles eastward, and soon we were away again, this time equipped for the thing in hand, splendidly equipped, it seemed, for what we should really need to do. We were all well mounted, and each of us carried a blanket, saddle, bridle, picket-pin, and lariat; each had a haversack, a canteen, a butcher knife, a tin plate and tin cup. We had Spencer rifles and Colt's revolvers, with rounds of ammunition for both; and each of us carried seven days' rations. Besides this equipment the pack mules bore a large additional store of ammunition, together with rations and hospital supplies.

Northward again we pushed, alert for every faint sign of Indians. Those keen-eyed scouts were a marvel to me. They read the ground, the streams, the sagebrush, and the horizon as a primer set in fat black type. Leader of them, and official guide, was a man named Grover, who could tell by the hither side of a bluff what was on the farther side. But for five days the trails were illusive, finally vanishing in a spread of faint footprints radiating from a centre telling us that the Indians had broken up and scattered over separate ways. And so again we seemed to have been deceived in this unmapped land.

We were beyond the Republican River now, in the very northwest corner of Kansas, and the thought of turning back toward civilization had come to some of us, when a fresh trail told us we were still in the Indian country. We headed our horses toward the southwest, following the trail that hugged the Republican River. It did not fade out as the others had done, but grew plainer each mile.

The whole command was in a fever of expectancy. Forsyth's face was bright and eager with the anticipation of coming danger. Lieutenant Beecher was serious and silent, while the guide, Sharp Grover, was alert and cool. A tenseness had made itself felt throughout the command. I learned early not to ask questions; but as we came one noon upon a broad path leading up to the main trail where from this union we looked out on a wide, well-beaten way, I turned an inquiring face toward Morton, who rode beside me. There was strength in the answer his eyes gave mine. He had what the latter-day students of psychology call "poise," a grip on himself. It is by such men that the Plains have been won from a desert demesne to fruitful fields.

"I gave you warning it was no boy's play," he said simply.

I nodded and we rode on in silence. We pressed westward to where the smaller streams combine to form the Republican River. The trail here led us up the Arickaree fork, a shallow stream at this season of the year, full of sand-bars and gravelly shoals. Here the waters lost themselves for many feet in the underflow so common in this land of aimless, uncertain waterways.

On the afternoon of the sixteenth of September the trail led to a little gorge through which the Arickaree passes in a narrower channel. Beyond it the valley opened out with a level space reaching back to low hills on the north, while an undulating plain spread away to the south. The grass was tall and rank in this open space, which closed in with a bluff a mile or more to the west. Although it was hardly beyond midafternoon, Colonel Forsyth halted the company, and we went into camp. We were almost out of rations. Our horses having no food now, were carefully picketed out to graze at the end of their lariats. A general sense of impending calamity pervaded the camp. But the Plainsmen were accustomed to this kind of thing, and the Civil War soldiers had learned their lesson at Gettysburg and Chickamauga and Malvern Hill. I was the green hand, and I dare say my anxiety was greater than that of any other one there. But I had a double reason for apprehension.

As we had come through the little gorge that afternoon, I was riding some distance in the rear of the line. Beside me was a boy of eighteen, fair-haired, blue-eyed, his cheek as smooth as a girl's. His trim little figure, clad in picturesque buckskin, suggested a pretty actor in a Wild West play. And yet this boy, Jack Stillwell, was a scout of the uttermost daring and shrewdness. He always made me think of Bud Anderson. I even missed Bud's lisp when he spoke.

"Stillwell," I said in a low tone as we rode along, "tell me what you think of this. Aren't we pretty near the edge? I've felt for three days as if an Indian was riding beside me and I couldn't see him. It's not the mirage, and I'm not locoed. Did you ever feel as if you were near somebody you couldn't see?"

The boy turned his fair, smooth face toward mine and looked steadily at me.

"You mustn't get to seein' things," he murmured. "This country turns itself upside down for the fellow who does that. And in Heaven's name we need every man in his right senses now. What do I think? Good God, Baronet! I think we are marching straight into Hell's jaws. Sandy knows it"—"Sandy" was Forsyth's military pet name—"but he's too set to back out now. Besides, who wants to back out? or what's to be gained by it? We've come out here to fight the Cheyennes. We're gettin' to 'em, that's all. Only there's too damned many of 'em. This trail's like the old Santa Fé Trail, wide enough for a Mormon church to move along. And as to feelin' like somebody's near you, it's more 'n feelin'; it's fact. There's Injuns on track of this squad every minute. I'm only eighteen, but I've been in the saddle six years, and I know a few things without seein' 'em. Sharp Grover knows, too. He's the doggondest scout that ever rode over these Plains. He knows the trap we've got into. But he's like Sandy, come out to fight, and he'll do it. All we've got to do is to keep our opinions to ourselves. They don't want to be told nothin'; they know."

The remainder of the company was almost out of sight as we rounded the shoulder of the gorge. The afternoon sunlight dazzled me. Lifting my eyes just then I saw a strange vision. What I had thought to be only a piece of brown rock, above and beyond me, slowly rose to almost a sitting posture before my blinking eyes, and a man, no, two men, seemed to gaze a moment after our retreating line of blue-coats. It was but an instant, yet I caught sight of two faces. Stillwell was glancing backward at that moment and did not see anything. At the sound of our horses' feet on the gravel the two figures changed to brown rock again. In the moment my eye had caught the merest glint of sunlight on an artillery bugle, a gleam, and nothing more.

"What's the matter, Baronet? You're white as a ghost. Are you scared or sick?" Stillwell spoke in a low voice. We didn't do any shouting in those trying days.

"Neither one," I answered, but I had cause to wonder whether I was insane or not. As I live, and hope to keep my record clear, the two figures I had seen were not strangers to me. The smaller of the two had the narrow forehead and secretive countenance of the Reverend Mr. Dodd. In his hand was an artillery bugle. Beyond him, though he wore an Indian dress, rose the broad shoulders and square, black-shadowed forehead of Father Le Claire.

"It is the hallucination of this mirage-girt land," I told myself. "The Plains life is affecting my vision, and then the sun has blinded me. I'm not delirious, but this marching is telling on me. Oh, it is at a fearful price that the frontier creeps westward, that homes are planted, and peace, blood-stained, abides with them."

So I meditated as I watched the sun go down on that September night on the far Colorado Plains by the grassy slopes and yellow sands and thin, slow-moving currents of the Arickaree.

CHAPTER XVII

IN THE VALLEY OF THE ARICKAREE

A blush as of roses
Where rose never grew!
Great drops on the bunch grass.
But not of the dew!
A taint in the sweet air
For wild bees to shun!
A stain that shall never
Bleach out in the sun!

—WHITTIER.

Stillwell was right. Sharp Grover knew, as well as the boy knew, that we were trapped, that before us now were the awful chances of unequal Plains warfare. A mere handful of us had been hurrying after a host, whose numbers the broad beaten road told us was legion. There was no mirth in that little camp that night in mid-September, and I thought of other things besides my strange vision at the gorge. The camp was the only mark of human habitation in all that wide and utterly desolate land. For days we had noted even the absence of all game—strong evidence that a host had driven it away before us. Everywhere, save about that winking camp fire was silence. The sunset was gorgeous, in the barbaric sublimity of its seas of gold and crimson atmosphere. And then came the rich coloring of that purple twilight. It is no wonder they call it regal. Out on the Plains that night it swathed the landscape with a rarer hue than I have ever seen anywhere else, although I have watched the sun go down into the Atlantic off the Rockport coast, and have seen it lost over the edge of the West Prairie beyond the big cottonwood above the farther draw. As I watched the evening shadows deepen, I remembered what Morton had told me in the little cabin back in the Saline country, "Who ever fights the Indians must make his will before the battle begins." Now that I was face to face with the real issue, life became very sweet to me. How grand over war and hate were the thoughts of peace and love! And yet every foot of this beautiful land must be bought with a price. No matter where the great blame lies, nor who sinned first in getting formal possession, the real occupation is won only by sacrifice. And I was confronted with my part of the offering. Strange thoughts come in such an hour. Sitting there in the twilight, I asked myself why I should want to live; and I realized how strong, after all, was the tie that bound me to Springvale; how under all my pretence of beginning a new life I had not really faced the future separated from the girl I loved. And then I remembered that it would mean nothing serious to her how this campaign ended. Oh! I was in the crucible now. I must prove myself the thing I always meant to be. God knew the heroic spirit I needed that lonely September night. As I sat looking out toward the west the years of my boyhood came back to me, and then I remembered O'mie's words when he told me of his struggle:

"It was to save a woman, Phil. He could only kill me. He wouldn't have been that good to her. You'd have done the same to save any woman, aven a stranger to you. Wait an' see."

I thought of the two women in the Solomon Valley, whom Black Kettle's band had dragged from their homes, tortured inhumanly, and at last staked out hand and foot on the prairie to die in agony under pitiless skies.

"When the day av choosin' comes," O'mie said, "we can't do no more 'n to take our places. We all do it. When you git face to face with a thing like that, somehow the everlastin' arms Dr. Hemingway preaches about is strong underneath you."

Oh, blessed O'mie! Had he told me that to give me courage in my hour of shrinking? Wherever he was to-night I knew his heart was with me, who so little deserved the love he gave me. At last I rolled myself snugly in my blanket, for the September evenings are cold in Colorado. The simple prayers of childhood came back to me, and I repeated the "Now I lay me" I used to say every night at Aunt Candace's knee. It had a wonderful meaning to me to-night. And once more I thought of O'mie and how his thin hand gripped mine when he said: "Most av all, don't niver forgit it, Phil, when the thing comes to you, aven in your strength. Most av all, above all sufferin', and natural longin' to live, there comes the reality av them words

Aunt Candace taught us: 'Though I walk through the valley av the shadow av death, I will fear no evil.'"

"It may be that's the Arickaree Valley for me," I said to myself. "If it is, I will fear no evil." And I stretched out on the brown grasses and fell asleep.

About midnight I wakened suddenly. A light was gleaming near. Some one stood beside me, and presently I saw Colonel Forsyth looking down into my face with kindly eyes. I raised myself on my elbow and watched him passing among the slumbering soldiers. Even now I can see Jack Stillwell's fair girl-face with the dim light on it as he slept beside me. What a picture that face would make if my pen were an artist's brush! At three in the morning I wakened again. It was very dark, but I knew some one was near me, and I judged instinctively it was Forsyth. It was sixty hours before I slept again.

For five days every movement of ours had been watched by Indian scouts. Night and day they had hung on our borders, just out of sight, waiting their time to strike. Had we made a full march on that sixteenth day of September, instead of halting to rest and graze our horses, we should have gone, as Stillwell predicted, straight into Hell's jaws. As it was, Hell rose up and crept stealthily toward us. For while our little band slept, and while our commander passed restlessly among us on that night, the redskins moved upon our borders.

Morning was gray in the east and the little valley was full of shadows, when suddenly the sentinel's cry of "Indians! Indians!" aroused the sleeping force. The shouts of our guards, the clatter of ponies' hoofs, the rattling of dry skins, the swinging of blankets, the fierce yells of the invading foe made a scene of tragic confusion, as a horde of redskins swept down upon us like a whirlwind. In this mad attempt to stampede our stock nothing but discipline saved us. A few of the mules and horses not properly picketed, broke loose and galloped off before the attacking force, the remaining animals held as the Indians fled away before the sharp fire of our soldiers.

"Well, we licked them, anyhow," I said to myself exultantly as we obeyed the instant orders to get into the saddle.

The first crimson line of morning was streaking the east and I lifted my face triumphantly to the new day. Sharp Grover stood just before me; his hand was on Forsyth's shoulder.

Suddenly he uttered a low exclamation. "Oh, heavens! General, look at the Indians."

This was no vision of brown rock and sun-blinded eyes. From every direction, over the bluff, out from the tall grass, across the slope on the south, came Indians, hundreds on hundreds. They seemed to spring from the sod like Roderick Dhu's Highland Scots, and people every curve and hollow. Swift as the wind, savage as hate, cruel as hell, they bore down upon us from every way the wind blows. The thrill of that moment is in my blood as I write this. It was then I first understood the tie between the commanding officer and his men. It is easy to laud the file of privates on dress parade, but the man who directs the file in the hour of battle is the real power. In that instant of peril I turned to Forsyth with that trust that the little child gives to its father. How cool he was, and yet how lightning-swift in thought and action.

In all the valley there was no refuge where we might hide, nor height on which we might defend ourselves. The Indians had counted on our making a dash to the eastward, and had left that way open for us. They had not reckoned well on Colonel Forsyth. He knew intuitively that the gorge at the lower end of the valley was even then filled with a hidden foe, and not a man of us would ever have passed through it alive. To advance meant death, and there was no retreat possible. Out in the middle of the Arickaree, hardly three feet above the river-bed, lay a little island. In the years to be when the history of the West shall be fully told, it may become one of the Nation's shrines. But now in this dim morning light it showed only an insignificant elevation. Its sandy surface was grown over with tall sage grasses and weeds.

A few wild plums and alder bushes, a clump of low willow shrubs, and a small cottonwood tree completed its vegetation.

"How about that island, Grover?" I heard Forsyth ask.

"It's all we can do," the scout answered; and the command: "Reach the island! hitch the horses!" rang through the camp.

It takes long to tell it, this dash for the island. The execution of the order was like the passing of a hurricane. Horses, mules, men, all dashed toward the place, but in the rush the hospital supplies and rations were lost. The Indians had not counted on the island, and they raged in fury at their oversight. There were a thousand savage warriors attacking half a hundred soldiers, and they had gloated over the fifty scalps to be taken in the little gorge to the east. The break in their plans confused them but momentarily, however.

On the island we tied our horses in the bushes and quickly formed a circle. The soil was all soft sand. We cut the thin sod with our butcher knives and began throwing up a low defence, working like fiends with our hands and elbows and toes, scooping out the sand with our tin plates, making the commencement of shallow pits. We were stationed in couples, and I was beside Morton when the onslaught came. Up from the undulating south, and down over the north bluff swept the furious horde. On they came with terrific speed, their blood-curdling yells of hate mingling with the wild songs, and cries and taunts of hundreds of squaws and children that crowded the heights out of range of danger, watching the charge and urging their braves to battle. Over the slopes to the very banks of the creek, into the sandy bed of the stream, and up to the island they hurled their forces, while bullets crashed murderously, and arrows whizzed with deadly swiftness into our little sand-built defence.

In the midst of the charge, twice above the din, I caught the clear notes of an artillery bugle. It was dim daylight now. Rifle-smoke and clouds of dust and gray mist shot through with flashes of powder, and the awful rage, as if all the demons of Hell were crying vengeance, are all in that picture burned into my memory with a white-hot brand. And above all these there come back to me the faces of that little band of resolute men biding the moment when the command to charge should be given. Such determination and such splendid heroism, not twice in a lifetime is it vouchsafed to many to behold.

We held our fire until the enemy was almost upon us. At the right instant our rifles poured out a perfect billow of death. Painted bodies reeled and fell; horses sank down, or rushed mad with pain, upon their fallen riders; shrieks of agony mingled with the unearthly yells; while above all this, the steady roar of our guns—not a wasted bullet in all the line—carried death waves out from the island thicket. To me that first defence of ours was more tragic than anything in the days and nights that followed it. The first hour's struggle seasoned me for the siege.

The fury of the Indian warriors and of the watching squaws is indescribable. The foe deflected to left and right, vainly seeking to carry their dead from the field with them. The effort cost many Indian lives. The long grass on either side of the stream was full of sharpshooters. The morning was bright now, and we durst not lift our heads above our low entrenchment. Our position was in the centre of a space open to attack from every arc of the circle. Caution counted more than courage here. Whoever stood upright was offering his life to his enemy. Our horses suffered first. By the end of an hour every one of them was dead. My own mount, a fine sorrel cavalry horse, given to me at Fort Hays, was the last sacrifice. He was standing near me in the brown bushes. I could see his superb head and chest as, with nostrils wide, and flashing eyes, he saw and felt the battle charge. Subconsciously I felt that so long as he was unhurt I had a sure way of escape. Subconsciously, too, I blessed the day that Bud Anderson taught O'mie and me to drop on the side of Tell Mapleson's pony and ride like a Plains Indian. But even as I looked up over my little sand ridge a bullet crashed into his broad chest. He plunged forward toward us, breaking his tether. He staggered to his knees, rose again with a lunge, and turning half way round reared his fore feet in agony and seemed about to fall into our pit. At that instant I heard a laugh just beyond the bushes, and a voice, not Indian, but English, cried exultingly, "There goes the last damned horse, anyhow."

It was the same voice that I had heard up on "Rockport" one evening, promising Marjie in pleading tones to be a "good Indian." The same hard, cold voice I had heard in the same place saying to me, as a promise before high heaven: "I will go. But I shall see you there. When we meet again my hand will be on your throat and—I don't care whose son you are."

Well, we were about to meet. The wounded animal was just above our pit. Morton rose up with lifted carbine to drive him back when from the same gun that had done for my horse came a bullet full into the man's face. It ploughed through his left eye and lodged in the bones beyond it. He uttered no cry, but dropped into the pit beside me, his blood, streaming from the wound, splashed hot on my forehead as he fell. I was stunned by his disaster, but he never faltered. Taking his handkerchief from his pocket, he bound it tightly about his head and set his rifle ready for the next charge. After that, nothing counted with me. I no longer shrank in dread of what might happen. All fear of life, or death, of pain, or Indians, or fiends from Hades fell away from me, and never again did my hand tremble, nor my heart-beat quicken in the presence of peril. By the warm blood of the brave man beside me I was baptized a soldier.

The force drew back from this first attempt to take the island, but the fire of the hidden enemy did not cease. In this brief breathing spell we dug deeper into our pits, making our defences stronger where we lay. Disaster was heavy upon us. The sun beat down pitilessly on the hot, dry earth where we burrowed. Out in the open the Indians were crawling like serpents through the tall grasses toward our poor house of sand, hoping to fall upon us unseen. They had every advantage, for we did not dare to let our bodies be exposed above the low breastworks, and we could not see their advance. Nearly one-half of our own men were dead or wounded. Each man counted for so much on that battle-girt island that day. Our surgeon had been struck in the first round and through all the rest of his living hours he was in a delirium. Forsyth himself, grievously wounded in both lower limbs, could only drag his body about by his arms. A rifle ball had grazed his scalp and fractured his skull. The pain from this wound was almost unbearable. But he did not loosen his grip on the military power delegated to him. From a hastily scooped-out pit where we laid him he directed the whole battle.

And now we girded on our armor for the supreme ordeal. The unbounded wrath of the Indians at their unlooked-for failure in their first attack told us what to expect. Our own guns were ready for instant use. The arms of our dead and wounded comrades were placed beside our own. No time was there in those awful hours to listen to the groans of the stricken ones nor to close the dying eyes. Not a soul of us in those sand-pits had any thought that we should ever see another sunset. All we could do was to put the highest price upon our lives. It was ten o'clock in the forenoon. The firing about the island had almost ceased, and the silence was more ominous than the noise of bullets. Over on the bluff the powers were gathering. The sunlight glinted on their arms and lighted up their fantastic equipments of war. They formed in battle array. And then there came a sight the Plains will never see again, a sight that history records not once in a century. There were hundreds of these warriors, the flower of the fierce Cheyenne tribe, drawn up in military order, mounted on great horses, riding bareback, their rifles held aloft in their right hands, the left hand grasping the flowing mane, their naked bodies hideously adorned with paint, their long scalp-locks braided and trimmed with plumes and quills. They were the very acme of grandeur in a warfare as splendid as it was barbaric. And I, who live to write these lines, account myself most fortunate that I saw it all.

They were arrayed in battle lines riding sixty abreast. It was a man of genius who formed that military movement that day. On they came in orderly ranks but with terrific speed, straight down the slope, across the level, and on to the island, as if by their huge weight and terrible momentum they would trample it into the very level dust of the earth, that the winds of heaven might scatter it broadcast on the Arickaree waters. Till the day of my death I shall hear the hoof-beats of that cavalry charge.

Down through the centuries the great commanders have left us their stories of prowess, and we have kept their portraits to adorn our stately halls of fame; and in our historic shrines we have preserved their records—Cyrus, Alexander, Leonidas at Thermopylæ, Hannibal crossing the Alps, Charles Martel at Tours, the white-plumed Henry of Navarre leading his soldiers in the battle of Ivry, Cromwell with his Ironsides—godly men who chanted hymns while they fought—Napoleon's grand finale at Waterloo, with his three thousand steeds mingling the sound of hoof-beats with the clang of cuirasses and the clash of sabres; Pickett's grand sweep at Gettysburg, and Hooker's charge up Lookout Mountain.

But who shall paint the picture of that terrific struggle on that September day, or write the tale of that swirl of Indian warriors, a thousand strong, as they swept down in their barbaric fury upon the handful of Anglo-Saxon soldiers crouching there in the sand-pits awaiting their onslaught? It was the old, old story retold that day on the Colorado plains by the sunlit waters of the Arickaree—the white man's civilization against the untamed life of the wilderness. And for that struggle there is only one outcome.

Before the advancing foe, in front of the very centre of the foremost line, was their leader, Roman Nose, chief warrior of the Cheyennes. He was riding a great, clean-limbed horse, his left hand grasping its mane. His right hand was raised aloft, directing his forces. If ever the moulds of Nature turned out physical perfection, she realized her ideal in that superb Cheyenne. He stood six feet and three inches in his moccasins. He was built like a giant, with a muscular symmetry that was artistically beautiful. About his naked body was a broad, blood-red silken sash, the ends of which floated in the wind. His war bonnet, with its two short, curved, black buffalo horns, above his brow, was a magnificent thing crowning his head and falling behind him in a sweep of heron plumes and eagle feathers. The Plains never saw a grander warrior, nor did savage tribe ever claim a more daring and able commander. He was by inherent right a ruler. In him was the culmination of the intelligent prowess and courage and physical supremacy of the free life of the broad, unfettered West.

On they rushed that mount of eager warriors. The hills behind them swarmed with squaws and children. Their shrieks of grief and anger and encouragement filled the air. They were beholding the action that down to the last of the tribe would be recounted a victory to be chanted in all future years over the graves of their dead, and sung in heroic strain when their braves went forth to conquest. And so, with all the power of heart and voice, they cried out from the low hill-tops. Just at the brink of the stream the leader, Roman Nose, turned his face a moment toward the watching women. Lifting high his right hand he waved them a proud salute. The gesture was so regal, and the man himself so like a king of men, that I involuntarily held my breath. But the set blood-stained face of the wounded man beside me told what that kingship meant.

As he faced the island again, Roman Nose rose up to his full height and shook his clenched fist toward our entrenchment. Then suddenly lifting his eyes toward the blue sky above him, he uttered a war-cry, unlike any other cry I have ever heard. It was so strong, so vehement, so full of pleading, and yet so dominant in its certainty, as if he were invoking the gods of all the tribes for their aid, yet sure in his defiant soul that victory was his by right of might. The unearthly, blood-chilling cry was caught up by all his command and reëchoed by the watchers on the hills till, away and away over the undulating plains it rolled, dying out in weird cadences in the far-off spaces of the haze-wreathed horizon.

Then came the dash for our island entrenchment. As the Indians entered the stream I caught the sound of a bugle note, the same I had heard twice before. On the edge of the island through a rift in the dust-cloud, I saw in the front line on the end nearest me a horse a little smaller than the others, making its rider a trifle lower than his comrades. And then I caught one glimpse of the rider's face. It was the man whose bullet had wounded Morton—Jean Pahusca.

We held back our fire again, as in the first attack, until the foe was almost upon us. With Forsyth's order, "Now! now!" our part of the drama began. I marvel yet at the power of that return charge. Steady, constant, true to the last shot, we swept back each advancing wave of warriors, maddened now to maniac fury. In the very moment of victory, defeat was breaking the forces, mowing down the strongest, and spreading confusion everywhere. A thousand wild beasts on the hills, frenzied with torture, could not have raged more than those frantic Indian women and shrieking children watching the fray.

With us it was the last stand. We wasted no strength in this grim crisis; each turn of the hand counted. While fearless as though he bore a charmed life, the gallant savage commander dared death at our hands, heeding no more our rain of rifle balls than if they had been the drops of a summer shower. Right on he pressed regardless of his fallen braves. How grandly he towered above them in his great strength and superb physique, a very prince of prowess, the type of leader in a land where the battle is always to the strong. And no shot of our men was able to reach him until our finish seemed certain, and the time-limit closing in. But down in the thick weeds, under a flimsy rampart of soft sand, crouched a slender fair-haired boy. Trim and pink-cheeked as a girl, young Stillwell was matching his cool nerve and steady marksmanship against the exultant dominance of a savage giant. It was David and Goliath played out in the Plains warfare of the Western continent. At the crucial moment the scout's bullet went home with unerring aim, and the one man whose power counted as a thousand warriors among his own people received his mortal wound. Backward he reeled, and dead, or dying, he was taken from the field. Like one of the anointed he was mourned by his people, for he had never known fear, and on his banners victory had constantly perched.

In the confusion over the loss of their leader the Indians again divided about the island and fell back out of range of our fire. As the tide of battle ebbed out, Colonel Forsyth, helpless in his sand pit, watching the attack, called to his guide.

"Can they do better than that, Grover?"

"I've been on the Plains since I was a boy and I never saw such a charge as that. I think they have done their level best," the scout replied.

"All right, then, we are good for them." How cheery the Colonel's voice was! It thrilled my spirits with its courage. And we needed courage, for just then, Lieutenant Beecher was stretching himself wearily before his superior officer, saying briefly:

"I have my death-wound; good-night." And like a brave man who had done his best he pillowed his head face downward on his arms, and spoke not any more on earth forever.

It has all been told in history how that day went by. When evening fell upon that eternity-long time, our outlook was full of gloom. Hardly one-half of our company was able to bear arms. Our horses had all been killed, our supplies and hospital appliances were lost. Our wounds were undressed; our surgeon was slowly dying; our commander was helpless, and his lieutenant dead. We had been all day without food or water. We were prisoners on this island, and every man of us had half a hundred jailers, each one a fiend in the high art of human torture.

I learned here how brave and resourceful men can be in the face of disaster. One of our number had already begun to dig a shallow well. It was a muddy drink, but, God be praised, it was water! Our supper was a steak cut from a slaughtered horse, but we did not complain. We gathered round our wounded commander and did what we could for each other, and no man thought of himself first. Our dead were laid in shallow graves, without a prayer. There was no time here for the ceremonies of peace; and some of the men, before they went out into the Unknown that night, sent their last messages to their friends, if we should ever be able to reach home again.

At nightfall came a gentle shower. We held out our hands to it, and bathed our fevered faces. It was very dark and we must make the most of every hour. The Indians do not fight by night, but the morrow might bring its tale of battles. So we digged, and shaped our stronghold, and told over our resources, and planned our defences, and all the time hunger and suffering and sorrow and peril stalked about with us. All night the Indians gathered up their dead, and all night they chanted their weird, blood-chilling death-songs, while the lamentations of the squaws through that dreadful night filled all the long hours with hideous mourning unlike any other earthly discord. But the darkness folded us in, and the blessed rain fell softly on all alike, on skilful guide, and busy soldier, on the wounded lying helpless in their beds of sand, on the newly made graves of those for whom life's fitful fever was ended. And above all, the loving Father, whose arm is never shortened that He cannot save, gave His angels charge over us to keep us in all our ways.

CHAPTER XVIII

THE SUNLIGHT ON OLD GLORY

The little green tent is made of sod,
And it is not long, and it is not broad,
But the soldiers have lots of room.
And the sod is a part of the land they saved,
When the flag of the enemy darkly waved,
A symbol of dole and gloom.

—WALT MASON.

"Baronet, we must have that spade we left over there this morning. Are you the man to get it?" Sharp Grover said to me just after dusk. "We've got to have water or die, and Burke here can't dig a well with his toe nails, though he can come about as near to it as anybody." Burke was an industrious Irishman who had already found water for us. "And then we must take care of these." He motioned toward a still form at my feet, and his tone was reverent.

"Over there" was the camp ground of the night before. It had been trampled by hundreds of feet. Our camp was small, and finding the spade by day might be easy enough. To grope in the dark and danger was another matter. Twenty-four hours before, I would not have dared to try. Nothing counted with me now. I had just risen from the stiffening body of a comrade whom I had been trying to compose for his final rest. I had no more sentiment for myself than I had for him. My time might come at any moment.

"Yes, sir, I'll go," I answered the scout, and I felt of my revolvers; my own and the one I had taken from the man who lay at my feet.

"Well, take no foolish chances. Come back if the way is blocked, but get the spade if you can. Take your time. You'd better wait an hour than be dead in a minute," and he turned to the next work before him.

He was guide, commander, and lieutenant all in one, and his duties were many. I slipped out in the danger-filled shadows toward our camping place of the night before. Every step was full of peril. The Indians had no notion of letting us slip through their fingers in the dark. Added to their day's defeats, we had slain their greatest warrior, and they would have perished by inches rather than let us escape now. So our island was guarded on every side. The black shadowed Plains were crossed and re-crossed by the braves silently gathering in their lost ones for burial. My scalp would have been a joy to them who had as yet no human trophy to gloat over. Surely a spade was never so valuable before. My sense of direction is fair and to my great relief I found that precious implement marvellously soon, but the creek lay between me and the island. Just at its bank I was compelled to drop into a clump of weeds as three forms crept near me and straightened themselves up in the gloom. They were speaking in low tones, and as they stood upright I caught their words.

"You made that bugle talk, anyhow, Dodd."

So Dodd was the renegade whom I had heard three times in the conflict. My vision at the gorge was not the insanity of the Plains, after all. I was listening ravenously now. The man who had spoken stood nearest me. There was a certain softness of accent and a familiar tone in his speech. As he turned toward the other two, even in the dim light, the outline of his form and the set of his uncovered head I knew.

"That's Le Claire, as true as heaven, all but the voice," I said to myself. "But I'll never believe that metallic ring is the priest's. It is Le Claire turned renegade, too, or it's a man on a pattern so like him, they couldn't tell themselves apart."

I recalled all the gentleness and manliness of the Father. Never an act of his was cruel, or selfish, or deceptive. True to his principles, he had warned us again and again not to trust Jean. And yet he had always seemed to protect the boy, always knew his comings and goings, and the two had grown yearly to resemble each other more and more in face and form and gesture. Was Le Claire a villain in holy guise?

I did not meditate long, for the third man spoke. Oh, the "good Indian"! Never could he conceal his voice from me.

"Now, what I want you to do is to tell them all which one he is. I've just been clear around their hole in the sand. I could have hit my choice of the lot. But he wasn't there."

No, I had just stepped out after the spade.

"If he had been, I'd have shot him right then, no matter what come next. But I don't want him shot. He's mine. Now tell every brave to leave him to me, the big one, nearly as big as Roman Nose, whiter than the others, because he's not been out here long. But he's no coward. The one with thick dark curly hair; it would make a beautiful scalp. But I want him."

"What will you do with him?" the man nearest to me queried.

"Round the bend below the gorge the Arickaree runs over a little strip of gravel with a ripple that sounds just like the Neosho above the Deep Hole. I'll stake him out there where he can hear it and think of home until he dies. And before I leave him I've got a letter to read to him. It'll help to keep Springvale in his mind if the water fails. I've promised him what to expect when he comes into my country."

"Do it," the smallest of the three spoke up. "Do it. It'll pay him for setting Bud Anderson on me and nearly killing me in the alley back of the courthouse the night we were going to burn up Springvale. I was making for the courthouse to get the papers to burn sure. I'd got the key and could have got them easy—and there's some needed burning specially—when that lispin' tow-head caught my arm and gave my head such a cut that I'll always carry the scar, and twisted my wrist so I've never been able to lift anything heavier than an artillery bugle since. Nobody ever knew it back there but Mapleson and Conlow and Judson. Funny nobody ever guessed Judson's part in that thing except his wife, and she kept it to herself and broke her heart and died. Everybody else said he was water-bound away from home. He wasn't twenty feet from his own house when the Whately girl come out. He was helpin' Jean then. Thought her mother'd be killed, and Whately'd never get home alive—as he didn't—and he'd get the whole store; greediest man on earth for money. He's got the store anyhow, now, and he's going to marry the girl he was helpin' Jean to take out of his way. That store never would have been burnt that night. I wish Jean had got her, though. Then I'd turned things against Tell Mapleson and run him out of town instead of his driving me from Springvale. Tell played a double game damned well. I'm outlawed and he's gettin' richer every day at home."

So spoke the Rev. Mr. Dodd, pastor of the Methodist Church South. It may be I needed the discipline of that day's fighting to hold me motionless and silent in the clump of grass beside these three men.

"Well, let's get up there and watch the fool women cry for their men." It was none other than Father Le Claire's form before me, but this man's voice was never that soft French tone of the good man's—low and musical, matching his kindly eyes and sweet smile. As the three slipped away I did the only foolish act of mine in the whole campaign: I rose from my hiding place, shouldered that spade, and stalked straight down the bank, across the creek, and up to our works in the centre of the island as upright and free as if I were walking up Cliff Street to Judge Baronet's front door. Jean's words had put into me just what I needed—not acceptance of the inevitable, but a power of resistance, the indomitable spirit that overcomes.

History is stranger than fiction, and the story of the Kansas frontier is more tragical than all the Wild West yellow-backed novels ever turned off the press. To me this campaign of the Arickaree has always read like a piece of bloody drama, so terrible in its reality, it puts the imagination out of service.

We had only one chance for deliverance, we must get the tidings of our dreadful plight to Fort Wallace, a hundred miles away. Jack Stillwell and another brave scout were chosen for the dangerous task. At midnight they left us, moving cautiously away into the black blank space toward the southwest, and making a wide detour from their real line of direction. The Indians were on the alert, and a man must walk as noiselessly as a panther to slip between their guards.

The scouts wore blankets to resemble the Indians more closely in the shadows of the night. They made moccasins out of boot tops, that their footprints might tell no story. In sandy places they even walked backward that they should leave no tell-tale trail out of the valley.

Dawn found them only three miles away from their starting place. A hollow bank overhung with long, dry grasses, and fronted with rank sunflowers, gave them a place of concealment through the daylight hours. Again on the second night they hurried cautiously forward. The second morning they were near an Indian village. Their only retreat was in the tall growth of a low, marshy place. Here they crouched through another long day. The unsuspecting squaws, hunting fuel, tramped the grasses dangerously near to them, but a merciful Providence guarded their hiding-place.

On the third night they pushed forward more boldly, hoping that the next day they need not waste the precious hours in concealment. In the early morning they saw coming down over the prairie the first guard of a Cheyenne village moving southward across their path. The Plains were flat and covertless. No tall grass, nor friendly bank, nor bush, nor hollow of ground was there to cover them from their enemies. But out before them lay the rotting carcass of an old buffalo. Its hide still hung about its bones. And inside the narrow shelter of this carcass the two concealed themselves while a whole village passed near them trailing off toward the south.

Insufficient food, lack of sleep, and poisonous water from the buffalo wallows brought nausea and weakness to the faithful men making their way across the hostile land to bring help to us in our dire extremity. It is all recorded in history how these two men fared in that hazardous undertaking. No hundred miles of sandy plain were ever more fraught with peril; and yet these two pressed on with that fearless and indomitable courage that has characterized the Saxon people on every field of conquest.

Meanwhile day crept over the eastern horizon, and the cold chill of the shadows gave place to the burning glare of the September sun. Hot and withering it beat down upon us and upon the unburied dead that lay all about us. The braves that had fallen in the strife strewed the island's edges. Their blood lay dark on the sandy shoals of the stream and stained to duller brown the trampled grasses. Daylight brought the renewal of the treacherous sharpshooting. The enemy closed in about us and from their points of vantage their deadly arrows and bullets were hurled upon our low wall of defence. And so the unequal struggle continued. Ours was henceforth an ambush fight. The redskins did not attack us in open charge again, and we durst not go out to meet them. And so the thing became a game of endurance with us, a slow wearing away of ammunition and food, a growing fever from weakness and loss of blood, a festering of wounds, the ebbing out of strength and hope; while putrid mule meat and muddy water, the sickening stench from naked bloated bodies under the blazing heat of day, the long, long hours of watching for deliverance that came not, and the certainty of the fate awaiting us at last if rescue failed us—these things marked the hours and made them all alike. As to the Indians, the passing of Roman Nose had broken their fighting spirit; and now it was a mere matter of letting us run to the end of our tether and then—well, Jean had hinted what would happen.

On the third night two more scouts left us. It seemed an eternity since Stillwell and his comrade had started from the camp. We felt sure that they must have fallen by the way, and the second attempt was doubly hazardous. The two who volunteered were quiet men. They knew what the task implied, and they bent to it like men who can pay on demand the price of sacrifice. Their names were Donovan and Pliley, recorded in the military roster as private scouts, but the titles they bear in the memory of every man who sat in that grim council on that night, has a grander sound than the written records declare.

"Boys," Forsyth said, lifting himself on his elbow where he lay in his sand bed, "this is the last chance. If you can get to the fort and send us help we can hold out a while. But it must come quickly. You know what it means for you to try, and for us, if you succeed."

The two men nodded assent, then girding on their equipments, they gave us their last messages to be repeated if deliverance ever came to us and they were never heard of again. We were getting accustomed to this now, for Death stalked beside us every hour. They said a brief good-bye and slipped out from us into the dangerous dark on their chosen task. Then the chill of the night, with its uncertainty and gloom, with its ominous silences broken only by the howl of the gray wolves, who closed in about us and set up their hunger wails beyond the reach of our bullets; and the heat of the day with its peril of arrow and rifle-ball filled the long hours. Hunger was a terror now. Our meat was gone save a few decayed portions which we could barely swallow after we had sprinkled them over with gunpowder. For the stomach refused them even in starvation. Dreams of banquets tortured our short, troubled sleep, and the waking was a horror. A luckless little coyote wandered one day too near our fold. We ate his flesh and boiled his bones for soup. And one day a daring soldier slipped out from our sand pit in search of food—anything—to eat in place of that rotting horseflesh. In the bushes at the end of the island, he found a few wild plums. Oh, food for the gods was that portion of stewed plums carefully doled out to each of us.

Six days went by. I do not know on which one the Sabbath fell, for God has no holy day in the Plains warfare. Six days, and no aid had come from Fort Wallace. That our scouts had failed, and our fate was decreed, was now the settled conclusion in every mind.

On the evening of this sixth day our leader called us about him. How gray and drawn his face looked in the shadowy gray light, but his eyes were clear and his voice steady.

"Boys, we've got to the end of our rope, now. Over there," pointing to the low hills, "the Indian wolves are waiting for us. It's the hazard of war; that's all. But we needn't all be sacrificed. You, who aren't wounded, can't help us who are. You have nothing here to make our suffering less. To stay here means—you all know what. Now the men who can go must leave us to what's coming. I feel sure now that you can get through together somehow, for the tribes are scattering. It is only the remnant left over there to burn us out at last. There is no reason why you should stay here and die. Make your dash for escape together to-night, and save your lives if you can. And"—his voice was brave and full of cheer—"I believe you can."

Then a silence fell. There were two dozen of us gaunt, hungry men, haggard from lack of sleep and the fearful tax on mind and body that tested human endurance to the limit—two dozen, to whom escape was not impossible now, though every foot of the way was dangerous. Life is sweet, and hope is imperishable. We looked into one another's face grimly, for the crisis of a lifetime was upon us. Beside me lay Morton. The handkerchief he had bound about his head in the first hour of battle had not once been removed. There was no other handkerchief to take its place.

"Go, Baronet," he said to me. "Tell your father, if you see him again, that I remembered Whately and how he went down at Chattanooga."

His voice was low and firm and yet he knew what was awaiting him. Oh! men walked on red-hot ploughshares in the days of the winning of the West.

Sharp Grover was sitting beside Forsyth. In the silence of the council the guide turned his eyes toward each of us. Then, clenching his gaunt, knotted hands with a grip of steel, he said in a low, measured voice:

"It's no use asking us, General. We have fought together, and, by Heaven, we'll die together."

In the great crises of life the only joy is the joy of self-sacrifice. Every man of us breathed freer, and we were happier now than we had been at any time since the conflict began. And so another twenty-four hours, and still another twenty-four went by.

> The sun came up and the sun went down,
> And day and night were the same as one.

And any evil chance seemed better than this slow dragging out of misery-laden time.

"Nature meant me to defend the weak and helpless. The West needs me," I had said to my father. And now I had given it my best. A slow fever was creeping upon me, and weariness of body was greater than pain and hunger. Death would be a welcome thing now that hope seemed dead. I thought of O'mie, bound hand and foot in the Hermit's Cave, and like him, I wished that I might go quickly if I must go. For back of my stolid mental state was a frenzied desire to outwit Jean Pahusca, who was biding his time, and keeping a surer watch on our poor battle-wrecked, starving force than any other Indian in the horde that kept us imprisoned.

The sunrise of the twenty-fifth of September was a dream of beauty on the Colorado Plains. I sat with my face to the eastward and saw the whole pageantry of morning sweep up in a splendor of color through stretches of far limitless distances. Oh! it was gorgeous, with a glory fresh from the hand of the Infinite God, whose is the earth and the seas. Mechanically I thought of the sunrise beyond the Neosho Valley, but nothing there could be half so magnificent as this. And as I looked, the thought grew firmer that this sublimity had been poured out for me for the last time, and I gazed at the face of the morning as we look at the face awaiting the coffin lid.

And even as the thought clinched itself upon me came the sentinel's cry of "Indians! Indians!"

We grasped our weapons at the shrill warning. It was the death-grip now. We knew as surely as we stood there that we could not resist this last attack. The redskins must have saved themselves for this final blow, when resistance on our part was a feeble mockery. The hills to the northward were black with the approaching force, but we were determined to make our last stand heroically, and to sell our lives as dearly as possible. As with a grim last measure of courage we waited, Sharp Grover, who stood motionless, alert, with arms ready, suddenly threw his rifle high in air, and with a shout that rose to heaven, he cried in an ecstasy of joy:

"By the God above us, it's an ambulance!"

To us for whom the frenzied shrieks of the squaws, the fiendish yells of the savage warriors, and the weird, unearthly wailing for the dead were the only cries that had resounded above the Plains these many days, this shout from Grover was like the music of heaven. A darkness came before me, and my strength seemed momentarily to go from me. It was but a moment, and then I opened my eyes to the sublimest sight it is given to the Anglo-American to look upon.

Like the passing of a hurricane, horses, mules, men, all dashed toward the place

Down from the low bluffs there poured a broad surge of cavalry, in perfect order, riding like the wind, the swift, steady hoof-beats of their horses marking a rhythmic measure that trembled along the ground in musical vibration, while overhead—oh, the grandeur of God's gracious dawn fell never on a thing more beautiful—swept out by the free winds of heaven to its full length, and gleaming in the sunlight, Old Glory rose and fell in rippling waves of splendor.

On they came, the approaching force, in a mad rush to reach us. And we who had waited for the superb charge of Roman Nose and his savage warriors, as we wait for death, saw now this coming in of life, and the regiment of the unconquerable people.

We threw restraint to the winds and shouted and danced and hugged each other, while we laughed and cried in a very transport of joy.

It was Colonel Carpenter and his colored cavalry who had made a dash across the country rushing to our rescue. Beside the Colonel at their head, rode Donovan the scout, whom we had accounted as dead. It was his unerring eye that had guided this command, never varying from the straight line toward our danger-girt entrenchment on the Arickaree.

Before Carpenter's approaching cavalry the Indians fled for their lives, and they who a few hours hence would have been swinging bloody tomahawks above our heads were now scurrying to their hiding-places far away.

Never tenderer hands cared for the wounded, and never were bath and bandage and food and drink more welcome. Our command was shifted to a clean spot where no stench of putrid flesh could reach us. Rest and care, such as a camp on the Plains can offer, was ours luxuriously; and hardtack and coffee, food for the angels, we had that day, to our intense satisfaction. Life was ours once more, and hope, and home, and civilization. Oh, could it be true, we asked ourselves, so long had we stood face to face with Death.

The import of this struggle on the Arickaree was far greater than we dreamed of then. We had gone out to meet a few foemen. What we really had to battle with was the fighting strength of the northern Cheyenne and Sioux tribes. Long afterwards it came to us what this victory meant. The broad trail we had eagerly followed up the Arickaree fork of the Republican River had been made by bands on bands of Plains Indians mobilizing only a little to the westward, gathering for a deadly purpose. At the full of the moon the whole fighting force, two thousand strong, was to make a terrible raid, spreading out on either side of the Republican River, reaching southward as far as the Saline Valley and northward to the Platte, and pushing eastward till the older settlements turned them back.

They were determined to leave nothing behind them but death and desolation. Their numbers and leadership, with the defenceless condition of the Plains settlers, give broad suggestion of what that raid would have done for Kansas. Our victory on the Arickaree broke up that combination of Indian forces, for all future time. It was for such an unknown purpose, and against such unguessed odds, that fifty of us led by the God of all battle lines, had gone out to fight. We had met and vanquished a foe two hundred times our number, aye, crippled its power for all future years. We were lifting the fetters from the frontier; we were planting the standards westward, westward. In the history of the Plains warfare this fight on the Arickaree, though not the last stroke, was one of the decisive struggles in breaking the savage sovereignty, a sovereignty whose wilderness demesne to-day is a land of fruit and meadow and waving grain, of peaceful homes and wealth and honor.

It was impossible for our wounded comrades to begin the journey to Fort Wallace on that day. When evening came, the camp settled down to quiet and security: the horses fed at their rope tethers, the fires smouldered away to gray ashes, the sun swung down behind the horizon bar, the gold and scarlet of evening changed to deeper hues and the long, purple twilight was on the silent Colorado Plains. Over by the Arickaree the cavalry men lounged lazily in groups. As the shades of evening gathered, the soldiers began to sing. Softly at first, but richer, fuller, sweeter their voices rose and fell with that cadence and melody only the negro voice can compass. And their song, pulsing out across the undulating valley wrapped in the twilight peace, made a harmony so wonderfully tender that we who had dared danger for days unflinchingly now turned our faces to the shadows to hide our tears.

We are tenting to-night on the old camp ground.
Give us a song to cheer
Our weary hearts, a song of home
And friends we love so dear.
Many are the hearts that are weary to-night,
Wishing for this war to cease,
Many are the hearts looking for the right
To see the dawn of peace.

So the cavalry men sang, and we listened to their singing with hearts stirred to their depths. And then with prayers of thankfulness for our deliverance, we went to sleep. And over on the little island, under the shallow sands, the men who had fallen beside us lay with patient, folded hands waiting beside the Arickaree waters till the last reveille shall sound for them and they enter the kingdom of Eternal Peace.

CHAPTER XIX

A MAN'S BUSINESS

> Mankind was my business; the common welfare was my business; charity, mercy, forbearance, and benevolence were all my business; the dealings of my trade were but a drop of water in the comprehensive ocean of my business.
>
> —DICKENS.

Every little community has its customs peculiar to itself. With the people of Springvale the general visiting-time was on Sunday between the afternoon Sabbath-school and the evening service. The dishes that were prepared on Saturday for the next day's supper excelled the warm Sunday dinner.

We come to know the heart and soul of the folks that fill up a little town, and when we get into the larger city we miss them oftener than we have the courage to say. Unselfishness and integrity and stalwart principles of right are not confined to the higher circles of society. A man may be hungry for friends on the crest of his popularity; he may long for the strong right hand of Christian fellowship in the centre of a brotherhood of churchmen. Cam Gentry and his good wife are among those whom in all my busy years of wide acquaintance with people of all ranks I account as genuine stuff. They were only common clay, generous, unselfish, clean of thought and act. Uneducated, with no high ideals, they gauged their way by the golden rule, and made the most of their time. A journey to Topeka was their "trip abroad"; beyond the newspapers they read little except the Bible; and they built their faith on the Presbyterian Church and the Republican party. But the cosy lighted tavern on winter nights, and its clean, cool halls and resting-places in the summer heat, are still a green spot in the memory of many a traveller. Transients and regulars at the Cambridge House delighted in this Sabbath evening spread.

"Land knows," Dollie Gentry used to declare, "if ever a body feels lonesome it's on Sunday afternoon between Sunday-school and evenin' service. Why, the blues can get you then, when they'd stan' no show ary other day er hour in the week. An' it stan's to reason a man, er woman, either, is livin' in a hotel because they ain't got no home ner nobody to make 'em feel glad to see 'em. If they're goin' to patronize the Cambridge House they're goin' to get the best that's comin' to 'em right then."

So the old dining-room was a joy at this time of the week, with all that a good cook can make attractive to the appetite.

Mary Gentry, sweet-tempered and credulous as in her childhood, grew up into a home-lover. We all wondered why John Anderson, who was studying medicine, should fancy Mary, plain good girl that she was. John had been a bashful boy and a hard student whom the girls failed to interest. But the home Mary made for him later, and her two sons that grew up in it, are justification of his choice of wife. The two boys are men now, one in Seattle, and one in New York City. Both in high places of trust and financial importance.

One October Sabbath afternoon, O'mie fell into step beside Marjie on the way from Sabbath-school. Since his terrible experience in the Hermit's Cave five years before, he had never been strong. We became so accustomed to his little hacking cough we did not notice it until there came a day to all of us when we looked back and wondered how we could have been so inattentive to the thing growing up before our eyes. O'mie was never anything but a good-hearted Irishman, and yet he had a keener insight into character and trend of events than any other boy or man I ever knew. I've always thought that if his life had been spared to mature manhood—but it wasn't.

"Marjie, I'm commissioned to invite you to the Cambridge House for lunch," O'mie said. "Mary wants to see you. She's got a lame arm, fell off a step ladder in the pantry. The papers on the top shelves had been on there fifteen minutes, and Aunt Dollie thought they'd better put up clean ones. That's the how. Dr. John Anderson's most sure to call professionally this evening, and Bill Mead's going to bring Bess over for tea, and there's still others on the outskirts, but you're specially wanted, as usual. Bud will be there, too. Says he wants to see all the Andersons once more before he leaves town, and he knows it's his last chance; for John's forever at the tavern, and Bill Mead is monopolizing Bess at home; and you know, Star-face, how Clayton divides himself around among the Whatelys and Grays over at Red Range and a girl he's got up at Lawrence."

"All this when I'm starving for one of Aunt Dollie's good lunches. Offer some other inducement, O'mie," Marjie replied laughingly.

"Oh, well, Tillhurst'll be there, and one or two of the new folks, all eligible."

"What makes you call me 'Star-face'? That's what Jean Pahusca used to call me." She shivered.

"Oh, it fits you; but if you object, I can make it, 'Moon-face,' or 'Sun-up.'"

"Or 'Skylight,' or 'Big Dipper'; so you can keep to the blue firmament. Where's Bud going?"

Out of the tail of his eye O'mie caught sight of Judson falling in behind them here and he answered carelessly:

"Oh, I don't know where Bud is going exactly. Kansas City or St. Louis, or somewhere else. You'll come of course?"

"Yes, of course," Marjie answered, just as Judson in his pompous little manner called to her:

"Marjory, I have invited myself up to your mother's for tea."

"Why, there's nobody at home, Mr. Judson," the girl said kindly; "I'm going down to Mary Gentry's, and mother went up to Judge Baronet's with Aunt Candace for lunch."

Nobody called my father's sister by any other name. To Marjie, who had played about her knee, Aunt Candace was a part of the day's life in Springvale. But the name of Baronet was a red rag to Judson's temper. He was growing more certain of his cause every day; but any allusion to our family was especially annoying, and this remark of Marjie's fired him to hasten to something definite in his case of courtship.

"When she's my wife," he had boasted to Tell Mapleson, "I'll put a stop to all this Baronet friendship. I won't even let her go there. Marjie's a fine girl, but a wife must understand and obey her lord and master. That's it; a wife must obey, or your home's ruined."

Nobody had ever accused Tell Mapleson's wife of ruining a home on that basis; for she had been one of the crushed-down, washed-out women who never have two ideas above their dish-pan. She had been dead some years, and Tell was alone. People said he was too selfish to marry again. Certainly matrimony was not much in his thoughts.

The talk at the tavern table that evening ran on merrily among the young people. Albeit, the Sabbath hour was not too frivolous, for we were pretty stanch in our Presbyterianism there. I think our love for Dr. Hemingway in itself would have kept the Sabbath sacred. He never found fault with our Sunday visiting. All days were holy to him, and his evening sermons taught us that frivolity, and idle gossip, and scandal are as unforgivable on week days as on the Sabbath Day. Somewhere in the wide courts of heaven there must be reserved an abode of inconceivable joy and peace for such men as he, men who preach the Word faithfully through the years, whose hand-clasp means fellowship, and in whose tongue is the law of kindness.

"Say, Clate, where's Bud going?" Somebody called across the table. Bud was beside Marjie, whose company was always at a premium in any gathering.

"Let him tell; it's his secret," Clayton answered. "I'll be glad when he's gone"—he was speaking across to Marjie now—"then I'll get some show, maybe."

"I'm going to hunt a wife," Bud sang out. "Can't find a thoul here who'll thtay with me long enough to get acquainted. I'm going out Wetht thomewhere."

"I'd stay with you a blamed sight longer if I wasn't acquainted with you than if I was," Bill Mead broke in. "It's because they do get acquainted that they don't stay, Bud; and anyhow, they can run faster out there than here, the girls can; they have to, to keep away from the Indians. And there's no tepee ring for the ponies to stumble over. Marjie, do you remember the time Jean Pahusca nearly got you? I remember it, for when I came to after the shock, I was standing square on my head with both feet in the air. All I could see was Bud dragging Jean's pony out of the muss. I thought he was upside down at first and the horses were walking like flies on the ceiling."

Marjie's memories of that moment were keen. So were O'mie's.

"Well, what ever did become of that Jean, anyhow? Anybody here seen him for five years?"

The company looked at one another. Bud's face was as innocent as a baby's. Lettie Conlow at the foot of the table encountered O'mie's eyes and her face flamed. Dr. John Anderson was explaining the happening to Tillhurst and some newcomers in Springvale to whom the story was interesting, and the whole table began to recall old times and old escapades of Jean's.

"Wasn't afraid of anything on earth," Bill Mead declared.

"Yeth he wath, brother," Bud broke in, while Bess Anderson blushed deeply at Bud's teasing name. Bill and Bess were far along the happy way of youth and love.

"Why, what did he fear?" Judson asked Dave Mead at the head of the table.

"Phil Baronet. He never would fight Phil. He didn't dare. He couldn't bear to be licked."

And then the conversation turned on me, and my virtues and shortcomings were reviewed in friendly gossip. Only Judson's face wore a sneer.

"I don't wonder this Jean was afraid of him," a recent-comer to the town declared.

"Oh, if he was afraid of this young man, this boy," Judson declared, "he would have feared something else; that's it, he'd been afraid of other things."

"He was," O'mie spoke up.

"Well, what was it, O'mie?" Dr. John queried.

"Ghosts," O'mie replied gravely. "Oh, I know," he declared, as the crowd laughed. "I can prove it to you and tell you all about it. I'll do it some day, but I'll need the schoolhouse and some lantern slides to make it effective. I may charge a small admission fee and give a benefit to defray Bud's expenses home from this trip."

"Would you really do that, O'mie?" Mary Gentry asked him.

But the query, "Where's Phil, now?" was going the rounds, and the answers were many. My doings had not been reported in the town, and gossip still was active concerning me.

"Up at Topeka," "Gone to St. Louis," "Back in Massachusetts." These were followed by Dave Mead's declaration:

"The best boy that ever went out of Springvale. Just his father over again. He'll make some place prouder than it would have been without him."

Nobody knew who started the story just then, but it grew rapidly from Tillhurst's side of the table that I had gone to Rockport, Massachusetts, to settle in my father's old home-town.

"Stands to reason a boy who can live in Kansas would go back to Massachusetts, doesn't it?" Dr. John declared scornfully.

"But Phil's to be married soon, to that stylish Miss Melrose. She's got the money, and Phil would become a fortune. Besides, she was perfectly infatuated with him."

"Well," somebody else asserted, "if he does marry her, he can bring her back here to live. My! but Judge Baronet's home will be a grand place to go to then. It was always good enough."

Amid all this clatter Marjie was as indifferent and self-possessed as if my name were a stranger's. Those who had always known her did not dream of what lay back of that sweet girl-face. She was the belle of Springvale, and she had too many admirers for any suspicion of the truth to find a place.

While the story ran on Bud turned to her and said in a low voice, "Marjie, I'm going to Phil. He needdth me now."

Nobody except Bud noticed how white the girl was, as the company rising from the table swept her away from him.

That night Dr. Hemingway's prayer was fervent with love. The boys were always on his heart, and he called us all by name. He prayed for the young men of Springvale, who had grown up to the life here and on whom the cares of citizenship, and the town's good name were soon to rest; and for the young men who would not be with us again: for Tell Mapleson, that the snares of a great city like St. Louis might not entrap him; for James Conlow, whose lines had led him away from us; for David Mead, going soon to the far-away lands where the Sierras dip down the golden slope to the Pacific seas; for August Anderson, also about to go away from us, that life and health might be his; and last of all for Philip Baronet. A deeper hush fell upon the company bowed in prayer.

"For Philip Baronet, the strong, manly boy whom we all love, the brave-hearted hero who has gone out from among us, and as his father did before him for the homes of a nation, so now the son has gone to fight the battles of the prairie domain, and to build up a wall of safety before the homes and hearthstones of our frontier." And then he offered thanksgiving to a merciful Father that, "in the awful conflict which Philip, with a little handful of heroes, has helped to wage against the savage red man, a struggle in which so many lives have gone out, our Philip has been spared." His voice broke here, and he controlled it by an effort, as in calm, low tones he finished his simple prayer with the earnest petition, "Keep Thou these our boys; and though they may walk through the valley of the shadow of death, may they fear no evil, for Thou art with them. Amen."

It was the first intimation the town had had of what I was doing. Springvale was not without a regard for me who had loved it always, and then the thought of danger to a fellow citizen is not without its appeal. I have been told that Judge Baronet and Aunt

Candace could not get down the aisle after service until after ten o'clock that night and that the tears of men as well as women fell fast as my father gave the words of the message sent to him by Governor Crawford on the evening before. Even Chris Mead, always a quiet, stern man, sat with head bowed on the railing of the pew before him during the recital. It was noted afterwards that Judson did not remain, but took Lettie Conlow home as soon as the doxology was ended. The next day my stock in Springvale was at a premium; for a genuine love, beside which fame and popularity are ashes and dust, was in the heart of that plain, good little Kansas town.

Bud called to say good-bye to Marjie, before he left home.

"Are you going out West to stay?" Marjie asked.

"I'm going to try it out there. Clate'th got all the law here a young man can get; he'th gobbled up Dave and Phil'th share of the thing. John will be the coming M. D. of the town, and Bill Mead already taketh to the bank like a duck to water. I'm going to try the Wetht. What word may I take to Phil for you?"

"There's nothing to say," Marjie answered.

To his words, "I hoped there might be," she only said gayly, "Good-bye, Bud. Be a good boy, and be sure not to forget Springvale, for we'll always love your memory."

And so he left her. He was a good boy, nor did he forget the town where his memory is green still in the hearts of all who knew him. His last thought was of Springvale, and he babbled of the Neosho, and fancied himself in the shallows down by the Deep Hole. He clung to me, as in his childhood, and begged me to carry him on my shoulders when waters of Death were rolling over him. I held his hand to the last, and when the silence fell, I stretched myself on the brown curly mesquite beside him and thanked God that He had let me know this boy. Ever more my life will be richer for the remembrance it holds of him.

Bud left Springvale in one of those dripping, chilly, wet days our Kansas Octobers sometimes mix in with their opal-hued hours of

Indian summer. That evening Tell Mapleson dropped into Judson's store and O'mie was let off early.

The little Irishman ran up the street at once to the Whately home. Mrs. Whately had retired. Eight o'clock was bed time for middle-aged people in our town. Marjie sat alone by the fire. How many times that summer we had talked of the long winter evenings we should spend together by that fireplace in Marjie's cosy sitting-room. And now she was beside the hearth, and I was far away. I might have been forgiven without a word had I walked in that evening and found her, as O'mie did, alone with her sad thoughts. Marjie never tried to hide anything from O'mie. She knew he could see through any pretence of hers. She knew, too, that he would keep sacred anything he saw.

"Marjie, I'm lonesome to-night."

Marjie gave him a seat beside the fire.

"What makes you lonesome, O'mie?" she asked gravely.

"The wrongs av the world bear heavily upon me."

Marjory looked at him curiously to see if he was joking.

"What I need to do is to shrive myself, I guess, and then get up an inquisition, with myself as chief inquisitor."

Marjie, studying the pictures in the burning coals, said nothing. O'mie also sat silent for a time.

"Marjie," he said at length, "when you see things goin' all wrong end to, and you know what's behind 'em, drivin' 'em wrong, what's your rale Presbyterian duty then? Let 'em go? or tend to somethin' else besides your own business? Honest, now, what's what?"

"I don't know what you're up to, O'mie." She was looking dreamily into the grate, the firelight on her young face and thoughtful brown eyes making a picture tenderly sweet and fair. In her mind was the image of Judge Baronet as he looked the night before, when he lifted his head after Dr. Hemingway's prayer for his son. And then maybe a picture of the graceless son himself came unbidden, and his eyes were full of love as when they looked down into hers on the day Rachel Melrose came into Judge Baronet's office demanding his attention. "What's the matter, O'mie? Is Uncle Cam being imposed on? You'd never stand that, I know."

"No, little girl, Cambridge Gentry can still take care of Cam's interest and do a kind act to more folks off-hand better than any other man I know. Marjie, it's Phil Baronet."

Marjie gave a start, but she made no effort to hide her interest.

"Little girl, he's been wronged, and lied about, and misunderstood, by a crowd av us who have knowed him day in and day out since he was a little boy. Marjory Whately, did anybody iver catch him in a lie? Did he iver turn coward in a place where courage was needed? Did he iver do a cruelty to a helpless thing, or fight a smaller boy? Did he iver decaive? Honestly, now, was there iver anything in all the years we run together that wasn't square and clane and fearless and lovin'?"

Marjie sat with bowed head before the flickering fire. When O'mie spoke again his voice was husky.

"Little girl, when I was tied hand and foot, and left to die in that dark Hermit's Cave, it was Phil Baronet who brought in the sunlight and a face radiant with love. When Jean Pahusca, drunk as a fury, was after you out on the prairie with that cruel knife ready, the knife I've seen him kill many a helpless thing with when he was drunk, when this Jean was ridin' like a fiend after you, Phil turned to me that day and his white agonized face I'll never forget. Now, Marjie, it's to right his wrong, and the wrongs of some he loves that I'm studyin' about. The week Phil came home from the rally I took a vacation. Shall I tell you why?"

Marjie nodded.

"Well, Star-face, it was laid on me conscience heavy to pay a part av the debt I owe to the boy who saved me life. I ain't got eyes fur nothin', and I see the clouds gatherin' black about that boy's head. Back of 'em was jealousy, that was a girl; hate, that was a man whose cruel, ugly deeds Phil had knocked down and trampled on and prevented from comin' to a harvest of sufferin'; and revenge, that was a rebel-hearted scoundrel who'd have destroyed this town but for Phil; and last, a selfish, money-lovin' son of a horse-thief who was grabbing for riches and pulling hard at the covers to hide some sins he'd never want to come to the light, being a deacon in the Presbyterian Church. All thim in one cloud makes a hurricane, and with 'em comes a shallow, selfish, pretty girl. Oh, it was a sight, Marjie. If I can do somethin' to keep shipwreck not only from them the storm's aimed at, but them that's pilin' up trouble fur themselves, too, I'm goin' to do it."

Marjie made no reply.

"So I took a vacation and wint off on a visit to me rich relatives in Westport."

Marjie could not help smiling now. O'mie had not a soul to call his next of kin.

"Oh, yis, I wint," he continued, "on tin days' holiday. The actual start to it was on the evenin' Phil got home from Topeka. The night of the party at Anderson's Lettie Conlow comes into the store just at closin'. I was behind a pile of ginghams fixin' some papers and cord below the counter. And Judson, being a fool by inheritance and choice of profession, takes no more notice of me than if I was a dog; says things he oughtn't to when he knows I'm 'round. But he forgits me in the pride of his stuck-uppityness. And I heard Judson say to her low, 'Now be sure to go right after dark and look in there again. You're sure you know just which crevice of the rock it is?' Lettie laughed and said, she'd watched it too long not to know. And so they arranged it, and I arranged my wrappin'-cord, and when I straightened up (I'm little, ye know), they didn't see my rid head by the pile of ginghams; and so she went away. When I got ready I wint, too. I trailed round after dark until I found meself under that point av rock by the bushes in the steep bend up-street. I was in a little corner full of crevices, when along comes Lettie. She seemed to be tryin' to get somethin' out of 'em, and her short fat arm couldn't reach it. Blamed inconvanient bein' little and short! She tried and tried and thin she said some ugly words only a boy has a right to say when he's cussin' somethin'. Just thin somethin' made a noise between her and the steps, and she made a rush for 'em and was gone. My eyes was gettin' catty and used to the dark now, and I could make out pretty sure it was Phil who sails up nixt, aisy, like he knowed the premises, and in his hand goes and he got out somethin' sayin' to himself—and me:

"'Well, Marjie tucked it in good and safe. I didn't know that hole was so deep.'

"Marjie, maybe if that hole's too deep for Lettie to reach clear in, there might be somethin' she's missed. I dunno'. But niver moind. I took me vacation, went sailin' out with Dever fur a rale splurge to Kansas City. Across the Neosho Dever turns the stage aside, U. S. mail and all, and lands me siven miles up the river and ferries me on this side again. Dever can keep the stillest of any livin' stage-driver whose business is to drive stage on the side and gossip on the main line. He never cheeped a chirp. I come back that same day and put in tin days studyin' things. I just turned myself into a holy inquisition for tin mortial days. Now, what I know has a value to Phil's good name, who has been accused of doing more diviltry than the thief on the cross. Marjie, I'm goin' to proceed now and turn on screws till the heretics squeal. It's not exactly my business; but—well, yes, it's the Lord's business to right the wrongs, and we must do His work now and then, 'unworthy though we be,' as Grandpa Mead says, in prayer meetin'."

"O'mie, you heard Dr. Hemingway's prayer last night?" Marjie asked, in a voice that quivered with tears.

"Oh, good God! Marjie, the men that's fighting the battles on the frontier, the fire-guards around them prairie homes, they are the salt of the earth." He dropped his head between his hands and groaned. Presently he rose to say good-night.

"Shall I do it, little sister? See to what's not my business at all, at all, and start a fire in this town big enough to light the skies clear to where Phil is this rainy night, and he can read a welcome home in it?"

"They said last night that he's going to be married soon to that Massachusetts girl. Maybe he wouldn't want to come if he did see it," Marjie murmured, turning her face away.

"Oh, maybe not, maybe not. Niver did want to get back when he was away. But, say, Marjie Star-face, Fort Wallace away out on the Plains ain't Rockport; and rich men's homes and all that gabble they was desecratin' the Sabbath with at supper last night—" O'mie broke off and took the girl's trembling hand in his. "Oh! I can look after that rascal's good name, but I don't dare to fix things up for you two, no matter what I know." So ran his thoughts.

The rain blew in a bitter gust as he opened the door. "Good-night, Marjie. It's an ugly night. Any old waterproof cloak to lend me, girlie?" he asked, but Marjie did not smile. She held the light as in the olden time she had shown us the dripping path, and watched the little Irishman trotting away in the darkness.

The Indian summer of 1868 in Kansas was as short as it was glorious. The next day was gorgeous after the rain, and the warm sunshine and light breeze drove all the dampness and chill away. In the middle of the afternoon Judson left the store to O'mie and went up to Mrs. Whately's for an important business conference. These conferences were growing frequent now, and dear Mrs. Whately's usually serene face wore a deeply anxious look after each one. Marjie had no place in them. It was not a part of Judson's plan to have her understand the business.

Fortune favored O'mie's inquisition scheme. Judson had hardly left the store when Lettie Conlow walked in. Evidently Judson's company on the Sunday evening before had given her a purpose in coming. In our play as children Lettie was the first to "get mad and call names." In her young womanhood she was vindictive and passionate.

"Good-afternoon, Lettie. Nice day after the rain," O'mie said, pleasantly.

She did not respond to his greeting, but stood before him with flashing eyes. She had often been called pretty, and her type is always considered handsome, for her coloring was brilliant, and her form attractive. This year she was the best dressed girl in town, although her father was not especially prosperous. Whether transplanting in a finer soil with higher culture might have changed her I cannot say, for the Conlow breed ran low and the stamp of the common grade was on Lettie. I've seen the same on a millionaire's wife; so it is in the blood, and not in the rank. No other girl in town broke the law as Lettie did, and kept her good name, but we had always known her. The boys befriended her more than the girls did, partly because we knew more of her escapades, and partly because she would sometimes listen to us. A pretty, dashing, wilful, untutored, and ill-principled girl, she was sowing the grain of a certain harvest.

"O'mie," she began angrily, "you've been talking about me, and you've been spying on me long enough; and I'm going to settle you now. You are a contemptible spy, and you're the biggest rascal in this town. That's what you are."

"Not by the steelyards, I ain't," O'mie replied. Passing from behind the counter and courteously offering her a chair. Then jumping upon the counter beside her he sat swinging his heels against it, fingering the yard-stick beside the pile of calicoes. "Not by the steelyards, I ain't the biggest. Tell Mapleson's lots longer, and James Conlow, blacksmith, and Cam Gentry, and Cris Mead are all bigger. But if you want to settle me, I'm ready. Who says I've been talking about you?"

"Amos Judson, and he knows. He's told me all about you."

O'mie's irrepressible smile spread over his face. "All about me? I didn't give him credit for that much insight."

"I'm not joking, and you must listen to me. I want to know why you tag after me every place I go. No gentleman would do that."

"Maybe not, nor a lady nather," O'mie interposed.

Lettie's face burned angrily.

"And you've been saying things about me. You've got to quit it. Only a dirty coward would talk about a girl as you do."

She stamped her foot and her pudgy hands were clenched into hard little knots. It was a cheap kind of fury, a flimsy bit of drama, but tragedies have grown out of even a lesser degree of unbridled temper. O'mie was a monkey to whom the ludicrous side of life forever appealed, and the sight of Lettie as an accusing vengeance was too much for him. The twinkle in his eye only angered her the more.

"Oh, you needn't laugh, you and Marjie Whately. How I hate her! but I've fixed her. You two have always been against me, I know. I've heard what you say. She's a liar, and a mean flirt, always trying to take everybody away from me; and as good as a pauper if Judson didn't just keep her and her mother."

"Marjie'd never try to get Judson away from Lettie," O'mie thought, but all sense of humor had left his face now. "Lettie Conlow," he said, leaning toward her and speaking calmly, "you may call me what you please—Lord, it couldn't hurt me—but you, nor nobody else, man or woman, praist or pirate, is comin' into this store while I'm alone in controllin' it, and call Marjie Whately nor any other dacent woman by any evil names. If you've come here to settle me, settle away, and when you get through my turn's comin' to settle; but if you say another word against Marjie or any other woman, by the holy Joe Spooner, and all the other saints, you'll walk right out that door, or I'll throw you out as I'd do anybody else in the same case, no matter if they was masculine, feminine, or neuter gender. Now you understand me. If you have anything more to say, say it quick."

Lettie was furious now, but the Conlow blood is not courageous, and she only ground her teeth and muttered: "Always the same. Nobody dares to say a word against her. What makes some folks so precious, I wonder? There's Phil Baronet, now,—the biggest swindle in this town. Oh, I could tell you a lot about him. I'll do it some day, too. It'll take more money to keep me still than Baronet's bank notes."

"Lettie," said O'mie in an even voice, "I'm waitin' here to be settled."

"Then let me alone. I'm not goin' to be forever tracked 'round like a thief. I'll fix you so you'll keep still. Who are you, anyhow? A nobody, poor as sin, living off of this town all these years; never knowing who your father nor mother is, nor nobody to care for you; the very trash of the earth, somebody's doorstep foundling, to set yourself up over me! You'd ought to 'a been run out of town long ago."

"I was, back in '63, an' half the town came after me, had to drag me back with ropes, they was so zealous to get me. I wasn't worth it, all the love and kindness the town's give me. Now, Lettie, what else?"

"Nothing except this. After what Dr. Hemingway said last night Springvale's gone crazy about Phil again. Just crazy, and he's sure to come back here. If he does"—she broke off a moment—"well, you know what you've been up to for four months, trackin' me, and tellin' things you don't know. Are you goin' to quit it? That's all."

"The evidence bein' in an' the plaintiff restin'," O'mie said gravely, "it's time for the defence in the case to begin.

"You saved me a trip, my lady, for I was comin' over this very evenin' to settle with you. But never mind, we can do it now. Judson's havin' one of his M. E. quarterly conferences up at the Whately house and we are free to talk this out. You say I'm a contemptible spy. Lettie, we're a pair of 'em, so we'll lave off the adjective or adverb, which ever it is, that does that for names of 'persons, places, and things that can be known or mentioned.' Some of 'em that can be known, can't aven be mentioned, though. Where were you, Lettie, whin I was spyin' and what were you doin' at the time yoursilf?"

"I guess I had a right to be there. It's a free country, and it was my own business, not somebody else's," the girl retorted angrily, as the situation dawned on her.

"Exactly," O'mie went on. "It's a free country and we both have a right to tend to our own business. Nobody has a right to tend to a business of sin and evil-doin' toward his neighbor, though, my girl. If I've tagged you and spied, and played the dirty coward, and ain't no gintleman, it was to save a good name, and to keep from exposure a name—maybe it's a girl's, none too good, I'm afraid—but it would niver come to the gossips through me. You know that."

Lettie did know it. O'mie and she had made mud pies together in the days when they still talked in baby words. It was because he was true and kind, because he was a friend to every man, woman, and child there, that Springvale loves his memory to-day.

"Second, I wish to Heaven I could make things right, but I can't. I wish you could, but some of 'em you won't and, Lettie, some of 'em you can't now.

"Third, you've heard what I said about you. Why, child, I've said the worst to you. No words comin' straight nor crooked to you, have I said of you I'd not say to yoursilf, face to face.

"And again now, girlie, you've talked plain here; came pretty near callin' me names, in fact. I can stand it, and I guess I deserve some of 'em. I am something of a rascal, and a consummate liar, I admit; but when you talk about a lot of scandal up your sleeve, more 'n bank notes can pay by blackmail, and your chance of fixin' Phil Baronet's character, Lettie, you just can't do it. You are too mad to be anything but foolish to-day, but I'm glad you did come to me; it may save more 'n Phil's name. Your own is in the worst jeopardy right now. You said, in conclusion, that I was trackin' you, and you ask, am I goin' to quit it? The defendant admits the charge, pleads guilty on that count, and throws himself on the mercy av the coort. But as to the question, am I goin' to quit it, I answer yes. Whin? Whin there's no more need fur it, and not one minute sooner. I may be the very trash av the earth, with no father nor mother nor annybody to care for me" (I can see, even now, the pathetic look that came sometimes into his laughing gray eyes. It must have been in them at that moment); "but I have sometimes been 'round when things I could do needed doin', and I'm goin' to be prisent now, and in the future, to put my hand up against wrong-doin' if I can." O'mie paused, while that little dry cough that brought a red spot to each cheek had its way.

"Now, Lettie, you've had your say with me, and your mind's relieved. It's my time to say a few things, and you must listen."

Lettie sat looking at the floor.

"I don't know why I have to listen," she spoke defiantly.

"Nor do I know why I had to listen to what you said. You don't need to, but I would if I was you. It may be all the better for you in a year if you do. You spake av bein' tagged wherever you go. Who begun it? I'll tell you. Back in the summer one day, two people drove out to the stone cabin, the haunted one, by the river in the draw below the big cottonwood. Somebody made his home there, somebody who didn't dare to show his face in Springvale by day, 'cause his hand's been lifted to murder his fellow man. But he hangs 'round here, skulkin' in by night to see the men he does business with, and meetin' foolish girls who ought never to trust him a minute. This man's waiting his chance to commit murder again, or worse. I know, fur I've laid fur him too many times. There's no cruel-hearted savage on the Plains more dangerous to the settlers on the frontier; not one av 'em 'ud burn a house, and kill men and children, and torture and carry off women, quicker than this miserable dog that a girl who should value her good name has been counsellin' with time and again, this summer, partly on account of jealousy, and partly because of a silly notion of bein' romantic. Back in June she made a trip to the cabin double quick to warn the varmint roostin' there. In her haste she dropped a bow of purple ribbon which with some other finery a certain little store-keeper gives her to do his spyin' fur him. It's a blamed lovely cabal in this town. I know 'em all by name.

"Spakin' of bein' paupers and bein' kept by Judson, Lettie—who is payin' the wages of sin, in money and fine clothes, right now? It's on the books, and I kape the books. But, my dear girl,"—O'mie looked straight into her black eyes—"they's books bein' kept of the purpose, price av the goods, and money. And you and him may answer for that. I can swear in coort only to what Judson spends on you; you know what for."

Lettie cowered down before her inquisitor, and her anger was mingled with fear and shame.

"This purple bow was found, identified. Aven Uncle Cam, short-sighted as he is, remembered who wore it that day; aven see her gallopin' into town and noticed she'd lost it. This same girl hung around the cliff till she found a secret place where two people put their letters. She comes in here and tells me I've no business taggin' her. What business had she robbin' folks of letters, stealin' 'em out, and givin' 'em into wicked hands? Lettie, you know whose letter you took when you could reach far enough to git it out, and you know where you put it.

"You said you could ruin Phil. It's aisy for a woman to do that, I admit. No matter how hard the church may be on 'em, and how much other women may cut 'em dead for doin' wrong things, a woman can go into a coort-room and swear a man's character away, an' the jury'll give her judgment every time. The law's a lot aisier with the women than the crowd you associate with is." O'mie's speech was broken off by his cough.

"Now to review this case a bit. The night av the Anderson's party you tried to get the letter Marjie'd put up for Phil. You didn't do it."

"I never tried," Lettie declared.

"How come the rid flowers stuck with the little burrs on your dress? They don't grow anywhere round here only on that cliff side. I pulled off one bunch, and I saw Phil pull off another when your skirts caught on a nail in the door. But I saw more 'n that. I stood beside you when you tried to get the letter, and I heard you tell Judson you had failed. I can't help my ears; the Almighty made 'em to hear with, and as you've said, I am a contemptible spy.

"You have given hints, mean ugly little hints, of what you could tell about Phil on that night. He took you home, as he was asked to do. But what took you to the top of the cliff at midnight? It was to meet Jean Pahusca, the dog the gallows is yappin' for now. You waited while he tried to kill Phil. He'd done it, too, if Phil hadn't been too strong to be killed by such as him. And then you and Jean were on your way out to his cabin whin the boys found you. You know Bill and Bud was goin' to Red Range, that night in the carriage when they overtook you. It was moonlight, you remember; and ridin' on the back seat was Cris Mead, silent as he always is, but he heard every word that was said. Bud come all the way back with you to keep your good name a little while longer; took chances on his own to save a girl's. It's Phil Baronet put that kind of loyalty into the boys av this town. No wonder they love him. Bud's affidavit's on file ready, when needed; and Bill is here to testify; and Cris Mead's name's good on paper, or in coort, or prayer meetin'. Lettie, you have sold yourself to two of the worst men ever set foot in this town."

"Amos Judson is my best friend; I'll tell him you said he's one of the two worst men in this town," Lettie cried.

"It's a waste av time; he knows it himself. Now, a girl who visits in lonely cabins at dead hours av the night, with men she knows is dangerous, oughtn't to ask why some folks are so precious. It's because they keep their bodies and souls sacred before Almighty God, and don't sell aither. You've accused me of tryin' to protect Phil, and of keepin' Marjie's name out of everything, and that I've been spyin' on you. Good God! Lettie, it's to keep you more 'n them. I was out after my own business, after things other folks ought to a' looked after and didn't, things strictly belongin' to me, whin I run across you everywhere, and see your wicked plan to ruin good names and break hearts and get money by blackmail. Lettie, it's not too late to turn back now. You've done wrong; we all do. But, little girl, we've knowed each other since the days I used to tie your apron strings when your short little fat arms couldn't reach to tie 'em, and I know you now. What have you done with Marjie's letter that you stole before it got to Phil?" His voice was kind, even tender.

"I'll never tell you!" Lettie blazed up like a fire brand.

"Aren't you willing to right the wrongs you've done, and save yourself, too?" His voice did not change.

"I'm going to leave here when I get ready. I'm going away, but not till I am ready, and—" She had almost yielded, but evil desire is a strong master. The spirit of her low-browed father gained control again, and she raised a stormy face to him who would have befriended her. "I'm going to do what I please, and go where I please; and I'll fix some precious saints so they'll never want to come back to this town; and some others'll wish they could leave it."

"All right, then," O'mie replied, as Lettie flung herself out of the door, "if you find me among those prisent when you turn some corner suddenly don't be surprised. I wonder," he went on, "who got that letter the last night the miserable Melrose girl was here, or the night after. I wonder how she could reach it when she couldn't get the other one. Maybe the hole had something in it, one of Phil's letters to Marjie, who knows? And that was why that letter did not get far enough back from her thievin' fingers. Oh, I'm mighty glad Kathleen Morrison give me the mitten for Jess Gray, one of them Red Range boys. How can a man as good and holy as I am manage the obstreperous girls? But," he added seriously, "this is too near to sin and disgrace to joke about now."

CHAPTER XX

THE CLEFT IN THE ROCK

And yet I know past all doubting truly,
A knowledge greater than grief can dim,
I know as he loved, he will love me duly,
Yea, better, e'en better, than I love him.

—JEAN INGELOW.

While O'mie and Lettie were acting out their little drama in the store that afternoon, Judson was up in Mrs. Whately's parlor driving home matters of business with a hasty and masterful hand. Marjie had slipped away at his coming, and for the second time since I had left Springvale she took the steep way up to our "Rockport." Had she known what was going on at home she might have stayed there in spite of her prejudices.

"It's just this way, Mrs. Whately," Judson declared, when he had formally opened the conference, "it's just this way. With all my efforts in your behalf, your business interest in the store has been eaten up by your expenditures. Of course I know you have always lived up to a certain kind of style whether you had the money or not; and I can understand, bein' a commercialist, how easy those things go. But that don't alter the fact that you'll have no more income from the store in a very few months. I'm planning extensive changes in the Winter for next Spring, and it'll take all the income. Do you see now?"

"Partly," Mrs. Whately replied faintly.

She was a sweet-spirited, gentle woman. She had been reared in a home of luxury. Her own home had been guarded by a noble, loving husband, and her powers of resource had never been called out. Of all the women I have ever known, she was least fitted to match her sense of honor, her faith in mankind, and her inexperience and lack of business knowledge against such an unprincipled, avaricious man as the one who domineered over her affairs.

Judson had been tricky and grasping in the day of his straightened circumstances, but he might never have developed into the scoundrel he became, had prosperity not fallen upon him by chance. Sometimes it is poverty, and sometimes it is wealth that plays havoc with a man's character and leads an erring nature into consummate villainy.

"Well, now, if you can see what I'm tellin' you, that you are just about penniless (you will be in a few months; that's it, you will be soon), then you can see how magnanimous a man can be, even a busy merchant, a—a commercialist, if I must use the word again. You'll not only be poor with nobody to support you, but you'll be worse, my dear woman, you'll be disgraced. That's it, just disgraced. I've kept stavin' it off for you, but it's comin'—ugly disgrace for you and Marjory."

Mrs. Whately looked steadily at him with a face so blanched with grief only a hard-hearted wretch like Judson could have gone on.

"I've been gettin' you ready for this for months, have laid my plans carefully, and I've been gradually puttin' the warnin' of it in your mind."

This was true. Judson had been most skilfully paving the way, else Mrs. Whately would not have had that troubled face and burdened spirit after each conference. The intimation of disaster had grown gradually to dreaded expectation with her.

"Do tell me what it is, Amos. Anything is better than this suspense. I'll do anything to save Marjie from disgrace."

"Now, that's what I've been a-waitin' for. Just a-waitin' till you was ready to say you'd do what's got to be done anyhow. Well, it's this. Whately, your deceased first husband"—Judson always used the numeral when speaking of a married man or woman who had passed away—"Whately, he made a will before he went to the war. Judge Baronet drawed it up, and I witnessed it. Now that will listed and disposed of an amount of property, enough to keep you and Marjie in finery long as you lived. That will and some other valuable papers was lost durin' the war (some says just when they was taken, but they don't know), and can't nowhere be found. Havin' entire care of the business in his absence, and bein' obliged to assoom control on his said demise at Chattanoogy, I naturally found out all about his affairs. To be short, Mrs. Whately, he never had the property he said he had. Nobody could find the money. There was an awful shortage. You can't understand, but in a word, he was a disgraced, dishonest man—a thief—that's it."

Mrs. Whately buried her face in her hands and groaned aloud.

"Now, Mrs. Whately, you mustn't take on and you must forget the past. It's the present day we're livin' in, and the future that's a-comin'. Nobody can control what's comin', but me." He rose up to his five feet and three inches, and swelled to the extent of his power. "Me." He tapped his small chest. "I'll come straight to the end of this thing. Phil Baronet's been quite a friend here, quite a friend. I've explained to you all about him. Now you know he's left town to keep from bein' mixed up in some things. They's some business of his father's he was runnin' crooked. You know they say, I heard it out at Fingal's Creek, that he left here on account of a girl he wanted to get rid of. And if they'd talk that way about one girl, they'll say Marjie was doin' wrong to go with him. You've all been friends of the Baronets. I never could see why; but now—well, you know Phil left. Now, it rests with me"—more tapping on that little quart-measure chest—"with me to keep things quiet and save his name from further talk, and save Marjie, too. Many a man, a business man, now, wouldn't have done as I'm doin'. I'll marry Marjie. That saves you from poverty. It saves Irving Whately's name from lastin' disgrace, and it saves Baronet's boy. I can control the men that's against Baronet, in the business matter—some land case—and I know the girl that the talk's all about; and it saves Marjory's name bein' mixed up with this boy of Judge Baronet's."

Had Judson been before Aunt Candace, she would have thrust him from the door with one lifting of her strong, shapely hand. Dollie Gentry would have cracked his head with her rolling pin before she let him go. Cris Mead's wife would have chased him clear to the Neosho; she was Bill Mead's own mother when it came to whooping things; but poor, gentle Mrs. Whately sat dumb and dazed in a grief-stricken silence.

"Give me your consent, and the thing's done. Marjie's only twenty. She'll come to me for safety soon as she knows what you do. She'll have to, to save them that's dearest to her. You and her father and her friendship for the Baronets ought to do somethin'; besides, Marjie needs somebody to look after her. She's a pretty girl and everybody runs after her. She'd be spoiled. And she's fond of me, always was fond of me. I don't know what it is about some men makes girls act so; but now, there's Lettie Conlow, she's just real fond of me." (Oh, the popinjay!) "You'll say yes, and say it now." There was a ring of authority in his last words, to which Mrs. Whately had insensibly come to yield.

She sat for a long time trying to see a way out of all this tangled web of her days. At last, she said slowly: "Marjie isn't twenty-one, but she's old for her years. I won't command her. If she will consent, so will I, and I'll do all I can."

Judson was jubilant. He clapped his hands and giggled hysterically.

"Good enough, good enough! I'll let it be quietly understood we are engaged, and I'll manage the rest. You must use all the influence you can with her. Leave nothing undid that you can do. Oh, joy! You'll excuse my pleasure, Mrs. Whately. The prize is as good as mine right now, though it may take a few months even to get it all completely settled. I'll go slow and quiet and careful. But I've won."

Could Mrs. Whately have seen clear into the man's cruel, cunning little mind, she would have been unutterably shocked at the ugly motives contending there. But she couldn't see. She was made for sunshine and quiet ways. She could never fathom the gloom. It was from her father that Marjie inherited all that strong will and courage and power to walk as bravely in the shadows as in the light, trusting and surefooted always.

Judson waited only until some minor affairs had been considered, and then he rose to go.

"I'm so sure of the outcome now," he said gleefully, "I'll put a crimp in some stories right away; and I'll just let it be known quietly at once that the matter's settled, then Marjie can't change it," he added mentally. "And you're to use all your influence. Good-evening, my dear Mrs. W. It'll soon be another name I may have for you."

Meanwhile, Marjie sat up on "Rockport," looking out over the landscape, wrapped in the autumn peace. Every inch of the cliff-side was sacred to her. The remembrance of happy childhood and the sweet and tender memories of love's young dream had hallowed all the ground and made the view of the whole valley a part of the life of the days gone by. The woodland along the Neosho was yellow and bronze and purple in the afternoon sunshine, the waters swept along by verdant banks, for the fall rains had given life to the brown grasses of August. Far up the river, the shapely old cottonwood stood in the pride of its autumn gold, outlined against a clear blue sky, while all the prairie lay in seas of golden haze about it. On the gray, jagged rocks of the cliff, the blood-red leaves of the vines made a rich warmth of color.

For a long time Marjie sat looking out over the valley. Its beauty appealed to her now as it had done in the gladsome days, only the appeal touched other depths of her nature and fitted her sadder mood. At last the thought of what might have been filled her eyes with tears.

"I'll go down to our post-office, as O'mie suggested," she declared to herself. "Oh, anything to break away from this hungry longing for what can never be!"

The little hidden cleft was vine-covered now, and the scarlet leaves clung in a lacework about the gray stone under which the crevice ran back clean and dry for an arm's length. It was a reflex action, and not a choice of will, that led Marjie to thrust her hand in as she had done so often before. Only cold stone received her touch. She recalled O'mie's picture of Lettie, short-necked, stubby Lettie, down there in the dark trying to stretch her fat arm to the limit of the crevice, and as she thought, Marjie slipped her own arm to its full length, down the cleft. Something touched her hand. She turned it in her fingers. It was paper—a letter—and she drew it out. A letter—my letter—the long, loving message I had penned to her on the night of the party at Anderson's. Clear and white, as when I put it there that moonlit midsummer night, when I thrust it in too far for my little girl to find without an effort.

Marjie carried it up to "Rockport" and sat down. She had no notion of when it was put there. She only knew it was from my pen.

"It's his good-bye for old times' sake," she mused.

And then she read it, slowly at first, as one would drink a last cup of water on the edge of a desert, for this was a voice from the old happy life she had put all away now. I had done better than I dreamed of doing in that writing. Here was Rachel Melrose set in her true light, the possibility of a visit, and the possibility of her words and actions, just as direct as a prophecy of what had really happened. Oh! it cleared away every reason for doubt. Even the Rockport of Rachel's rapturous memory, I declared I detested because only our "Rockport" meant anything to me. And then she read of her father's dying message. It was the first time she had known of that, and the letter in her trembling hands pulsed visibly with her strong heart-throbs. Then came the closing words:

"Good-night, my dear, dear girl, my wife that is to be, and know now and always there is for me only one love. In sunny ways or shadow-checkered paths, whatever may come, I cannot think other than as I do now. You are life of my life; and so again, good-night."

The sun was getting low in the west when Marjie with shining face came slowly down Cliff Street toward her home. Near the gate she met my father. His keen eyes caught something of the Marjie he had loved to see. Something must have happened, he knew, and his heartbeats quickened at the thought. Down the street he had met Judson with head erect walking with a cocksure step.

The next day the word was brought directly to him that Amos Judson and Marjory Whately were engaged to be married.

In George Eliot's story of "The Mill on the Floss," the author gives to one chapter the title, "How a Hen Takes to Stratagem." The two cases are not parallel; and yet I always think of this chapter-heading when I recall what followed Amos Judson's admonition to Mrs. Whately, to use her influence in his behalf. When Marjie's mother had had time to think over what had come about, her conscience upbraided her. Away from the little widower and with Marjie innocent of all the trouble—free-spirited, self-dependent Marjie—the question of influence did not seem so easy. And yet, she knew Amos Judson well enough to know that he was already far along in fulfilling his plans for the future. For once in her life Mrs. Whately resolved to act on her own judgment, and to show that she had been true to her promise to use all her influence.

"Daughter, Judge Baronet wants to see you this afternoon. I'm going down to his office now on a little matter of business. Will you go over and see how Mary Gentry's arm is, and come up to the courthouse in about half an hour?"

Mrs. Whately's face was beaming, for she felt somehow that my father could help her out of any tangle, and if he should advise Marjie to this step, it would surely be the right thing for her to do.

"All right, mother, I'll be there," Marjie answered.

The hours since she found that precious letter had been alternately full of joy and sadness. There was no question in her mind about the message in the letter. But now that she was the wrong-doer in her own estimation, she did not spare herself. She had driven me away. She had refused to hear any explanation from me, she had returned my last note unopened. Oh, she deserved all that had come to her. And bitterest of all was the thought that her own letter that should have righted everything with me, I must have taken from the rock. How could I ever care for a girl so mean-spirited and cruel as she had been to me? Lettie couldn't get letters out, O'mie had said; and in the face of what she had written, she had still refused to see me, had shown how jealous-hearted and narrow-minded she could be. What could I do but leave town? So ran the little girl's sad thoughts; and then hope had its way again, for hers was always a sunny spirit.

"I can only wait and see what will come. Phil is proud and strong, and everybody loves him. He will make new friends and forget me."

And then the words of my letter, "In sunny ways, or shadow-checkered paths, I cannot think of you other than as I do now. You are life of my life," she read over and over. And so with shining eyes and a buoyant step, she went to do her mother's bidding that afternoon.

Judge Baronet had had a hard day. Coupled with unusual business cares was the story being quietly circulated regarding Judson's engagement. He had not thought how much his son's happiness could mean to him.

"And yet, I let him go to discipline him. Oh, we are never wise enough to be fathers. It is only a mother who can understand," and the memory of the woman glorified to him now, the one love of all his years, came back to him.

It was in this mood that Mrs. Whately found him.

"Judge Baronet, I've come to get you to help me." She went straight to her errand as soon as she was seated in the private office. "Marjie will be here soon, and I want you to counsel her to do what I've promised to help to bring about. She loves you next to her own father, and you can have great influence with her."

And then directly and frankly came the whole story of Judson's plan. Mrs. Whately did not try to keep anything back, not even the effort to shield my reputation, and she ended with the assurance that it must be best for everybody for this wedding to take place, and Amos Judson hoped it might be soon to save Irving's name.

"I've not seen Marjie so happy in weeks as she was last night," she added. "You know Mr. Tillhurst has been paying her so much attention this Fall, and so has Clayton Anderson. And Amos has been going to Conlow's to see Lettie quite frequently lately. I guess maybe that has helped to bring Marjie around a little, when she found he could go with others. It's the way with a girl, you know. You'll do what you can to make Marjie see the right if she seems unwilling to do what I've agreed she may do. For after all," Mrs.

Whately said thoughtfully, "I can't feel sure she's willing, because she never did encourage Amos any. But you'll promise, won't you, for the sake of my husband? Oh, could he do wrong! I don't believe he did, but he can't defend himself now, and I must protect Marjie's name from any dishonor."

It was a hard moment for the man before her, the keen discriminating intelligent master of human nature. The picture of the battle field at Missionary Ridge came before his eyes, the rush and roar of the conflict was in his ears, and Irving Whately was dying there. "I hope they will love each other. If they do, give them my blessing." Clearly came the words again as they sounded on that day. And here was Irving Whately's wife, Marjie's mother, in the innocence of her soul, asking that he should help to give his friend's daughter to a man whom he was about to call to judgment for heinous offences. And maybe,—oh, God forbid it,—maybe the girl herself was not unwilling, since it was meant for the family's welfare. What else could that look on her face last night have meant? Oh, he had been a foolish father, over-fond, maybe, of a foolish boy; but somehow he had hoped that sweet smile and the light in Marjie's eyes might have meant word from Fort Wallace. What he might have said to the mother, he never knew, for Marjie herself came in at that moment, and Mrs. Whately took her leave at once.

Marjie was never so fair and womanly as now. The brisk walk in the October air had put a pink bloom on her cheeks. Her hair lay in soft fluffy little waves about her head, and her big brown eyes, clear honest eyes, were full of a radiant light. My father brought my face and form back to her as he always did, and the last hand-clasp in that very room, the last glance from eyes full of love; and the memory was sweet to her.

"Mother said you wanted to see me," she said, "so I came in."

My father put her in his big easy-chair and sat down near her. His back was toward the window, and his face was shadowed, while his visitor's face was full in the light.

"Yes, Marjie, your mother has asked me to talk with you." I wonder at the man's self-control. "She is planning, or consenting to plans for your future, and she wants me to tell you I approve them. You seem very happy to-day."

A blush swept over the girl's face, and then the blood ebbed back leaving it white as marble. Men may abound in wisdom, but the wisest of them may not always interpret the swift bloom that lights the face of a girl and fades away as swiftly as it comes.

"She is consenting," my father assumed.

"If you are satisfied with the present arrangement, I do not need to say anything. I do not want to, anyhow. I only do it for the sake of your mother, for the sake of the wife of my best friend. For his sake too, God bless his memory!"

Marjie's confusion deepened. The words of my letter telling of her father's wishes were burning in her brain. With the thought of them, this hesitancy on the part of Judge Baronet brought a chill that made her shiver. Could it be that her mother was trying to influence my father in her favor? Her good judgment and the knowledge of her mother's sense of propriety forbade that. So she only murmured,

"I don't understand. I have no plans. I would do anything for my father, I don't know why I should be called to say anything," and then she broke down entirely and sat white and still with downcast eyes, her two shapely little hands clenched together.

"Marjie, this is very embarrassing for me," my father said kindly, "and as I say, it is only for Irving's sake I speak at all. If you feel you can manage your own affairs, it is not right for anybody to interfere," how tender his tones were, "but, my dear girl, maybe years and experience can give me the right to say a word or two for the sake of the friendship that has always been between us, a friendship future relations will of necessity limit to a degree. But if you have your plans all settled, I wish to know it. It will change the whole course of some proceedings I have been preparing ever since the war; and I want to know, too, this much for the sake of the man who died in my arms. I want to know if you are perfectly satisfied to accept the life now opening to you."

Marjie had seen my father every day since I left home. Every day he had spoken to her, and a silent sort of parental and filial love had grown up between the two. The sudden break in it had come to both now.

Women also may abound in wisdom but the wisest of them may not always interpret correctly.

"He had planned for Phil to marry Rachel, had sent him East on purpose. He was so polite to her when she was here. I have broken up his plans and his friendship is to be limited." So ran the girl's thoughts. "But I have no plans. I don't know what he means. Nothing new is opening to me."

A new phase of womanhood began suddenly for her, a call for self-dependence, for a judgment of her own, not the acceptance of events. When she spoke again, her sweet voice had a clear ring in it that startled the man before her.

"Judge Baronet, I do not know what you are talking about. I do not know of any plans for the future. I do not know what mother said to you. If I am concerned in the plans you speak of, I have a right to know what they are. If you are asked to approve of my doing, I certainly ought to know of what you mean to approve."

She had risen from her chair and was standing before him. Oh, she was pretty, and with this grace of womanly self-control, her beauty and her dignity combined into a new charm.

"Sit down, Marjie," my father said in kind command. "You know the purpose of Amos Judson's visit with your mother yesterday?"

"Business, I suppose," Marjie answered carelessly, "I am not admitted to these conferences." She smiled. "You know I wanted to talk with you about some business affairs some time ago, but—"

"Yes, I know, I understand," my father assured her. They both remembered only too well what had happened in that room on her last visit. For she had not been inside of the courthouse since the day of Rachel's sudden appearance there.

"Judge Baronet thinks I have nothing to bring Phil. I've heard everywhere how Phil wants a rich wife, and yet the Baronets have more property than anybody else here." So Marjie concluded mentally and then she asked innocently:

"How can Amos Judson's visit make this call here necessary?"

At last the light broke in. "She doesn't know anything yet, that's certain. But, by heavens, she must know. It's her right to know," my father thought.

"Marjie, your mother, in the goodness of her heart, and because of some sad and bitter circumstances, came here to-day to ask me to talk with you. I do this for her sake. You must not misunderstand me." He laid his hand a moment on her arm, lying on the table.

And then he told her all that her mother had told to him. Told it without comment or coloring, sparing neither Phil, nor himself nor her father in the recital. If ever a story was correctly reported in word and spirit, this one was.

"She shall have Judson's side straight from me first, and we'll depend on events for further statement," he declared to himself.

"Now, little girl, I'm asked to urge you for your own good name, for your mother's maintenance, and your own, for the sake of that boy of mine, and for my own good, as well, and most of all for the sake of your father's memory, revered here as no other man who ever lived in Springvale—for all these reasons, I'm asked to urge you to take this man for your husband."

He was standing before her now, strong, dignified, handsome, courteous. Nature's moulds hold not many such as he. Before him rose up Marjie. Her cloak had fallen from her shoulders, and lay over the arm of her chair. Looking steadily into his face with eyes that never wavered in their gaze, she replied:

"I may be poor, but I can work for mother and myself. I'm not afraid to work. You and your son may have done wrong. If you have, I cannot cover it by any act of mine, not even if I died for you. I don't believe you have done wrong. I do not believe one word of the stories about Phil. He may want to marry a rich girl," her voice wavered here, "but that is his choice; it is no sin. And as to protecting my father's name, Judge Baronet, it needs no protection. Before Heaven, he never did a dishonest thing in all his life. There has been a tangling of his affairs by somebody, but that does not change the truth. The surest way to bring dishonor to his name is for me to marry a man I do not and could not love; a man I believe to be dishonest in money matters, and false to everybody. It is no disgrace to work for a living here in Kansas. Better girls than I am do it. But it is a disgrace here and through all eternity to sell my soul. As I hope to see my father again, I believe he would not welcome me to him if I did. Good and just as you are, you are using your influence all in vain on me."

Judge Baronet felt his soul expand with every word she uttered. Passing round the table, he took both her cold hands in his strong, warm palms.

"My daughter," neither he nor the girl misunderstood the use of the word here, "my dear, dear girl, you are worthy of the man who gave up his life on Missionary Ridge to save his country. God bless you for the true-hearted, noble woman that you are." He gently stroked the curly brown locks away from her forehead, and stooping kissed it, softly, as he would kiss the brow of a saint.

Marjie sank down in her seat, and as she did so my letter fell from the pocket of the cloak she had thrown aside. As Judge Baronet stooped to pick it up, he caught sight of my well-known handwriting on the envelope. He looked up quickly and their eyes met. The wild roses were in her cheeks now, and the dew of teardrops on her downcast lashes. He said not a word, but laid the letter face downward in her lap. She put it in her pocket and rose to go.

"If you need me, Marjie, I have a force to turn loose against your enemies, and ours. And you will need me. As a man in this community I can assure you of that. You never needed friends as you will in the days before you now. I am ready at your call. And let me assure you also, that in the final outcome, there is nothing to fear. Good-bye."

He looked down into her upturned face. Something neither would have put into words came to both, and the same picture came before each mind. It was the picture of a young soldier out at Fort Wallace, gathering back the strength the crucial test of a Plains campaign had cost him.

"There'll be the devil to pay," my father said to himself, as he watched Marjie passing down the leaf-strewn walk, "but not a hair of her head shall suffer. When the time comes, I'll send for Judson, as I promised to do."

And Marjie, holding the letter in her hand thrust deep in her cloak pocket, felt strength and hope and courage pulsing in her veins, and a peace that she had not known for many days came with its blessing to her troubled soul.

CHAPTER XXI

THE CALL TO SERVICE

We go to rear a wall of men on Freedom's Southern line,
And plant beside the cotton-tree the rugged Northern pine!

—WHITTIER.

"Phil Baronet, you thon of a horthe-thief, where have you been keeping yourthelf? We've been waiting here thinthe Thummer before latht to meet you."

That was Bud Anderson's greeting. Pink-cheeked, sturdy, and stubby as a five-year-old, he was standing in my path as I slipped from my horse in front of old Fort Hays one October day a fortnight after the rescue of Colonel Forsyth's little company.

"Bud, you tow-headed infant, how the dickens and tomhill did you manage to break into good society out here?" I cried, as we clinched in each other's arms, for Bud's appearance was food to my homesick hunger.

"When you git through, I'm nixt into the barber's chair."

I had not noticed O'mie leaning against a post beside the way, until that Irish brogue announced him.

"Why, boys, what's all this delegation mean?"

"Aw," O'mie drawled. "You've been elected to Congress and we're the proud committy av citizens in civilians' clothes, come to inform you av your elevation."

"You mean you've come to get first promise of an office under me. Sorry, but I know you too well to jeopardize the interest of the Republican party and the good name of Kansas by any rash promises. It's dinner time, and I'm hungry. I don't believe I'll ever get enough to eat again."

Oh, it was good to see them, albeit our separation had amounted to hardly sixty days. Bud had been waiting for me almost a week; and O'mie, to Bud's surprise, had come upon him unannounced that morning. The dining-room was crowded; and as soon as dinner was over we went outside and sat down together where we could visit our fill unmolested. They wanted to know about my doings, but I was too eager to hear all the home news to talk of myself.

"Everybody all right when I left," Bud asserted. "I got off a few dayth before thith mitherable thon of Erin. Didn't know he'd tag me, or I'd have gone to Canada." He gave O'mie an affectionate slap on the shoulder as he spoke.

"Your father and Aunt Candace are well, and glad you came out of the campaign you've been makin' a record av unfadin' glory in. Judge Baronet was the last man I saw when I left town," O'mie said.

"Why, where was Uncle Cam?" I asked.

"Oh, pretendin' to be busy somewheres. Awful busy man, that Cam Gentry." O'mie smiled at the remembrance. He knew why tender-hearted Cam had fled from a good-bye scene. "Dave Mead's goin' to start to California in a few days." He rattled on, "The church supper in October was the biggest they've had yet. Dever's got a boil on the back of his neck, and Jim Conlow's drivin' stage for him. Jim had a good job in Topeka, but come back to Springvale. Can't keep the Conlows corralled anywhere else. Everybody else is doing fine except Grandma Mead. She's failin'. Old town looked pretty good to me when I looked back at it from the east bluff of the Neosho."

It had looked good to each one of us at the same place when each started out to try the West alone. Somehow we did not care to talk, for a few minutes.

"What brought you out here, Bud?" I asked to break the spell.

"Oh, three or four thingth. I wanted to thee you," Bud answered. "You never paid me that fifteen thenth you borrowed before you went to college."

"And then," he continued, "the old town on the Neosho'th too thmall for me. Our family ith related to the Daniel Boone tribe of Indianth, and can't have too big a crowd around. Three children of the family are at home, and I wanted to come out here anyhow. I'd like to live alwayth on the Plainth and have a quiet grave at the end of the trail where the wind blowth thteady over me day after day."

We were lounging against the side of the low building now in the warm afternoon sunshine, and Bud's eyes were gazing absently out across the wide Plains. Although I had been away from home only two months, I felt twenty years older than this fair-haired, chubby boy, sitting there so full of blooming life and vigor. I shivered at the picture his words suggested.

"Don't joke, Bud. There's a grave at the end of most of the trails out here. The trails aren't very long, some of 'em. The wind sweeps over 'em lonely and sad day after day. They're quiet enough, Heaven knows. The wrangle and noise are all on the edge of 'em, just as you're getting ready to get in."

"I'm not joking, Phil. All my life I have wanted to get out here. It'th a fever in the blood."

We talked a while of the frontier, of the chances of war, and of the Indian raids with their trail of destruction, death, torture and captivity of unspeakable horror.

The closing years of the decade of the sixties in American history saw the closing events of the long and bitter, but hopeless struggle of a savage race against a superior civilized force. From the southern bound of British America to the northern bound of old Mexico the Plains warfare was waged.

The Western tribes, the Cheyenne and Arapahoe, and Kiowa, and Brule, and Sioux and Comanche were forced to quarter themselves on their reservations again and again with rations and clothing and equipments for all their needs. With fair, soft promises in return from their chief men these tribes settled purringly in their allotted places. Through each fall and winter season they were "good

Indians," wards of the nation; their "untutored mind saw God in clouds, or heard him in the wind."

Eastern churches had an "Indian fund" in their contribution boxes, and very pathetic and beautifully idyllic was the story the sentimentalists told, the story of the Indian as he looked in books and spoke on paper. But the Plains had another record, and the light called History is pitiless. When the last true story is written out, it has no favoring shadows for sentimentalists who feel more than they know.

Each Winter the "good Indians" were mild and gentle. But with the warmth of Spring and the fruitfulness of summer, with the green grasses of the Plains for their ponies, with wild game in the open, and the labor of the industrious settler of the unprotected frontier as a stake for the effort, the "good Indian" came forth from his reservation. Like the rattlesnake from its crevice, he uncoiled in the warm sunshine, grew and flourished on what lay in his pathway, and full of deadly venom he made a trail of terror and death.

This sort of thing went on year after year until, in the late Summer of 1868, the crimes of the savages culminated in those terrible raids through western Kansas, whose full particulars even the official war records deem unfit to print.

Such were the times the three of us from Springvale were discussing on the south side of the walls of old Fort Hays in the warm sunshine of an October afternoon.

We were new to the Plains and we did not dream of the tragedies that were taking place not many miles away from the shadow of the Fort on that October afternoon, tragedies whose crimes we three would soon be called forth to help to avenge. For even as we lounged idly there in the soft sunshine, and looked away through shimmering seas of autumn haze toward the still land where Bud was to find his quiet grave at the end of the trail—as we talked of the frontier and its needs, up in the Saline Valley, a band of Indians was creeping stealthily upon a cornfield where a young man was gathering corn. In his little home just out of sight was a pretty, golden-haired girl, the young settler's bride of a few months.

Through the window she caught sight of her husband's horse racing wildly toward the house. She did not know that her husband, wounded and helpless, lay by the river bank, pierced by Indian arrows. Only one thought was hers, the thought that her husband had been hurt—maybe killed—in a runaway. What else could this terrified horse with its flying harness ends mean? She rushed from the house and started toward the field.

A shout of fiendish glee fell on her ears. She was surrounded by painted savage men, human devils, who caught her by the arms, dragged her about by her long silky, golden hair, beat her brutally in her struggles to free herself, bound her at last, and thrusting her on a pony, rode as only Indians ride, away toward the sunset. And their captive, the sweet girl-wife of gentle birth and gentle rearing, the happy-hearted young home-maker on the prairie frontier, singing about her work an hour before, dreaming of the long, bright years with her loved one—God pity her! For her the gates of a living Hell had swung wide open, and she, helpless and horror-stricken, was being dragged through them into a perdition no pen can picture. And so they rode away toward the sunset.

On and on they went through days and days of unutterable blackness, of suffering and despair. On, until direction and space were lost to measure. For her a new, pitiless, far-off heaven looked down on a new agonized earth. The days ran into months, and no day had in it a ray of hope, a line of anything but misery.

And again beyond the Saline, where the little streams turn toward the Republican River, in another household the same tragedy of the times was being played, with all its settings of terror and suffering. Here the grown-up daughter of the home, a girl of eighteen years, was wrenched from arms that clung to her, and, bound on a pony's back, was hurried three hundred miles away into an unknown land. For her began the life of a slave. She was the victim of brute lust, the object of the vengeful jealousy of the squaws. The starved, half-naked, wretched girl, whose eighteen years had been protected in the shelter of a happy Christian home, was now the captive laborer whose tasks strong men would stagger under. God's providence seemed far away in those days of the winning of the prairie.

Fate, by and by, threw these two women together. Their one ray of comfort was the sight of one another. And for both the days dragged heavily by, the two women of my boyhood's dreams. Women of whose fate I knew nothing as we sat by the south side of old Fort Hays that afternoon forty years ago.

"Did you know, boys, that General Sheridan is not going to let those tribes settle down to a quiet winter as they've been allowed to do every year since they were put on their reservations?" I asked O'mie and Bud. "I've been here long enough to find out that these men out here won't stand for it any longer," I went on. "They're MEN on these Plains, who are doing this homesteading up and down these river valleys, and you write every letter of the word with a capital."

"What'th going to be done?" Bud queried.

"Sheridan's going to carry a campaign down into their own country and lick these tribes into behaving themselves right now, before another Summer and another outbreak like that one two months ago."

"What's these Kansas men with their capital letters got to do with it?" put in O'mie.

"Governor Crawford has issued a call at Sheridan's command, for a Kansas regiment to go into service for six months, and help to do this thing up right. It means more to these settlers on the boundary out here than to anybody else. And you just see if that regiment isn't made up in a hurry."

I was full of my theme. My two months beyond the soft, sheltered life of home had taught me much; and then I was young and thought I knew much, anyhow.

"What are you going to do, Phil?" O'mie asked.

"I? I'm going to stay by this thing for a while. The Baronets were always military folks. I'm the last of the line, and I'm going to give my fighting strength, what little I have, to buy these prairies for homes and civilization. I'm going to see the Indian rule broken here, or crawl into the lonely grave Bud talks about and pull the curly mesquite over me for a coverlet. I go to Topeka to-morrow to answer Governor Crawford's call for volunteers for a cavalry company to go out on a winter campaign against the rascally redskins. They're going to get what they need. If you mix up with Custer, you'll see."

"And when the campaign's over," queried O'mie, "will you stay in the army?"

"No, O'mie, I'll find a place. The world is wide. But look here, boy. You haven't told me how you got pried loose and kicked out yet. Bud's an exception. The rest of us boys had a reason for leaving the best town on earth."

"You're just right, begorra!" O'mie replied with warmth. "I was kicked out av town by His Majesty, the prophet Amos, only you've got to spell it with an 'f' instead av a 'ph.'"

"Now, O'mie, confess the whole sin at once, please."

O'mie looked up with that sunshiny face that never stayed clouded long, and chuckled softly. "Judson's on the crest right now. Oh, let him ride. He's doomed, so let him have his little strut. He comes to me a few days backward into the gone on, and says, says he, important and commercial like, 'O'mie, I shall not need you any more. I've got a person to take your place.' 'All right,' I responds, respectful, 'just as you please. When shall I lave off?' 'To-morrow mornin',' he answers, an' looks at me as if to say, 'Nothin' left for you but the poor-house.' And indade, a clerk under Judson don't make no such bank account as he made under Irving Whately. I ain't ready to retire yet."

"And do you mean to say that because Amos Judson turned you off and cut you out of his will, you had to come out to this forsaken land? I thought better of the town," I declared.

"Oh, don't you mind! Cris Mead offered me a place in the bank. Dr. Hemingway was fur havin' me fill his pulpit off an' on. He's gettin' old. An' Judge Baronet was all but ready to adopt me in the place av a son he'd lost. But I knowed the boy'd soon be back."

O'mie gave me a sidelong glance, but I gave no hint of any feeling.

"No, I was like Bud, ready to try the frontier," he added more seriously. "I'm goin' down with you to join this Kansas regiment."

"Now what the deuce can you do in the army, O'mie?" I could not think of him anywhere but in Springvale.

"I want to live out av doors till I get rid av this cough," he answered. "And ye know I can do a stunt in the band. Don't take giants to fiddle and fife. Little runts can do that. Who do you reckon come to Springvale last month?"

"Give it up," I answered.

"Father Le Claire."

"Oh, the good man!" Bud exclaimed.

"Where has he been? and where was he going?" I asked coldly.

O'mie looked at me curiously. He was shrewder than Bud, and he caught the tone I had meant to conceal.

"Where? Just now he's gone to St. Louis. He's in a hospital there. He's been sick. I never saw him so white and thin as whin he left. He told me he expected to be with the Osages this Winter."

"I'm glad of that," I remarked.

"Why?" O'mie spoke quickly.

"Oh, I was afraid he might go out West. It's hard on priests in the West."

O'mie looked steadily at me, but said nothing.

"Who taketh your plathe, O'mie?" Bud asked.

"That's the beauty av it. It's a lady," O'mie answered.

Somehow my heart grew sick. Could it be Marjie, I wondered. I knew money matters were a problem with the Whatelys, but I had hoped for better fortune through my father's help. Maybe, though, they would have none of him now any more than of myself. When

Marjie and I were engaged I did not care for her future, for it was to be with me, and my burden was my joy then. Not that earning a living meant any disgrace to the girl. We all learned better than that early in the West.

"Well, who be thaid lady?" Bud questioned.

"Miss Letitia Conlow," O'mie answered with a grave face.

"Oh, well, don't grieve, O'mie; it might be worse. Cheer up!" I said gayly.

"It couldn't be, by George! It just couldn't be no worse." O'mie was more than grave, he was sad now. "Not for me, bedad! I'm glad." He breathed deeply of the sweet, pure air of the Plains. "I can live out here foine, but there's goin' to be the divil to pay in the town av Springvale in the nixt six months. I'm glad to be away."

The next day I left the fort for Topeka. My determination to stay in the struggle was not merely a young man's love of adventure, nor was my declaration of what would be done to the Indian tribes an idle boast. The tragic days of Kansas were not all in its time of territorial strife and border ruffianism. The story of the Western Plains—the short grass country we call it now—in the decade following the Civil War is a tragedy of unparalleled suffering and danger and heroism. In the cold calculation of the official reports the half-year I had entered on has its tabulated record of one hundred and fifty-eight men murdered, sixteen wounded, forty-one scalped, fourteen women tortured, four women and twenty-four children carried into captivity. And nearly all this record was made in the Saline and Solomon and Republican River valleys in Kansas.

The Summer of the preceding year a battalion of soldiers called the Eighteenth Kansas Cavalry spent four months on the Plains. Here they met and fought two deadly foes, the Indians and the Asiatic cholera. Theirs was a record of bravery and endurance; and their commander, Major Horace L. Moore, keeps always a place in my own private hall of fame.

Winter had made good Indians out of the savage wretches, as usual; but the Summer of 1868 brought that official count of tragedy with all the unwritten horror that history cannot burden itself to carry. Only one thing seemed feasible now, to bear the war straight into the heart of the Indian country in a winter campaign, to deal an effectual blow to the scourge of the Plains, this awful menace to the frontier homes. General Sheridan had asked Kansas to furnish a cavalry regiment for United States military service for six months.

The capital city was a wide-awake place that October. The call for twelve hundred men was being answered by the veterans of the Plains and by the young men of Kansas. The latter took up the work as many a volunteer in the Civil War began it—in a sort of heyday of excitement and achievement. They gave little serious thought to the cost, or the history their record was to make. But in the test that followed they stood, as the soldiers of the nation had stood before them, courageous, unflinching to the last. Little notion had those rollicking young fellows of what lay before them—a winter campaign in a strange country infested by a fierce and cunning foe who observed no etiquette of civilized warfare.

At the Teft House, where Bud and O'mie and I stopped, I met Richard Tillhurst. We greeted each other cordially enough.

"So you're here to enlist, too," he said. "I thought maybe you were on your way home. I am going to enlist myself and give up teaching altogether if I can pass muster." He was hardly of the physical build for a soldier. "Have you heard the news?" he went on. "Judson and Marjory are engaged. Marjie doesn't speak of it, of course, but Judson told Dr. Hemingway and asked him to officiate when the time comes. Mrs. Whately says it's between the young people, and that means she has given her consent. Judson spends half his time at Whately's, whether Marjie's there or not. There's something in the air down there this Fall that's got everybody keyed up one way or another. Tell Mapleson's been like a boy at a circus, he's so pleased over something; and Conlow has a grin on his face all the time. Everybody seems just unsettled and anxious, except Judge Baronet. Honestly, I don't see how that town could keep balanced without him. He sails along serene and self-possessed. Always knows more than he tells."

"I guess Springvale is safe with him, and we can go out and save the frontier," I said carelessly.

"For goodness' sake, who goes there?" Tillhurst pushed me aside and made a rush out of doors, as a lady passed before the windows. I followed and caught a glimpse of the black hair and handsome form of Rachel Melrose. At the same moment she saw me. Her greeting lacked a little of its former warmth, but her utter disregard of anything unpleasant having been between us was positively admirable. Her most coquettish smiles, however, were for Tillhurst, but that didn't trouble me. Our interview was cut short by the arrival of the stage from the south just then, and I turned from Tillhurst to find myself in my father's embrace. What followed makes one of the sacred memories a man does not often put into print.

We wanted to be alone, so we left the noisy hotel and strolled out toward the higher level beyond the town. There was only brown prairie then stretching to the westward and dipping down with curve and ravine to the Kaw River on the one side and the crooked little Shunganunga Creek on the other. Away in the southwest the graceful curve of Burnett's Mound, a low height like a tiny mountain-peak, stood out purple and hazy in the October sunlight. A handful of sturdy young people were taking their way to Lincoln College, the little stone structure that was to be dignified a month later by a new title, Washburn College, in honor of its great benefactor, Ichabod Washburn.

"Why did the powers put the State Capitol and the College so far from town, I wonder," I said as we loitered about the walls of the former.

"For the same reason that the shortsighted colonists of the Revolution put Washington away off up the Potomac, west of the thirteen States," my father answered. "We can't picture a city here now, but it will be built in your day if not in mine."

And then we walked on until before us stood that graceful little locust tree, the landmark of the prairie. Its leaves were falling in golden showers now, save as here and there a more protected branch still held its summer green foliage.

"What a beautiful, sturdy little pioneer!" my father exclaimed. "It has earned a first settler's right to the soil. I hope it will be given the chance to live, the chance most of the settlers have had to fight for, as it has had to stand up against the winds and hold its own against the drouth. Any enterprising city official who would some day cut it down should be dealt with by the State."

We sat down by the tree and talked of many things, but my father carefully avoided the mention of Marjie's name. When he gave the little girl the letter that had fallen from her cloak pocket he read her story in her face, but he had no right or inclination to read it aloud to me. I tried by all adroit means to lead him to tell me of the Whatelys. It was all to no purpose. On any other topic I would have quitted the game, but—oh, well, I was just the same foolish-hearted boy that put the pink blossoms on a little girl's brown curls and kissed her out in the purple shadows of the West Draw one April evening long ago. And now I was about to begin a dangerous campaign where the hazard of war meant a nameless grave for a hundred, where it brought after years of peace and honor to one. I must hear something of Marjie. The love-light in her brown eyes as she gave me one affectionate glance when I presented her to Rachel Melrose in my father's office—that pledge of her heart, I pictured over and over in my memory.

"Father, Tillhurst says he has heard that Amos Judson and Marjie are engaged. Are they?" I put the question squarely. My father was stripping the gold leaves one by one off a locust spray.

"Yes, I have heard it, too," he replied, and to save my life I could not have judged by word or manner whether he cared one whit or not. He was studying me, if toying with a locust branch and whistling softly and gazing off at Burnett's Mound are marks of study. He had nothing of himself to reveal. "I have heard it several times," he went on. "Judson has made the announcement quietly, but generally."

He threw away the locust branch, shook down his cuff and settled it in his sleeve, lifted his hat from his forehead and reset it on his head, and then added as a final conclusion, "I don't believe it."

He had always managed me most skilfully when he wanted to find out anything; and when the time came that I began in turn to manage him, being of his own blood, the game was interesting. But before I knew it, we had drifted far away from the subject, and I had no opportunity to come back to it. My father had found out all he wanted to know.

"Phil, I must leave on the train for Kansas City this evening," he said as we rose to go back to town. "I'm to meet Morton there, and we may go on East together. He will have the best surgeons look after that wound of his, Governor Crawford tells me."

Then laying his hand affectionately on my shoulder he said, "I congratulate you on the result of your first campaign. I had hoped it would be your last; but you are a man, and must choose for yourself. Yet, if you mean to give yourself to your State now, if you choose a man's work, do it like a man, not like a schoolboy on a picnic excursion. The history of Kansas is made as much by the privates down in the ranks as by the men whose names and faces adorn its record. You are making that record now. Make it strong and clean. Let the glory side go, only do your part well. When you have finished this six months and are mustered out, I want you to come home at once. There are some business matters and family matters demanding it. But I must go to Kansas City, and from there to New York on important business. And since nobody has a lease on life, I may as well say now that if you get back and I'm not there, O'mie left his will with me before he went away."

"His will? Now what had he to leave? And who is his beneficiary?"

"That's all in the will," my father said, smiling, "but it is a matter that must not be overlooked. In the nature of things the boy will go before I do. He's marked, I take it; never has gotten over the hardships of his earliest years and that fever in '63. Le Claire came back to see him and me in September."

"He did? Where did he come from?"

My father looked at me quickly. "Why do you ask?" he queried.

"I'll tell you when we have more time. Just now I'm engaged to fight the Cheyennes, the Arapahoes, the Comanches, and the Kiowas, in which last tribe my friend Jean Pahusca has pack right. He was in that gang of devils that fought us out on the Arickaree."

For once I thought I knew more than my father, but he replied quietly, "Yes, I knew he was there. His tether may be long, but its limit will be reached some day."

"Who told you he was there, father?" I asked.

"Le Claire said so," he answered.

"Where was he at that time?" I was getting excited now.

"He spent the week in the little stone cabin out by the big cottonwood. Took cold and had to go to St. Louis to a hospital for a week or two."

"He was in the haunted cabin the third week in September," I repeated slowly; "then I don't know black from white any more."

My father smiled at me. "They call that being 'locoed' out on the Plains, don't they?" he said with a twinkle in his eye. "You have a delusion mixed up in your gray matter somewhere. One thing more," he added as an unimportant afterthought, "I see Miss Melrose is still in Topeka."

"Yes," I answered.

"And Tillhurst, too," he went on. "Well, there has been quite a little story going around Conlow's shop and the post-office and Fingal's Creek and other social centres about you two; and now when Tillhurst gets back (he'll never make the cavalry), he's square, but a little vain and thin-skinned, and he may add something of color and interest to the story. Let it go. Just now it may be better so."

I thought his words were indefinite, for one whose purposes were always definite, and in the wisdom of my youth I wondered whether he really wanted me to follow Rachel's leading, or whether he was, after all, inclined to believe Judson's assertion about his engagement, and family pride had a little part to play with him. It was unlike John Baronet to stoop to a thing like that.

"Father," I said, "I'm going away, too. I may never come back, and for my own sake I want to assure you of one thing: no matter what Tillhurst may say, if Rachel Melrose were ten times more handsome, if she had in her own name a fortune such as I can never hope to acquire myself, she would mean nothing to me. I care nothing for the stories now"—a hopelessness would come into my voice—"but I do not care for her either. I never did, and I never could."

My eyes were away on Burnett's Mound, and the sweet remembrance of Marjie's last affectionate look made a blur before them. We stood in silence for some time.

"Phil," said John Baronet in a deep, fervent tone, "I have a matter I meant to take up later, but this is a good time. Let the young folks go now. This is a family matter. Years ago a friend of the older Baronets died in the East leaving some property that should sooner or later come to me to keep in trust for you. This time was to be at the death of the man and his wife who had the property for their lifetime. Philip, you have been accused by the Conlow-Judson crowd of wanting a rich wife. I also am called grasping by Tell Mapleson's class. And," he smiled a little, "indeed, Iago's advice to Roderigo, 'Put money in thy purse,' was sound philosophy if the putting be honestly done. But this little property in the East that should come to you is in the hands of a man who is now ill, probably in his last sickness. He has one child that will have nothing else left to her. Shall we take this money at her father's death?"

"Why, father, no. I don't want it. Do you want it?"

I knew him too well to ask the question. Had I not seen the unselfish, kindly, generous spirit that had marked all his business career? Springvale never called him grasping, save as his prosperity grated on men of Mapleson's type.

"Will you sign a relinquishment to your claim, and trust to me that it is the best for us to do?" he asked.

"Just as soon as we get to an inkstand," I answered. Nor did I ever hold that such a relinquishment is anything but Christian opportunity.

That evening I said good-bye to my father, and when I saw him again it was after I had gone through the greatest crisis of these sixty years. On the same train that bore my father to the East were his friend Morton and his political and professional antagonist, Tell Mapleson. The next day I enlisted in Troop A of the Nineteenth Kansas Cavalry, and was quartered temporarily in the State House, north of Fifth Street, on Kansas Avenue. Tillhurst was not admitted to the regiment, as my father had predicted. Neither was Jim Conlow, who had come up to Topeka for that purpose. Good-natured, shallow-pated "Possum," no matter where he found work to do, he sooner or later drifted back to Springvale to his father's forge. He did not realize that no Conlow of the Missouri breed ought ever to try anything above a horse's hoofs, in cavalry matters. The Lord made some men to shoe horses, and some to ride them. The Conlows weren't riders, and Jim's line was turned again to his father's smithy.

Tillhurst took his failure the more grievously that Rachel, who had been most gracious to him at first, transferred her attentions to me. And I, being only a man and built of common clay, with my lifetime hope destroyed, gave him good reason to believe in my superior influence with the beautiful Massachusetts girl. I had a game to play with Rachel, for Topeka was full of pretty girls, and I made the most of my time. I knew somewhat of the gayety the Winter on the Plains was about to offer. As long as I could I held to the pleasures of the civilized homes and sheltered lives. And with all and all, one sweet girl-face, enshrined in my heart's holy of holies, held me back from idle deception and turned me from temptation.

CHAPTER XXII

THE NINETEENTH KANSAS CAVALRY

"The regiments of Kansas have glorified our State on a hundred battle fields, but none served her more faithfully, or endured more in her cause than the Nineteenth Kansas Cavalry."

—HORACE L. MOORE.

When Camp Crawford was opened, northeast of town, between the Kaw River and the Shunganunga Creek, I went into training for regular cavalry service, thinking less of pretty girls and more of good horses with the passing days. I had plenty of material for both themes. Not only were there handsome young ladies in the capital city, but this call for military supplies had brought in superb cavalry mounts. Every day the camp increased its borders. The first to find places were the men of the Eighteenth Kansas Regiment, veterans of the exalted order of the wardens of civilization. Endurance was their mark of distinction, and Loyalty their watchword. It was the grief of this regiment, and especially of the men directly under his leadership, that Captain Henry Lindsey was not made a Major for the Nineteenth. No more capable or more popular officer than Lindsey ever followed an Indian trail across the Plains.

It was from the veterans of this Eighteenth Cavalry, men whom Lindsey had led, that we younger soldiers learned our best lessons in the months that followed. Those were my years of hero-worship. I had gone into this service with an ideal, and the influence of such men as Morton and Forsyth, the skill of Grover, and the daring of Donovan and Stillwell were an inspiration to me. And now my captain was the same Pliley, who with Donovan had made that hundred-mile dash to Fort Wallace to start a force to the rescue of our beleaguered few in that island citadel of sand.

The men who made up Pliley's troop were, for the most part, older than myself, and they are coming now to the venerable years; but deep in the heart of each surviving soldier of that company is admiration and affection for the fearless, adroit, resourceful Captain, the modest, generous-hearted soldier.

On the last evening of our stay in Topeka there was a gay gathering of young people, where, as usual, the soldier boys were the lions. Brass buttons bearing the American Eagle and the magic inscription "U. S." have ever their social sway.

Rachel had been assigned to my care by the powers that were. After Tillhurst's departure I had found my companions mainly elsewhere, and I would have chosen elsewhere on this night had I done the choosing. On the way to her aunt's home Rachel was more charming than I had ever found her before. It was still early, and we strolled leisurely on our way and talked of many things. At the gate she suddenly exclaimed:

"Philip, you leave to-morrow. Maybe I shall never see you again; but I'm not going to think that." Her voice was sweet, and her manner sincere. "May I ask you one favor?"

"Yes, a dozen," I said, rashly.

"Let's take one more walk out to our locust tree."

"Oh, blame the locust tree! What did it ever grow for?" That was my thought but I assented with a show of pleasure, as conventionality demands. It was a balmy night in early November, not uncommon in this glorious climate. The moon was one quarter large, and the dim light was pleasant. Many young people were abroad that evening. When we reached the swell where the tree threw its lacy shadows on its fallen yellow leaves, my companion grew silent.

"Cheer up, Rachel," I said. "We'll soon be gone and you'll be free from the soldier nuisance. And Dick Tillhurst is sure to run up here again soon. Besides, you have all Massachusetts waiting to be conquered."

She put her little gloved hand on my arm.

"Philip Baronet, I'm going to ask you something. You may hate me if you want to."

"But I don't want to," I assured her.

"I had a letter from Mr. Tillhurst to-day. He does want to come up," she went on; "he says also that the girl you introduced to me in your father's office, what's her name?—I've forgotten it."

"So have I. Go on!"

"He says she is to be married at Christmas to somebody in Springvale. You used to like her. Tell me, do you care for her still? You could like somebody else just as well, couldn't you, Phil?"

I put my hand gently over her hand resting on my arm, and said nothing.

"Could you, Phil? She doesn't want you any more. How long will you care for her?"

"Till death us do part," I answered, in a low voice.

She dropped my arm, and even in the shadows I could see her eyes flash.

"I hate you," she cried, passionately.

"I don't blame you," I answered like a cold-blooded brute. "But, Rachel, this is the last time we shall be together. Let's be frank, now. You don't care for me. It is for the lack of one more scalp to dangle at your door that you grieve. You want me to do all the caring. You could forget me before we get home."

Then the tears came, a woman's sure weapon, and I hated myself more than she hated me.

"I can only wound your feelings, I always make you wretched. Now, Rachel, let's say good-bye to-night as the best of enemies and the worst of friends. I haven't made your stay in Kansas happy. You will forget me and remember only the pleasant people here."

When she bade me good-bye at her aunt's door, there was a harshness in her voice I had not noted before.

"If she really did care for me she wouldn't change so quickly. By Heaven, I believe there is something back of all this love-making. Charming a dog as he is, Phil Baronet in himself hasn't that much attraction for her," I concluded, and I breathed freer for the thought. When I came long afterwards to know the truth about her, I understood this sudden change, as I understood the charming pretensions to admiration and affection that preceded it.

The next day our command started on its campaign against the unknown dangers and hardships and suffering of the winter Plains. It was an imposing cavalcade that rode down the broad avenue of the capital city that November day when we began our march. Up from Camp Crawford we passed in regular order, mounted on our splendid horses, riding in platoon formation. At Fourth Street we swung south on Kansas Avenue. At the head of the column twenty-one buglers rode abreast, Bud Anderson and O'mie among them. Our Lieutenant-Colonel, Horace L. Moore, and his staff followed in order behind the buglers. Then came the cavalry, troop after troop, a thousand strong, in dignified military array, while from door and window, side-walk and side-street, the citizens watched our movements and cheered us as we passed. Six months later the remnants of that well-appointed regiment straggled into Topeka like stray dogs, and no demonstration was given over their return. But they had done their work, and in God's good time will come the day "to glean up their scattered ashes into History's golden urn."

A few miles out from Topeka we were overtaken by Governor Crawford. He had resigned the office of Chief Executive of Kansas to take command of our regiment. The lustre of the military pageantry began to fade by the time we had crossed the Wakarusa divide, and the capital city, nestling in its hill-girt valley by the side of the Kaw, was lost to our view. Ours was to be a campaign of endurance, of dogged patience, of slow, grinding inactivity, the kind of campaign that calls for every resource of courage and persistence from the soldier, giving him in return little of the inspiration that stimulates to conquest on battle fields. The years have come and gone, and what the Nineteenth Kansas men were called to do and to endure is only now coming into historical recognition.

Our introduction to what should befall us later came in the rainy weather, bitter winds, insufficient clothing, and limited rations of our journey before we reached Fort Beecher, on the Arkansas River. To-day, the beautiful city of Wichita marks the spot where the miserable little group of tents and low huts, called Fort Beecher, stood then. Fifty miles east of this fort we had passed the last house we were to see for half a year.

The Arkansas runs bottomside up across the Plains. Its waters are mainly under its bed, and it seems to wander aimlessly among the flat, lonely sand-bars, trying helplessly to get right again. Beyond this river we looked off into the Unknown. Somewhere back of the horizon in that shadowy illimitable Southwest General Sheridan had established a garrison on the Canadian River, and here General Custer and his Seventh United States Cavalry were waiting for us. They had forage for our horses and food and clothing for ourselves. We had left Topeka with limited supplies expecting sufficient reinforcement of food and grain at Fort Beecher to carry us safely forward until we should reach Camp Supply, Sheridan's stopping-place, wherever in the Southwest that might be. Then the two regiments, Custer's Seventh and the Kansas Nineteenth, were together to fall upon the lawless wild tribes and force them into submission.

Such was the prearranged plan of campaign, but disaster lay between us and this military force on the Canadian River. Neither the Nineteenth Cavalry commanders, the scouts, nor the soldiers knew a foot of that pathless mystery-shrouded, desolate land stretching away to the southward beyond the Arkansas River. We had only a meagre measure of rations, less of grain in proportion, and there was no military depot to which we could resort. The maps were all wrong, and in the trackless wastes and silent sand-dunes of the Cimarron country gaunt Starvation was waiting to clutch our vitals with its gnarled claws; while with all our nakedness and famine and peril, the winter blizzard, swirling its myriad whips of stinging cold came raging across the land and caught us in its icy grip.

I had learned on the Arickaree how men can face danger and defy death; I had only begun to learn how they can endure hardship.

It was mid-November when our regiment, led by Colonel Crawford, crossed the Arkansas River and struck out resolutely toward the southwest. Our orders were to join Custer's command at Sheridan's camp in the Indian Territory, possibly one hundred and fifty miles away. We must obey orders. It is the military man's creed. That we lacked rations, forage, clothing, and camp equipment must not deter us, albeit we had not guides, correct maps, or any knowledge of the land we were invading.

My first lesson in this campaign was the lesson of comradeship. My father had put me on a horse and I had felt at home when I was so short and fat my legs spread out on its back as if I were sitting on a floor. I was accounted a fair rider in Springvale. I had loved at first sight that beautiful sorrel creature whose bones were bleaching on the little island in Colorado, whose flesh a gnawing hunger had forced me to eat. But my real lessons in horsemanship began in Camp Crawford, with four jolly fellows whom I came to know and love in a way I shall never know or love other men—my comrades. Somebody struck home to the soldier heart ever more when he wrote:

> There's many a bond in this world of ours,
> Ties of friendship, and wreaths of flowers,
> And true-lover's knots, I ween;
> The boy and girl are sealed with a kiss;
> But there's never a bond, old friend, like this,—
> We have drunk from the same canteen.

Such a bond is mine for these four comrades. Reed and Pete, Hadley and John Mac were their camp names, and I always think of them together. These four made a real cavalry man of me. It may be the mark of old age upon me now, for even to-day the handsome automobile and the great railway engine can command my admiration and awe; but the splendid thoroughbred, intelligent, and quivering with power, I can command and love.

The bond between the cavalry man and his mount is a strong one, and the spirit of the war-horse is as varied and sensitive as that of his rider. When our regiment had crossed the Arkansas River and was pushing its way grimly into the heart of the silent stretches of desolation, our horses grew nervous, and a restless homesickness possessed them. Troop A were great riders, and we were quick to note this uneasiness.

"What's the matter with these critters, Phil?" Reed, who rode next to me, asked as we settled into line one November morning.

"I don't know, Reed," I replied. "This one is a dead match for the horse I rode with Forsyth. The man that killed him laughed and said, 'There goes the last damned horse, anyhow.'"

"Just so it ain't the first's all I'm caring for. You'll be in luck if you have the last," the rider next to Reed declared.

"What makes you think so, John?" I inquired.

"Oh, that's John Mac for you," Reed said laughing. "He's homesick."

"No, it's the horses that's homesick," John Mac answered. "They've got horse sense and that's what some of us ain't got. They know they'll never get across the Arkansas River again."

"Cheerful prospect," I declared. "That means we'll never get across either, doesn't it?"

"Oh, yes," John answered grimly, "we'll get back all right. Don't know as this lot'd be any special ornament to kingdom come, anyhow; but we'll go through hell on the way comin' or goin'; now, mark me, Reed, and stop your idiotic grinning."

Whatever may have given this nervousness to the horses, so like a presentiment of coming ill, they were all possessed with the same spirit, and we remembered it afterwards when their bones were bleaching on the high flat lands long leagues beyond the limits of civilization.

The Plains had no welcoming smile for us. The November skies were clouded over, and a steady rain soaked the land with all its appurtenances, including a straggling command of a thousand men floundering along day after day among the crooked canyons and gloomy sandhills of the Cimarron country. In vain we tried to find a trail that should lead us to Sheridan's headquarters at Camp Supply, on the Canadian River. Then the blizzard had its turn with us. Suddenly, as is the blizzard's habit, it came upon us, sheathing our rain-sodden clothing in ice. Like a cloudburst of summer was this winter cloudburst of snow, burying every trail and covering every landmark with a mocking smoothness. Then the mercury fell, and a bitter wind swept the open Plains.

We had left Fort Beecher with five days' rations and three days' forage. Seven days later we went into bivouac on a crooked little stream that empties its salty waters into the Cimarron. It was a moonless, freezing night. Fires were impossible, for there was no wood, and the buffalo chips soaked with rain were frozen now and buried under the snow. A furious wind threshed the earth; the mercury hovered about the zero mark. Alkali and salt waters fill the streams of that land, and our food supply was a memory two days old.

How precious a horse can become, the Plains have taught us. The man on foot out there is doomed. All through this black night of perishing cold we clung to our frightened, freezing, starving horses. We had put our own blankets about them, and all night long we led them up and down. The roar of the storm, the confusion from the darkness, the frenzy from hunger drove them frantic. A stampede among them there would have meant instant death to many of us, and untold suffering to the dismounted remainder. How slowly the cold, bitter hours went by! I had thought the burning heat of the Colorado September unendurable. I wondered in that time of freezing torment if I should ever again call the heat a burden.

There were five of us tramping together in one little circle that night—Reed and John Mac, and Pete and Hadley, with myself. In all the garrison I came to know these four men best. They were near my own age; their happy-go-lucky spirit and their cheery laughter were food and drink. They proved to me over and over how kind-hearted a soldier can be, and how hard it is to conquer a man who wills himself unconquerable. Without these four I think I should never have gotten through that night.

Morning broke on our wretched camp at last, and we took up the day's march, battling with cold and hunger over every foot of ground. On the tenth day after we crossed the Arkansas River the crisis came. Our army clothes were waiting for us at Camp Supply. Rain and ice and the rough usage of camp life had made us ragged already, and our shoes were worn out. And still the cold and storm stayed with us. We wrapped pieces of buffalo hide about our bare feet and bound the horses' nose-bags on them in lieu of cavalry boots. Our blankets we had donated to our mounts, and we had only dog tents, well adapted to ventilation, but a very mockery at sheltering.

Our provisions were sometimes reduced to a few little cubes of sugar doled out to each from the officers' stores. The buffalo, by which we had augmented our food supply, were gone now to any shelter whither instinct led them. It was rare that even a lone forsaken old bull of the herd could be found in some more sheltered spot.

At last with hungry men and frenzied horses, with all sense of direction lost, with a deep covering of snow enshrouding the earth, and a merciless cold cutting straight to the life centres, we went into camp on the tenth night in a little ravine running into Sand Creek, another Cimarron tributary, in the Indian Territory. We were unable to move any farther. For ten days we had been on the firing line, with hunger and cold for our unconquerable foes. We could have fought Indians even to the death. But the demand on us was for endurance. It is a woman's province to suffer and wait and bear. We were men, fighting men, but ours was the struggle of resisting, not attacking, and the tenth night found us vanquished. Somebody must come to our rescue now. We could not save ourselves. In the dangerous dark and cold, to an unknown place, over an unknown way, somebody must go for us, somebody must be the sacrifice, or we must all perish. The man who went out from the camp on Sand Creek that night was one of the two men I had seen rise up from the sand-pits of the Arickaree Island and start out in the blackness and the peril to carry our cry to Fort Wallace—Pliley, whose name our State must sometime set large in her well-founded, well-written story.

With fifty picked men and horses he went for our sakes, and more, aye, more than he ever would claim for himself. He was carrying rescue to homes yet to be, he was winning the frontier from peril, he was paying the price for the prairie kingdom whose throne and altar are the hearthstone.

"Camp Starvation," we christened our miserable, snow-besieged stopping-place. We had fire but we were starving for food. Our horses were like wild beasts in their ravenous hunger, tearing the clothing from the men who came too carelessly near to their rope tethers.

That splendid group of mounts that had pranced proudly down Kansas Avenue less than a month before, moving on now nearly seven days without food, dying of cruel starvation, made a feature of this tragical winter campaign that still puts an ache into my soul. Long ago I lost most of the sentiment out of my life, but I have never seen a hungry horse since that Winter of '68 that I let go unfed if it lay within my power to bring it food.

The camp was well named. It was Hadley and Reed and Pete and John Mac, that good-natured quartet, who stood sponsors for that title. We were a pitiful lot of fellows in this garrison. We mixed the handful of flour given to us with snow water, and, wrapping the unsalted dough around a sagebrush spike, we cooked it in the flames, and ate it from the stick, as a dog would gnaw a bone. The officers put a guard around the few little hackberry trees to keep the men from eating the berries and the bark. Not a scrap of the few buffalo we found was wasted. Even the entrails cleansed in the snow and eaten raw gives hint of how hungry we were.

At last in our dire extremity it was decided to choose five hundred of the strongest men and horses to start under the command of Lieutenant-Colonel Horace L. Moore, without food or tents, through the snow toward the Beulah Land of Camp Supply. Pliley had been gone for three days. We had no means of knowing whether his little company had found Sheridan's Camp or were lost in the pathless snows of a featureless land, and we could not hold out much longer.

I was among the company of the fittest chosen to make this journey. I was not yet twenty-two, built broad and firm, and with all the heritage of the strength and endurance of the Baronet blood, I had a power of resistance and recoil from conditions that was marvellous to the veterans in our regiment.

It was mid-forenoon of the fifth of November when the Nineteenth Kansas moved out of Camp Crawford by the Shunganunga and marched proudly down the main thoroughfare of Topeka at the auspicious beginning of its campaign. Twenty days later, Lieutenant-Colonel Moore again headed a marching column, this time, moving out of Camp Starvation on Sand Creek—five hundred ragged, hungry men with famishing horses, bearing no supplies, going, they could only guess whither, and unable even to surmise how many days and nights the going would consume. It was well for me that I had an ideal. I should have gone mad otherwise, for I was never meant for the roving chance life of a Plains scout.

When our division made its tentless bivouac with the sky for a covering on the first night out beyond the Cimarron River from Camp Starvation, the mercury was twenty degrees below zero. Even a heart that could pump blood like mine could hardly keep the fires of the body from going out. There was a full moon somewhere up in the cold, desolate heavens lighting up a frozen desolate land. I shiver even now at the picture my memory calls up. In the midst of that night's bitter chill came a dream of home, of the warm waters of the Neosho on August afternoons, of the sunny draw, and—Marjie. Her arms were about my neck, her curly head was nestling against my shoulder, the little ringlets about her temples touched my cheek. I lifted her face to kiss her, but a soft shadowy darkness crept between us, and I seemed to be sinking into it deeper and deeper. It grew so black I longed to give up and let it engulf me. It was so easy a thing to do.

Then in a blind stupidity I began to hear a voice in my ears, and to find myself lunging back and forth and stumbling lamely on my left foot. The right foot had no feeling, no power of motion, and I forgot that I had it.

"What are you doing, Pete?" I asked, when I recognized who it was that was holding me.

Pete was like an elder brother, always doing me a kind service.

"Trying to keep you from freezing to death," he replied.

"Oh, let me go. It's so easy," I answered back drowsily.

"By golly, I've a notion to do it." Pete's laugh was a tonic in itself. "Here you and your horse are both down, and you can't stand on one of your feet. I'll bet it's froze, and you about to go over the River; and when a fellow tries to pull you back you say, 'Oh, let me go!' You darned renegade! you ought to go."

He was doing his best for me all the time, and he had begun none too soon, for Death had swooped down near me, and I was ready to give up the struggle. The warmth of the horse's body had saved one foot, but as to the other—the little limp I shall always have had its beginning in that night's work.

The next day was Thanksgiving, although we did not know it. There are no holy days or gala days to men who are famishing. That day the command had no food except the few hackberries we found and the bark of the trees we gnawed upon. It was the hardest day of all the march.

Pete, who had pulled me back from the valley of the shadow the night before, in his search for food that day, found a luckless little wild-cat. And that cat without sauce or dressing became his Thanksgiving turkey.

The second night was bitterly cold, and then came a third day of struggling through deep snows on hilly prairies, and across canyon-guarded bridgeless streams. The milestones of our way were the poor bodies of our troop horses that had given up the struggle, while their riders pushed resolutely forward.

On the fourth day out from Camp Starvation we came at sundown to the edge of a low bluff, beyond which lay a fertile valley. If Paradise at life's eventide shall look as good to me, it will be worth all the cares of the journey to make an abundant entrance therein.

Out of the bitter cold and dreary snow fields, trackless and treeless, whereon we had wandered starving and uncertain, we looked down on a broad wooded valley sheltering everything within it. Two converging streams glistening in the evening light lay like great bands of silver down this valley's length. Below us gleamed the white tents of Sheridan's garrison, while high above them the Stars and Stripes in silent dignity floated lightly in the gentle breeze of sunset.

That night I slept under a snug tent on a soft bed of hay. And again I dreamed as I had dreamed long ago of the two strange women whom I was struggling to free from a great peril.

General Sheridan had expected the Kansas regiment to make the journey from Fort Beecher on the Arkansas to his station on the Canadian River in four or five days. Our detachment of five hundred men had covered it in fourteen days, but we had done it on five days' rations, and three days' forage. Small wonder that our fine horses had fallen by the way. It is only the human organism backed by a soul, that can suffer and endure.

Pliley and his fifty men who had left us the night we went into camp on Sand Creek had reached Sheridan three days in advance of us, and already relief was on its way to those whom we had left beyond the snow-beleaguered canyons of the Cimarron. The whole of our regiment was soon brought in and this part of the journey and its hardships became but a memory. Official war reports account only for things done. No record is kept of the cost of effort. The glory is all for the battle lists of the killed or wounded, and yet I account it the one heroic thing of my life that I was a Nineteenth Kansas Cavalry man through that November of 1868 on the Plains.

CHAPTER XXIII

IN JEAN'S LAND

> All these regiments made history and left records of unfading glory.

While the Kansas volunteers had been floundering in the snow-heaped sand-dunes of the Cimarron country, General Sheridan's anxiety for our safety grew to gravest fears. General Custer's feeling was that of impatience mingled with anxiety. He knew the tribes were getting farther away with every twenty-four hours' delay, and he shaped his forces for a speedy movement southward. The young general's military genius was as strong in minute detail as in general scope. His command was well directed. Enlisted under him were a daring company of Osage scouts, led by Hard Rope and Little Beaver, two of the best of this ever loyal tribe. Forty sharpshooters under Colonel Cook, and a company of citizen scouts recruited by their commanding officer, Pepoon, were added to the regular soldiery of the Seventh Cavalry.

These citizen scouts had been gathered from the Kansas river valleys. They knew why they had come hither. Each man had his own tragic picture of the Plains. They were a silent determined force which any enemy might dread, for they had a purpose to accomplish—even the redemption of the prairie from its awful peril.

The November days had slipped by without our regiment's appearance. The finding of an Indian trail toward the southwest caused Sheridan to loose Custer from further delay. Eagerly then he led forth his willing command out of Camp Supply and down the trail toward the Washita Valley, determined to begin at once on the winter's work.

The blizzard that had swept across the land had caught the Indian tribes on their way to the coverts of the Wichita Mountains, and forced them into winter quarters. The villages of the Cheyenne, the Kiowa, and the Arapahoe extended up and down the sheltering valley of the Washita for many miles. Here were Black Kettle and his band of Cheyenne braves—they of the loving heart at Fort Hays, they who had filled all the fair northern prairie lands with terror, whose hands reeked with the hot blood of the white brothers they professed to love. In their snug tepees were their squaws, fat and warm, well clothed and well fed. Dangling from the lodge poles were scalps with the soft golden curls of babyhood. No comfort of savage life was lacking to the papooses here. And yet, in the same blizzards wherein we had struggled and starved, half a score of little white children torn from their mothers' clinging arms, these Indians had allowed to freeze to death out on the Plains, while the tribes were hurrying through the storm to the valley. The fathers of some of these lost children were in that silent company under Pepoon, marching now with the Seventh Cavalry down upon the snow-draped tepees of Black Kettle and his tribe.

Oh, the cost of it all! The price paid out for a beautiful land and sheltered homes, and school privileges and Sabbath blessings! It was for these that men fought and starved and dared, and at last died, leaving only a long-faded ripple in the prairie sod where an unmarked grave holds human dust returned to the dust of the earth.

In the shelter of the Washita Valley on that twenty-seventh day of November, God's vengeance came to these Indians at the hands of General Custer. He had approached their village undiscovered. As the Indians had swooped down on Forsyth's sleeping force; as the yells of Black Kettle's braves had startled the sleeping settlers at dawn on Spillman Creek, the daybreak now marked the beginning of retribution. While the Seventh Cavalry band played "Garry Owen" as a signal for closing in, Custer's soldiery, having surrounded the village, fell upon it and utterly destroyed it. Black Kettle and many of his braves were slain, the tepees were burned, the Indians' ponies were slaughtered, and the squaws and children made captives.

News of this engagement reached Sheridan's garrison on the day after our arrival, with the word also that Custer, unable to cope with the tribes swarming down the Washita River, was returning to Camp Supply with his spoils of battle.

"Did you know, Phil," Bud Anderson said, "that Cuthter'th to have a grand review before the General and hith thtaff when he geth here to-morrow, and that'th all we'll thee of the thircuth. My! but I wish we could have been in that fight; don't you?"

"I don't know, Bud, I'd hate to come down here for nothing, after all we've gone through; but don't you worry about that; there'll be plenty to be done before the whole Cheyenne gang is finished."

"It'll be a sight worth seein' anyhow, this parade," O'mie declared. "Do you remember the day Judge Baronet took his squad out av Springvale, Phil? What a careless set av young idiots we were then?"

Did I remember? Could I be the same boy that watched that line of blue-coats file out of Springvale and across the rocky ford of the Neosho that summer day? It seemed so long ago; and this snow-clad valley seemed the earth's end from that warm sunny village. But Custer's review was to come, and I should see it.

It was years ago that this review was made, and I who write of it have had many things crowded into the memory of each year. And yet, I recall as if it were but yesterday that parade of a Plains military review. It was a magnificent sunlit day. The Canadian Valley, smooth and white with snow, rose gently toward the hills of the southwest. Across this slope of gleaming whiteness came Custer's command, and we who watched it saw one of those bits of dramatic display rare even among the stirring incidents of war.

Down across the swell, led by Hard Rope and Little Beaver, came the Osage scouts tricked out in all the fantastic gear of Indian war coloring, riding hard, as Indians ride, cutting circles in the snow, firing shots into the air, and chanting their battle songs of victory. Behind them came Pepoon's citizen scouts. Men with whom I had marched and fought on the Arickaree were in that stern, silent company, and my heart thumped hard as I watched them swinging down the line.

And then that splendid cavalry band swept down the slope riding abreast, their instruments glistening in the sunlight, and their horses stepping proudly to the music as the strains of "Garry Owen to Glory" filled the valley.

Behind the band were the prisoners of war, the Cheyenne widows and orphans of Black Kettle's village riding on their own ponies in an irregular huddle, their bright blankets and Indian trinkets of dress making a division in that parade, the mark of the untrained and uncivilized. After these were the sharpshooters led by their commander, Cook, and then—we had been holding our breath for this—then rode by column after column in perfect order, dressed to the last point of military discipline, that magnificent Seventh Cavalry, the flower of the nation's soldiery, sent out to subdue the Plains. At their head was their commander, a slender young man of twenty-nine summers, lacking much the fine physique one pictures in a leader of soldiers. But his face, from which a tangle of long yellow curls fell back, had in it the mark of a master.

This parade was not without its effect on us, to whom the ways of war were new. Well has George Eliot declared "there have been no great nations without processions." The unwritten influence of that thrilling act of dramatic display somehow put a stir in the blood and loyalty and patriotism took stronger hold on us.

We had come out to break the red man's power by a winter invasion. Camp Supply was abandoned, and the whole body made its way southward to Fort Cobb. To me ours seemed a tremendous force. We were two thousand soldiers, with commanders, camp officials, and servants. Our wagon train had four hundred big Government wagons, each drawn by six mules. We trailed across the Plains leaving a wide and well marked path where twenty-five hundred cavalry horses, with as many mules, tramped the snow.

The December of the year 1868 was a terror on the Plains. No fiercer blizzard ever blew out of the home of blizzards than the storms that fell upon us on the southward march.

Down in the Washita Valley we came to the scene of Custer's late encounter. Beyond it was a string of recently abandoned villages clustering down the river in the sheltering groves where had dwelt Kiowa, Arapahoe, and Comanche, from whose return fire Custer saved himself by his speedy retreat northward after his battle with Black Kettle's band.

A little company of us were detailed to investigate these deserted quarters. The battle field had a few frozen bodies of Indians who had been left by the tribe in their flight before the attack of the Seventh Cavalry. There were also naked forms of white soldiers who had met death here. In the villages farther on were heaps of belongings of every description, showing how hasty the exodus had been. In one of these villages I dragged the covering from a fallen snow-covered tepee. Crouched down in its lowest place was the body of a man, dead, with a knife wound in the back.

"Poor coward! he tried hard to get away," Bud exclaimed.

"Some bigger coward tried to make a shield out of him, I'll guess," I replied, lifting the stiff form with more carefulness than sentiment. As I turned the body about, I caught sight of the face, which even in death was marked with craven terror. It was the face of the Rev. Mr. Dodd, pastor of the Springvale Methodist Church South. In his clenched dead hands he still held a torn and twisted blanket. It was red, with a circle of white in the centre.

On the desolate wind-swept edge of a Kiowa village Bud and I came upon the frozen body of a young white woman. Near her lay her two-year-old baby boy. With her little one, she had been murdered to prevent her rescue, on the morning of Custer's attack on the Cheyennes, murdered with the music of the cavalry band sounding down the valley, and with the shouts and shots of her own people, ringing a promise of life and hope to her.

Bud hadn't been with Forsyth, and he was not quite ready for this. He stooped and stroked the woman's hair tenderly and then lifted a white face up toward me. "It would have happened to Marjie, Phil, long ago, but for O'mie. They were Kiowath, too," he said in a low voice.

After that moment there was no more doubt for me. I knew why I had been spared in Colorado, and I consecrated myself to the fighting duty of an American citizen, "Through famine and fire and frost," I vowed to myself, "I give my strength to this work, even unto death if God wills it."

Tenderly, for soldiers can be tender, the body of the mother and her baby were wrapped in a blanket and placed in one of the wagons, to be carried many miles and to wait many days before they were laid to rest at last in the shadow of Fort Arbuckle.

I saw much of O'mie. In the army as in Springvale, he was everybody's friend. But the bitter winter did not alleviate that little hacking cough of his. Instead of the mild vigor of the sunny Plains, that we had looked for was the icy blast with its penetrating cold, as sudden in its approach as it was terrible in its violence. Sometimes even now on winter nights when the storms sweep across the west prairie and I hear them hurl their wrathful strength against this stanch stone house with its rounded turret-like corners, I remember how the wind blew over our bivouacs, and how we burrowed like prairie dogs in the river bank, where the battle with the storm had only one parallel in all this campaign. That other battle comes later.

But with all and all we could live and laugh, and I still bless the men, Reed and Hadley and John Mac and Pete, whose storm cave was near mine. Without the loud, cheery laugh from their nest I should have died. But nobody said "die." Troop A had the courage of its convictions and a breezy sense of the ludicrous. I think I could turn back at Heaven's gate to wait for the men who went across the Plains together in that year of Indian warfare.

This is only one man's story. It is not an official report. The books of history tell minutely how the scattered tribes submitted. Overwhelmed by the capture of their chief men, on our march to Fort Cobb, induced partly by threatened danger to these captive chiefs, but mostly by bewilderment at the presence of such a large force in their country in midwinter, after much stratagem and time-gaining delays they came at last to the white commander's terms, and pitched their tepees just beyond our camp. Only one tribe remained unsubdued: the Cheyennes, who with trick and lie, had managed to elude all the forces and escape to the southwest.

We did not stay long at Fort Cobb. The first week of the new year found us in a pleasanter place, on the present site of Fort Sill. It was not until after the garrison was settled here that I saw much of these Indian tribes, whom Custer's victory on the Washita, and diplomatic handling of affairs afterwards, had brought into villages under the guns of our cantonment.

I knew that Satanta and Lone Wolf, chief men of the Kiowas, were held as hostages, but I had not been near them. Satanta was the brute for whom the dead woman with her little one had been captured. Her form was mouldering back to earth in her grave at Fort Arbuckle, while he, well clothed and well fed, was a gentleman prisoner of war in a comfortable lodge in our midst.

The East knew little of the Plains before the railroads crossed them. Eastern religious papers and church mission secretaries lauded Satanta as a hero, and Black Kettle, whom Custer had slain, as a martyr; while they urged that the extreme penalty of the civil law be meted out to Custer and Sheridan in particular, and to the rest of us at wholesale.

One evening I was sent by an officer on some small errand to Satanta's tent. The chief had just risen from his skin couch, and a long band of black fur lay across his head. In the dim light it gave his receding forehead a sort of square-cut effect. He threw it off as I entered, but the impression it made I could not at once throw off. The face of the chief was for the moment as suggestive of Jean Pahusca's face as ever Father Le Claire's had been.

"If Jean is a Kiowa," I said to myself, "then this scoundrel here must be his mother's brother." I had only a few words with the man, but a certain play of light on his cunning countenance kept Jean in my mind continually.

When I turned to go, the tent flap was pulled back for me from the outside and I stepped forth and stood face to face with Jean Pahusca himself, standing stolidly before me wrapped in a bright new red blanket. We looked at each other steadily.

"You are in my land now. This isn't Springvale." There was still that French softness in his voice that made it musical, but the face was cruel with a still relentless, deadly cruelty that I had never seen before even in his worst moods.

The Baronets are not cowardly by nature, but something in Jean always made me even more fearless. To his taunting words, "This isn't Springvale," I replied evenly, "No, but this is Phil Baronet still."

He gave me a swift searching look, and turning, disappeared in the shadows beyond the tents.

"I owe him a score for his Arickaree plans," I said to myself, "and his scalp ought to come off to O'mie for his attempt to murder the boy in the Hermit's Cave. Oh, it's a grim game this. I hope it will end here soon."

As I turned away I fell against Hard Rope, chief of the Osage scouts. I had seen little of him before, but from this time on he shadowed my pathway with a persistence I had occasion to remember when the soldier life was forgotten.

The beginning of the end was nearer than I had wished for. All about Fort Sill the bluffy heights looked down on pleasant little valleys. White oak timber and green grass made these little parks a delight to the eye. The soldiers penetrated all the shelving cliffs about them in search of game and time-killing leisure.

The great lack of the soldier's day is seclusion. The mess life and tent life and field life may develop comradeship, but it cannot develop individuality. The loneliness of the soldier is in the barracks, not in the brief time he may be by himself.

Beyond a little brook Bud and I had by merest chance found a small cove in the low cliff looking out on one of these valleys, a secluded nook entered by a steep, short climb. We kept the place a secret and called it our sanctuary. Here on the winter afternoons we sat in the warm sunshine sheltered from the winds by the rocky shelf, and talked of home and the past; and sometimes, but not often, of the future. On the day after I saw Jean at the door of Satanta's tent, Bud stole my cap and made off to our sanctuary. I had adorned it with turkey quills, and made a fantastic head-gear out of it. Soldiers do anything to kill time; and jokes and pranks and child's play, stale and silly enough in civil life, pass for fun in lieu of better things in camp.

It was a warm afternoon in February, and the soldiers were scattered about the valley hunting, killing rattlesnakes that the sunshine had tempted out on the rocks before their cave hiding-places, or tramping up and down about the river banks. Hearing my name called, I looked out, only to see Bud disappearing and John Mac, who had mistaken him for me, calling after him. John Mac, leading the other three, Hadley and Reed and Pete, each with his hands on the shoulders of the one before him, were marching in locked step across the open space.

"The rascal's heading for the sanctuary," I said to myself. "I'll follow and surprise him."

I had nearly reached the foot of the low bluff when a pistol shot, clear and sharp, sounded out; and I thought I heard a smothered cry in the direction Bud had taken. "Somebody hunting turkey or killing snakes," was my mental comment. Rifles and revolvers were popping here and there, telling that the boys were out on a hunting bout or at target practice. As I rounded a huge bowlder, beyond which the little climb to our cove began, I saw Bud staggering toward me. At the same time half a dozen of the boys, Pete and Reed and John Mac among them, came hurrying around the angle of another projecting rock shelf.

Bud's face was pallid, and his blue eyes were full of pathos. I leaped toward him, and he fell into my arms. A hole in his coat above his heart told the story,—a bullet and internal bleeding. I stretched him out on the grassy bank and the soldiers gathered around him.

"Somebody's made an awful mistake," John Mac said bitterly. "The boys are hunting over on the other side of the bluff. We heard them shooting turkey, and then we heard one shot and a scream. The boys don't know what they've done."

"I'm glad they don't," I murmured.

"We were back there; you can't get down in front," Reed said. They did not know of our little nest on the front side of the bluff.

"I'm all right, Phil," Bud said, and smiled up at me and reached for my hand. "I'm glad you didn't come. I told O'mie latht night where to find it." And then his mind wandered, and he began to talk of home.

"Run for the surgeon, somebody," one of the boys urged; and John Mac was off at the word.

"It ain't no use," Pete declared, kneeling beside the wounded boy. "He's got no need for a surgeon."

And I knew he was right. I had seen the same thing before on reeking sands under a blazing September sky.

I took the boy's head in my lap and held his hand and stroked that shock of yellow hair. He thought he was at Springvale and we were in the Deep Hole below the Hermit's Cave. He gripped my hand tightly and begged me not to let him go down. It did not last long. He soon looked up and smiled.

"I'm thafe," he lisped. "Your turn, now, Phil."

The soldiers had fallen back and left us two together. John Mac and Reed had hastened to the cantonment for help, but Pete knew best. It was useless. Even now, after the lapse of nearly forty years, the sorrow of that day lies heavy on me. "Accidental death" the official record was made, and there was no need to change it, when we knew better.

That evening O'mie and I sat together in the shadowy twilight. There was just a hint of spring in the balmy air, and we breathed deeply, realizing, as never before, how easy a thing it is to cut off the breath of life. We talked of Bud in gentle tones, and then O'mie said: "Lem me tell you somethin', Phil. I was over among the Arapahoes this afternoon, an' I saw a man, just a glimpse was all; but you never see a face so like Father Le Claire's in your life. It couldn't be nobody else but that praist; and yet, it couldn't be him, nather."

"Why, O'mie?" I asked.

"It was an evil-soaked face. And yet it was fine-lookin'. It was just like Father Le Claire turned bad."

"Maybe it was Father Le Claire himself turned bad," I said. "I saw the same man up on the Arickaree, voice and all. Men sometimes lead double lives. I never thought that of him. But who is this shadow of Jean Pahusca's—a priest in civilization, a renegade on the Plains? Not only the face and voice of the man I saw, but his gait, the set of his shoulders, all were Le Claire to a wrinkle."

"Phil, it couldn't have been him in September. The praist was at Springvale then, and he went out on Dever's stage white and sick, hurrying to Kansas City. Oh, begorra, there's a few extry folks more 'n I can use in this world, annyhow."

We sat in silence a few minutes, the shadow of the bowlder concealing us. I was just about to rise when two men came soft-footed out of the darkness from beyond the cliff. Passing near us they made their way along the little stream toward the river. They were talking in low tones and we caught only a sentence or two.

"When are you going to leave?" It was Jean Pahusca's voice.

"Not till I get ready."

The tone had that rich softness I heard so often when Father Le Claire chatted with our gang of boys in Springvale, but there was an insolence in it impossible to the priest. O'mie squeezed my hand in the dark and rising quickly he followed them down the stream. The boy never did know what fear meant. They were soon lost in the darkness and I waited for O'mie's return. He came presently, running swiftly and careless of the noise he made. Beyond, I heard the feet of a horse in a gallop, a sound the bluff soon shut off.

"Come, Phil, let's get into camp double quick for the love av all the saints."

Inside the cantonment we stopped for breath, and as soon as we could be alone, O'mie explained.

"Whoiver that man with Jean was, he's a 'was' now for good. Jean fixed him."

"Tell me, O'mie, what's he done?" I asked eagerly.

"They seemed to be quarrellin'. I heard Jean say, 'You can't get off too quick; Satanta has got men hired to scalp you; now take my word.' An' the Le Claire one laughed, oh, hateful as anything could be, and says, 'I'm not afraid of Satanta. He's a prisoner.' Bedad! but his voice is like the praist's. They're too much alike to be two and too different somehow to be one. But Phil, d'ye know that in the rumpus av Custer's wid Black Kittle, Jean stole old Satanta's youngest wife and made off wid her, and wid his customary cussedness let her freeze to death in them awful storms. Now he's layin' the crime on this praist-renegade and trying to git the Kiowas to scalp the holy villain. That's the row as I made it out between 'em. They quarrelled wid each other quite fierce, and the Imitation says, 'You are Satanta's tool yourself'; and Jean said somethin' I couldn't hear. Then the Imitation struck at him. It was dark, but I heard a groan and something like the big man went plunk into the river. Then Jean made a dash by me, and he's on a horse now, and a mile beyont the South Pole by this time. 'Tain't no pony, I bet you, but a big cavalry horse he's stole. He put a knife into what went into the river, so it won't come out. That Imitation isn't Le Claire, but nather is he anybody else now. Phil, d'ye reckon this will iver be a dacent civilized country? D'ye reckon these valleys will iver have orchards and cornfields and church steeples and schoolhouses in 'em, and little homes, wid children playin' round 'em not afraid av their lives?"

"I don't know," I answered, "but orchards and cornfields and church steeples and schoolhouses and little homes with children unafraid, have been creeping across America for a hundred years and more."

"So they have; but oh, the cost av it all! The Government puts the land at a dollar and a quarter an acre, wid your courage and fightin' strength and quickest wits, and by and by your heart's blood and a grave wid no top cover, like a fruit tart, sometimes, let alone a tomb-stone, as the total cost av the prairie sod. It's a great story now, aven if nobody should care to read it in a gineration or so."

So O'mie philosophized and I sat listening, whittling the while a piece of soft pine, the broken end of a cracker box.

"Now, Phil, where did you get that knife?" O'mie asked suddenly.

"That's the knife I found in the Hermit's Cave one May day nearly six years ago, when I went down there after a lazy red-headed Irishman. I found it to-day down in my Saratoga trunk. See the name?" I pointed to the script lettering, spelling out slowly—"Jean Le Claire."

"Well, give it to me. I got it away from the 'good Injun' first." O'mie deftly wrenched it out of my hand. "Let me kape it, Phil. I've a sort of fore-warnin' I may nade it soon."

"Keep it if you want to, you grasping son of Erin," I replied carelessly.

We were talking idly now, to hide the heaviness of our sorrow as we thought of Bud down under the clods, whose going had left us two so lonely and homesick.

Two days later when I found time to slip away to our sanctuary and be alone for a little while, my eye fell upon my feather-decked hat, crushed and shapeless as if it had been trampled on, lying just at the corner where I came into the nook. I turned it listlessly in my hands and stood wrapped in sorrowful thought. A low chuckle broke the spell, and at the same moment a lariat whizzed through the air and encircled my body. A jerk and I was thrown to the ground, my arms held to my sides. Almost before I could begin to struggle the coils of the rope were deftly bound about me and I was helpless as a mummy. Then Jean Pahusca, deliberate, cruel, mocking, sat down beside me. The gray afternoon was growing late, and the sun was showing through the thin clouds in the west. Down below us was a beautiful little park with its grove of white-oak trees, and beyond was the river. I could see it all as I lay on the sloping shelf of stone—the sky, and the grove and the bit of river with the Arapahoe and Kiowa tepees under the shadow of the fort, and the flag floating lazily above the garrison's tents. It was a peaceful scene, but near me was an enemy cutting me off from all this serenity and safety. In his own time he spoke deliberately. He had sat long preparing his thought.

"Phil Baronet, you may know now you are at the end of your game. I have waited long. An Indian learns to wait. I have waited ever since the night you put the pink flowers on her head—Star-face's. You are strong, you are not afraid, you are quick and cunning, you are lucky. But you are in my land now. You have no more strength, and your cunning and courage and luck are useless. They don't know where you are. They don't know about this place." He pointed toward the tents as he spoke. "When they do find you, you won't do them any good." He laughed mockingly but not unmusically. "They'll say, 'accidental death by hunters,' as they said of Bud. Bah! I was fooled by his hat. I thought he was you. But he deserved it, anyhow."

So that was what had cut him off. Innocent Bud! wantonly slain, by one the law might never reach. The thought hurt worse than the thongs that bound me.

"Before I finish with you I'll let you have more time to think, and here is something to think about. It was given to me by a girl who loved you, or thought she did. She found it in a hole in the rock where Star-face had put it. Do you know the writing?"

He held a letter before my eyes. In Marjie's well known hand I read the inscription, "Philip Baronet, Rockport, Cliff Street."

"It's a letter Star-face put in the place you two had for a long time. I never could find it, but Lettie did. She gave it to me. There was another letter deeper in, but this was the only one she could get out. Her arm was too short. Star-face and Amos Judson were married Christmas Day. You didn't know that."

How cruelly slow he was, but it was useless to say a word. He had no heart. No plea for mercy would move him to anything but fiendish joy that he could call it forth. At last he opened the letter and read aloud. He was a good reader. All his schooling had developed his power over the English language, but it gave him nothing else.

Slowly he read, giving me time to think between the sentences. It was the long loving letter Marjie wrote to me on the afternoon that Rachel and I went to the old stone cabin together. It told me all the stories she had heard, and it assured me that in spite of them all her faith in me was unshaken.

"I know you, Phil," she had written at the end, "and I know that you are all my own."

I understood everything now. Oh, if I must die, it was sweet to hear those words. She had not gotten my letter. She had heard all the misrepresentation, and she knew all the circumstances entangling everything. What had become of my letter made no difference; it was lost. But she loved me still. And I who should have read this letter out on "Rockport" in the August sunset, I was listening to it now out on this gray rock in a lonely land as I lay bound for the death awaiting me. But the reading brought joy. Jean watching my face saw his mistake and he cursed me in his anger.

"You care so much for another man's wife? So! I can drive away your happiness as easily as I brought it to you," he argued. "I go back to Springvale. Nobody knows when I go. Bud's out of the way; O'mie won't be there. Suddenly, silently, I steal upon Star-face when she least thinks of me. I would have been good to her five years ago. I can get her away long and long before anybody will know it. Tell Mapleson will help me sure. Now I sell her, on time, to one buck. When I get ready I redeem her, and sell her to another. You know that woman you and Bud found in Satanta's tepee on the Washita? I killed her myself. The soldiers went by five minutes afterwards,—she was that near getting away. That's what Star-face will come to by and by. Satanta is my mother's brother. I can surpass him. I know your English ways also. When you die a little later, remember what Star-face is coming to. When I get ready I will torture her to death. You couldn't escape me. No more can she. Remember it!"

The sun was low in the west now, and the pain of my bonds was hard to bear, but this slow torture of mind made them welcome. They helped me not to think. After a long silence Jean turned his face full toward me. I had not spoken a word since his first quick binding of my limbs.

"When the last pink is in the sky your time will come," he laughed. "And nobody will know. I'll leave you where the hunter accidentally shot you. Watch that sunset and think of home."

He shoved me rudely about that I might see the western sky and the level rays of the sun, as it sank lower and lower. I had faced death before. I must do it sometime, once for all. But life was very dear to me. Home and Marjie's love. Oh, the burden of the days had been more grievous than I had dreamed, now that I understood. And all the time the sun was sinking. Keeping well in the shadow that no eye from below might see him, Jean walked toward the edge of the shelf.

"It will be down in a minute more; look and see," he said, in that soft tone that veiled a fiend's purpose. Then he turned away, and glancing out over the valley he made a gesture of defiance at the cantonment. His back was toward me. The red sun was on the horizon bar, half out of sight.

"Though I walk through the valley of the shadow of death, I will fear no evil." The arm of the All Father was round about me then, and I put my trust in Him.

As Jean turned to face the west the glow of the sinking ball of fire dazzled his eyes a moment. But that was long enough, for in that instant a step fell on the rock beside me. A leap of lightning swiftness put a form between my eyes and the dying day; the flash of a knife—Jean Le Claire's short sharp knife—glittered here; my bonds were cut in a twinkling; O'mie, red-headed Irish O'mie, lifted me to my feet, and I was free.

CHAPTER XXIV

THE CRY OF WOMANHOOD

The women have no voice to speak, but none can check your pen—
Turn for a moment from your strife and plead their cause, O men!

—KIPLING.

After all, it was not Tillhurst, but Jim Conlow, who had a Topeka story to tell when he went back to Springvale; and it was Lettie who edited and published her brother's story. Lettie had taken on a new degree of social importance with her elevation to a clerkship in Judson's store, and she was quick to take advantage of it.

Tillhurst, when he found his case, like my own, was hopeless with Marjie, preferred that Rachel's name and mine should not be linked together. Also a degree of intimacy had developed suddenly between Tell Mapleson and the young teacher. The latter had nothing to add when Lettie enlarged on Rachel's preference for me and my devotion to her while the Nineteenth Kansas was mobilizing in Topeka.

"And everybody knows," Lettie would declare, "that she's got the money, and Phil will never marry a poor girl. No, sir! No Baronet's going to do that."

Although it was only Lettie who said it, yet the impression went about and fixed itself somehow, that I had given myself over to a life of luxury. I, who at this very time was starving of hunger and almost perishing of cold in a bleak wind-swept land. And to me for all this, there were neither riches nor glory, nor love.

Springvale was very gay that winter. Two young lawyers from Michigan, fresh from the universities, set up a new firm over Judson's store where my father's office had been before "we planted him in the courthouse, where he belongs," as Cam Gentry used to declare. A real-estate and money-loaning firm brought three more young men to our town, while half a dozen families moved out to Kansas from Indiana and made a "Hoosiers' Nest" in our midst. And then Fingal's Creek and Red Range and all the fertile Neosho lands were being taken by settlers. The country population augmented that of the town, nor was the social plane of Springvale lowered by these farmers' sons and daughters, who also were of the salt of the earth.

"For an engaged girl, Marjory Whately's about the most popular I ever see," Dollie Gentry said to Cam one evening, when the Cambridge House was all aglow with light and full of gay company.

Marjie, in a dainty white wool gown with a pink sash about her waist, and pink ribbons in her hair, had just gone from the kitchen with three or four admiring young fellows dancing attendance upon her.

"How can anybody help lovin' her?" Dollie went on.

Cam sighed, "O Lordy! A girl like her to marry that there pole cat! How can the Good Bein' permit it?"

"'Tain't between her and her Maker; it's all between Mrs. Whately and Amos," Dollie asserted. "Now, Cam, has anybody ever heard her say she was engaged? She goes with one and another. Cris Mead's wife says she always has more company'n she can make use of any ways. It's like too much canned fruit a'most. Mis' Mead loves Marjie, and she's so proud of her. Marjie don't wear no ring, neither, not a one, sence she took off Phil Baronet's."

Springvale had sharp eyes; and the best-hearted among us could tell just how many rings any girl did or didn't wear.

"Well, by hen!" Cam declared, "I'm just goin' to ask herself myself."

"No, you ain't, Cam Gentry," Dollie said decisively.

"Now, Dollie, don't you dictate to your lord and master no more. I won't stand it." Cam squinted up at her from his chair in a ludicrous attempt to frown. "Worst hen-pecked man in town, by golly."

"I ain't goin' to dictate to no fool, Cam. If you want to be one, I can't help it. I must go and set bread now." And Dollie pattered off singing "Come Thou Fount," in a soft little old-fashioned tune.

"Marjie, girl, I knowed you when you was in bib aperns, and I knowed your father long ago. Best man ever went out to fight and never got back. They's as good a one comin' back, though, some day," he added softly, and smiled as the pink bloom on Marjie's cheeks deepened. "Marjie, don't git mad at an old man like your Uncle Cam. I mean no harm."

It was the morning after the party. Marjie, who had been helping Mary Gentry "straighten up," was resting now by the cosy fireplace, while Dollie and Mary prepared lunch.

"Go ahead, Uncle Cam," the girl said, smiling. "I couldn't get mad at you, because you never would do anything unkind."

"Well, little sweetheart, honest now, and I won't tell, and it's none of my doggoned business neither; but be you goin' to marry Amos Judson?"

There was no resentment in the girl's face when she heard his halting question, but the pink color left it, and her white cheeks and big brown eyes gave her a stateliness Cam had never seen in her before.

"No, Uncle Cam. It makes no difference what comes to me, I could not marry such a man. I never will."

"Oh, Lord bless you, Marjie!" Cam closed his eyes a moment. "They's a long happy road ahead of you. I can see it with my good inside eyes that sees further'n these things I use to run the Cambridge House with. 'Tain't my business, I'm a gossipin' inquisitive old pokeyer-nose, but I've always been so proud of you, little blossom. Yes, we're comin', Dollie, if you've got a thing a dyspeptic can eat."

He held the door for Marjie to pass before him to the dining-room. Cam was not one of the too-familiar men. There was a gentleman's heart under the old spotted velvet "weskit," as he called his vest, and with all his bad grammar, a quaint dignity and purity of manner and speech to women.

But for all this declaration of Marjie's, Judson was planning each day for the great event with an assurance that was remarkable.

"She'll be so tangled up in this, she'll have to come to terms. There ain't no way out, if she wants to save old Whately's name from dishonor and keep herself out of the hired-girl class," he said to Tell Mapleson. "And besides, there's the durned Baronet tribe that all the Whatelys have been so devoted to. That's it, just devoted to 'em. Now they'll come in for a full share of disgrace, too."

The little man had made a god of money so long he could not understand how poverty and freedom may bring infinitely more of blessing than wealth and bonds. So many years, too, he had won his way by trickery and deception, he felt himself a man of Destiny in all he under-took. But one thing he never could know—I wonder if men ever do know—a woman's heart. He had not counted on having to reckon with Marjie, having made sure of her mother. It was not in his character to understand an abiding love.

There was another type of woman whom he misjudged—that of Lettie Conlow. In his dictatorial little spirit, he did not give a second thought beyond the use he could make of her in his greedy swooping in of money.

"O'mie knows too much," Judson informed his friend. "He's better out of this town. And Lettie, now, I can just do anything with Lettie. You know, Mapleson, a widower's really more attractive to a girl than a young man; and as for me, well, it's just in me, that's all. Lettie likes me."

Whatever Tell thought, he counselled care.

"You can't be too careful, Judson. Girls are the unsafest cattle on this green earth. My boy fancied Conlow's girl once. I sent him away. He's married now, and doing well. Runs on a steamboat from St. Louis to New Orleans. I'd go a little slow about gettin' a girl like Lettie in here."

They came slowly toward us, the two captive women for whom we waited

"Oh, I can manage any girl on earth. Old maids and young things'll come flockin' round a man with money. Beats all."

This much O'mie had overheard as the two talked together in tones none too low, in Judson's little cage of an office, forgetting the clerk arranging the goods for the night.

When Judson had found out how Mrs. Whately had tried to help his cause by appealing to my father, his anger was a fury. Poor Mrs. Whately, who had meant only for the best, beset with the terror of disgrace to Marjie through the dishonorable acts of her father, tried helplessly to pacify him. Between her daughter and herself a great gulf opened whenever Judson's name was mentioned; but in everything else the bond between them was stronger than ever.

"She is such a loving, kind daughter, Amos," Mrs. Whately said to the anxious suitor. "She fills the house with sunshine, and she is so strong and self-reliant. When I spoke to her about our coming poverty, she only laughed and held up her little hands, and said, 'They 're equal to it.' The very day I spoke to her she began to do something. She found three music pupils right away. She's been giving lessons all this Fall, and has all she can give the time to. And when I hinted about her father's name being disgraced, she kissed his picture and put it on the Bible and said, 'He was true as truth. I won't disgrace myself by ever thinking anything else.' And last of all, because she did so love Phil once" (poor Mrs. Whately was the worst of strategists here), "when I tried to put his case she said indifferently, 'If he did wrong, let him right it. But he didn't.' Now, Amos, you must talk to her yourself. I don't know what John Baronet advised her to do."

Talking to Marjie was the thing Amos could not do, and the mention of John Baronet was worse than the recollection of that callow stripling, Phil. The widower stormed and scolded and threatened, until Mrs. Whately turned to him at last and said quietly:

"Amos, I think we will drop the matter now. Go home and think it over."

He knew he had gone too far, and angry as he was, he had the prudence to hold his tongue. But his purpose was undaunted. His temper was not settled, however, when Mapleson called on him later in the day. Lettie was busy marking down prices on a counter full of small articles and the two men did not know how easily they could be overheard. Judson had no reason to control himself with Tell, and his wrath exploded then and there. Neither did Mapleson have need for temperance, and their angry tones rose to a pitch they did not note at the time.

"I tell you, Amos," Lettie heard Tell saying, "you've got to get rid of this Conlow girl, or you're done for. Phil's lost that Melrose case entirely; and he's out where a certain Kiowa brave we know is creepin' on his trail night and day. He'll never come back. If his disappearance is ever checked up to Jean, I'll clear the Injun. You can't do a thing to the Baronets. If this thing gets up to Judge John, you're done for. I'll never stand by it a minute. You can't depend on me. Now, let her go."

"I tell you I'm going to marry Marjie, Lettie or no Lettie. Good Lord, man! I 've got to, or be ruined. It's too late now. I can get rid of this girl when I want to, but I'll keep her a while."

Lettie dropped her pencil and crept nearer to the glass partition over the top of which the angry words were coming to her ears. Her black eyes dilated and her heart beat fast, as she listened to the two men in angry wrangle.

"He's going to marry Marjie. He'll be ruined if he doesn't. And he says that after all he has promised me all this Fall and Winter! Oh!" She wrung her hands in bitterness of soul. Judson had not counted on having to reckon with Lettie, any more than with Marjie.

That night at prayer meeting, a few more prominent people were quietly let into the secret of the coming event, and the assurance with which the matter was put left little room for doubt.

John Baronet sat in his office looking out on the leafless trees of the courthouse yard and down the street to where the Neosho was glittering coldly. It was a gray day, and the sharp chill in the air gave hint of coming rough weather.

Down the street came Cris Mead on his way to the bank, silent Cris, whose business sense and moral worth helped to make Springvale. He saw my father at the window, and each waved the other a military salute. Presently Father Le Claire, almost a stranger to Springvale now, came up the street with Dr. Hemingway, but neither of them looked toward the courthouse. Other folks went up and down unnoted, until Marjie passed by with her music roll under her arm. Her dark blue coat and scarlet cap made a rich bit of color on the gray street, and her fair face with the bloom of health on her cheek, her springing step, and her quiet grace, made her a picture good to see. John Baronet rose and stood at the window watching her. She lifted her eyes and smiled a pleasant good-morning greeting and went on her way. Some one entered the room, and with the picture of Marjie still in his eyes, he turned to see Lettie Conlow. She was flashily dressed, and a handsome new fur cape was clasped about her shoulders. Self-possession, the lifetime habit of the lawyer and judge, kept his countenance impassive. He bade her a courteous good-morning and gave her a chair, but the story he had already read in her face made him sick at heart. He knew the ways of the world, of civil courts, of men, and of some women; so he waited to see what turn affairs would take. His manner, however, had that habitual dignified kindliness that bound people to him, and made them trust him even when he was pitted with all his strength against their cause.

Lettie had boasted much of what she could do. She had refused all of O'mie's well-meant counsel, and she had been friends with envy and hatred so long that they had become her masters.

It must have been a strange combination of events that could take her now to the man upon whom she would so willingly have brought sorrow and disgrace. But a passionate, wilful nature such as hers knows little of consistency or control.

"Judge Baronet," Lettie began in a voice not like the bold belligerent Lettie of other days, "I've come to you for help."

He sat down opposite her, with his back to the window.

"What can I do for you, Lettie?"

"I don't know," the girl answered confusedly. "I don't know—how much to tell you."

John Baronet looked steadily at her a moment. Then he drew a deep breath of relief. He was a shrewd student of human nature, and he could sometimes read the minds of men and women better than they read themselves. "She has not come to accuse, but to get my help," was his conclusion.

"Tell me the truth, Lettie, and as much of it as I need to know," he said kindly. "Otherwise, I cannot help you at all."

Lettie sat silent a little while. A struggle was going on within her, the strife of ill-will against submission and penitent humiliation. Some men might not have been able to turn the struggle, but my father understood. The girl looked up at length with a pleading glance. She had helped to put misery in two lives dear to the man before her. She had even tried to drag down to disgrace the son on whom his being centred. In no way could she interest him, for his ideals of life were all at variance with hers. Small wonder, if distrust and an unforgiving spirit should be his that day. But as this man of wide experience and large ideals of right and justice looked at this poor erring girl, he put away everything but the determination to help her.

"Lettie," he said in that deep strong voice that carried a magnetic power, "I know some things you do not want to tell. It is not what you have done, but what you are to do that you must consider now."

"That's just it, Mr. Baronet," Lettie cried. "I've done wrong, I know, but so have other people. I can't help some things I've done to some folks now. It's too late. And I hated 'em."

The old sullen look was coming back, and her black brows were drawn in a frown. My father was quick to note the change.

"Never mind what can't be helped, Lettie," he said gravely. "A good many things right themselves in spite of our misdoing. But let's keep now to what you can do, to what I can do for you." His voice was full of a stern kindness, the same voice that had made me walk the straight line of truth and honor many a time in my boyhood.

"You can summon Amos Judson here and make him do as he has promised to do." Lettie cried, the hot tears filling her eyes.

"Tell me his promise first," her counsel said. And Lettie told him her story. As she went on from point to point, she threw reserve to the winds, and gave word to many thoughts she had meant to keep from him. When she had finished, John Baronet sat with his eyes on the floor a little while.

"Lettie, you want help, and you need it; and you deserve it on one condition only," he said slowly.

"What's that?" she asked eagerly.

"That you also be just to others. That's fair, isn't it?"

"Yes, it is," she agreed. Her soul was possessed with a selfish longing for her own welfare, but she was before a just and honorable judge now, in an atmosphere of right thinking.

"You know my son Phil, have known him many years. Although he is my boy, I cannot shield him if he does wrong. Sin carries its own penalty sooner or later. Tell me the truth now, as you must answer for yourself sometime before the almighty and ever-living God, has Philip Baronet ever wronged you?"

How deep and solemn his tones were. They drove the frivolous trifling spirit out of Lettie, and a sense of awe and fear of lying suddenly possessed her. She dropped her eyes. The old trickery and evil plotting were of no avail here. She durst do nothing but tell the truth.

"He never did mistreat me," she murmured, hardly above a whisper.

"He took you home from the Andersons' party the night Dave Mead was at Red Range?" queried my father.

Lettie nodded.

"Of his own choice?"

She shook her head. "Amos asked him to," she said.

"And you told him good-bye at your own door?"

Another nod.

"Did you see him again that night?"

"Yes." Lettie's cheeks were scarlet.

"Who took you home the second time?"

A confusion of face, and then Lettie put her head on the table before her.

"Tell me, Lettie. It will open the way for me to help you. Don't spare anybody except yourself. You need not be too hard on yourself. Those who should befriend you can lay all the blame you can bear on your shoulders." He smiled kindly on her.

"Judge Baronet, I was a bad girl. It was Amos promising me jewelry and ribbons if I'd do what he wanted, making me think he would marry me if he could. I hated a girl because—" She stopped, and her cheeks flamed deeply.

"Never mind about the girl. Tell me where you were, and with whom."

"I was out on the West Prairie, just a little way, not very far. I was coming home."

"With Phil?" My father did not comment on the imprudence of a girl out on the West Prairie at this improper hour.

"No, no. I—I came home with Bud Anderson." Then, seeing only the kind strong pitying face of the man before her, she told him all he wanted to know. Would have told him more, but he gently prevented her, sparing her all he could. When she had finished, he spoke, and his tones were full of feeling.

"In no way, then, has Philip ever done you any wrong? Have you ever known him to deceive anybody? Has he been a young man of double dealing, coarse and rude with some company and refined with others? A father cannot know all that his children do. James Conlow has little notion of what you have told me of yourself. Now don't spare my boy if you know anything."

"Oh, Judge Baronet, Phil never did a thing but be a gentleman all his life. It made me mad to see how everybody liked him, and yet I don't know how they could help it." The tears were streaming down her cheeks now.

And then the thought of her own troubles swept other things away, and she would again have begged my father to befriend her, but his kind face gave her comfort.

"Lettie, go back to the store now. I'll send a note to Judson and call him here. If I need you, I will let you know. If I can do it, I will help you. I think I can. But most of all, you must help yourself. When you are free of this tangle, you must keep your heart with all diligence. Good-bye, and take care, take care of every step. Be a good woman, Lettie, and the mistakes and wrong-doing of your girlhood will be forgotten."

As Lettie went slowly down the walk, to the street, my father looked steadily after her. "Wronged, deceived, neglected, undisciplined," he murmured. "If I set her on her feet, she may only drop again. She's a Conlow, but I'll do my best. I can't do otherwise. Thank God for a son free from her net."

CHAPTER XXV

JUDSON SUMMONED

Though the mills of the gods grind slowly,
Yet they grind exceeding small.

—FRIEDRICH VON LOGAN.

Half an hour later Amos Judson was hurrying toward the courthouse with a lively strut in his gait, answering a summons from Judge Baronet asking his immediate presence in the Judge's office.

The irony of wrong-doing lies much in the deception it practices on the wrong-doer, blunting his sense of danger while it blunts his conscience, leading him blindly to choose out for himself a way to destruction. The little widower was jubilant over the summons to the courthouse.

"Good-morning, Baronet," he cried familiarly as soon as he was inside the door of the private office. "You sent for me, I see."

My father returned his greeting and pointed to a chair. "Yes, I sent for you. I told you I would when I wanted to see you," he said, sitting down across the table from the sleek little man.

"Yes, yes, I remember, so you did. That's it, you did. I've not been back since, knowing you'd send for me; and then, I'm a business man and can't be loafing. But now this means business. That's it, business; when a man like Baronet calls for a man like me, it means something. After all, I'm right glad that the widow did speak to you. I was a little hard on her, maybe. But, confound it, a mother-in-law's like a wife, only worse. Your wife's got to obey, anyhow. The preacher settles that, but you must up and make your mother-in-law obey. Now ain't that right? You waited a good while; but I says, 'Let him think. Give him time.' That's it, 'give him time.' But to tell the truth I was getting a little nervous, because matters must be fixed up right away. I don't like to boast, but I've got the whip hand right now. Funny how a man gets to the top in a town like this." Oh, the poor little knave! Whom the gods destroy they first make silly, at least.

"And by the way, did you settle it with the widow, too? I hope you did. You'd be proud of me for a son, now Phil's clear out of it. And you and Mrs. Whately'd make the second handsomest couple in this town." He giggled at his own joke. "But say now, Baronet, it's took you an awful time to make up your mind. What's been the matter?" His familiarity and impudence were insufferable in themselves.

"I hadn't all the evidence I needed," my father answered calmly.

In spite of his gay spirits and lack of penetration that word "evidence" grated on Judson a little.

"Don't call it 'evidence'; sounds too legal, and nobody understands the law, not even the lawyers." He giggled again. "Let's get to business." A harsher tone in spite of himself was in his voice.

"We will begin at once," my father declared. "When you were here last Summer I was not ready to deal with you. The time has come for us to have an understanding. Do you prefer any witness or counsel, or shall we settle this alone?"

Judson looked up nervously into my father's face, but he read nothing there.

"I—well, I don't know quite what you mean. No, I don't want no witnesses, and I won't have 'em, confound it. This is between us as man to man; and don't you try to bring in no law on this, because you know law books. This is our own business and nobody else's. I'd knock my best friend out of the door if he come poking into my private matters. Why, man alive! this is sacred. That's it—an affair of the heart. Now be careful." His voice was high and angry and his self-control was slipping.

"Amos Judson, I've listened patiently to your words. Patiently, too, I have watched your line of action, for three years. Ever since I came home from the war I have followed your business methods carefully."

The little man before him was turning yellow in spite of his self-assurance and reliance on his twin gods, money and deception, to carry him through any vicissitude. He made one more effort to bring the matter to his own view.

"Now, don't be so serious, Baronet. This is a little love affair of mine. If you're interested, all right; if not, let it go. That's it, let it go, and I'm through with you." He rose to his feet.

"But I'm not through with you. Sit down. I sent for you because I wanted to see you. I am not through with this interview. Whether it's to be the last or not will depend on conditions."

Judson was very uncomfortable and blindly angry, but he sat as directed.

"When I came home, I found you in possession of all the funds left by my friend, Irving Whately, to his wife and child. A friend's interest led me to investigate the business fallen to you. Irving begged me, when his mortal hours were few, to befriend his loved ones. It didn't take long to discover how matters were shaping themselves. But understanding and belief are one thing, and legal evidence is another."

"What was it your business?" Judson stormed. My father rose and, going to his cabinet, he took from an inner drawer a folded yellow bit of paper torn from a note book. Through the centre of it was a ragged little hole, the kind a bullet might have cut.

"This," he said, "was in Whately's notebook. We found it in his pocket. The bullet that killed him went through it, and was deadened a trifle by it, sparing his life a little longer. These words he had written in camp the night before that battle at Missionary Ridge:

"'If I am killed in battle I want John Baronet to take care of my wife and child.' It was witnessed by Cris Mead and Howard Morton. Morton's in the hospital in the East now, but Cris is down in the bank. Both of their signatures are here."

Judson sat still and sullen.

"This is why it was my business to find out, at least, if all was well with Mrs. Whately and her daughter. It wasn't well, and I set about making it well. I had no further personal interest than this then. Later, when my son became interested in the Whately family, I dropped the matter—first, because I could not go on without giving a wrong impression of my motives; and secondly, because I knew my boy could make up to Marjie the loss of their money."

"Phil hasn't any property," the widower broke in, the ruling passion still controlling him.

"None of Whately's property, no," my father replied; "but he has a wage-earning capacity which is better than all the ill-begotten property anybody may fraudulently gather together. Anyhow, I reasoned that if my boy and Whately's girl cared for each other, I would not be connected with any of their property matters. I have, however, secured a widow's pension and some back-pay for Mrs. Whately, and not a minute too soon." He smiled a little. "Oh, yes, Tell Mapleson went East on the same train I did in October. I just managed to outwit him in time, and all his affidavits and other documents were useless. He would have cut off that bit of assistance from a soldier's widow to help your cause. It would have added much value to your stock if Irving Whately's name should have been so dishonored at Washington that his wife should receive no pension for his service and his last great sacrifice. But so long as Phil and Marjie were betrothed, I let your business alone."

Judson could not suppress a grin of satisfaction.

"Now that there is no bond other than friendship between the two families, and especially since Marjie has begged me to take hold of it, I have probed this business of yours to the bottom. Don't make any mistake," he added, as Judson took on a sly look of disbelief. "You will be safer to accept that fact now. Drop the notion that your tracks are covered. I've waited for some time, so that one sitting would answer."

There was a halting between cowardly cringing and defiance, overlaid all with a perfect insanity of anger; for Judson had lost all self-control.

"You don't know one thing about my business, and you can't prove a word you say, you infernal, lying, old busybody, not one thing," he fairly hissed in his rage.

John Baronet rose to his full height, six feet and two inches. Clasping his hands behind his back he looked steadily down at Judson until the little man trembled. No bluster, nor blows, could have equalled the supremacy of that graceful motion and that penetrating look.

"It takes cannon for the soldier, the rope for the assassin, the fist for the rowdy; but, by Heaven! it's a ludicrous thing to squander gunpowder when insect powder will accomplish the same results. I told you, I had waited until I had the evidence," he said. "Now you are going to listen while I speak."

It isn't the fighter, but the man with the fighting strength, who wins the last battle. Judson cowered down in his chair and dropped his eyes, while my father seated himself and went on.

"Before Irving Whately went to the war he had me draw up a will. You witnessed it. It listed his property—the merchandise, the real estate, the bank stock, the cash deposits, and the personal effects. One half of this was to become Marjie's at the age of twenty (Marjie was twenty on Christmas Day), and the whole of it in the event of her mother's death. He did not contemplate his wife's second marriage, you see. That will, with other valuable papers, was put into the vault here in the courthouse for safe keeping, and you carried the key. While most of the loyal, able-bodied men were fighting for their country's safety, you were steadily drawing on the bank account in the pretence of using it for the store. Nobody can find from your bookkeeping how matters were in that business during those years.

"On the night Springvale was to be burned, you raided the courthouse, taking these and other papers away, because you thought the courthouse was to be burned that night. Mapleson got mixed up in his instructions, you remember, and Dodd nearly lost his good name in his effort to get these same papers out of the courthouse to burn them. You and Tell didn't 'tote fair' with him, and he thought you were here in town. You wouldn't have treated the parson well, had your infamous scheme succeeded. But you were not in town. You left your sick baby and faithful wife to carry that will and that property-list out to the old stone cabin, where you hid them. You meant to go back and destroy them after you had examined them more carefully. But you never could find them again. They were taken from your hiding-place and put in another place. You thought you were alone out there; also you thought you had outwitted Dodd. You could manage the Methodist Church South, but you failed to reckon with the Roman Catholics. While you were searching the draw to get back across the flood, Father Le Claire, wet from having swum the Neosho up above there, stopped to rest in the gray of the morning. You didn't see him, but he saw you."

My father paused and, turning his back on the cowardly form in the chair, walked to the window. Presently he sat down again.

"Mrs. Whately was crushed with grief over her husband's death; she was trustful and utterly ignorant in business matters; and in these circumstances you secured her signature to a deed for the delivery of all her bank stock to you. She had no idea what all that paper meant. She only wanted to be alone with her overwhelming sorrow. I need not go through that whole story of how steadily, by fraud, and misuse, and downright lie, you have eaten away her property, getting everything into your own name, until now you would turn the torture screw and force a marriage to secure the remnant of the Whately estate, you greedy, grasping villain!

"But defrauding Irving Whately's heirs and getting possession of that store isn't the full limit of your 'business.' You and Tell Mapleson, after cutting Dodd and Conlow out of the game, using Conlow only as a cat's paw, you two have been conducting a systematic commerce on commission with one Jean Pahusca, highway robber and cut-throat, who brings in money and small articles of value stolen in Topeka and Kansas City and even St. Louis, with the plunder that could be gathered along the way, all stored in the old stone cabin loft and slipped in here after dark by as soft-footed a scoundrel as ever wore a moccasin. You and Tell divide the plunder and promise Jean help to do his foes to death—fostering his savage blood-thirsty spirit."

"You can't prove that. Jean's word's no good in law; and you never found it out through Le Claire. He's Jean's father; Dodd says so." Judson was choking with rage.

"The priest can answer that charge for himself," my father said calmly. "No, it was your head clerk, Thomas O'Meara, who took a ten days' vacation and stayed at night up in the old stone cabin for his health. You know he has weak lungs. He found out many things, even Jean's fear of ghosts. That's the Indian in Jean. The redskin doesn't live that isn't afraid of a ghost, and O'mie makes a good one. This traffic has netted you and Mapleson shamefully large amounts.

"Where's my evidence?" he asked, as Judson was about to speak. "Ever since O'mie went into the store, your books have been kept, and incidentally your patronage has increased. That Irishman is shrewd and to the last penny accurate. All your goods delivered by Dever's stage, or other freight, with receipts for the same are recorded. All the goods brought in through Jean's agency have been carefully tabulated. This record, sworn to before old Joseph Mead, Cris's father, as notary, and witnessed by Cam Gentry, Cris Mead, and Dr. Hemingway, lies sealed and safe in the bank vault.

"One piece of your trickery has a double bearing; here, and in another line. Your books show that gold rings, a watch chain, sundry articles of a woman's finery charged to Marjory Whately, taken from her mother's income, were given as presents to another girl. Among them are a handsome fur collar which Lettie Conlow had on this very morning, and some beautiful purple ribbon, a large bow of which fastened with a valuable pin set with brilliants I have here."

He opened a drawer of his desk and lifted out the big bow of purple ribbon which Lettie lost on the day Marjie and I went out to the haunted cabin. "In your stupid self-conceit you refused to grant a measure of good common sense and powers of observation to those about you. I have seen your kind before; but not often, thank God!"

My father paused, and the two sat in silence for a few moments. Judson evidently fancied his case closed and he was beginning to hunt for a way out, when his accuser spoke again.

"Your business transactions, however, rank as they are, cannot equal your graver deeds. Human nature is selfish, and a love of money has filled many a man's soul with moth and rust. You are not the only man who, to get a fortune, turned the trick so often that when an opportunity came to steal, he was ready and eager for the chance. Some men never get caught, or being known, are never brought to the bar of account; but you have been found out as a thief and worse than a thief; you have tried to destroy a good man's reputation. With words that were false, absolutely false, you persuaded a defenceless woman that her noble husband—wearing now the martyr's crown of victory—you persuaded her, I say, that this man had done the things you yourself have done in his name—that he was a business failure, a trickster, and an embezzler. With Tell Mapleson and James Conlow and some of that Confederate gang from Fingal's Creek, swearing to false affidavits, you made Mrs. Whately believe that his name was about to be dishonored for wrongs done in his business and for fraudulent dealing which you, after three years of careful sheltering, would no longer hide unless she gave her daughter to you in marriage. For these days of wearing grief to Mrs. Whately you can never atone. You and Tell, as I said a while ago, almost succeeded in your scheme at Washington. To my view this is infinitely worse than taking Irving Whately's property.

"All this has been impersonal to me, except as the wrongs and sorrows of a friend can hurt. But I come now to my own personal interest. And where that is concerned a man may always express himself."

Judson broke out at this point unable to restrain himself further.

"Baronet, you needn't mind. You and me have nothing in the world in common."

My father held back a smile of assent to this.

"All I ever did was to suggest a good way for you to help Mrs. Whately, best way in the world you could help her if you really feel so bad about her. But you wouldn't do it. I just urged it as good for all parties. That's it, just good for all of us; and it would have been, but I didn't command you to it, just opened the way to help you."

My father did not repress the smile this time, for the thought of Judson commanding him was too much to bear unsmilingly. The humor faded in a moment, however, and the stern man of justice went on with his charge.

"You tried to bring dishonor upon my son by plans that almost won, did win with some people. You adroitly set on foot a tale of disgraceful action, and so well was your work done that only Providence prevented the fulfilling of your plans."

"He is a fast young man; I have the evidence," Judson cried defiantly. "He's been followed and watched by them that know. I guess if you take Jean Pahusca's word about the goods you'll have to about the doings of Phil Baronet."

"No doubt about Phil being followed and watched, but as to taking Jean Pahusca's word, I wouldn't take it on oath about anything, not a whit more than I would take yours. When a man stands up in my court and swears to tell the truth the whole truth, and nothing but the truth, he must first understand what truth is before his oath is of any effect. Neither Jean nor you have that understanding. Let me tell you a story: You asked Phil to escort Lettie Conlow home one night in August. About one o'clock in the morning Phil went from his home down to the edge of the cliff where the bushes grow thick. What took him there is his own business. It is all written in a letter that I can get possession of at any time that I need it, Lettie was there. Why, I do not know. She asked him to go home with her, but he refused to do so."

Judson would have spoken but my father would not permit it here.

"She started out to that cabin at that hour of the night to meet you, started with Jean Pahusca, as you had commanded her to do, and you know he is a dangerous, villainous brute. He had some stolen goods at the cabin, and you wanted Lettie to see them, you said. If she could not entrap Phil that night, Jean must bring her out to this lonely haunted house. You led the prayer meeting that week for Dr. Hemingway. Amos Judson, so long as such men as you live, there is still need for guardian angels. One came to this poor wilful erring girl that night in the person of Bud Anderson, who not only made her tell where she was going, but persuaded her to turn back, and he saw her safe within her own home."

"It's Phil that's deceived her and been her downfall. I can prove it by Lettie herself. She's a very warm friend and admirer of mine."

"She told me in this room not two hours ago that Phil had never done her wrong. It was she who asked to have you summoned here this morning, although I was ready for you anyhow."

The end of Judson's rope was in sight now. He collapsed in his chair into a little heap of whining fear and self-abasement.

"Your worst crime, Judson, is against this girl. You have used her for your tool, your accomplice, and your villainously base purposes. You bribed her, with gifts she coveted, to do your bidding. You lived a double life, filling her ears with promises you meant only to break. Even your pretended engagement to Marjie you kept from her, and when she found it out, you declared it was false. And more, when with her own ears she heard you assert it as a fact, you sought to pacify her with promises of pleasures bought with sin. You are a property thief, a receiver of stolen goods, a defamer of character. Your hand was on the torch to burn this town. You juggled with the official records in the courthouse. You would basely deceive and marry a girl whose consent could be given only to save her father's memory from stain, and her mother from a broken heart. And greatest and blackest of all, you would utterly destroy the life and degrade the soul of one whose erring feet we owe it to ourselves to lead back to straight paths. On these charges I have summoned you to this account. Every charge I have evidence to prove beyond any shadow of question. I could call you before the civil courts at once. That I have not done it has not been for my son's sake, nor for Marjie's, nor her mother's, but for the sake of the one I have no personal cause to protect, the worst one connected with this business outside of yourself and that scoundrel Mapleson—for the sake of a woman. It is a man's business to shield her, not to drag her down to perdition. I said I would send for you when it was time for you to come again, when I was ready for you. I have sent for you. Now you must answer me."

Judson, sitting in a crumpled-up heap in the big armchair in John Baronet's private office, tried vainly for a time to collect his forces. At last he turned to the one resource we all seek in our misdoing: he tried to justify himself by blaming others.

"Judge Baronet," his high thin voice always turned to a whine when he lowered it. "Judge Baronet, I don't see why I'm the only one you call to account. There's Tell Mapleson and Jim Conlow and the Rev. Dodd and a lot more done and planned to do what I'd never 'a dreamed of. Now, why do I have to bear all of it?"

"You have only your part to bear, no more; and as to Tell Mapleson, his time is coming."

"I think I might have some help. You know all the law, and I don't know any law." My father did not smile at the evident truth of the last clause.

"You can have all the law, evidence, and witnesses you choose. You may carry your case up to the highest court. Law is my business; but I'll be fair and say to you that a man's case is sometimes safer settled out of court, if mercy is to play any part. I've no cause to shield you, but I'm willing you should know this."

"I don't want to go to court. Tell's told me over and over I'd never have a ghost of a show"—he was talking blindly now—"I want somebody to shake you loose from me. That's it, I want to get rid of you."

"How much time will it require to get your counsel and come here again?"

If a man sells his soul for wealth, the hardest trial of his life comes when he first gets face to face with the need of what money cannot buy; that is, loyalty. Such a trial came to Judson at this moment. Mapleson had warned him about Baronet, but in his puny egotistic narrowness he thought himself the equal of the best. Now he knew that neither Mapleson nor any other of the crew with whom he had been a law-breaker would befriend him.

"They ain't one of 'em 'll stand by a fellow when he's down, not a one," the little man declared.

"No, they never do; remember that," John Baronet replied.

"Well, what is it you want?" he whined.

"What are you going to do? Settle this in court or out of it?"

"Out of it, out of it," Judson fairly shrieked. "I'd be put out of the Presbyterian Church if this gets into the courts. I've got a bank account I'm not ashamed of. How much is it going to take to settle it? What's the least will satisfy you?"

"Settle it? Satisfy me? Great heavens! Can a career like this be atoned for with a bank check and interest at eight per cent?" My father's disgust knew no bounds.

"You are going to turn over to the account of Marjory Whately an amount equal to one-half the value of Whately's estate at the time of his death, with a legal rate of interest, which according to his will she was to receive at the age of twenty. The will," my father went on, as he read a certain look in Judson's face, "is safe in the vault of the courthouse, and there are no keys available to the box that holds it. Also, you are going to pay in money the value of all the articles charged to Marjory Whately's account and given to other people, mostly young ladies, and especially to Lettie Conlow. Your irregular business methods in the management of that store since O'mie began to keep your records you are going to make straight and honest by giving all that is overdue to your senior partner, Mrs. Irving Whately. Furthermore, you are going to give an account for the bank stock fraudulently secured in the days of Mrs. Whately's deep sorrow. This much for your property transactions. You can give it at once or stand suit for embezzlement. I have the amounts all listed here. I know your bank account and property possession. Will you sign the papers now?"

"But—but," Judson began. "I can't. It'll take more than half, yes, all but two-thirds, I've got to my name. I can't do it. I'll have to hire to somebody if I do."

"You miserable cur, the pity is you can't make up all that you owe but that cannot be proved by any available record. Only one thing keeps me back from demanding a full return for all your years of thieving stewardship."

"Isn't that all?" Judson asked.

"Not yet. You cannot make returns for some things. If it were all a money proposition it would be simple. The other thing you are going to do, now mark me, I've left you the third of your gains for it. You are going to make good your promise to Lettie Conlow, and you will do it now. You will give her your name, the title of wife. Your property under the Kansas law becomes hers also; her children become the heirs to your estate. These, with an honest life following, are the only conditions that can save you from the penitentiary, as an embezzler, a receiver of stolen goods, a robber of county records, a defamer of innocent men, an accomplice in helping an Indian to steal a white girl, and a libertine.

"I shall not release the evidence, nor withdraw the power to bring you down the minute you break over the restrictions. Amos Judson," (there was a terrible sternness in my father's voice, as he stood before the wretched little man), "there is an assize at which you will be tried, there is a bar whose Judge knows the heart as well as the deed, and for both you must answer to Him, not only for the things in which I give you now the chance to redeem yourself, but for those crimes for which the law may not now punish you. There is here one door open beside the one of iron bars, and that is the door to an honest life. Redeem your past by the future."

For the person who could have seen John Baronet that day, who could have heard his deep strong voice and felt the power of his magnetic personality, who could have been lifted up by the very strength of his nobility so as to realize what a manhood such as his can mean—for one who could have known all this it were easy to see to how hard a task I have set my pen in trying to picture it here.

"No man's life is an utter failure until he votes it so himself." My father did not relax his hold for a moment. "You must square yours by a truer line and lift up to your own plane the girl you have promised to marry, and prosperity and happiness such as you could never know otherwise will come to you. On this condition only will you escape the full penalty of the law."

The little widower stood up at last. It had been a terrible grilling, but his mind and body, cramped together, seemed now to expand.

"I'll do it, Judge Baronet. Will you help me?"

He put out his hand hesitatingly.

My father took it in his own strong right hand. No man or woman, whether clothed upon with virtue or steeped in vice, ever reached forth a hand to John Baronet and saw in his face any shadow of hesitancy to receive it. So supreme to him was the ultimate value of each human soul. He did not drop the hand at once, but standing there, as father to son he spoke:

"I have been a husband. Through all these long years I have walked alone and lonely, yearning ever for the human presence of my loved one lying these many years under the churchyard grasses back at old Rockport. Judson, be good to your wife. Make her happy. You will be blessed yourself and you will make her a true good woman."

There was a quiet wedding at the Presbyterian parsonage that evening. The name of only one witness appeared on the marriage certificate, the name in a bold hand of John Baronet.

CHAPTER XXVI

O'MIE'S INHERITANCE

In these cases we still have judgment here.

—SHAKESPEARE.

True to his word, Tell Mapleson's time followed hard on the finishing up of Judson. My father did not make a step until he was sure of what the next one would be. That is why the supreme court never reversed his decisions. When at last he had perfected his plans, Tell Mapleson grew shy of pushing his claims. But Tell was a shrewd pettifogger, and his was a different calibre of mind from Judson's. It was not until my father was about to lay claim in his client's behalf to the valuable piece of land containing the big cottonwood and the haunted cabin, that Tell came out of hiding. This happened on the afternoon following the morning scene with Judson. And aside from the task of the morning, the news of Bud Anderson's untimely death had come that day. Nobody could foretell what next this winter's campaign might hold for the Springvale boys out on the far Southwest Plains, and my father's heart was heavy.

Tell Mapleson was tall and slight. He was a Southern man by birth, and he always retained something of the Southern air in his manner. Active, nervous, quick-witted, but not profound, he made a good impression generally, especially where political trickery or nice turns in the law count for coin. Professionally he and my father were competitors; and he might have developed into a man of fine standing, had he not kept store, become postmaster, run for various offices, and diffused himself generally, while John Baronet held steadily to his calling.

In the early afternoon Tell courteously informed my father that he desired an interview with the idea of adjusting differences between the two. His request was granted, and a battle royal was to mark the second half of the day. John Baronet always called this day, which was Friday, his black but good Friday.

"Good-afternoon, Mr. Mapleson, have a chair."

"Good-afternoon, Judge. Pretty stiff winter weather for Kansas."

So the two greeted each other.

"You wanted to see me?" my father queried.

"Yes, Judge. We might as well get this matter between us settled here as over in the court-room, eh?"

My father smiled. "Yes, we can afford to do that," he said. "Now, Mapleson, you represent a certain client in claiming a piece of property known as the north half of section 29, range 14. I also represent a claim on the same property. You want this settled out of court. I have no reason to refuse settlement in this way. State your claim."

Mapleson adjusted himself in his chair.

"Judge, the half section of land lying upon the Neosho, the one containing among other appurtenances the big cottonwood tree and the stone cabin, was set down in the land records as belonging to one Patrick O'Meara, the man who took up the land. He was a light-headed Irishman; he ran off with a Cheyenne squaw, and not long afterwards was killed by the Comanches. This property, however, he gave over to a friend of his, a Frenchman named Le Claire, connected in a business way with the big Choteau Fur-trading Company in St. Louis. This Frenchman brought his wife and child here to live. I knew them, for they traded at the 'Last Chance' store. That was before your day here, Baronet. Le Claire didn't live out in that cabin long, for his only child was stolen by the Kiowas, and his wife, in a frenzy of grief drowned herself in the Neosho. Then Le Claire plunged off into the Plains somewhere. Later he was reported killed by the Kiowas. Now I have the evidence, the written statement signed by this Irishman, of the turning of the property into Le Claire's hands. Also the evidence that Le Claire was not killed by the Indians. Instead, he was legally married to a Kiowa squaw, a sister of Chief Satanta, who is now a prisoner of war with General Custer in the Indian Territory. By this union there was one child, a son, Jean Pahusca he is called. To this son this property now belongs. There can be no question about it. The records show who entered the land. Here is the letter sworn to in my store by this same man, left by him to be given to Le Claire when he should come on from St. Louis. The Irishman was impatient to join these Cheyennes he'd met on a fur-hunting trip way up on the Platte, and with his affidavit before old Judge Fingal (he also was here before you) he left this piece of land to the Frenchman."

Mapleson handed my father a torn greasy bit of paper, duly setting forth what he had claimed.

"Now, to go on," he resumed. "This Kiowa marriage was a legal one, for the Frenchman had a good Catholic conscience. This marriage was all right. I have also here the affidavit of the Rev. J. J. Dodd, former pastor of the Methodist Church South in Springvale. At the time of this marriage Dodd, who was then stationed out near Santa Fé, New Mexico, was on his way east with a wagon train. Near Pawnee Rock Le Claire with a pretty squaw came to the train legally equipped and was legally married by Dodd. As a wedding fee he gave this letter of land grant to Dodd. 'Take it,' he said, 'I'll never use it. Keep it, or give it away.' Dodd kept it."

"Until when?" my father asked.

Mapleson's hands twitched nervously.

"Until he signed it over to me," he replied. "I have everything secured," he added, smiling, and then he went on.

"Le Claire soon got tired of the Kiowas of course, and turned priest, repented of all his sins, renounced his wife and child, and all his worldly goods. It will be well for him to keep clear of old Satanta in his missionary journeys to the heathen, however. You know this priest's son, Jean Pahusca. He got into some sort of trouble here during the war, and he never comes here any more. He has assigned to me all his right to this property, on a just consideration and I am now ready to claim my own, by force, if necessary, through the courts. But knowing your position, and that you also have a claim on the same property, I figured it could be adjusted between us. Baronet, there isn't a ghost of a show for anybody else to get a hold on this property. Every legal claimant is dead except this half-breed. I have papers for every step in the way to possession; and as a man whose reputation for justice has never been diminished, I don't believe you will pile up costs on your client, nor deal unfairly with him. Have you any answer to my claim?"

At that moment the door opened quietly and Father Le Claire entered. He was embarrassed by his evident intrusion and would have retreated but my father called him in.

"You come at a most opportune time, Father Le Claire. Mapleson here has been proving some things to me through your name. You can help us both."

John Baronet looked at both men keenly. Mapleson's face had a look of pleasure as if he saw not only the opportunity to prove his cause, but the chance to grill the priest, whose gentle power had time and again led the Indians from his "Last Chance" saloon on annuity days, when the peaceful Osages and Kaws came up for their supplies. The good Father's face though serious, even apprehensive, had an undercurrent of serenity in its expression hard to reconcile with fear of accusation.

"Mr. Mapleson, will you repeat to Le Claire what you have just told me and show him your affidavits and records?" John Baronet asked.

"Certainly," Tell replied, and glibly he again set forth his basis to a claim on the valuable property. "Now, Le Claire," he added, "Baronet and I have about agreed to arbitrate for ourselves. Your name will never appear in this. The records are seldom referred to, and you are as safe with us as if you'd never married that squaw of old Satanta's household. We are all men here, if one is a priest and one a judge and the other a land-owner."

Le Claire's face never twitched a muscle. He turned his eyes upon the judge inquiringly, but unabashed.

"Will you help us out of this, Le Claire?" my father asked. "If you choose I will give you my claim first."

"Good," said Mapleson. "Let him hear us both, and his word will show us what to do."

"Well, gentlemen," my father began, "by the merest chance a few years ago I came upon the entry of the land in question. It was entered in the name of Patrick O'Meara. Happening to recall that the little red-headed orphan chore-boy down at the Cambridge House bore the same name, I made some inquiry of Cam Gentry about the boy's origin and found that he was an orphan from the Osage Mission, and had been brought up here by one of the priests who stopped here a day or two on his way from the Osage to St. Mary's, up on the Kaw. Cam and Dollie were kind to the child, and he begged the priest to stay with them. The good man consented, and while the guardianship remained with the people of the Mission, O'mie grew up here. It seemed not impossible that he might have some claim on this land. Everything kept pointing the fact more and more clearly to me. Then I was called to the war."

Tell Mapleson's mobile face clouded up a bit at this.

"But I had by this time become so convinced that I called in Le Claire here and held a council with him. He told me some of what he knew, not all, for reasons he did not explain" (my father's eyes were on the priest's face), "but if it is necessary he will tell."

"Now that sounds like a threat," Mapleson urged. Somehow, shrewd as he was, solid as his case appeared to himself, the man was growing uncomfortable. "I've known Le Claire's story for years. I never questioned him once. I had my papers from Dodd. Le Claire long ago renounced the world. His life has proved it. The world includes the undivided north half of section 29, range 14. That's Jean Pahusca's. It's too late now for his father to try to get it away from him, Baronet. You know the courts won't stand for it." Adroit as he was, the Southern blood was beginning to show in Tell's nervous manner and flashing eyes.

"When I came back from the war," my father went on, ignoring the interruption, "I found that the courthouse records had been juggled with. Some of them, with some other papers, had been stolen. It happened on a night when for some reason O'mie, a harmless, uninfluential Irish orphan, was hunted for everywhere in order to be murdered. Why? He stood in the way of a land-claim, and human life was cheap that night."

Tell Mapleson's face was ashy gray with anger; but no heed was given to him, as my father continued.

"It happened that Jean Pahusca, who took him out of town by mistake and left him unconscious and half dead on the bank of Fingal's Creek, was ordered back by the ruffians to find his body, and if he was alive to finish him in any way the Indian chose. That same night the courthouse was entered, and the record of this land-entry was taken."

"I have papers showing O'Meara's signing it over—" Tell began; but my father waved his hand and proceeded.

"Briefly put, it was concealed in the old stone cabin by one Amos Judson. Le Claire here was a witness to the transaction."

The priest nodded assent.

"But for reasons of his own he did not report the theft. He did, however, remove the papers from their careless hiding-place in an old chest to a more secure nook in the far corner of the dark loft. Before I came home he had left Springvale, and business matters called him to France. He has not been here since, until last September when he spent a few days out at the cabin. The lead box had been taken from the loft and concealed under the flat stone that forms the door step, possibly by some movers who camped there and did some little harm to the property.

"I have the box in the bank vault now. Le Claire turned it over to me. There is no question as to the record. Two points must be settled, however. First, did O'Meara give up the land he entered? And second, is the young man we call O'mie heir to the same? Le Claire, you are just back from the Osage Mission?"

The priest assented.

"Now, will you tell us what you know of this case?"

A sudden fear seized Tell Mapleson. Would this man lie now to please Judge Baronet? Tell was a good reader of human nature, and he had thoroughly believed in the priest as a holy man, one who had renounced sin and whose life was one long atonement for a wild, tragic, and reckless youth. He disliked Le Claire, but he had never doubted the priest's sincerity. He could have given any sort of bribe had he deemed the Frenchman purchasable.

"Just one word please, Judge," he said suavely. "Look here, Le Claire, Baronet's a good lawyer, a rich man, and a popular man with a fine reputation; but by jiminy! if you try any tricks with me and vary one hair from the truth, I'll have you before the civil and church courts so quick you'll think the Holy Inquisition's no joke. If you'll just tell the truth nobody's going to know through me anything about your former wives, nor how many half-breed papooses claim you. And I know Baronet here well enough to know he never gossips."

Le Claire turned his dark face toward Mapleson, and his piercing black eyes seemed to look through the restless lawyer fidgeting in his chair. In the old days of the "Last Chance" saloon the two had played a quiet game, each trying to outwit the other—the priest for the spiritual and financial welfare of the Indian pensioners, Mapleson for his own financial gain. Yet no harsh word had ever passed between them. Not even after Le Claire had sent his ultimatum to the proprietor of the "Last Chance," "Sell Jean Pahusca another drink of whiskey and you'll be removed from the Indian agency by order from the Secretary of Indian affairs at Washington."

"Mr. Mapleson, I hope the truth will do you no harm. It is the only thing that will avail now, even the truth I have for years kept back. I am no longer a young man, and my severe illness in October forced me to get this business settled. Indeed, I in part helped to bring matters to an issue to-day."

Mapleson was disarmed at once by the priest's frankness. He had waited long to even up scores with the Roman Catholic who had kept many a dollar from his till.

"You are right, gentlemen, in believing that I hold the key to this situation. The Judge has asked two questions: 'Did Patrick O'Meara ever give up his title to the land?' and 'Is O'mie his heir, and therefore the rightful owner?' Let me tell you first what I know of O'mie.

"His mother was a dear little Irish woman who had come, a stranger, to New York City and was married to Patrick O'Meara when she was quite young. They were poor, and after O'mie was born, his father decided to try the West. Fate threw him into the way of a Frenchman who sent him to St. Louis to the employment of a fur-trading company in the upper Missouri River country. O'Meara knew that the West held large possibilities for a poor man. He hoped in a short time to send for his wife and child to join him."

The priest paused, and his brow darkened.

"This Frenchman, although he was of noble birth, had all the evil traits and none of the good ones of all the generations, and withal he was a wild, restless, romantic dreamer and adventurer. You two do not know what heartlessness means. This man had no heart, and yet," the holy man's voice trembled, "his people loved him—will always love his memory, for he could be irresistibly charming and affectionate when he chose. To make this painful story short, he fell in love—madly as only he could love—with this pretty little auburn-haired Irish woman. He had a wife in France, but Mrs. O'Meara pleased him for the time; and he was that kind of a beast.

"O'Meara came to Springvale, and finding here a chance to get hold of a good claim, he bought it. He built a little cabin and sent money to New York for his wife and child to join him here. Mails were slow in preterritorial days. The next letter O'Meara had from New York was from this Frenchman telling him that his wife and child were dead. Meanwhile the villain played the kind friend and brother to the little woman and helped her to prepare for her journey to the West. He had business himself in St. Louis. He would precede her there and accompany her to her husband's new home. Oh, he knew how to deceive, and he was as charming in manner as he was dominant in spirit. No king ever walked the earth with a prouder step. You have seen Jean Pahusca stride down the streets of

Springvale, and you know his regal bearing. Such was this Frenchman.

"In truth," the priest went on, "he had cause to leave New York. Word had come to him that his deserted French wife was on her way to America. This French woman was quick-tempered and jealous, and her anger was something to flee from.

"It is a story of utter baseness. From St. Louis to Springvale Mrs. O'Meara's escort was more like a lover than a friend and business director of her affairs. This land was an Osage reservation then. O'Meara's half-section claim was west of here. The home he built was that little stone cabin near where the draw breaks through the bluff up the river, this side of the big cottonwood."

Le Claire paused and sat in silence for a while.

"Much as I have dealt with all sorts of people," he continued, "I never could understand this Frenchman's nature. Fickle and heartless he was to the very core. The wild frontier life attracted him, and he, who could have adorned the court of France or been a power in New York's high circles, plunged into this wilderness. When they reached the cabin the cause for his devoted attentions was made plain. O'Meara was not there, had indeed been gone for weeks. Letters left at Springvale directed to this Frenchman read:

"'I'm gone for good. A pretty Cheyenne squaw away up on the Platte is too much for me. Tell Kathleen I'm never coming back. So she is free to do what she wants to. You may have this ground I have preëmpted, for your trouble. Good-bye.'

"This letter, scrawled on a greasy bit of paper, was so unlike anything Patrick O'Meara had ever said, its spirit was so unlike his genial true-hearted nature that his wife might have doubted it. But she was young and inexperienced, alone and penniless with her baby boy in a harsh wilderness. The message broke her heart. And then this man used all the force of his power to win her. He showed her how helpless she was, how the community here would look upon her as his wife, and now since she was deserted by her husband, the father of her child, her only refuge lay with him, her true lover.

"The woman's heart was broken, but her fidelity and honor were founded on a rock. She scorned the villain before her and drove him from her door. That night she and O'mie were alone in that lonely little cabin. The cruel dominant nature of the man was aroused now, and he determined to crush the spirit of the only woman who had ever resisted him. Two days later a band of Kiowas was passing peaceably across the Plains. Here the Frenchman saw his chance for revenge by conniving with the Indians to seize little O'mie playing on the prairie beyond the cabin.

"The women out in Western Kansas have had the same agony of soul that Kathleen O'Meara suffered when she found her boy was stolen. In her despair she started after the tribe, wandering lost and starving many days on the prairie until a kind-hearted Osage chief found her and took her to our blessed Mission down the river. Here a strange thing happened. Before she had been there a week, her husband, Thomas O'Meara, came from a trapping tour on the Arkansas River. With him was a little child he had rescued from the Kiowas in a battle at Pawnee Rock. It was his own child, although he did not know it then. In this battle he was told that a Frenchman had been killed. The name was the same as that of the Frenchman he had known in New York. Can you picture the joy of that reunion? You who have had a wife to love, a son to cherish?"

My father's heart was full. All day his own boy's face had been before him, a face so like to the woman whose image he held evermore in sacred memory.

"But their joy was short-lived, for Mrs. O'Meara never recovered from her hardships on the prairie; she died in a few weeks. Her husband was killed by the Comanches shortly after her death. His claim here he left to his son, over whom the Mission assumed guardianship. O'mie was transferred to St. Mary's for some reason, and the priest who started to take him there stopped here to find out about his father's land. But the records were not available. Fingal, for whom Fingal's Creek was named, also known as Judge Fingal, held possession of all the records, and—how, I never knew—but in some way he prevented the priest from finding out anything. Fingal was a Southern man; he met a violent death that year. You know O'mie's story after that." Le Claire paused, and a sadness swept over his face.

"But that doesn't finish the Frenchman's story," he continued presently.

"The night that O'mie's mother left her home in the draw, the French woman who had journeyed far to find her husband came to Springvale. You know what she found. The belongings of another woman. It was she who slipped into the Neosho that night. The Frenchman was in the fight at Pawnee Rock. After that he disappeared. But he had entered a formal claim to the land as the husband of Patrick O'Meara's widow, heir to her property. You see he held a double grip. One through the letter—forged, of course—the other through the claim to a union that never existed."

"Seems to me you've a damned lot to answer for," Tell Mapleson hissed in rage. "If the Church can make a holy man out of such a villain, I'm glad I'm a heretic."

"I'm answering for it," the priest said meekly. Only my father sat with face impassive and calm.

"This half-section of land in question is the property of Thomas O'Meara, son and heir to Patrick O'Meara, as the records show. These stolen records I found where Amos Judson had hastily concealed them, as Judge Baronet has said. I put them in the dark loft for safer keeping, for I felt sure they were valuable. When I came to look for them, they had been moved again. I supposed the one who first took them had recovered them, and I let the matter go. Meanwhile I was called home. When I came here last Fall I found matters still unsettled, and O'mie still without his own. I spent several days in the stone cabin searching for the lost papers. The weather was bad, and you know of my severe attack of pneumonia. But I found the box. In the illness that followed I was kept from Springvale longer than I wished. When I came again O'mie had gone."

The priest paused and sat with eyes downcast, and a sorrowful face.

"Is this your story?" Tell queried. "Your proof of O'mie's claim you consider incontestable, but how about these affidavits from the Rev. Mr. Dodd who married you to the Kiowa squaw? How—"

But Le Claire lifted his hand in commanding gesture. A sudden sternness of face and attitude of authority seemed to clothe him like a garment.

"Gentlemen, there is another story. A bitter, painful story. I have never told it, although it has sometimes almost driven me from the holy sanctuary because of my silence."

It was a deeply impressive moment, for all three of the men realized the importance of the occasion.

"My name," said the priest, "is Pierre Rousseau Le Claire. I am of a titled house of France. We have only the blood of the nobility in our veins. My father had two sons, twins—Pierre the priest, and Jean the renegade, outlawed even among the savages; for his scalp will hang from Satanta's tepee pole if the chance ever comes. Mapleson, here, has told you the truth about his being married to a sister of Chief Satanta. He also is the father of Jean Pahusca. You have noticed the boy's likeness to me. If he, being half Indian, has such a strong resemblance to his family, you can imagine how much alike we are, my brother and myself. In form and gesture, everything—except—well, I have told you what his nature was, and—you have known me for many years. And yet, I have never ceased to pray for him, wicked as he is. We played together about the meadows and vine-clad hill slopes of old France, in our happy boyhood. We grew up and loved and might both have been happily wedded there,—but—I've told you his story. There is nothing of myself that can interest you. That letter of Mapleson's, purporting to be from Patrick O'Meara, is a mere forgery. I have just come up from the Mission. The records and letters of O'Meara have all been kept there. This handwriting would not stand, in court, Mapleson. The land was O'Meara's. It is now O'mie's."

Mapleson sat with rigid countenance. For almost fifteen years he had matched swords with John Baronet. He had felt so sure of his game, he had guarded every possible loophole where success might escape him, he had paved every step so carefully that his mind, grown to the habitual thought of winning, was stunned by the revelation. Like Judson in the morning, his only defence lay In putting blame on somebody else.

"You are the most accomplished double-dealer I ever met," he declared to the priest. "You pretend to follow a holy calling, you profess a love for your brother, and yet you are trying to rob his child of his property. You are against Jean Pahusca, son of the man you love so much. Is that the kind of a priest you are?"

"The very kind—even worse," Le Claire responded. "I went back to France before my aged father died. My mother died of a broken heart over Jean long ago. While our father yet lived I persuaded him to give all his estate—it was large—to the Holy Church. He did it. Not a penny of it can ever be touched."

Mapleson caught his breath like a drowning man.

"It spoiled a beautiful lawsuit, I know," Le Claire continued looking meaningly at him. "For that fortune in France, put into the hands of Jean Pahusca's attorneys here, would have been rich plucking. It can never be. I fixed that before our father's death. Why?"

"Yes, you narrow, grasping robber of orphans, why?" Tell shouted in his passion.

"For the same reason that I stood between Jean Pahusca and this town until he was outlawed here. The half-breed cares nothing for property except as it can buy revenge and feed his appetites. He would sell himself for a drink of whiskey. You know how dangerous he is when drunk. Every man in this town except Judge Baronet and myself has had to flee from him at some time or other. Sober, he is a devil—half Indian, half French, and wholly fiendish. Neither he nor his father has any property. I used my influence to prevent it. I would do it again. Jean Le Claire has forfeited all claims to inheritance. So have I. Among the Indians he is a renegade. I am only a missionary priest trying as I may to atone for my own sins and for the sins of my father's son, my twin brother. That, gentlemen, is all I can say."

"We are grateful to you, Le Claire," John Baronet said. "Mapleson said before you began that your word would show us what to do. It has shown us. It is now time, when some deeds long past their due, must be requited." He turned to Tell sitting defiantly there casting mentally in every direction for some legal hook, some cunning turn, by which to win victory away from defeat.

"Tell Mapleson, the hour has come for us to settle more than a property claim between an Irish orphan and a half-breed Kiowa. And now, if it was wise to settle the other matter out of court, it will be a hundred times safer to settle this here this afternoon. You have grown prosperous in Springvale. In so far as you have done it honestly, I rejoice. You know yourself that I have more than once proved my sincerity by turning business your way, that I could as easily have put elsewhere."

Tell did know, and with something of Southern politeness, he nodded assent.

"You are here now to settle with me or to go before my court for some counts you must meet. You have been the headpiece for all the evil-doing that has wrecked the welfare of Springvale and that has injured reputation, brought lasting sorrow, even cost the life of many citizens. Sooner or later the man who does that meets his own crimes face to face, and their ugly powers break loose on him."

"What do you mean?" Tell's voice was suppressed, and his face was livid.

"I mean first: you with Dick Yeager and others, later in Quantrill's band, in May of 1863 planned the destruction of this town by mob violence. The houses were to be burned, every Union man was to be murdered with his wife and children, except such as the Kiowa and Comanche Indians chose to spare. My own son was singled out as the choicest of your victims. Little O'mie, for your own selfish ends, was not to be spared; and Marjory Whately, just blooming into womanhood, you gave to Jean Pahusca as his booty. Your plan failed, partly through the efforts of this good man here, partly through the courage and quick action of the boys of the town, but mainly through the mercy of Omnipotent God, who sent the floods to keep back the forces of Satan. That Marjory escaped even in the midst of it all is due to the shrewdness and sacrifice of the young man you have been trying to defraud—O'mie.

"In the midst of this you connived with others to steal the records from the courthouse. You were a treble villain, for you set the Rev. Mr. Dodd to a deed you afterwards held over him as a threat and drove him from the town for fear of exposure, forcing him to give you the papers he held against Jean Le Claire's claims to the half-section on the Neosho. Not that his going was any loss to Springvale. But Dodd will never trouble you again. He cast his lot with the Dog Indians of the plains, and one of them used him for a shield in Custer's battle with Black Kettle's band last December. He had not even Indian burial.

"Those deeds against Springvale belong to the days of the Civil War, but your record since proves that the man who planned them cannot be trusted as a safe citizen in times of peace. Into your civil office you carried your war-time methods, until the Postmaster-General cannot deal longer with you. Your term of office expires in six days. Your successor's commission is already on its way here. This much was accomplished in the trip East last Fall." My father spoke significantly.

"It wasn't all that was accomplished, by Heaven! There's a lawsuit coming; there's a will that's to be broken that can't stand when I get at it. You are mighty good and fine about money when other folks are getting it; but when it's coming to you, you're another man." Tell's voice was pitched high now.

"Father Le Claire, let me tell you a story. Baronet's a smooth rascal and nobody can find him out easily. But I know him. He has called me a thief. It takes that kind to catch a thief, maybe. Anyhow, back at Rockport the Baronets were friends of the Melrose family. One of them, Ferdinand, was drowned at sea. He had some foolish delusion or other in his head, for he left a will bequeathing all his property to his brother James Melrose during his lifetime. At his death all Ferdinand's money was to go to John Baronet in trust for his son Phil. Baronet, here, sent his boy back East to school in hopes that Phil would marry Rachel Melrose, James's daughter, and so get the fortune of both Ferdinand and James Melrose. He went crazy over the girl; and, to be honest, for Phil's a likable young fellow, the girl was awfully in love with him. Baronet's had her come clear out here to visit them. But, you'll excuse me for saying it, Judge, Phil is a little fast. He got tangled up with a girl of shady reputation here, and Rachel broke off the match. Now, last October the Judge goes East. You see, he's well fixed, but that nice little sum looks big to him, and he's bound Phil shall have it, wife or no wife. But there's a good many turns in law. While Baronet was at Rockport before I could get there, being detained at Washington" (my father smiled a faint little gleam of a smile in his eyes more than on his lip)—"before I could get to Rockport, Mr. Melrose dies, leaving his wife and Rachel alone in the world. Now, I'm retained here as their attorney. Tillhurst is going on to see to things for me. It's only a few thousand that Baronet is after, but it's all Rachel and her mother have. The Melroses weren't near as rich as the people thought. That will of Ferdinand's won't hold water, not even salt water. It'll go to pieces in court, but it'll show this pious Judge, who calls his neighbors to account, what kind of a man he is. The money's been tied up in some investments and it will soon be released."

Le Claire looked anxiously toward my father, whose face for the first time that day was pale. Rising he opened his cabinet of private papers and selected a legal document.

"This seems to be the day for digging up records," he said in a low voice. "Here is one that may interest you and save time and money. What Mapleson says about Ferdinand Melrose is true. We'll pass by the motives I had in sending Phil East, and some other statements. When I became convinced that love played no part in Phil's mind toward Rachel Melrose, I met him in Topeka in October and gave him the opportunity of signing a relinquishment to all claims on the estate of Ferdinand Melrose. Phil didn't care for the girl; and as to the money gotten in that way" (my father drew himself up to his full height), "the oxygen of Kansas breeds a class of men out here who can make an honest fortune in spite of any inheritance, or the lack of it. I put my boy in that class."

I was his only child, and a father may be pardoned for being proud of his own.

"When I reached Rockport," he continued, "Mr. Melrose was ill. I hurried to him with my message, and it may be his last hours were more peaceful because of my going. Rachel will come into her full possessions in a short time, as you say. Mapleson, will you renounce your retainer's fees in your interest in the orphaned?"

It was Tell's bad day, and he swore sulphureously in a low tone.

"Now I'll take up this matter where I left off," John Baronet said. "While O'mie was taking a vacation in the heated days of August, he slept up in the stone cabin. Jean Pahusca, thief, highwayman, robber, and assassin, kept his stolen goods there. Mapleson and his mercantile partner divided the spoils. O'mie's sense of humor is strong, and one night he played ghost for Jean. You know the redskin's inherent fear of ghosts. It put Jean out of the commission goods business. No persuasion of Mapleson's or his partner's could induce Jean to go back after night to the cabin after this reappearance of the long quiet ghost of the drowned woman."

Le Claire could not repress a smile.

"I think I unconsciously played the same role in September out there, frightening a little man away one night. I was innocent of any harm intended."

"It did the work," my father replied. "Jean cut for the West at once, and joined the Cheyennes for a time—and with a purpose." Then as he looked straight at Tell, his voice grew stern, and that mastery of men that his presence carried made itself felt.

"Jean has bought the right to the life of my son. His pay for the hundreds of dollars he has turned into the hands of this man was that Mapleson should defame my son's good name and drive him from Springvale, and that Jean in his own time was to follow and assassinate him. Mapleson here was in league to protect Jean from the law if the deed should ever be traced to his door. With these conditions in addition, Mapleson was to receive the undivided one-half of section 29, range 14.

"Tell Mapleson, I pass by the crime of forging lies against the name of Irving Whately; I pass by the plotted crimes against this town in '63; I ignore the systematic thievery of your dealings with the half-breed Jean Pahusca; but, by the God in heaven, my boy is my own. For the crime of seeking to lay stain upon his name, the crime of trying to entangle him hopelessly in a scandal and a legal prosecution with a sinful erring girl, the crime of lending your hand to hold the coat of the man who should stone him to death,—for these things, I, the father of Philip Baronet, give you now twenty-four hours to leave Springvale and the State. If at the end of that time you are within the limits of Kansas, you must answer to me in the court-room over there; and, Tell Mapleson, you know what's before you. I came to the West to help build it up. I cannot render my State a greater service than by driving you from its borders; and so long as I live I shall bar your entrance to a land that, in spite of all it has to bear, grows a larger crop of honest men with the conquest of each acre of the prairie soil."

CHAPTER XXVII

SUNSET BY THE SWEETWATER

And we count men brave who on land and wave fear not to die; but still,
Still first on the rolls of the world's great souls are the men who have feared to kill.

—EDMUND VANCE COOKE.

Jean Pahusca turned at the sound of O'mie's step on the stone. The red sun had blinded his eyes and he could not see clearly at first. When he did see, O'mie's presence and the captive unbound and staggering to his feet, surprised the Indian and held him a moment longer. The confusion at the change in war's grim front passed quickly, however,—he was only half Indian,—and he was himself again. He darted toward us, swift as a serpent. Clutching O'mie by the throat and lifting him clear of the rock shelf the Indian threw him headlong down the side of the bluff, crashing the bushes as he fell. The knife that had cut the cords that bound me, the same knife that would have scalped Marjie and taken the boy's life in the Hermit's Cave, was flung from O'mie's hand. It rang on the stone and slid down in the darkness below. Then the half-breed hurled himself upon me and we clinched there by the cliff's edge for our last conflict.

I was in Jean's land now. I had come to my final hour with him. The Baronets were never cowardly. Was it inherited courage, or was it the spirit of power in that letter, Marjie's message of love to me, that gave me grace there? Followed then a battle royal, brute strength against brute strength. All the long score of defeated effort, all the jealousy and hate of years, all the fury of final conflict, all the mad frenzy of the instinct of self-preservation, all the savage lust for blood (most terrible in the human tiger), were united in Jean. He combined a giant's strength and an Indian's skill with the dominant courage and coolness of a son of France. Against these things I put my strength in that strange struggle on the rocky ledge in the gathering twilight of that February day. The little cove on the bluff-side, was not more than fifteen feet across at its widest place. The shelf of sloping stone made a fairly even floor. In this little retreat I had been bound and unable to move for an hour. My muscles were tense at first. I was dazed, too, by a sudden deliverance from the slow torture that had seemed inevitable for me. The issue, however, was no less awful than swift. I had just cause for wreaking vengeance on my foeman. Twice he had attempted to take O'mie's life. The boy might be dead from the headlong fall at this very minute, for all I knew. The clods were only two days old on Bud Anderson's grave. Nothing but the skill and sacrifice of O'mie had saved Marjie from this brute's lust six years before. While he lived, my own life was never for one moment safe. And more than everything else was the possibility of a fate for Marjie too horrible for me to dwell upon. All these things swept through my mind like a lightning flash.

If ever the Lord in the moment of supreme peril gave courage and self-control, these good and perfect gifts were mine in that evening's strife. With the first plunge he had thrown me, and he was struggling to free his hand from my grasp to get at my throat; his knee was on my chest.

"You're in my land now," he hissed in my ear.

"Yes, but this is Phil Baronet still," I answered with a calmness so dominant, it stayed the struggle for a moment. I was playing on him the same trick by which he had so often deceived us,—the pretended relaxation of all effort, and indifference to further strife. In that moment's pause I gained my lost vantage. Quick as thought I freed my other hand, and, holding still his murderous grip from my throat, I caught him by the neck, and pushing his head upward, I gave him such a thrust that his hold on me loosened a bit. A bit only, but that was enough, for when he tightened it again, I was on my feet and the strife was renewed—renewed with the fierceness of maddened brutes, lashed into fury. Life for one of us meant death for the other, and I lost every humane instinct in that terrible struggle except the instinct to save Marjie first, and my own life after hers. Civilization slips away in such a battle, and the fighter is only a jungle beast, knowing no law but the unquenchable thirst for blood. The hand that holds this pen is clean to-day, clean and strong and gentle. It was a tiger's claw that night, and Jean's hot blood following my terrific blow full in his face only thrilled me with savage courage. I hurled him full length on the stone, my heavy cavalry boot was on his neck, and I would have stamped the life out of him in an instant. But with the motion of a serpent he wriggled himself upward; then, catching me by the leg, he had me on one knee, and his long arms, like the tentacles of a devil-fish, tightened about me. Then we rolled together over and under, under and over. His hard white teeth were sunk in my shoulder to cut my life artery. I had him by the long soft hair, my fingers tangled in the handfuls I had torn from his head. And every minute I was possessed with a burning frenzy to strangle him. Every desire had left my being now, save the eagerness to conquer, and the consciousness of my power to fight until that end should come.

We were at the cliff's edge now, my head hanging over; the blood was rushing toward my clogging brain; the sharp rock's rim, like a stone knife, was cutting my neck. Jean loosened his teeth from my shoulder, and his murderous hand was on my throat. In that supreme crisis I summoned the very last atom of energy, the very limit of physical prowess, the quickness and cunning which can be called forth only by the conflict with the swift approach of death.

Nature had given me a muscular strength far beyond that of most men. And all my powers had been trained to swift obedience and almost unlimited endurance. With this was a nervous system that matched the years of a young man's greatest vigor. Strong drink and tobacco had never had the chance to play havoc with my steady hand or to sap the vitality of my reserve forces. Even as Jean lifted me by the throat to crush my head backward over that sharp stone ledge, I put forth this burst of power in a fierceness so irresistible that it hurled him from me, and the struggle was still unended. We were on our feet again in a rage to reach the finish. I had almost ceased to care to live. I wanted only to choke the breath from the creature before me. I wanted only to save from his hellish power the victims who would become his prey if he were allowed to live.

Instinct led me to wrestle with my assailant across the ledge toward the wall that shut in about the sanctuary, just as, a half-year before, on our "Rockport" fighting ground, I strove to drag him through the bushes toward Cliff Street, while he tried to fling me off the projecting rock. And so we locked limb and limb in the horrible contortion of this savage strife. Every muscle had been so wrenched, no pain or wound reported itself fairly to the congested brain. I had nearly reached the wall, and I was making a frantic effort to fling the Indian against it. I had his shoulder almost upon the rocky side, and my grip was tight about him, when he turned on me the same trick I had played in the early part of this awful game. A sudden relaxation threw me off my guard. The blood was streaming from a wound on my forehead, and I loosed my hold to throw back my long hair from my face and wipe the trickling drops from my eyes. In that fatal moment my mind went blank, whether from loss of blood or a sudden blow from Jean, I do not know. When I did know myself, I seemed to have fallen through leagues of space, to be falling still, until a pain, so sharp that it was a blessing, brought me to my senses. The light was very dim, but my right hand was free. I aimed one blow at Jean's shoulder, and he fell by the cliff's edge, dragging me with him, my weight on his body. His left hand hung over the cliff-side. I should have finished with him then, but that the fallen hand, down in the black shadows, had closed over a knife sticking in the crevice just below the edge of the bluff—Jean Le Claire's knife, that had been flung from O'mie's grip as he fell.

I caught its gleam as the half-breed flashed it upward in a swift stab at my heart and my breath hung back. I leaped from him in time to save my life, but not quickly enough to keep the villainous thing from cutting a long jagged track across my thigh, from which spurted a crimson flood. There could be only one thing evermore for us two. A redoubled fury seized me, and then there swept up in me a power for which I cannot account, unless it may be that the Angel of Life, who guards all the passes of the valley of the shadow, sometimes turns back the tide for us. A sudden calmness filled me, a cool courage contrasting with Jean's frenzy, and I set my teeth together with the grip of a bulldog. Jean had leaped to his feet as I sprang back from his knife-thrust, and for the first time since the fight began we stood apart for half a minute.

"I may die, but I'll never be cut to death. It must be an equal fight, and when I go, Jean Pahusca, you are going with me. I'll have that knife first and then I'll kill you with my own hands, if my breath goes out at that same instant."

There must have been something terrible in my voice for it was the voice of a strong man going down to death, firm of purpose, and unafraid.

The feel of the weapon gave the Indian renewed energy. He sprang at me with a maniac's might. He was a maniac henceforth. Three times we raged across the narrow fighting ground. Three times I struck that murderous blade aside, but not without a loss of my own blood for each thrust, until at last by sheer virtue of muscle against muscle, I wrenched it from Jean's hand, dripping with my red life-tide. And even as I seized it, it slipped from me and fell, this time to the ledges far below. Then hell broke all bounds for us, and what followed there in that shadowy twilight, I care not to recall much less to set it down here.

I do not know how long we battled there, nor whose blood most stained the stone of that sanctuary, nor how many times I was underneath, nor how often on top of my assailant. Not all the struggles of my sixty years combined, and I have known many, could equal that fight for life.

There came a night in later time when for what seemed an age to me, I matched my physical power and endurance against the terrible weight of broken timbers of a burning bridge that was crushing out human lives, in a railroad wreck. And every second of that eternity-long time, I faced the awful menace of death by fire. The memory of that hour is a pleasure to me when contrasted with this hand to hand battle with a murderer.

It ended at last—such strife is too costly to endure long—ended with a form stretched prone and helpless and whining for mercy before a conqueror, whose life had been well-nigh threshed out of him; but the fallen fighter was Jean Pahusca, and the man who towered over him was Phil Baronet.

The half-breed deserved to die. Life for him meant torturing death to whatever lay in his path. It meant untold agony for whomsoever his hand fell upon. And greater to me than these then was the murderous conflict just ended, in which I had by very miracle escaped death again and again. Men do not fight such battles to weep forgiving tears on one another's necks when the end comes. When the spirit of mortal strife possesses a man's soul, the demons of hell control it. The moment for a long overdue retribution was come. As we had clinched and torn one another there Jean's fury had driven him to a maniac's madness. The blessed heritage of self-control, my endowment from my father, had not deserted me. But now my hand was on his throat, my knee was planted on his chest, and by one twist I could end a record whose further writing would be in the blood of his victims.

I lifted my eyes an instant to the western sky, out of which a clear, sweet air was softly fanning my hot blood-smeared face. The sun had set as O'mie cut my bonds. And now the long purple twilight of the Southwest held the land in its soft hues. Only one ray of iridescent light pointed the arch above me—the sun's good-night greeting to the Plains. Its glory held me by a strange power. God's mercy was in that radiant shaft of beauty reaching far up the sky, keeping me back from wilful murder.

And then, because all pure, true human love is typical of God's eternal love for his children, then, all suddenly, the twilight scene slipped from me. I was in my father's office on an August day, and Marjie was beside me. The love light in her dear brown eyes, as they looked steadily into mine, was thrilling my soul with joy. I felt again the touch of her hand as I felt it that day when I presented her to Rachel Melrose. Her eyes were looking deep into my soul, her hand was in my hand, the hand that in a moment more would take the life of a human being no longer able to give me blow for blow. I loosed my clutch as from a leprous wound, and the Indian gasped again for mercy. Standing upright, I spurned the form grovelling now at my feet.

Lifting my bloody right hand high above me, I thanked God I had conquered in a greater battle. I had won the victory over my worser self.

But I was too wise to think that Jean should have his freedom. Stepping to where the cut thongs that had bound me lay, I took the longest pieces and tied the half-breed securely.

All this time I had fogotten O'mie. Now it dawned upon me that he must be found. He might be alive still. The fall must have been broken somehow by the bushes. I peered over the edge of the bluff into the darkness of the valley below.

"O'mie!" I called, "O'mie!"

"Present!" a voice behind me responded.

I turned quickly. Standing there in the dim light, with torn clothing, and tumbled red hair, and scratched face was the Irish boy, bruised, but not seriously hurt.

"I climbed down and round and up and got back as soon as I come too," he said, with that happy-go-lucky smile of his. "Bedad! but you've been makin' some history, I see. Git up, you miserable cur, and we'll march ye down to General Custer. You take entirely too many liberties wid a Springvale boy what's knowed you too darned long already."

We lifted Jean, and keeping him before us we hurried him into the presence of the fair-haired commander to whom we told our story, failing not to report on the incident witnessed by O'mie on the river bank two nights before, when Jean sent his murdered father's body into the waters below him.

"And so that French renegade is dead, is he," Custer mused, never lifting his eyes from the ground. He had heard us through without query or comment, until now. "I knew him well. First as a Missionary priest to the Osages. He was a fine man then, but the Plains made a devil of him; and he deserved what he got, no doubt.

"Now, as to this half-breed, why the devil didn't you kill him when you had the chance? Dead Indians tell no tales; but the holy Church and the United States Government listen to what the live ones tell. You could have saved me any amount of trouble, you infernal fool."

I stood up before the General. There was as great a contrast in our appearance as in our rank. The slight, dapper little commander in full official dress and perfect military bearing looked sternly up at the huge, rough private with his torn, bloody clothing and lacerated hands. Custer's yellow locks had just been neatly brushed. My own dark hair, uncut for months, hung in a curly mass thrown back from my scarred face.

I gave him a courteous, military salute. Then standing up to my full height, and looking steadily down at the slender, graceful man before me, I said:

"I may be a fool, General, but I am a soldier, not a murderer."

Custer made no reply for a time.

He sat down and, turning toward Jean Pahusca, he studied the young half-breed carefully. Then he said briefly,

"You may go now."

We saluted and passed from his tent. Outside we had gone only a few steps, when the General overtook us.

"Baronet," he said, "you did right. You are a soldier, the kind that will yet save the Plains."

He turned and entered his tent again.

"Golly!" O'mie whistled softly. "It's me that thinks Jean Pahusca, son av whoever his father may be, 's got to the last and worst piece av his journey. I'm glad you didn't kill him, Phil. You're claner 'n ever in my eyes."

We strolled away together in the soft evening shadows, silent for a time.

"Tell me, O'mie," I said at last, "how you happened to find me up there two hours ago?"

"I was trailin' you to your hidin'-place. Bud, Heaven bless him, told me where your little sanctuary was, the night before he—went away." There were tears in O'mie's voice, but soldiers do not weep. "I had hard work to find the path. But it was better so maybe."

"You were just in time, you red-headed angel. Life is sweet." I breathed deeply of the pleasant air. "Oh, why did Bud have to give it up, I wonder."

We sat down behind the big bowlder round which Bud, wounded unto death, had staggered toward me only a few days before.

"Talk, O'mie; I can't," I said, stretching myself out at full length.

"I was just in time to see Jean spring his trap on you. I waited and swore, and swore and waited, for him to give me the chance to get betwane you and the pollutin' pup! It didn't come until the sun took his face full and square, and I see my chance to make two steps. He's so doggoned quick he'd have caught me, if it hadn't been for that blessed gleam in his eyes. He wa'n't takin' no chances. By the way," he added as an afterthought, "the General says we break camp soon. Didn't say it to me, av course. Good-night now. Sleep sweet, and don't get too far from your chest protector,—that's me." He smiled good-bye with as light a heart as though the hours just past had been full of innocent play instead of grim tragedy.

February on the Plains was slipping into March when the garrison at Fort Sill broke up for the final movement. This winter campaign, as war records run, had been marked by only one engagement, Custer's attack on the Cheyenne village on the Washita River. But the hurling of so large a force as the Fort Sill garrison into the Indian stronghold in the depth of winter carried to the savage mind and spirit a deeper conviction of our power than could have been carried by a score of victories on the green prairies of summer. For the Indian stronghold, be it understood, consisted not in mountain fastnesses, cunning hiding-places, caves in the earth, and narrow passes guarded by impregnable cliffs. This was no repetition of the warfare of the Celts among the rugged rocks of Wales, nor of the Greeks at Thermopylæ, nor of the Swiss on Alpine footpaths. This savage stronghold was an open, desolate, boundless plain, fortified by distances and equipped with the slow sure weapons of starvation. That Government was a terror to the Indian mind whose soldiers dared to risk its perils and occupy the land at this season of the year. The withered grasses; the lack of fuel; the absence of game; the salty creeks, which mock at thirst; the dreary waves of wilderness sand; the barren earth under a wide bleak sky; the never-ending stretch of unbroken plain swept by the fierce winter blizzard, whose furious blast was followed by a bitter perishing weight of cold,—these were the foes we had had to fight in that winter campaign. Our cavalry horses had fallen before them, dying on the way. Only a few of those that reached Fort Sill had had the strength to survive even with food and care. John Mac prophesied truly when he declared to us that our homesick horses would never cross the Arkansas River again. Not one of them ever came back, and we who had gone out mounted now found ourselves a helpless intantry.

Slowly the tribes had come to Custer's terms. When delay and cunning device were no longer of any avail they submitted—all except the Cheyennes, who had escaped to the Southwest.

Spring was coming, and the Indians and their ponies could live in comfort then. It was only in the winter that United States rations and tents were vital. With the summer they could scorn the white man's help, and more: they could raid again the white man's land, seize his property, burn his home, and brain him with their cruel tomahawks; while as to his wife and children, oh, the very fiends of hell could not devise an equal to their scheme of life for them. The escape of the Cheyennes from Custer's grasp was but an earnest of what Kiowa, Arapahoe and Comanche could do later. These Cheyennes were setting an example worthy of their emulation. Not quite, to the Cheyenne's lordly spirit, not quite had the cavalry conquered the Plains. And now the Cheyenne could well gloat over the failure of the army after all it had endured; for spring was not very far away, the barren Staked Plains, in which the soldier could but perish, were between them and the arm of the Government, and our cavalrymen were now mere undisciplined foot-soldiers. It was to subdue this very spirit, to strike the one most effectual blow, the conquest of the Cheyennes, that the last act of that winter campaign was undertaken. This, and one other purpose. I had been taught in childhood under Christian culture that it is for the welfare of the home the Government exists. Bred in me through many generations of ancestry was the high ideal of a man's divine right to protect his roof-tree and to foster under it those virtues that are built into the nation's power and honor. I had had thrust upon me in the day of my young untried strength a heavy sense of responsibility. I had known the crushing anguish of feeling that one I loved had fallen a prey to a savage foe before whose mastery death is a joy. I was now to learn the truth of all the teaching along the way. I was to see in the days of that late winter the finest element of power the American flag can symbolize—the value set upon the American home, over which it is a token of protection. This, then, was that other purpose of this campaign—the rescue of two captive women, seized and dragged away on that afternoon when Bud and O'mie and I leaned against the south wall of old Fort Hays in the October sunshine and talked of the hazard of Plains warfare. But of this other purpose the privates knew nothing at all. The Indian tribes, now full of fair promises, were allowed to take up their abode on their reservations without further guarding. General Custer, with the Seventh United States Regiment, and Colonel Horace L. Moore, in full command of the Nineteenth Kansas Cavalry, were directed to reach the Cheyenne tribe and reduce it to submission.

A thousand men followed the twenty-one buglers on their handsome horses, in military order, down Kansas Avenue in Topeka, on that November day in 1868, when the Kansas volunteers began this campaign. Four months later, on a day in early March, Custer's regiment with the Nineteenth, now dismounted cavalry, filed out of Fort Sill and set their faces resolutely to the westward. Infantry marching was new business for the Kansas men, but they bent to their work like true soldiers. After four days a division came, and volunteers from both regiments were chosen to continue the movement. The remainder, for lack of marching strength, was sent up on the Washita River to await our return in a camp established up there under Colonel Henry Inman.

Reed, one of my Topeka comrades, was of those who could not go farther. O'mie was not considered equal to the task. I fell into Reed's place with Hadley and John Mac and Pete, when we started out at last to conquer the Cheyennes, who were slipping ever away from us somewhere beyond the horizon's rim. The days that followed, finishing up that winter campaign, bear a record of endurance unsurpassed in the annals of American warfare.

I have read the fascinating story of Coronado and his three hundred Spanish knights in their long weary march over a silent desolate level waste day after day, pushing grimly to the northward in their fruitless search for gold. What did this band of a thousand weary men go seeking as they took the reverse route of Coronado's to the Southwest over these ceaslessly crawling sands? Not the discoverer's fame, not the gold-seeker's treasure led them forth through gray interminable reaches of desolation. They were going now to put the indelible mark of conquest by a civilized Government, on a crafty and dangerous foe, to plough a fire-guard of safety about the frontier homes.

Small heed we gave to this history-making, it is true, as we pressed silently onward through those dreary late winter days. It was a soldier's task we had accepted, and we were following the flag. And in spite of the sins committed in its name, of the evil deeds protected by its power, wherever it unfurls its radiant waves of light "the breath of heaven smells wooingly"; gentle peace, and rich prosperity, and holy love abide ever more under its caressing shadow.

We were prepared with rations for a five days' expedition only. But weary, ragged, barefoot, hungry, sleepless, we pressed on through twenty-five days, following a trail sometimes dim, sometimes clearly written, through a region the Indians never dreamed we could cross and live. The nights chilled our famishing bodies. The short hours of broken rest led only to another day of moving on. There were no breakfasts to hinder our early starting. The meagre bit of mule meat doled out sparingly when there was enough of this luxury to be given out, eaten now without salt, was our only food. Our clothing tattered with wear and tear, hung on our gaunt frames. Our lips did not close over our teeth; our eyes above hollow cheeks stared out like the eyes of dead men. The bloom of health had turned to a sickly yellow hue; but we were all alike, and nobody noted the change.

As we passed from one deserted camp to another, it began to seem a will-o'-the-wisp business, an elusive dream, a long fruitless chasing after what would escape and leave us to perish at last in this desert. But the slender yellow-haired man at the head of the column had an indomitable spirit, and an endurance equalled only by his courage and his military cunning. Under him was the equally indomitable Kansas Colonel, Horace L. Moore, tried and trained in Plains warfare. Behind them straggled a thousand soldiers. And still the March days dragged on.

Then the trails began to tell us that the Indians were gathering in larger groups and the command was urged forward with more persistent purpose. We slept at night without covering under the open sky. We hardly dared to light fires. We had nothing to cook, and a fire would reveal our whereabouts to the Indians we were pursuing. A thousand soldiers is a large number; but even a thousand men, starving day after day, taxing nerve and muscle, with all the reserve force of the body feeding on its own unfed store of energy; a thousand men destitute of supplies, cut off by leagues of desert sands from any base of reinforcement, might put up only a weak defence against the hundreds of savages in their own habitat. It was to prevent another Arickaree that Custer's forces kept step in straggling lines when rations had become only a taunting mockery of the memory.

The map of that campaign is kept in the archives of war and its official tale is all told there, told as the commander saw it. I can tell it here only as a private down in the ranks.

In the middle of a March afternoon, as we were silently swinging forward over the level Plains, a low range of hills loomed up. Beyond them lay the valley of the Sweetwater, a tributary of the Canadian River. Here, secure in its tepees, was the Cheyenne village, its inhabitants never dreaming of the white man's patience and endurance. Fifteen hundred strong it numbered, arrogant, cunning, murderous. The sudden appearance of our army of skeleton men was not without its effect on the savage mind. Men who had crossed the Staked Plains in this winter time, men who looked like death already, such men might be hard to kill. But lying and trickery still availed.

There was only one mind in the file that day. We had come so far, we had suffered such horrors on the way, these men had been guilty of such atrocious crimes, we longed fiercely now to annihilate this band of wretches in punishment due for all it had cost the nation. I thought of the young mother and her baby boy on the frozen earth between the drifts of snow about Satanta's tepee on the banks of the Washita, as Bud and I found her on the December day when we searched over Custer's battle field. I pictured the still forms lying on their blankets, and the long line of soldiers passing reverently by, to see if by chance she might be known to any of us—this woman, murdered in the very hour of her release; and I gripped my arms in a frenzy. Oh, Satan takes fast hold on the heart of a man in such a time, and the Christ dying on the cross up on Calvary, praying "Father forgive them for they know not what they do," seems only a fireside story of unreal things.

In the midst of this opportunity for vengeance just, and long overdue, comes Custer's lieutenant with military courtesy to Colonel Moore, and delivers the message, "The General sends his compliments, with the instructions not to fire on the Indians."

Courtesy! Compliments! Refrain from any rudeness to the wards of the Government! I was nearly twenty-two and I knew more than Custer and Sheridan and even President Grant himself just then. I had a sense of obedience. John Baronet put that into me back in Springvale years ago. Also I had extravagant notions of military discipline and honor. But for one brief moment I was the most lawless mutineer, the rankest anarchist that ever thirsted for human gore to satisfy a wrong. Nor was I alone. Beside me were those stanch fellows, Pete and John Mac, and Hadley. And beyond was the whole line of Kansas men with a cause of their own here. Before my fury left me, however, we were all about face, and getting up the valley to a camping-place.

I might have saved the strength the passion of fury costs. Custer knew his business and mine also. Down in that Cheyenne village, closely guarded, were two captive women, the women of my boyhood dream, maybe. The same two women who had been carried from their homes up in the Solomon River country in the early Fall. What they had endured in these months of captivity even the war records that set down plain things do not deem fit to enter. One shot from our rifles that day on the Sweetwater would have meant for them the same fate that befell the sacrifice on the Washita, the dead woman on the deserted battle field. It was to save these two, then, that we had kept step heavily across the cold starved Plains. For two women we had marched and suffered on day after day. Who shall say, at the last analysis, that this young queen of nations, ruling a beautiful land under the Stars and Stripes, sets no value on the homes of its people, nor holds as priceless the life and safety even of two unknown women.

Very adroitly General Custer visited, and exchanged compliments, and parleyed and waited, playing his game faultlessly till even the quick-witted Cheyennes were caught by it. When the precise moment came the shrewd commander seized the chief men of the village and gave his ultimatum—a life for a life. The two white women safe from harm must be brought to him or these mighty men must become degraded captives. Then followed an Indian hurricane of wrath and prayers and trickery. It availed nothing except to prolong the hours, and hunger and cold filled another night in our desolate camp.

Day brought a renewal of demand, a renewal of excuse and delay and an attempt to outwit by promises. But a second command was more telling. The yellow-haired general's word now went forth: "If by sunset to-morrow night these two women are not returned to my possession, these chiefs will hang."

So Custer said, and the grim selection of the gallows and the preparation for fulfilment of his threat went swiftly forward. The chiefs were terror-stricken, and anxious messages were sent to their people. Meanwhile the Cheyenne forces were moving farther and farther away. The squaws and children were being taken to a safe distance, and a quick flight was in preparation. So another night of hunger and waiting fell upon us. Then came the day of my dream long ago. The same people I knew first on the night after Jean Pahusca's attempt on Marjie's life, when we were hunting our cows out on the West Prairie, came now in reality before me.

The Sweetwater Valley spread out under the late sunshine of a March day was rimmed about by low hills. Beyond these, again, were the Plains, the same monotony of earth beneath and sky above, the two meeting away and away in an amethyst fold of mist around the world's far bound. There were touches of green in the brown valley, but the hill slopes and all the spread of land about them were gray and splotched and dull against a blue-gray sickly sky. The hours went by slowly to each anxious soldier, for endurance was almost at its limit. More heavily still they must have dragged for the man on whom the burden of command rested. High noon, and then the afternoon interminably long and dull, and by and by came the sunset on the Sweetwater Valley, and a new heaven and a new earth were revealed to the sons of men. Like a chariot of fire, the great sun rolled in all its gorgeous beauty down the west. The eastern sky grew radiant with a pink splendor, and every brown and mottled stretch of distant landscape was touched with golden light or deepened into richest purple, or set with a roseate bound of flame. Somewhere far away, a feathery gray mist hung like a silvery veil toning down the earth from the noonday glare to the sunset glory. Down in the very middle of all this was a band of a thousand men; their faded clothing, their uncertain step, their knotted hands, and their great hungry eyes told the price that had been paid for the drama this sunset hour was to bring. Slowly the moments passed as when in our little sanctuary above the pleasant parks at Fort Sill I had watched the light measured out. And then the low hills began to rise up and shut out the crimson west as twilight crept toward the Sweetwater Valley.

Suddenly, for there had been nothing there a moment before, all suddenly, an Indian scout was outlined on the top of the low bluff nearest us. Motionless he sat on his pony a moment, then he waved a signal to the farther height beyond him. A second pony and a second Indian scout appeared. Another signal and then came a third Indian on a third pony farther away. Each Indian seemed to call out another until a line of them had been signalled from the purple mist, out of which they appeared to be created. Last of all and farthest away, was a pony on which two figures were faintly outlined. Down in the valley we waited, all eyes looking toward the hills as these two drew nearer. Up in a group on the bluff beyond the valley the Indians halted. The two riders of the pony slipped to the ground. With their arms about each other, in close embrace, they came slowly toward us, the two captive women for whom we waited. It was a tragic scene, such as our history has rarely known, watched by a thousand men, mute and motionless, under its spell. Even now, after the lapse of nearly four decades, the picture is as vivid as if it were but yesterday that I stood on the Texas Plains a soldier of twenty-two years, feeling my heart throbs quicken as that sunset scene is enacted before me.

We had thought ourselves the victims of a hard fate in that winter of terrible suffering; but these two women, Kansas girls, no older than Marjie, home-loving, sheltered, womanly, a maiden and a bride of only a few months—shall I ever forget them as they walked into my life on that March day in the sunset hour by the Sweetwater? Their meagre clothing was of thin flour sacks with buckskin moccasins and leggins. Their hair hung in braids Indian fashion. Their haggard faces and sad eyes told only the beginning of their story. They were coming now to freedom and protection. The shadow of Old Glory would be on them in a moment; a moment, and the life of an Indian captive would be but a horror-seared memory.

Then it was that Custer did a graceful thing. The subjection of the Cheyennes could have been accomplished by soldiery from Connecticut or South Carolina, but it was for the rescue of these two, for the protection of Kansas homes, that the Nineteenth Kansas Cavalry had volunteered. Stepping to our commander, Colonel Moore, Custer asked that the Kansas man should go forward to meet the captives. With a courtesy a queen might have coveted the Colonel received them—two half-naked, wretched, fate-buffeted women.

The officers nearest wrapped their great coats about them. Then, as the two, escorted by Colonel Moore and his officers next of rank, moved forward toward General Custer, who was standing apart on a little knoll waiting to receive them, a thousand men watching breathless with uncovered heads the while, the setting sun sent down athwart the valley its last rich rays of glory, the motionless air was full of an opalescent beauty; while softly, sweetly, like dream music never heard before in that lonely land of silence, the splendid Seventh Cavalry band was playing "Home Sweet Home."

CHAPTER XXVIII

THE HERITAGE

It is morning here in Kansas, and the breakfast bell is rung!
We are not yet fairly started on the work we mean to do;
We have all the day before us, and the morning is but young,
And there's hope in every zephyr, and the skies are bright and blue.

—WALT MASON.

It was over at last, the long painful marching; the fight with the winter's blizzard, the struggle with starvation, the sunrise and sunset and starlight on wilderness ways—all ended after a while. Of the three boys who had gone out from Springvale and joined in the sacrifice for the frontier, Bud sleeps in that pleasant country at Fort Sill. The summer breezes ripple the grasses on his grave, the sunbeams caress it lovingly and the winter snows cover it softly over—the quiet grave he had wished for and found all too soon. Dear Bud, "not changed, but glorified," he holds his place in all our hearts. For O'mie, the winter campaign was the closing act of a comic tragedy, and I can never think sadly of the brave-hearted happy Irishman. He was too full of the sunny joy of existence, his heart beat with too much of good-will toward men, to be remembered otherwise than as a bright-faced, sweet-spirited boy whose span of years was short. How he ever endured the hardships and reached Springvale again is a miracle, and I wonder even now, how, waiting patiently for the inevitable, he could go peacefully through the hours, making us forget everything but his cheery laugh, his affectionate appreciation of the good things of the world, and his childlike trust in the Saviour of men.

His will was a simple thing, containing the bequest of all his possessions, including the half-section of land so long in litigation, and the requests regarding his funeral. The latter had three wishes: that Marjie would sing "Abide With Me" at the burial service, that he might lie near to John Baronet's last resting-place in the Springvale cemetery, and that Dave and Bill Mead, and the three Andersons, with myself would be his pall bearers. Dave was on the

Pacific slope then, and O'mie himself had helped to bear Bud to his final earthly home. One of the Red Range boys and Jim Conlow filled these vacant places. Reverently, as for one of the town's distinguished men, there walked beside us Father Le Claire and Judge Baronet, Cris Mead and Henry Anderson, father of the Anderson boys, Cam Gentry and Dever. Behind these came the whole of Springvale. It was May time, a year after our Southwest campaign, and the wild flowers of the prairie lined his grave and wreaths of the pink blossoms that grow out in the West Draw were twined about his casket. He had no next of kin, there were no especial mourners. His battle was ended and we could not grieve for his abundant entrance into eternal peace.

Three of us had gone out with the Nineteenth Kansas Cavalry, and I am the third. While we were creeping back to life at Camp Inman on the Washita after that well-nigh fatal expedition across the Staked Plains to the Sweetwater, I saw much of Hard Rope, chief man of the Osage scouts. I had been accustomed to the Osages all my years in Kansas. Neither this tribe, nor our nearer neighbors, the Kaws, had ever given Springvale any serious concern. Sober, they were law-abiding enough, and drunk, they were no more dangerous than any drunken white man. Bitter as my experience with the Indian has been, I have always respected the loyal Osage. But I never sought one of this or any other Indian tribe for the sake of his company. Race prejudice in me is still strong, even when I give admiration and justice free rein. Indians had frequent business in the Baronet law office in my earlier years, and after I was associated with my father there was much that brought them to us. Possibly the fact that I did not dislike the Osages is the reason I hardly gave them a thought at Fort Sill. It was not until afterwards that I recalled how often I had found the Osage scouts there crossing my path unexpectedly. On the day before we broke camp at the Fort, Hard Rope came to my tent and sat down beside the door. I did not notice him until he said slowly:

"Baronet?"

"Yes," I replied.

"Tobacco?" he asked.

"No, Hard Rope," I answered, "I have every other mark of a great man except this. I don't smoke."

"I want tobacco," he continued.

What made me accommodating just then I do not know, but I suddenly remembered some tobacco that Reed had left in my tent.

"Hard Rope," I said, "here is some tobacco. I forgot I had it, because I don't care for it. Take it all."

The scout seized it with as much gratitude as an Indian shows, but he did not go away at once.

"Something else now?" I questioned not unkindly.

"You Judge Baronet's son?"

I nodded and smiled.

He came very close to me, putting both hands on my shoulders, and looking steadily into my eyes he said solemnly, "You will be safe. No evil come near you."

"Thank you, Hard Rope, but I will keep my powder dry just the same," I answered.

All the time in the Inman camp the scout shadowed me. On the evening before our start for Fort Hays to be mustered out of service he came to me as I sat alone beside the Washita, breathing deeply the warm air of an April twilight. I had heard no word from home since I left Topeka in October. Marjie must be married, as Jean had said. I had never known the half-breed to tell a lie. It was so long ago that that letter of hers to me had miscarried. She thought of course that I had taken it and even then refused to stay at home. Oh, it was all a hopeless tangle, and now I might be dreaming of another man's wife. I had somehow grown utterly hopeless now. Jean—oh, the thought was torture—I could not feel sure about him. He might be shadowing her night and day. Custer did not tell me what had become of the Indian, and I had seen on the Sweetwater what such as he could do for a Kansas girl. As I sat thus thinking, Hard Rope squatted beside me.

"You go at sunrise?" pointing toward the east.

I merely nodded.

"I want to talk," he went on.

"Well, talk away, Hard Rope." I was glad to quit thinking.

What he told me there by the rippling Washita River I did not repeat for many months, but I wrung his hand when I said good-bye. Of all the scouts with Custer that we left behind when we started northward, none had so large a present of tobacco as Hard Rope.

My father had demanded that I return to Springvale as soon as our regiment was mustered out. Morton was still in the East, and I had no foothold in the Saline Valley as I had hoped in the Fall to have. Nor was there any other place that opened its doors to me. And withal I was homesick—desperately, ravenously homesick. I wanted to see my father and Aunt Candace, to look once more on the peaceful Neosho and the huge oak trees down in its fertile valley. For nearly half a year I had not seen a house, nor known a civilized luxury. No child ever yearned for home and mother as I longed for Springvale. And most of all came an overwhelming eagerness to see Marjie once more. She was probably Mrs. Judson now, unless Jean—but Hard Rope had eased my mind a little there—and I had no right even to think of her. Only I was young, and I had loved her so long. All that fierce battle with myself which I fought out on the West Prairie on the night she refused to let me speak to her had to be fought over again. And this time, marching northward over the April Plains toward Fort Hays, this time, I was hopelessly vanquished. I, Philip Baronet, who had fought with fifty against a thousand on the Arickaree; who had gone with Custer to the Sweetwater in the dreary wastes of the Texas desert; I who had a little limp now and then in my right foot, left out too long in the cold, too long made to keep step in weary ways on endlessly wearing marches; I who had lost the softness of the boy's physique and who was muscled like a man, with something of the military bearing hammered mercilessly upon me in the days of soldier life—I was still madly in love with a girl who had refused all my pleadings and was even now, maybe, another man's wife. Oh, cold and terror and starvation were all bad enough, but this was unendurable.

"I will go home as my father wishes," I said. "I do not need to stay there, but I will go now for a while and feel once more what civilization means. Then—I will go to the Plains, or somewhere else." So I argued as we came one April day into Fort Hays. Letters from home were awaiting me, urging me to come at once; and I went, leaving O'mie to follow later when he should have rested at the Fort a little.

All Kansas was in its Maytime glory. From the freshly ploughed earth came up that sweet wholesome odor that like the scent of new-mown hay carries its own traditions of other days to each of us. The young orchards—there were not many orchards in Kansas then—were all a blur of pink on the hill slopes. A thousand different blossoms gemmed the prairies, making a perfect kaleidoscope of brilliant hues, that blended with the shifting shades of green. Along the waterways the cottonwood's silvery branches, tipped with tender young leaves fluttering in the soft wind, stood up proudly above the scrubby bronze and purple growths hardly yet in bud and leaf. From every gentle swell the landscape swept away to the vanishing line of distances in billowy seas of green and gold, while far overhead arched the deep-blue skies of May. Fleecy clouds, white and soft as foam, drifted about in the limitless fields of ether. The glory of the new year, the fresh sweet air, the spirit of budding life, set the pulses a-tingle with the very joy of being. Like a dream of Paradise lay the Neosho Valley in its wooded beauty, with field and farm, the meadow, and the open unending prairie rolling away from it, wave on wave, in the Maytime grace and grandeur. Through this valley the river itself wound in and out, glistening like molten silver in the open spaces, and gliding still and shadowy by overhanging cliff and wooded covert.

"Dever," I said to the stage driver when we had reached the top of the divide and looked southward to where all this magnificence of nature was lavishly spread out, "Dever, do you remember that passage in the Bible about the making of the world long ago, 'And God saw that it was good'? Well, here's where all that happened."

Dever laughed a crowing laugh of joy. He had hugged me when I took the stage, I didn't know why. When it came to doing the nice thing, Dever had a sense of propriety sometimes that better-bred folk might have envied. And this journey home proved it.

"I've got a errant up west. D'ye's lief come into town that way?" he asked me.

Would I? I was longing to slip into my home before I ran the gantlet of all the streets opening on the Santa Fé Trail. I never did know what Dever's "errant" was, that led him to swing some miles to the west, out of the way to the ford of the Neosho above the old stone cabin where Father Le Claire swam his horse in the May flood six years before. He gave no reason for the act that brought me over a road, every foot sacred to the happiest moments of my life. Past the big cottonwood, down into the West Draw where the pink blossoms called in sweet insistent tones to me to remember a day when I had crowned a little girl with blooms like these, a day when my life was in its Maytime joy. On across the prairie we swung to the very borders of Springvale, which was nestling by the river and stretching up the hillslope toward where the bluff breaks abruptly. I could see "Rockport" gray and sun-flecked beyond its sheltering line of green bushes.

Just as we turned toward Cliff Street Dever said carelessly,

"Lots of changes some ways sence I took you out of here last August. Judson, he's married two months ago."

The warm sunny glorious world turned drab and cold to me with the words.

"What's the matter, Baronet?—you're whiter'n a dead man!"

"Just a little faint. Got that way in the army," I answered, which was a lie.

"Better now? As I was sayin', Judson and Lettie has been married two months now. Kinder surprised folks by jinin' up sudden; but—oh, well, it's a lot better quick than not at all sometimes."

I caught my breath. My "spell" contracted in the army was passing. And here were Cliff Street and the round turret-like corners of Judge Baronet's stone-built domicile. It was high noon, and my father had just gone into the house. I gave Dever his fare and made the hall door at a leap. My father turned at the sound and—I was in his arms. Then came Aunt Candace, older by more than ten months. Oh, the women are the ones who suffer most. I had not thought until that moment what all this winter of absence meant to Candace Baronet. I held her in my strong arms and looked down into her love-hungry eyes. Men are such stupid unfeeling brutes. I am, at least; for I had never read in this dear woman's face until that instant what must have been written there all these years,—the love that might have been given to a husband and children of her own, this lonely, childless woman had given to me.

"Aunty, I'll never leave you again," I declared, as she clung to me, and patted my cheeks and stroked my rough curly hair.

We sat down together to the midday meal, and my father's blessing was like the benediction of Heaven to my ears.

Springvale also had its measure of good breeding. My coming was the choicest news that Dever had had to give out for many a day, and the circulation was amazing in its rapid transit. I had a host of friends here where I had grown to manhood, and the first impulse was to take Cliff Street by storm. It was Cam Gentry who counselled better methods.

"Now, by hen, let's have some sense," he urged, "the boy's jest got here. He's ben through life and death, er tarnation nigh akin to it. Let's let him be with his own till to-morror. Jest ac like we'd had a grain o' raisin' anyhow, and wait our turn. Ef he shows hisself down on this 'er street we'll jest go out and turn the Neoshy runnin' north for an hour and a half while we carry him around dry shod. But now, to-day, let him come out o' hidin', and we'll give him welcome; but ef he stays up there with Candace, we'll be gentlemen fur oncet ef it does purty nigh kill some of us."

"Cam is right," Cris Mead urged. "If he comes down here he'll take his chances, but we'll hold our fire on the hill till to-morrow."

"Well, by cracky, the Baronets never miss prayer meeting, I guess. Springvale will turn out to-night some," Grandpa Mead declared.

And so while I revelled in a home-coming, thankful to be alone with my own people, the best folks on earth were waiting and dodging about, but courteously abstaining from rushing in on our sacred home rights.

In the middle of the afternoon Cam Gentry called to Dollie to come to his aid.

"Jest tie the end of this rope good and fast around this piazzer post," he said.

His wife obeyed before she noted that the other end was fastened around Cam's right ankle. To her wondering look he responded:

"Ef I don't lariat myself to something, like a old hen wanting to steal off with her chickens, I'll be up to Baronet's spite of my efforts, I'm that crazy to see Phil once more."

Through the remainder of the May afternoon he sat on the veranda, or hopped the length of his tether to the side-walk and looked longingly up toward the high street, that faced the cliff, but his purpose did not change.

Springvale showed its sense of delicacy in more ways than this. Marjie was the last to hear of my leaving when all suddenly I turned my back on the town nearly ten months before. And now, while almost every family had discussed my return—anything furnishes a little town a sensation—the Whately family had had no notice served of the momentarily interesting topic. And so it was that Marjie, innocent of the suppressed interest, went about her home, never dreaming of anything unusual in the town talk of that day.

The May evening was delicious in its balmy air and the deepening purple of its twilight haze. The spirit of the springtime, wooing in its tone of softest music, voiced a message to the sons and daughters of men. Marjie came out at sunset and slowly took her way through the sweetness of it all up to the "Rockport" of our childhood, the trysting place of our days of love's young dream. Her fair face had a womanly strength and tenderness now, and her form an added grace over the curves of girlhood. But her hair still rippled about her brow and coiled in the same soft folds of brown at the back of her head. Her cheeks had still the pink of the wild rose bloom, and the dainty neatness in dress was as of old.

She came to the rock beyond the bushes and sat down alone looking dreamily out over the Neosho Valley.

"You'll go to prayer meeting, Phil?" Aunt Candace asked at supper.

"Yes, but I believe I'll go down the street first. Save a place for me. I want to see Dr. Hemingway next to you of all Springvale." Which was my second falsehood for that day. I needed prayer meeting.

The sunset hour was more than I could withstand. All the afternoon I had been subconsciously saying that I must keep close to the realities. These were all that counted now. And yet when the evening came, all the past swept my soul and bore every resolve before it. I did not stop to ask myself any questions. I only knew that, lonely as it must be, I must go now to "Rockport" as I had done so many times in the old happy past, a past I was already beginning numbly to feel was dead and gone forever. And yet my step was firm and my head erect, as with eager tread I came to the bushes guarding our old happy playground. I only wanted to see it once more, that was all.

The limp had gone from my foot. It was intermittent in the earlier years. I was combed and groomed again for social appearing. Aunt Candace had hung about my tie and the set of my coat, and for my old army head-gear she had resurrected the jaunty cap I had worn home from Massachusetts. With my hands in my pockets, whistling softly to abstract my thoughts, I slipped through the bushes and stood once more on "Rockport."

And there was Marjie, still looking dreamily out over the valley. She had not heard my step, so far away were her thoughts. And the picture, as I stood a moment looking at her—will the world to come hold anything more fair, I wondered. It was years ago, I know, but so clearly I recall it now it could have been a dream of yesterday. Before me were the gray rock, the dark-green valley, the gleaming waters of the Neosho, the silvery mist on the farther bluff iridescent with the pink tints of sunset reflected on the eastern sky, the quiet loveliness of the May twilight, and Marjie, beautiful with a girlish winsomeness, a woman's grace, a Madonna's tenderness.

"Were you waiting for me, dearie? I am a little late, but I am here at last."

I spoke softly, and she turned quickly at the sound of my voice. A look of dazed surprise as she leaped to her feet, and then the reality dawned upon her.

"Come, sweetheart," I said. "I have been away so long, I'm hungering for your welcome."

I held out my hands to her. Her face was very white as she made one step toward me, and then the love-light filled her brown eyes, the glorious beauty of the pink blossoms swept her cheek. I put my arms around her and drew her close to me, my own little girl, whom I had loved and thought I had lost forever.

"Oh, Phil, Phil, are you here again? Are you—" she put her little hand against my hair curling rebelliously over my cap's brim. "Are you mine once more?"

"Am I, Marjie? Six feet of me has come back; but, little girl, I have never been away. I have never let you go out of my life. It was only the mechanical action that went away. Phil Baronet stayed here! Oh, I know it now—I was acting out there; I was really living here with you, my Marjie, my own."

I held her in my arms as I spoke, and we looked out at the sweet sunset prairie. The big cottonwood, shapely as ever, was outlined against the horizon, which was illumined now with all the gorgeous grandeur of the May evening. The level rays of golden light fell on us, as we stood there, baptizing us with its splendor.

"Oh, Marjie, it was worth all the suffering and danger to have such a home-coming as this!" I kissed her lips and pushed back the little ringlets from her white forehead.

"It is vouchsafed to a man sometimes to know a bit of heaven here on earth," Father Le Claire had said to me out on this rock six years before. It was a bit of heaven that came down to me in the purple twilight of that May evening, and I lifted my face to the opal skies above me with a prayer of thankfulness for the love that was mine once more. In that hour of happiness we forgot that there was ever a storm cloud to darken the blue heavens, or ever a grief or a sin to mar the joy of living. We were young, and we were together. Over the valley swept the sweet tones of the Presbyterian Church bell. Marjie's face, radiant with light, was lifted to mine.

"I must go to prayer meeting, Phil. I shall see you again—to-morrow?" She put the question hesitatingly, even longingly.

"Yes, and to-night. Let's go together. I haven't been to prayer meeting regularly. We lost out on that on the Staked Plains."

"I must run home and comb my hair," she declared; and indeed it was a little tumbled. But from the night I first saw her, a little girl in her father's moving-wagon, with her pink sun-bonnet pushed back from her blowsy curls, her hair, however rebellious, was always a picture.

"Go ahead, little girl. I will run home, too. I forgot something. I will be down right away."

Going home, I may have walked on Cliff Street, but my head was in the clouds, and all the songs that the morning-stars sing together—all the music of the spheres—was playing itself out for me in the shadowy twilight as I went along.

At the gate Aunt Candace and my father were waiting for me.

"You needn't wait," I cried. "I will be there presently."

"Oh, joined the regular army this time," my father said, smiling. "Sorry we can't keep you, Phil." But I gave no heed to him.

"Aunt Candace," I said in a low voice. "May I see you just a minute? I want to get something."

"It's in the top drawer in my room, Phil. The key is in the little tray on my dresser," Aunt Candace said quietly. She always understood me.

When I reached the Whately home, Marjie was waiting for me at the gate. I took her little hand in my own strong big one.

"Will you wear it again for me, dearie?" I asked, holding up my mother's ring before her.

"Always and always, Phil," she murmured.

Isn't it Longfellow who speaks of "the lovely stars, the forget-me-nots of the angels," blossoming "in the infinite meadows of heaven"? They were all a-bloom that May night, and dewy and sweet lay the earth beneath them. We were a little late to prayer meeting. The choir was in its place and the audience was gathered in the pews. Judge Baronet always sat near the front, and my place was between him and Aunt Candace when I wasn't in the choir. Bess Anderson was just finishing a voluntary as we two went up the aisle together. I hadn't thought of making a sensation, I thought only of Marjie. Passing around the end of the chancel rail I gently led her by the arm up the three steps to the choir place, and turning, faced all the town as I went to my seat beside my father. I was as happy as a lover can be; but I didn't know how much of all this was written on my countenance, nor did I notice the intense hush that fell on the company. I had faced the oncoming of Roman Nose and his thousand Cheyenne warriors; there was no reason why I should feel embarrassed in a prayer meeting in the Presbyterian Church at Springvale. The service was short. I remember not one word of it except the scripture lesson. That was the Twenty-third Psalm:

The Lord is my shepherd; I shall not want.
He maketh me to lie down in green pastures;
He leadeth me beside the still waters.
He restoreth my soul;
He leadeth me in the paths of righteousness for His name's sake.
Yea, though I walk through the valley of the shadow of death,
I will fear no evil; for Thou art with me.

These words had sounded in my ears on the night before the battle on the Arickaree, and again in the little cove on the low bluff at Fort Sill, the night Jean Pahusca was taunting me through the few minutes he was allowing me to live. That Psalm belonged to the days when I was doing my part toward the price paid out for the prairie homes and safety and peace. But never anybody read for me as Dr. Hemingway read it that evening. With the close of the service came a prayer of thanksgiving for my return. Then for the first time I was self-conscious. What had I done to be so lovingly and reverently welcomed home? I bowed my head in deep humility, and the tears welled up. Oh, I could look death calmly between the eyes as I had watched it creeping toward me on the heated Plains of the Arickaree, and among the cold starved sand dunes of the Cimarron, but to be lauded as a hero here in Springvale—the tears would come. Where were Custer, and Moore, and Forsyth, and Pliley, and Stillwell, and Morton, if such as I be called a hero?

Cam Gentry didn't lead the Doxology that night, he chased it clear into the belfry and up into the very top of the steeple; and his closing burst of melody "Praise Father, Son, and Holy Ghost," had, as Bill Mead declared afterwards, a regular "You-couldn't-have-done-it-better-Lord-if-you-had-been-there-yourself" ring to it.

Then came the benediction, fervent, holy, gentle, with Dr. Hemingway's white face (crowned now with snowy hair) lifted up toward heaven. After that I never could remember, save that there was a hush, then a clamor, that was followed pretty soon by embraces from the older men and women, pounding thumps from the younger men and handshaking with the girls. And all the while, with a proprietary sense I had found myself near Marjie, whom I kept close beside me now, her brown head just above my shoulder.

More than once in the decades since then it has been my fortune to return to Springvale and be met at the railway station and escorted home by the town band. Sometimes for political service, sometimes for civic effort, and once because by physical strength and great daring and quick cool courage I saved three human lives in a terrible wreck; but never any ovation was like that prayer meeting in the Presbyterian Church nearly forty years ago.

The days that followed my home-coming were busy ones, for my place in the office had been vacant. Clayton Anderson had devoted himself to the Whately affairs, although nobody but those in the secret knew when Judson gave up proprietorship and went on a clerk's pay again where he belonged. Springvale was kind to Judson, as it has always been to the man who tries honestly to make good in this life's struggle. It is in the Kansas air, this broader charity, this estimation of character, redeemed or redeemable.

My father did not tell me of his part in the Whately business affairs at once, and I did not understand when, one evening, some time later, Aunt Candace said at the supper table:

"Dollie Gentry tells me Dr. John (so we called John Anderson now), reports a twelve-pound boy over at Judsons'. They are going to christen him 'John Baronet Judson.' Aren't you proud of the name, John?"

"I am of the Judson part," my father answered, with that compression of the lips that sometimes kept back a smile, and sometimes marked a growing sternness.

I met O'mie at Topeka and brought him to Springvale. It was not until in May of the next year that he went away from us and came not back any more, save in loving remembrance.

In August Tillhurst went East. Somehow I was not at all surprised when the Rockport, Massachusetts, weekly newspaper, that had come to our house every Tuesday while we had lived on Cliff Street, contained the notice of the marriage of Richard Tillhurst and Rachel Agnes Melrose. The happy couple, the paper said, would reside in Rockport.

"They may reside at the bottom of the sea for all that I care," I said thoughtlessly, not understanding then the shadow that fell for the moment on my aunt's serene face.

Long afterwards when she slept beside my father in the quiet Springvale cemetery on the bluff beyond Fingal's Creek, I found among her letters the romance of her life. I knew then for the first time that Rachel's uncle, the Ferdinand Melrose whose life was lost at sea, was the one for whom this brave kind woman had mourned. Loving as the Baronets do, even unto death, she had gone down the lonely years, forgetting herself in the broad, beautiful, unselfish life she gave to those about her.

It was late in the August of the following year, when the Kansas prairies were brownest and the summer heat the fiercest, that I was met at the courthouse door one afternoon by a lithe, coppery Osage Indian boy, who handed me a bundle, saying, "From Hard Rope, for John Baronet's son."

"Well, all right, sonny; only it's about time for the gentleman in there to be known as Philip Baronet's father. He never fought the Cheyennes. He's just the father of the man who did. What's the tariff due on this junk?"

The Osage did not smile, but he answered mildly enough, "What you will pay."

I was not cross with the world. I could afford to be generous, even at the risk of having the whole Osage tribe trailing at my heels, and begging for tobacco and food and trinkets. I loaded that young buck to the guards with the things an Indian prizes, and sent him away.

Then in my own office I undid the bundle. It was the old scarlet blanket with the white circular centre, the pattern Jean Pahusca always wore. This one was dirty and frayed and splotched. I turned from it with loathing. In the folds of the cloth a sealed letter was securely fastened. Some soldier had written it for Hard Rope, and the penmanship and language were more than average fine. But the story it told I could not exult over, although a sense of lifted pressure in some corner of my mind came with the reading.

Briefly it recited that Jean Pahusca, Kiowa renegade, was dead. Custer's penalty for him had been to give him over to the Kiowas as their captive. When the tribe left Fort Sill in March, Satanta had had him brought bound to the Kiowa village then on the lower Washita. His crime, committed on the day of Custer's fight with Black Kettle, was the heinous one of stealing his Uncle Satanta's youngest and favorite wife, and leaving her to perish miserably in the cold of that

December month in which we also had suffered. His plan had been to escape from the Kiowas and reach the Cheyennes on the Sweetwater before we did, to meet me there, and this time, to give no moment for my rescue. So Hard Rope's message ran. But this was not all. The punishment that fell on Jean Pahusca was in proportion to his crime, as an Indian counts justice. He was sold as a slave to the Apaches and carried captive to the mountains of Old Mexico. Nor was he ever liberated again. Up above the snow line, with the passes guarded (for Jean was as dangerous to his mother's race as to his father's), he had fretted away his days, dying at last of cold and cruel neglect among the dreary rocks of the icy peaks. This much information Hard Rope's letter brought. I burned both the letter and the blanket, telling no one of them except my father.

"This Hard Rope was for some reason very friendly to me on your account," I said. "He told me on the Washita the night before we left Camp Inman that he had shadowed Jean all the time he was at Fort Sill, and had more than once prevented the half-breed from making an attack on me. He promised to let me know what became of Pahusca if he ever found out. He has kept his word."

"I know Hard Rope," my father said. "I saved his life one annuity day long ago. Tell Mapleson had made Jean Pahusca drunk. You know what kind of a beast he was then. And Tell had run this Osage into Jean's path, where he would be sure to lose his life, and Tell would have the big pile of money Hard Rope carried. That's the kind of beast Tell was. An Indian has his own sense of obligation; and then it is a good asset to be humane all along the line anyhow, although I never dreamed I was saving the man who was to save my boy."

"Shall we tell Le Claire?" I asked.

"Only that both Jean and his father are dead. We'll spare him the rest. Le Claire has gone to St. Louis to a monastery. He will never be strong again. But he is one of the kings of the earth; he has given the best years of his manhood to build up a kingdom of peace between the white man and the savage. No record except the Great Book of human deeds will ever be able to show how much we owe to men like Le Claire whose influence has helped to make a loyal peaceful tribe like the Osages. The brutal fiendishness of the Plains Indians is the heritage of Spanish cruelty toward the ancestors of the Apache and Kiowa and Arapahoe and Comanche, and you can see why they differ from our tribes here in Eastern Kansas. Le Claire has done his part toward the purchase of the Plains, and I am glad for the quiet years before him."

It was the custom in Springvale for every girl to go up to Topeka for the final purchases of her bridal belongings. We were to be married in October. In the late September days Mrs. Whately and her daughter spent a week at the capital city. I went up at the end of the visit to come home with them. Since the death of Irving Whately nothing had ever roused his wife to the pleasure of living like this preparation for Marjie's marriage, and Mrs. Whately, still a young and very pretty woman, bloomed into that mature comeliness that carries a grace of permanence the promise of youth may only hint at. She delighted in every detail of the coming event, and we two most concerned were willing to let anybody look after the details. We had other matters to think about.

"Come, little sweetheart," I said one night after supper at the Teft House, "your mother is to spend the evening with a friend of hers. I want to take you for a walk."

Strange how beautiful Topeka looked to me this September. It had all the making of a handsome city even then, although the year since I came up to the political rally had brought no great change except to extend the borders somewhat. Like two happy young lovers we strolled out toward the southwest, past the hole in the ground that was to contain the foundation of the new wings for the State Capitol, past Washburn College, and on to where the slender little locust tree waved its dainty lacy branches in graceful welcome.

"Marjie, I want you to see this tree. It's not the first time I have been here. Rachel—Mrs. Tillhurst—and I came here a few times." Marjie's hand nestled softly against my arm. "I always made faces at it as soon as I got away from it; but it is a beautiful little tree, and I want to put you with it in my mind. It was here last Fall that my father said he didn't believe that you were engaged to Amos Judson."

"Didn't believe," Marjie cried; "why, Phil, he knew I wasn't. I told him so when he was asked to urge me to marry Amos."

"He urge you to marry Amos! Now Marjie, girl, I hate to be hard on the gentleman; but if he did that it's my duty to scalp him, and I will go home and do it."

But Marjie explained. We sat in the moonlight by the locust-tree just as Rachel and I had done; only now Topeka and the tree and the silvery prairie and the black-shadowed Shunganunga Creek, winding down toward the Kaw through many devious turns, all seemed a fairy land which the moonbeams touched and glorified for us two. I can never think of Topeka, even to-day, with its broad avenues and beautiful shaded parks and paved ways, its handsome homes and churches and colleges, with all these to make it a proud young city—I can never think of it and leave out that sturdy young locust, grown now to a handsome tree. And when I think of it I do not think of the beautiful black-haired Eastern girl, with her rich dress and aristocratic manner. But always that sweet-faced, brown-eyed Kansas girl is with me there. And the open prairie dipping down to the creek, and the purple tip of Burnett's Mound, make a setting for the picture.

One October day when the wooded valley of the Neosho was in its autumn glory, when the creeping vines on the gray stone bluff were aflame with the frost's rich scarlet painting, and the west prairies were all one shimmering sea of gold flecked with emerald and purple; while above all these curved the wide magnificent skies of Kansas, unclouded, fathomless, and tenderly blue; when the peace of God was in the air and his benediction of love was on all the land,—on such a day as this, the clear-toned old Presbyterian Church bell rang the wedding chimes for Marjory Whately and Philip Baronet.

Loving hands had made the church a bower of autumn coloring with the dainty relief of pink and white asters against the bronze richness of the season. Bess Anderson played the wedding march, as we two came up the aisle together and met Dr. Hemingway at the chancel rail. I was in my young manhood's zenith, and I walked the earth like a king. Marjie wore my mother's wedding veil. Her white gown was soft and filmy, a fabric of her mother's own choosing, and her brown wavy hair was crowned with orange blossoms.

Springvale talked of that wedding for many a moon, for there was not a feature of the whole beautiful service, even to the very least appointment, that was not perfect in its simplicity and harmonious in its blending with everything about it.

Among the guests in the Baronet home, where everybody came to wish us happiness, was my father's friend and my own hero, Morton of the Saline Valley. Somehow I needed his presence that day. It kept me in touch with my days of greatest schooling. The quiet, forceful friend, who had taught me how to meet the realities of life like a man, put into my wedding a memory I shall always treasure. O'mie was still with us then. When his turn came to greet us he held Marjie's hand a moment while he slyly showed her a poor little bunch of faded brown blossoms which he crumpled to dust in his fingers.

"I told you I wouldn't keep them no longer'n till I caught the odor of them orange blooms. They are the little pink wreath two other fellows threw away out in the West Draw long ago. The rale evidence of my good-will to you two is locked up in Judge Baronet's safe."

We laughed, but we did not understand. Not until the Irish boy's will was read, more than half a year later, when the pink flowers were blooming again in the West Draw, did we comprehend the measure of his good-will. For by his legal last wish all his possessions, including the land, with the big cottonwood and the old stone cabin, became the property of Marjory Whately and her heirs and assigns forever.

Out there in later years we built our country home. The breezes of summer are always cool there, and from every wide window we can see the landscape the old cottonwood still watches over. Above the gateway to the winding road leading up from the West Draw is inscribed the name we gave the place,

O'MIE-HEIM.

Sixty years, and a white-haired, young-hearted young man I am who write these lines. For many seasons I have sat on the Judge's bench. Law has been my business on the main line, with land dealings on the side, and love for my fellowmen all along the way. Half a century of my life has run parallel with the story of Kansas, whose beautiful prairies have been purchased not only with the coin of the country, but with the coin of courage and unparalleled endurance. To-day the rippling billows of yellow wheat, the walls on walls of black-green corn, the stretches of emerald alfalfa set with its gems of amethyst bloom; orchard and meadow, grove and grassy upland, where cattle pasture; populous cities and churches and stately college halls; the whirring factory wheels, the dust of the mines, the black oil derrick and the huge reservoirs of natural gas, with the slender steel pathways of the great trains of traffic binding these together; and above all, the sheltered happy homes, where little children play never dreaming of fear; where sweet-browed mothers think not of loneliness and anguish and peril—all these are the splendid heritage of a land whose law is for the whole people, a land whose God is the Lord.

Slowly, through tribulation, and distress, and persecution, and famine, and nakedness, and peril, and sword; through fire and flood; through summer's drought and winter's blizzard; through loneliness, and fear, and heroism, and martyrdom too often at last, the brave-hearted, liberty-loving, indomitable people have come into their own, paying foot by foot, the price that won this prairie kingdom in the heart of the West.

Down through the years of busy cares, of struggle and achievement, of hopes deferred and victories counted, my days have run in shadow and sunshine, with more of practical fact than of poetic dreaming. And through them all, the call of the prairie has sounded in my soul, the voice of a beautiful land, singing evermore its old, old song of victory and peace. Aye, and through it all, beside me, cheering each step, holding fast my hand, making life always fine and beautiful and gracious for me, has been my loved one, Marjie, the bride of my young manhood, the mother of my sons and daughters, the light of my life.

It is for such as she, for homes her kind have made, that men have fought and dared and died, fulfilling the high privilege of the American citizen, the privilege to safeguard the hearthstones of the land above which the flag floats a symbol of light and law and love.

And I who write this know—for I have learned in the years whose story is here only a half-told thing under my halting pen—I know that however fiercely the storms may beat, however wildly the tempests may blow, however bitter the fighting hours of the day may be, beyond the heat and burden of it all will come the quiet eventide for me, and for all the sons and daughters of this prairie land I love. Though the roar of battle fill all the noontime, in the blessed twilight will come the music of *"HOME, SWEET HOME."*

Lightning Source UK Ltd.
Milton Keynes UK
UKHW040719070722
405516UK00001B/71

9 781034 812906